D0385159

Providence Rag

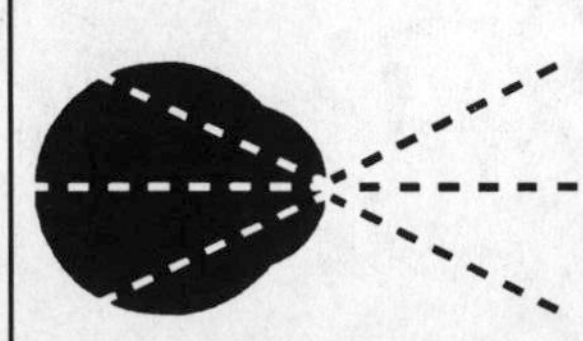

This Large Print Book carries the Seal of Approval of N.A.V.H.

PROVIDENCE RAG

BRUCE DESILVA

THORNDIKE PRESS
A part of Gale, Cengage Learning

Farmington Hills, Mich • San Francisco • New York • Waterville, Maine
Meriden, Conn • Mason, Ohio • Chicago

A Liam Mulligan Novel.
Thorndike Press, a part of Gale, Cengage Learning.

This is a work of fiction. All of the characters, organizations, and events portrayed in this novel are either products of the author's imagination or are used fictitiously.

Thorndike Press® Large Print Crime Scene.
The text of this Large Print edition is unabridged.
Other aspects of the book may vary from the original edition.
Set in 16 pt. Plantin.

LIBRARY OF CONGRESS CATALOGING-IN-PUBLICATION DATA

DeSilva, Bruce.
Providence Rag / by Bruce DeSilva. — Large print edition.
pages ; cm. — (Thorndike Press large print crime scene) (A Liam Mulligan novel)
ISBN 978-1-4104-6903-8 (hardcover) — ISBN 1-4104-6903-4 (hardcover)
1. Journalists—Fiction. 2. Providence (R.I.)—Fiction. 3. Large type books. I. Title.
PS3604.E7575P78 2014b
813'.6—dc23 2014006576

Published in 2014 by arrangement with Tom Doherty Associates, LLC

Printed in Mexico
1 2 3 4 5 6 7 18 17 16 15 14

For my children, Richard,
Melanie, and Jeremy;
and for *their* children,
Alexandra, Jason, Anthony,
Lillian, Ella, Benjamin, and Josephine.
No father or grandfather
has ever been more blessed.
And for my wife's granddaughter,
the irrepressible Mikaila,
whom we were privileged
to raise to adulthood and
who has kept us both young.

AUTHOR'S NOTE

This novel was inspired by two of Rhode Island's most notorious murder cases. However, the tale told in these pages is in no way intended to be a true account of the killers, their victims, the police who investigated the crimes, the lawyers and judges who adjudicated the cases, the jailers who confined the guilty, or the journalists who told their stories. The characters' personalities, actions, thoughts, and dialogue are entirely the product of the author's imagination. Although I have named a few characters after old friends, they bear scant resemblance to them. For example, the real Don Sockol is a Rhode Island educator and former journalist, not a Corrections Department clerk. A handful of real people, including Boston Red Sox World Series hero Curt Schilling, are mentioned in passing. However, only three of them — Roomful of Blues vocalist Phil Pemberton, WPRO radio newsman Ron St. Pierre, and CNN correspondent Nancy Grace — have speaking parts; and they are permitted only a few lines of fictional action or dialogue. Rhode Island geography is as accurate as I can make it, but I have played around a bit with space and time. For example, Hopes, the newspaper bar where I drank decades ago when I reported the news for the *Providence Journal,* is long gone, but I enjoyed resurrecting it for this story. I also borrowed the colorful nickname of a former Rhode Island attorney general; but the fictional and real Attila the Nun are nothing alike, and the character's actions and dialogue are entirely imaginary.

Some humans ain't human.

— John Prine

PART I
PRECOCIOUS BOYS

May 1989

The child holds the Mason jar up to the light and studies the wriggling mass inside. The quivering antennae, the thrashing legs, the compound eyes, the gossamer wings folded tight against segmented green abdomens. The unmown field behind his house is alive with them. He'd spent half the morning stalking these bits of life, snatching them from the waving blades of switchgrass with his big, strong hands.

On his knees now, he opens the jar, snares one with a thick finger, and screws the lid on tight. He places the prisoner on one of the flat stones that litter the field and holds it down with his left thumb. Then he reaches into the hip pocket of his jeans and extracts his 5× magnifying glass. The sun is high, and the glass focuses its wrath into a tight beam.

A wing curls into ash.

The grasshopper struggles, its six legs making a faint scratching sound as they rake the stone. The boy burns the legs off one by one, and the scratching stops. Carefully, he amputates each antenna. A brown, unblinking eye stares up at him, pleading for an end to this. He stares back, savoring the moment. Then he drags the beam across the abdomen to the eye, instantly obliterating it.

A thin curl of white smoke rises as he bores through to the knot of ganglia that passes for a brain. The boy bends close, sniffs. The aroma reminds him of meat frying in his mother's kitchen.

With a start, he feels a swelling in his jeans.

He wonders: Am I God?

1

June 1992

After her live-in boyfriend was transferred to the graveyard shift, Becky Medeiros fell into the evening habit of lounging around the house in her underwear. Or sometimes in the nude. She kept the front and side curtains drawn after dark, but the house backed up on a wooded lot, so she was often careless with the rear windows.

The neighborhood potheads had discovered her habit. After sundown, they often gathered beneath the low branches of a large white pine ten yards from her back fence to pass a joint and enjoy the show. Later, police would find a disturbance in the thick blanket of pine needles. Forty-five discarded roaches and a scattering of torn Doritos bags and Snickers wrappers told them someone had been lurking there on and off for weeks.

Becky was an attractive young woman. Slim waist, long muscular legs, small firm breasts. A dancer's body. The watchers whispered crude jokes and imagined what it would be like to screw her. All but one of them. He harbored a different fantasy.

It had been an unusually hot and dry Rhode Island spring; but on the evening of Friday, June 5, the temperature fell into the low sixties, and threatening clouds shimmered like embers beneath the setting sun. Shortly before ten, it began to rain. Only a few drops penetrated the pine's thick branches, but the weather had kept the other peepers away. This time, he had the hiding place all to himself.

He yanked a handkerchief from the front pocket of his hoodie, wiped raindrops from his binoculars, and raised them to his eyes. There she was, naked in the warm glow of her bedside lamp as she stretched and twisted to a yoga instructional video flashing blue on the small television above her bureau. She bent at the waist now, right hand touching left ankle, her ass an offering.

From weeks of watching, he knew she rarely turned in before *Late Night* signed off. But tonight she killed the TV after David Letterman's monologue and slipped out of the bedroom. A moment later, the bathroom light snapped on, narrow beams leaking between the cracks of the venetian blinds.

He swept the binoculars back and forth from the bathroom to the bedroom until, ten minutes later, she reappeared wrapped in a hot-pink towel. She dropped the towel to the floor, sat on the edge of her bed, and turned off the bedside lamp.

He lingered under the tree, giving her time to fall asleep. Then he laid his binoculars in the pine needles, crawled out from under the branches, vaulted her white picket fence, and crossed the wet grass to the rear door. There, an overhead lamp was burning. He reached up and gave the bulb a twist, extinguishing the light.

He tried the door. It was locked. He considered breaking a pane of glass to reach the inside latch, but that would make too much noise. Instead, he edged along the back of the house, looking for another way inside.

The kitchen window was open a crack. Perhaps Becky had forgotten to close it. Perhaps she had wanted to let the cool night air in. He pried off the screen and eased the window up. Then he sat on his haunches, removed his size twelve Nikes, placed them in the grass, and hoisted himself into the dark house.

He landed with a thud on the dinette table, knocking over the salt and pepper shakers. They rolled off the edge and shattered. He slid off the table, got to his feet, and froze, listening to the sounds of the dark house. At first, he heard only the ticking of a clock. Then the refrigerator clicked on and hummed to itself. He broke into a nervous sweat. After three or four minutes, he was desperately thirsty.

When he was confident that Becky had not awakened, he padded across the linoleum to the refrigerator, opened the door, and saw several cans of Diet Coke, a carton of orange juice, and a sippy cup half filled with milk. He grabbed the OJ and gulped, dribbling some down the front of his hoodie.

He set the carton on the counter and had just closed the refrigerator when the bedroom door creaked. He spun toward the hallway and saw Becky standing there in the nude. Perhaps the racket he'd made had roused her after all. Or maybe she'd just gotten up to go to the bathroom. She knew who he was. She'd often seen him riding his bike through the neighborhood and throwing a football in the street.

She opened her mouth to scream.

He charged into the hallway, grabbed her by the throat, and slammed her against the wall. Her head dented the plasterboard. Stunned, she slumped to the floor. He dashed back to the kitchen, clawed through the drawers under the counter, and pulled out an eight-inch chef's knife.

In the hallway, Becky staggered to her feet, her left temple dribbling blood. He lowered a shoulder and flew at her, hitting her the way he'd seen Andre Tippett, the New England Patriots' all-star linebacker, T-bone running backs on TV. She went down hard, landing on her back. He pounced and raised the knife. She screamed and deflected the blade with her arms.

Becky was young and strong. She battled ferociously in that cramped space. But he outweighed her by 130 pounds. In a minute, maybe less, she lay motionless, her breathing ragged, blood bubbling from the holes in her chest.

"Mama?"

He looked up and saw the little one standing a few feet away, rubbing the sleep from her eyes. She was dressed in My Little Pony pajamas like the ones his sister used to wear. He rose to his knees, swung the knife, and cut her down. Then he turned back to Becky, stabbing with such force that the steel blade snapped off at the handle.

Becky's screams had made his ears ring in

that narrow hallway. Had her cries alarmed the neighbors? He got to his feet, stepped through an archway into the living room, and padded across the carpet to the front window. Pulling the curtain aside, he pressed his forehead against the glass and peered out. Nothing was stirring.

He returned to the kitchen, drew two more knives from a drawer, and went back to work on Becky, stabbing her in the chest and abdomen long after he was certain she was dead. Finally he clambered to his feet, his face, hands, and hoodie drenched in her blood, and rinsed himself off at the kitchen sink.

Then he walked back to the hallway, stood over the bodies, unzipped his fly, and freed his erection. He spit on his right palm, stared at the woman, and moved his fist rhythmically, glorying in the power he'd felt as the knife penetrated her skin again and again. He threw back his head and moaned.

When he was done, he reached down and jerked a heart-shaped silver locket from the slim chain around Becky's neck — a keepsake to hold whenever he relived this night.

Stepping over the bodies, he entered Becky's room, tore a mint-green satin comforter from her bed, and threw it on the floor. He stripped off the matching sheet, carried it into the hallway, and draped it over the dead. Then he walked back to the kitchen and peeked out the open window. The same stillness greeted him. Satisfied that no one was watching, he shoved the dinette table aside and climbed out.

He sat on his rump in the grass, pulled off the bloody socks, and put his shoes back on, not bothering with the laces. It was raining harder now. Taking the socks with him, he sprinted across the backyard and jumped the fence. He fetched his binoculars from beneath the white pine. Then he pulled off his hoodie and did a poor job of hiding it and his socks, cramming them under some brush in the wooded lot.

Ten minutes later, he sneaked into his family's sleeping house and crept up the stairs to the second floor. There he showered before flopping into bed, feeling euphoric but exhausted. Clutching Becky's locket in his hand, he fell into a blissful, dream-rich sleep.

2

The 911 call was logged in at 6:34 A.M. The caller was so distraught that the dispatcher couldn't make sense of anything he was saying. She got him to calm down long enough to tell her where he was and sent a two-man patrol car with no clear idea of what they'd find when they got there.

Seven minutes later, Patrolmen Oscar Hernandez and Phil Rubino screeched up to the house and saw a man on his knees on the front walk. He was screaming, and his hands and shirt were drenched in scarlet.

Hernandez drew his gun and covered the guy while Rubino shoved him face-first to the ground, pulled his arms back, and cuffed him. They asked him his name. He couldn't stop screaming. Rubino dug the wallet out of the man's pants and found a Rhode Island driver's license identifying him as Walter Miller, 34. He lived there. The officers checked him over and determined that he wasn't injured. The blood belonged to somebody else.

Miller finally stopped screaming. He appeared catatonic now. The officers read him his *Miranda* rights, locked him in the back of the patrol car, and called for backup. Then they argued about what to do next. Hernandez wanted to sit tight until backup arrived. Rubino figured somebody inside the house was badly hurt and might die if they waited. He left his partner with the suspect and raced up the front walk with his weapon in his hand.

The front door was ajar. Rubino rapped on it, identified himself as a police officer, and stepped inside. Bloody shoe prints marched across the beige living room carpet, marking a path between the front door and an archway that led to the back of the house. A second blood trail, this one made by larger feet, stretched from the archway to the living room's picture window and back again.

Skirting the gore, Rubino crossed the living room, stepped through the arch, and entered a hallway. There, the walls were splashed with blood, and the hardwood floor was slick with it.

The bodies of two females, an adult and a child, were lying faceup, partially draped with a red-stained sheet. The heads and necks of the victims were exposed, as if someone had pulled the covering aside to take a look. Rubino hesitated, unable to reach the victims without stepping in their blood. Then he went to them, checked for pulses, and found none. His eyes lingered on the little girl longer than he wanted them to.

He exited the house just as backup arrived, called the dispatcher, and asked her, in a measured professional voice, to send detectives. Then he sat on the hood of the patrol car and wept.

Warwick chief of detectives Andrew Jennings and his partner, Detective Charlie Mello, arrived shortly after seven A.M. They found Hernandez standing guard over Miller. Other patrolmen were watching the house's exits to make sure no one got in — or out.

Jennings opened the back door of the patrol car and spoke to the suspect. He didn't respond. His eyes were wild and unfocused.

Mello and Hernandez kicked in the back door, and Rubino and Jennings entered through the front. No one noticed Rubino's slight hesitation. They searched all six rooms and the garage. They found no one left alive.

The officers exited the house and called for the medical examiner.

August 1989

That damned mouse. That's what his mother keeps calling it. She buys three spring-loaded bar traps, the kind that snap the neck, and places them in the corners of her cheerful yellow kitchen. That night his father throws them out, goes down to the Ace Hardware store on West Shore Road, and returns with a live-catch trap. He can't bear to kill anything, not since those things he did in the war.

Next morning, the boy rises early. He wanders into the kitchen in his Red Sox pajamas, opens the refrigerator, takes out a quart of orange juice, and drinks straight from the carton. That's when he hears it, a furious scratching. He gets down on his hands and knees on the black-and-white checkerboard floor and peers into the metal trap. A mouse, eyes bright with panic, is trying mightily to claw its way out.

It's a little brown-and-white field mouse. The

boy thinks it's cute.

He runs up the stairs to his room and tugs on jeans, sneakers, and a T-shirt. The shirt has the rap group Public Enemy's logo, a figure in a rifle's crosshairs, on the front. He tiptoes down the hall to the den and finds his father's cigar lighter by the ashtray on the desk. It's a butane torch lighter, the kind that works like a little flamethrower. He goes down the stairs to the kitchen, picks up the trap, tucks it under his arm, and goes outside.

The boy is very happy that his father threw out the kill-traps.

A dead mouse wouldn't be this much fun.

A dead mouse wouldn't scream.

3

June 1992

Liam Mulligan's earliest memory was of his father returning home from his milk delivery route, collapsing into his platform rocker, and pulling out his Comet harmonica. Later, when Mulligan was in his teens, his dad would fold himself into that chair every night and play along with a scratchy Son Seals, Buddy Guy, or Muddy Waters record, even though the chemo had drained him.

That's how Mulligan learned to love the blues — although no one would have mistaken his father for Little Walter.

Saturday afternoon, Mulligan flipped through his late father's records, selected Son Seals's *Bad Axe* LP, and placed it gently on the family turntable. Then he fetched that old harmonica from its place of honor on the mantel. Settling into that same squeaking rocker, he tapped his left foot to the first few bars of "Don't Pick Me for Your

Fool." Then he put the harmonica to his lips and honked along with the blues man's guitar. No one, Mulligan figured, was going to mistake *him* for Little Walter either.

The album had wound its way to the fifth cut, "Cold Blood," when his mother stuck her head out of the kitchen. She paused for a moment to listen, the sound of the harmonica conjuring warm memories of her husband.

"Liam? You have a phone call."

"Who is it?"

"Some guy from the paper."

Probably the sports editor with a question about the last story Mulligan had turned in. The one about Coach Frank "Happy" Dobbs's struggle to recruit players for the sad Brown University basketball program. He got up and wandered into the kitchen, where the wall phone was mounted beside the wheezing fifteen-year-old Frigidaire.

"Tell him you're on vacation," his mother whispered, and handed him the receiver.

"Mulligan."

"Sorry to disturb your Saturday afternoon, Mr. Mulligan. Was that your girlfriend who answered the phone?"

"My mother."

"You live with your mother?"

"She needs help with the rent. Who am I

talking to?"

"Ed Lomax, the city editor. Can you give us a hand with a breaking story?"

"Give you a hand with a story?" Ever since middle school, Mulligan had repeated questions while pondering his answer. It was a habit he was trying to break. "I think you got the wrong guy, Mr. Lomax. I work in sports."

"I'm aware of that, Mulligan, but the summer vacation schedule has left us shorthanded. I asked the sports editor if he could spare someone. He offered you."

"I just started *my* vacation."

"Then reschedule."

Mulligan didn't say anything.

"Or if you prefer," Lomax said, "I could pay you overtime."

"Overtime? I could use the money. What do you need?"

"There's been a double murder in Warwick. Hardcastle, our lead police reporter, has been at the scene since this morning, but the police are stonewalling him. Meet him there and see what you can do to help."

Mulligan wasn't sure what he'd be able to accomplish aside from standing around looking like a sportswriter. But overtime was overtime.

"Okay. Gimme the address."

■ ■ ■ ■

It was nearly five P.M. by the time Mulligan braked his rusting seven-year-old Yugo to a stop a block from the crime scene. That was as close as he could get. The suburban street was clogged with police cars, TV satellite vans, and a medical examiner's wagon. He was just climbing out when a uniformed officer bellowed at him.

"Get that heap of junk outta here!"

"Please don't talk to Citation that way, Officer," Mulligan said. "He's very sensitive about his looks."

"You *named* your Yugo?"

"Yes, sir."

"After a *racehorse*?"

"No. After the three speeding tickets I got the first week I owned him."

"That clunker goes fast enough to get speeding tickets?"

"This little honey can do forty in a school zone."

The cop chuckled, his face softening a little. "Still gotta move it. No unauthorized vehicles allowed on the street."

"I'm with *The Providence Dispatch.*"

"Oh. Got some ID?"

Mulligan pulled out his wallet and flashed

his press card.

"Shoulda showed me that in the first place."

Yellow crime scene tape had been strung across the trunks of four red maples that bordered the front yard of a white-shingled ranch-style house. Outside the tape, a gaggle of print, radio, and TV reporters milled around on the sidewalk. None of them appeared to be doing anything. Mulligan recognized Billy Hardcastle, a rawboned redneck who had hired on with the *Dispatch* after five years as the police reporter at the *Arkansas Democrat-Gazette.*

"I'm Mulligan."

"I know who you are," Hardcastle said. "You cover sports. You see any sports goin' on here?"

"Mr. Lomax sent me to give you some help."

Mulligan extended his right hand. Hardcastle ignored it.

"I *told* that SOB I don't need no goddamn help."

"You don't?"

"I don't. And I sure as hell don't have time to wet-nurse a rookie. Jesus! What the fuck was Lomax thinkin'?"

Mulligan shrugged.

"Now that I'm here, is there something

you'd like me to do?"

"Yeah. Leave."

"What if I talk to the neighbors, see if they know anything?"

"You don't think I thought of that? I'm way ahead of you, kid."

"What's everybody standing around for?"

"The chief's gonna come out in a few minutes and tell us what the hell's going on. I expect you to be gone by then."

"Maybe I could —"

"Maybe you could shut your pie hole and keep the fuck outta my way."

"Sure. I can do that."

So Mulligan, who'd never been this close to a murder, kept the fuck outta Hardcastle's way. He stood silently on the sidewalk and scanned the faces gathered around the house. The cops with their drained eyes. The frightened neighbors standing on the other side of the street. The print and broadcast journalists hungry for a headline. Hardcastle was right. He didn't belong here.

Forty minutes dragged by before Chief Walter Bennett of the Warwick PD strode out the front door of the murder house and approached the police line. Reporters shouted questions. The chief held up both hands to silence them.

"Here's what I can tell you. We have two

victims, Becky Medeiros, twenty-eight, of this address, and her four-year-old daughter, Jessica. Next of kin has been notified, so it's okay to report the names. We have a suspect in custody. That is all I am prepared to say at this time."

As he turned away, reporters hurled questions.

"When were they killed?"

"Who discovered the bodies?"

"Were they shot?"

"Did you recover the murder weapon?"

"Were drugs involved?"

The chief turned back to face them.

"They were killed sometime late last night or early this morning. Everything else is still under investigation."

"Hey, Chief!" Hardcastle shouted. "The neighbors say Becky's live-in boyfriend, Walter Miller, was taken away in handcuffs this morning. Can you confirm that he's your suspect?"

"We are still in the preliminary stages of our investigation," Bennett said, his narrowed eyes locked on Hardcastle. "If you print that name, you will never get so much as a head nod from anyone in this department. Do I make myself clear?"

He turned away abruptly, stomped up the

front walk, and disappeared inside the house.

"Big friggin' deal," Hardcastle muttered. "That prick never tells us shit anyway."

"That mean you're going with the name?" Mulligan asked.

Hardcastle smirked and headed for his car.

The rest of the reporters sprinted for their vehicles, too. Doors slammed. Engines roared to life. Minutes later, Mulligan stood alone on the sidewalk, a single uniformed patrolman eyeing him warily from the other side of the police line.

Mulligan turned and looked around. Neighbors who had been watching from across the street were drifting away, scuttling down the sidewalks and slipping back inside their houses. After a few minutes, the only ones left were two teenage boys on bicycles. One was a short, skinny kid in a Boston Celtics T-shirt with Kevin McHale's number 32 on the back. The other was a tall, heavyset kid wearing a Red Sox jersey with Mo Vaughn's number 42. The big kid was black, a rarity in this lily-white neighborhood. His wine-red twenty-six-inch Schwinn racer looked like a toy between his thighs.

What the heck, Mulligan figured. Since I'm here, I might as well ask a few questions. As he crossed the street and approached the two boys, they started to head out.

"Hey! Hold up."

"What do *you* want?" the short, skinny one snapped.

"I'm wondering if either of you saw what happened here this morning."

"Naw," the skinny kid said.

"I did," the other boy said.

"You *did*?" the skinny one said.

"Yeah."

"What's your name?" Mulligan asked.

"Kwame."

"Kwame what?"

"Kwame Diggs."

"How old are you?"

"Thirteen."

That was a surprise. Mulligan would have pegged him for a high school senior, maybe a starting lineman on the Veterans Memorial football team.

"You live around here?"

"Uh-huh."

"Where?"

"The green house right over there."

"Can you tell me what you saw?"

"You a cop?"

"I'm a reporter."

"He's lyin'," the skinny kid said. "Don't

tell him nothin', Kwame."

"You got something against the police?" Mulligan asked.

The skinny kid didn't say anything.

"Look, here's my press pass," Mulligan said, pulling it out of his pocket and showing it to them.

"You gonna put my name in the paper?" Kwame asked.

"Put your name in the paper? Only if you want me to."

"Yeah? That would be fuckin' cool!"

"Okay, then. I bet there were a lot of sirens going off here early this morning. Did they wake you up?"

"Uh-huh," Kwame said.

"So what did you do?"

"Pulled on some clothes and ran over to see what was up."

"And?"

"Couple of cops were putting handcuffs on a guy and shoving him in the back of a police car."

"Did you recognize him?"

"Yeah. Walter Miller."

"Walter Miller? He lives there, right?"

"Uh-huh. He moved in about six months ago."

"Did you notice anything unusual about him this morning?"

"Hell, yeah. He had blood all over him."

"Anything else?"

"He was screamin' and cryin' and shit."

"He must be the one who done it," the skinny kid butted in.

"Anything besides the blood make you think that?" Mulligan asked.

The skinny kid looked blank.

"Did Miller and Becky fight a lot?"

"I don't know nothin' about that," the skinny kid said.

"Me either," Kwame said, "but ain't it always the boyfriend who done it?"

"Where'd you hear that?"

"That Law & Order show on TV."

With that, the two friends took off down the street. Mulligan watched them go, then walked around the neighborhood to see if anyone else would talk to him. Those who did hadn't seen anything worth putting in the paper. After an hour he gave it up, walked back to the murder house, and chatted up the uniform behind the police tape.

"Must be terrible in there," Mulligan said.

"So I hear, but I haven't been inside. If I had, I couldn't tell you anything anyway."

"Bodies been removed?"

"Hours ago."

"Remember anything else like this ever happening in this neighborhood?"

"I don't remember anything *this* brutal happening in the whole damn state. At least not since Eric Kessler butchered the Freeman boy back in the eighties."

It was early evening now, the light leaking from the sky. Mulligan was still chatting up the uniform when a streetlight across the road snapped on. It was time to pack it in. He'd have to return to the paper and tell Lomax he had nothing to show for more than three hours of work.

He'd just fished the car keys out of his pocket when a detective, a tall, lanky guy with thickly muscled forearms, strode purposefully out of the murder house and headed for an unmarked car parked on the street.

Before he reached it, Mulligan intercepted him.

January 1990

It's a sunny, unseasonably warm Saturday morning, but the boy is planted in front of the TV, transfixed by an episode of *Danger Mouse. . . .* He wishes the two crows, Leatherhead and Stiletto Mafiosa, would finally get hold of the little do-gooder and twist his head off.

But cartoons are never that cool.

On the front porch, someone is talking to his mother. He mutes the television to catch the gist and hears their next-door neighbor, Mrs. Bigsby, blubbering about something.

"I'm so sorry," the boy's mother says. "I can't imagine who could have done such a terrible thing."

The old bat must have found her ugly little mutt this morning, stuffed in the trash can behind her garage. Muzzle tied shut with twine. Tail, ears, and feet hacked off. And who knows how many stab wounds? The boy doesn't. He lost count.

"We had Frieda for seven years," Mrs. Bigsby says. "She was our best friend. We loved her so much."

Friend.

Love.

Words the boy hears often around the house. He's even learned to use them. Still, they are mystifying. He has no idea what they mean.

He shrugs and turns the volume back up.

4

June 1992

"Excuse me. I'm Mulligan. A reporter for the *Dispatch.*"

"I've got nothing for you, Mulligan," the detective said.

"Look, I know that Becky Medeiros's boyfriend, Walter Miller, was arrested here this morning, and that he had blood all over him."

The detective gave him a hard look and said, "Get in the car."

"Why? Am I under arrest?"

"Just get in the damn car."

He opened the front passenger-side door, and Mulligan slid in. The detective slammed the door shut, walked around the unmarked Crown Vic, and got behind the wheel.

"Don't put Miller's name in the paper," the detective said.

"Why not?"

"Because he didn't do it."

"He didn't do it? The chief said a suspect was in custody. Does that mean you've arrested someone else?"

"No."

"Aw, hell," Mulligan said.

"Yeah," the detective said.

They both sat there and thought about that for a moment.

"You look familiar," the detective finally said, "but I don't know why. I don't remember seeing your sorry ass around the station."

"You haven't. I usually cover college sports."

"Wait a minute. Are you *Liam* Mulligan? Didn't you play for the Friars?"

"I'm surprised you'd remember. I was Dickey Simpkins' backup, so I didn't get much playing time."

"I know. I'm a big Providence College fan. Got me a pair of season tickets right behind the visitors' bench." He extended his hand, and Mulligan shook it. "I'm Andy Jennings. PC Class of '71."

"Nice to meet you, Detective Jennings. I just wish it were under better circumstances."

"Call me Andy."

"Well, Andy, you and I have a mutual problem."

"And what would that be?"

"You know Hardcastle?"

"Yeah. He's an asshole."

"I agree. And I'm pretty sure he's planning to name Miller as a suspect in tomorrow's paper."

"So stop him."

"Stop him? He won't listen to me. I was sent to help him out, but he gave me the brush-off."

Jennings sighed, cranked the ignition, turned on the headlights, and pulled away from the curb.

"Where are we going?"

"You'll find out when we get there."

As he turned onto West Shore Road, the detective snapped the radio on and tuned it to WPRO, a local news and talk station.

"Lincoln Chafee, son of former U.S. senator John Chafee, formally announced his candidacy for mayor of Warwick this afternoon," newsman Ron St. Pierre was saying. He cued a tape of the candidate's statement, then cut it short to break in with a bulletin.

"This just in. Warwick police have arrested Walter Miller, a thirty-four-year-old Narragansett Electric employee, in connection with the overnight murder of his girlfriend, Becky Medeiros, and her four-year-old daughter. We'll have more on this breaking story at the top of the hour."

"Aw, shit," Jennings said. "I was afraid that was gonna happen. After what he's been through, the poor bastard doesn't need this." He rubbed his jaw and added, "Guess I'm gonna have to call the station — and your editor — to set the record straight."

"Two out of three Rhode Islanders read the *Dispatch,*" Mulligan said, "so it's the best way to straighten out anything. But there's still a problem. If all we have is a short statement from you, the story will get buried inside the metro section where most people will never see it."

Jennings didn't say anything.

"But maybe we can fix that."

"How?"

"If you give me enough details about what happened inside that house, the story might end up on page one."

Jennings gave him a sideways glance. "Bet that would get you in solid with your boss, huh?"

"It would. And it would really piss off Hardcastle."

"I'm all for that," Jennings said, "but I gotta give this some thought."

He turned onto Greenwich Avenue and pulled into Dunkin' Donuts. Inside, they ordered two cups of coffee, black for Jennings and lots of milk and sugar for Mulligan. They found a table, and the detective took a sip.

"Sit tight," he told Mulligan. Then he got up and walked outside.

Through the window, Mulligan watched the detective pull a mobile phone out of his jacket and make a call.

In April, after the *Dispatch*'s best advertising quarter in a decade, editors had bought Nokia mobile phones for the entire reporting staff. Mulligan fished the newfangled toy out of his pants and punched in a number.

"City desk, Lomax."

"It's Mulligan, Mr. Lomax."

"Where the hell have you been? Hardcastle got back two hours ago."

"I'm developing a source."

"Got something for me?"

"Not yet, but I'm working on it."

"Oh, really? Hardcastle says you're useless."

"Useless, huh? Give me another hour to prove him wrong."

Before Lomax could reply, Mulligan ended the call and turned the phone off. Outside the window, Jennings was still talking, gesturing emphatically with his free hand. It was fifteen minutes before the detective tucked the phone into his pocket and strolled back inside.

"You called the chief?" Mulligan asked.

"Yup."

"And?"

"He says this will have to be off the record."

"Off the record? That means I can't use it."

"Oh, right. I meant not for attribution. The chief wants you to say it came from a source close to the investigation. That work for you?"

"Sure thing," Mulligan said.

Jennings looked out the window and composed his thoughts.

"Becky Medeiros and Walter Miller were planning to get married," he said. "They already sent out invitations and ordered flowers. Becky picked out dresses for herself and Jessica, her daughter from her first marriage, at Ana's Bridal Boutique in East Providence."

"You know that how?"

"A little detective work."

Mulligan pulled out a notebook and pen and started scribbling.

"The neighbors never heard the couple fight. They say Miller doted on the little girl, always bringing her presents, playing with her in the yard, taking walks with her around the neighborhood."

"So what happened this morning?"

Jennings ran down what he'd found when he'd arrived at the murder house. Occasionally, he consulted his notes. Mostly he talked with his eyes closed, as if a video of the scene were playing inside his head.

"Jessica bled out from one slice across the throat. But Becky? In twenty years on the job, I've never seen anything like it. The killer really went to town on her."

Mulligan dropped his Bic on the table and rubbed his eyes with the backs of his hands. This wasn't the kind of story he had signed on for. Jennings drained his coffee and ordered another for both of them. Mulligan ignored his. The first cup felt like acid in his stomach.

"By afternoon, the front yard was full of cops," Jennings said. "The sidewalk was crawling with reporters shouting questions and snapping pictures of everything that moved. The mayor and two city councilmen showed up to grandstand for the TV cameras. It was a goddamned circus. The chief figured we better make a public statement and announce that we had a suspect in custody."

"He thought you had your guy?"

"At the time, we all did. When you find the boyfriend at the scene of a murder and his hands and shirt are covered in blood, what else are you supposed to think?"

He took off his glasses, rubbed his jaw, and went on with the story.

Jennings and his partner, Detective Mello, drove Miller to the police station. They photographed him, confiscated his clothes, cleaned him up, fingerprinted him, and asked if he wanted a lawyer. He didn't. They stuck him in an interrogation room, gave him a cup of coffee, and managed to get him calmed down enough to tell his story.

The previous evening, he'd helped Becky tuck Jessica into bed, kissed them both good-bye, and headed to his overnight job at Narragansett Electric. He finished work at six A.M. and drove home, stopping off at the Dunkin' Donuts drive-in window on Post Road to pick up a couple of doughnuts for himself, a toasted cinnamon-raisin bagel for Becky, and two large coffees. He pulled his car into the garage, entered the house through the connecting door, and set the food and coffee on the kitchen counter. Then he turned toward the hallway and saw a scene from a slaughterhouse.

He rushed into the hall, slipped on the

blood-slick floor, and nearly fell. He pulled the sheet aside, saw the bodies, and completely lost it.

Did he touch anything besides the sheet?

Miller didn't know.

Mello left the interrogation room and got on the phone to check out Miller's story. It was after six P.M. by the time he tracked down Miller's supervisor at home. Yes, Miller had gotten to work on time at ten P.M. and hadn't left until six A.M. He was sure of it.

"About an hour ago, the medical examiner put the time of death at somewhere between one and three A.M.," Jennings said, "and Miller was released with an apology. Officer Hernandez drove him to Rhode Island Hospital, where I imagine they're giving him tranquilizers and psychological counseling."

"I've got some questions," Mulligan said.

"Shoot."

"Did the medical examiner say how many times Becky was stabbed?"

"Forty-eight."

"Forty-eight?" Mulligan's stomach lurched. He took a moment to compose himself, then pressed on.

"You said the killer twisted the bulb over

the back door to extinguish the light. How could you possibly know that?"

"Officer Rubino was stationed outside that door all day to keep unauthorized personnel from entering the house. Around eight o'clock, it was starting to get dark; so he opened the door, reached in, and hit the switch for the outside light. Nothing happened. He figured the bulb might have been loose, so he reached up to fiddle with it. Fortunately, I'd just stepped outside for a cigarette. I saw what Rubino was about to do and shouted, 'Stop!' As it turned out, the killer left us a perfect thumbprint on the sixty-watt Sylvania."

Mulligan didn't know much about what detectives did, but that sounded like good police work to him. That Jennings could rattle off the wattage and make of the bulb without consulting his notes seemed doubly impressive.

"What do you make of the two blood trails in the living room?"

"One of them was made by size nine dress shoes," Jennings said. "That was Miller tracking blood as he ran across the living room and out the front door."

"And the other one?"

"After the killer butchered his victims, he walked through the living room in his stocking feet."

"He did? What for?"

"To look out the picture window. He was probably checking to see if Becky's screams roused the neighbors. He left a blood smear on the curtains and a print of his forehead on the glass."

"Why wasn't he wearing shoes?"

"We figure he took them off before he broke in so he wouldn't make as much noise when he creeped the place."

"How did he get in?"

"He found an unlocked window at the rear of the house, pried the screen off, and crawled inside."

"Think he left the same way?"

"Can't say for sure."

"Any idea who could have done this?"

"Not yet. Any more questions?"

"Yeah. How do you spell Rubino?"

October 1990

The scientific method.

The boy sits at a school desk that is uncomfortably small for him and pays close attention as the teacher explains it. You form a hypothesis. Then you design an experiment to test it.

He's a solid B student. He likes to read, and history intrigues him, but math and science usually bore him. Not today. This concept appeals to him. It's not something you learn just to get a passing grade. It's something you can *use.* He decides to try it himself.

That afternoon, he thinks up his hypothesis. Then he tests it. He jumps with glee when his hypothesis proves to be correct.

Cats do burn faster than dogs.

5

June 1992

It was nearly ten P.M. by the time Mulligan stepped off the elevator into the *Dispatch*'s football-field-size newsroom, where three-quarters of the paper's 340 journalists worked. The rest were posted in Washington and in nine suburban bureaus that covered local news in every one of Rhode Island's thirty-nine cities and towns.

At this hour, more than half of the desks were empty. At the others, reporters were pounding out late-breaking news, copy editors were writing headlines, layout men were dummying pages, and photo editors were cropping the last few pictures for the fat Sunday edition. Lomax, who had started work twelve hours earlier, was still at his post at the city desk. He practically lived there.

" 'Bout time you showed up," he said. "The murder story's bare-bones. Got anything we can use to fill it out?"

"I do," Mulligan said.

"Type up your notes and give them to Hardcastle. Be quick about it. We're already crowding deadline."

"Sure thing, Mr. Lomax."

"And shoot me a hard copy. I want to see what you came up with."

Minutes after he turned in the notes, Lomax and Hardcastle hustled over to Mulligan's desk. Lomax was grinning. Hardcastle wasn't.

"Who's your source for all this?" Hardcastle demanded.

"Nearly all of it came from Detective Jennings."

"*Nearly* all?"

"I also talked to a thirteen-year-old neighborhood kid."

"You expect us to use information from a fuckin' *kid*?"

"He told me Miller was covered with blood when the police arrested him. Jennings tried to hold that back, but when I told him I already knew about it, he confirmed it."

"Big fuckin' deal," Hardcastle said. "I had that already." Without another word, he turned and stomped back to his desk.

"Maybe you're not useless after all,"

Lomax said. "Why don't you head on home now and get some rest?"

"If it's okay with you, Mr. Lomax, I'd like to hang around so I can read the story when Hardcastle's done with it."

"Sure thing. And kid?"

"Yes, sir?"

"Your notes put the murder house on Oakhurst Street. It's Oakhurst *Avenue.* Don't make a mistake like that again."

Thirty minutes later, Mulligan sat at his desk reading the finished copy. Hardcastle may be a jerk, he thought, but the guy can really write. As Mulligan headed for the elevator, he overheard Lomax and Hardcastle squabbling at the city desk.

"Why'd you leave Mulligan's name off of this?" Lomax asked.

"Cuz there's no way I'm sharing a byline with a fuckin' sportswriter."

"Fine," the city editor said. "Have it your way."

Next morning, Mulligan slept till noon. When he woke, he pulled on a Red Sox T-shirt and an old pair of jeans, trudged barefoot down the stairs from his mother's second-floor walk-up in the city's Mount Hope neighborhood, and fetched the Sunday paper from the stoop. The murder story was below the fold on page one. The two-column headline said:

Killer At Large in Double Slaying

It carried a single byline:

By L. S. A. Mulligan

By the time he got back upstairs, his mother had set the kitchen table with mugs of strong coffee and plates of pancakes and bacon. Together they ate and read the entire paper front to back, passing the sections back and forth. As his mother cleared the table, Mulligan spent an extra few minutes with the sports, where his piece on Coach Happy Dobbs was displayed on the section front. Then he rose and went to the sink to wash the dishes.

His mother sat back down at the table, cut out her son's two bylined stories, and stuck them on the refrigerator.

"I'm so proud of you, Liam."

"Thanks, Mom."

After drying the dishes, Mulligan stood in front of the refrigerator and studied the photograph that accompanied the murder story. Somehow, the *Dispatch* had gotten hold of a Medeiros family snapshot. According to the caption, it had been taken a couple of weeks ago at Misquamicut State Beach in Westerly. Jessica was on her knees, her brow furrowed in concentration as she dumped a yellow plastic shovel full of wet sand on top of a lopsided sand castle. Her mother and Miller sat behind her, grinning with their entire beings. Becky's blond hair, backlit by the sun, looked as if it were on fire.

Mulligan stared at the photo for a long time. Then he took the scissors from the kitchen table, cut out the picture, folded it, and slipped it into a vinyl sleeve in his wallet.

He walked into the living room, dropped into the platform rocker, and turned on the Red Sox–Royals game in time to see Frank Viola throw the first pitch to Brian McRae. In the third, the Sox took the lead when Wade Boggs doubled in Ellis Burks. Mulligan didn't care. He pulled out his cell and made a call.

"Mom," he shouted. "I'm going out for a while."

"Okay, hon. Can you pick up a loaf of bread on your way back?"

Ten minutes later, Mulligan pushed through the door of Hopes, the local press hangout, and took a seat at the bar. The Sox game was playing on the overhead TV. Boston had fallen behind by a run, and Viola was in a jam with runners on first and third. Not that it mattered. The Sox were going nowhere. If it weren't for the pathetic Seattle Mariners, they were probably the worst team in the league.

Lee Dykas, the nightside reporter who owned the place, wandered over and thunked a bottle of Bud in front of Mulligan.

"Your tab's getting a little long," he said. "Want to settle up?"

"Thursday. Right after I get paid."

"Okay. By the way, grcat job yesterday. The first one's on me."

"Thanks, Lee."

"Thought you should know Hardcastle was in here running his mouth about you last night."

"That so?"

"Yeah. Told everyone who would listen how you poached his story."

"Doesn't surprise me."

"Don't let it bother you. Hardcastle's a dick."

Mulligan was on his second bottle when Rosella Morelli came through the door in jeans and a tank top, pausing to let her eyes adjust to the dark. No matter how many times he saw her, he was always thrown by her Sicilian good looks. Huge dark eyes, raven hair cropped close to her head, wide shoulders, slim waist. She glided to the bar, claimed the stool next to Mulligan, and wrapped her impossibly long legs around it. At six feet five, she was an inch taller than him.

"Need some company?"

"Yeah. Thanks for coming, Rosie."

Mulligan and Rosie had been playmates in kindergarten and friends all through grade school, then dated off and on in their teens. She was the first girl Mulligan ever kissed. She lied and told him it was her first kiss, too. During their senior year at Providence's Hope High School, he took her to the prom.

One summer night after graduation, when Rosie's parents were out of town, she and Mulligan got sloshed on Pabst while watching *When Harry Met Sally* at a theater in East Providence. Mulligan squirmed and Rosie giggled when Sally, played by Meg Ryan, faked an explosive orgasm inside Manhattan's crowded Katz's Delicatessen. When an older woman diner told a waiter, "I'll have what she's having," Rosie howled. Then she tossed Mulligan a sultry look and whispered, "Yeah. Me too."

Later, as they made out in Rosie's living room, she pulled her T-shirt over her head and unfastened her bra. Then she rose and slid her shorts and panties from her hips. She grabbed Mulligan by the hand, pulled him up from the couch, and led him upstairs to her bedroom. She told him it was going to be her first time. He lied and told her it was going to be his first, too. They giggled as they crawled into bed. But when it was over, neither spoke. They just held each other in the dark until they fell asleep.

In the morning, they avoided eye contact as they pulled on their clothes. They drove in silence to the diner in Kennedy Plaza. After their coffee was delivered, Rosie raised her eyes from her cup, looked into Mulligan's eyes, and said, "It wasn't what I expected."

"I know," he said. "I felt like I was making love to my sister."

Nearly five years later, their families were still mystified that Mulligan hadn't popped the question, but he and Rosie never twisted the sheets again. Now, as he pictured the lithe body beneath the boyish clothes she had always favored, he still felt nothing but, well, friendship. The movie that had inspired them to leap into bed was the story of their lives, but with an alternate ending. Harry and Sally were lifelong friends who finally realized they were in love. Mulligan and Rosie were lifelong friends whose brief sexual encounter had convinced them that's what they'd always be.

Dykas dropped a Bud in front of Rosie, checked Mulligan's bottle, fetched him another from the cooler, and turned to watch the Royals scampering around the bases.

"What's wrong?" Rosie asked. "I thought you'd be on top of the world today."

"I feel more like it's on top of me."

"Want to talk about it?"

Mulligan just shook his head. He picked up his beer and took a pull.

"How's the training going?" he asked.

"Great. One more week and I'll be a full-fledged Providence firefighter. They already told me I'll be assigned to the station in our old neighborhood."

"Good for you. That'll be me cheering right up front at graduation. I might even pull the fire alarm to celebrate." He pulled a cheap cigar out of his shirt pocket and set fire to it. "You know, Rosie, we've talked about this before, but I still don't understand why you turned down that offer from the New York Liberty."

She'd been a star at Rutgers, breaking every career scoring and rebounding record for the Scarlet Knights and even making the cover of *Sports Illustrated*. After her senior season, she was the second player chosen in the WNBA draft.

"That was a children's game," she said. "Now I want to do something important."

"Not me."

"You're kidding, right?"

"Nope."

She swiveled on her stool and draped an arm over his shoulder.

"What happened to becoming the next Seymour Hersh?"

"I'm over that. I took the sportswriting job to get my foot in the door, figuring once they saw what I could do, I could maybe work my way onto the investigative team. But now I just want to get back to covering the Brown Bears and the Friars."

"That's your dream? Writing about sweaty ballers for the rest of your life?"

"It's what I'm cut out for."

"What makes you say *that*?"

"They get elbowed, tackled, or thrown out at third, but nobody gets stabbed."

Rosie stretched out her arms and wrapped him up in a hug.

"I could hold you here until you come to

your senses."

That sounded fine to Mulligan. He felt like hiding there for the rest of his life.

Mulligan stopped at the Cumberland Farms on North Main Street, grabbed a loaf of Wonder Bread, and asked the girl behind the counter for a package of Garcia y Vega cigars. To him, they tasted like shredded cardboard laced with citronella, but on a rookie sports reporter's pay, they were the best smokes he could afford.

As he slid back into Citation, his mobile phone rang.

"Mulligan."

"It's Lomax. What time can you get in tomorrow?"

"I thought I was back on vacation."

"I'd like you to stick with the murder case for a while."

Jennings's recounting of the horrors inside Becky Medeiros's house flashed through Mulligan's mind. He didn't want anything more to do with stories like that.

"The murder case? Can't Hardcastle handle it?"

"The Warwick PD is shutting him out. Apparently there's some bad history there. I need you on this, Mulligan. You're the only one the cops are talking to."

"I've got plans to spend the week in Boston," Mulligan lied. "Got seats for the whole Sox home stand."

"I'll find a way to make it up to you. Suppose I have the sports editor add you to our World Series coverage in the fall? How's that sound?"

Mulligan could see there was no way to talk Lomax out of this.

"All right, Mr. Lomax. I'll be on it first thing Monday morning."

"Good. And Mulligan?"

"Yeah?"

"Call me Ed."

6

"You look tired, Andy."

"I've got a right to. I've barely slept the last four weeks."

"Still no leads?" Mulligan asked.

"Nothing but dead ends."

It was Fourth of July weekend, the temperature peaking at ninety-six degrees outside the air-conditioned sanctuary of the Fraternal Order of Police lodge on Tanner Avenue in Warwick; but the Medeiros case had grown as cold as the inside of a morgue drawer.

"The tip I gave you didn't go anywhere?"

"Ralph Branco *was* obsessed with Becky. You got that part right. The greasy little creep dated her a few times after her divorce, and he couldn't stand it that she had the sense to dump him for Miller. But his alibi for the night of the murders checks out. And he wears a size ten shoe. No way he could have made those footprints on the rug."

Jennings drained his bottle of Narragansett and asked for another.

"How'd you find out about him?" he asked Mulligan. "We'd totally missed that."

"His name came up in a bar conversation with a couple of locals last week."

Jennings raised an eyebrow.

"I've been asking around," Mulligan said. "Same as you."

"Makes me wonder what else we missed," Jennings said, pausing to take another swallow. "Half the force has been working on this. We've questioned everyone we can think of who might have had contact with Becky. Postal workers. Meter readers. Trash collectors. Gutter cleaners. Landscapers. When that didn't pan out, we widened it to people she dealt with away from home. Gas station attendants, checkout clerks, bank tellers, pharmacists, co-workers, hairdressers, her manicurist, her doctor, her friends. Her ex-husband, of course. A couple of them had sheets, but none of them matched the physical evidence, and none of them seemed to have a reason to kill her. As far as we can tell, no one did."

"So now what?"

"Now we go back to the beginning and

start over. The killer was sloppy and careless. He left physical evidence all over the place. If his prints were on file, the bastard would already be in custody. The prosecutor says that once we find him, the conviction's gonna be a slam dunk. But if this was just a random crime of opportunity, we may never figure out who did it."

"Unless he kills again," Mulligan said.

April 1991

Street football. Five kids on each side. No tackling, just touch, which cuts down on the ways the boy can hurt people.

Eddie hasn't shown up today, so they have to let the dumb girl play. Jenny *is* fast. The boy has to give her that. She's tall, too. Taller than any of the guys. Except him, of course. Long, gangly legs like a colt that just dropped out of its mama. Ugly metal braces on her buckteeth. A blackhead on her nose that she doesn't have the sense to pop. And no tits on her skinny-ass chest.

He's pissed off just looking at her, split out to his right as if she thinks he would actually throw *her* the ball. It's bad enough that they're letting the bitch play. Why does she have to be on *his* team?

The boy grunts, "Hut!," takes the snap, and drops back to pass. He always plays quarter-back because he can throw the ball farther and straighter than any of the others. He looks left and sees Vinnie, the little Italian kid, churning his stubby legs as he tries to get open. Fat chance of that. Then he glances right and sees that Jenny has beaten her defender by a good five yards.

The street is nearly empty of cars today. The only vehicle in sight is Becky Medeiros's Toyota Celica, parked at the right-side curb about thirty yards away.

Jenny is looking back over her shoulder now, waving her arm and calling for the ball. What the hell. He rears back and lets the football fly, aiming for the yellow "Smile. God Loves You" bumper sticker on the back of the car.

The throw leads her right into it, just as he intended. She hits the back of the car with a thud and falls hard to the pavement.

The other kids rush to her side. The boy hangs back, not wanting them to see how hard he is laughing. He sticks around, admiring his handiwork, until the ambulance comes to take her away.

7

June 1994

Mulligan finished his phone interview with Big East Conference commissioner Mike Tranghese, hung up, and started typing.

The conference's four big-time football schools, Syracuse, Boston College, Pittsburgh, and Miami, were threatening to secede. If they went through with it, they'd take the league's lucrative CBS-TV contract with them, leaving the remaining six teams, including Providence College, in the lurch. It was a big story. If Mulligan could get it in print before anyone else broke it, he'd make national news.

"Mulligan?"

"Not now."

"This is urgent."

"So's what I'm doing."

"Mulligan, look at me and pay attention."

He looked up and saw Lomax hovering over his desk.

"What is it?" He turned back to the keyboard and kept typing.

"There's been another multiple murder in Warwick."

Mulligan raised his hands from the keys.

"Look, Ed, I've got a big story on my hands. Can't this wait?"

"How big?"

Mulligan told him.

"Okay. But as soon as you're done, come see me."

Mulligan finished the story, turned it in, and answered the sports editor's questions about his sources. It was an hour before he reluctantly made his way toward the city editor's desk. He wanted nothing more to do with murders, yet the memory of Becky Medeiros's face in that family photograph propelled him across the room.

He pulled up a chair across from Lomax and asked, "What do we know?"

"We've got three victims," Lomax said. "Connie Stuart, age thirty-three, and her two daughters, ages eight and twelve. They were killed sometime late last night or early this morning. Other than that, the cops aren't saying anything."

"What does this have to do with me?"

"The scene is just a couple of blocks from where Becky Medeiros and her daughter were butchered two years ago."

"Oh, hell."

"Yeah. Hardcastle's at the scene, but as usual the Warwick cops are stonewalling him. I thought maybe you could tap the source you cultivated on the Medeiros case."

Mulligan took a deep breath and slowly expelled it.

"I'd rather not," he said. "I'm not an 'if it bleeds, it leads' kind of guy. I still have nightmares from the last time you sucked me in."

Lomax leaned back in his chair and gave Mulligan an appraising look.

"This is a big story, kid. I'd hate to get beat on it."

Mulligan didn't say anything.

"I wouldn't ask if I didn't really need you on this."

"You can't find somebody else?"

"Not somebody with your source."

Mulligan looked at his feet and shook his head.

"Look," Lomax said. "Sometimes you have to accept an assignment you don't want. It's part of being a professional."

Mulligan had heard the line before. It was the standard boilerplate *Dispatch* editors used on reluctant reporters. And it was meant to be a conversation stopper.

"Okay, Ed," Mulligan said. "I'll see what I can do."

He went back to his desk and dialed the phone.

"Detective Jennings."

"Hi, Andy. It's Mulligan."

"Got no time for you now, kid. Get back to me in a few days."

Mulligan thanked him and hung up. Then he pulled out his wallet, removed the yellowing newspaper photograph of the Medeiros family, and smoothed it out on his desk. The picture reminded him, as if he needed reminding, of why he didn't want to cover stories like this.

It also reminded him of why somebody should.

8

Three days dragged by before Jennings found the time to meet Mulligan at Dunkin' Donuts on Greenwich Avenue in Warwick. Three days in which Mulligan and Hardcastle had to listen to Lomax rant about tight-lipped cops and about reporters who couldn't come up with anything about a goddamned triple murder.

It was the same doughnut shop where Mulligan and Jennings had their first conversation two years earlier. Since then, it had become their spot, the two of them getting together once or twice a month to share their passion for the PC Friars and the Boston Red Sox. Jennings was already there, nursing a cup of black coffee, when Mulligan strolled in and dropped into the booth.

"Hey, Mulligan. How's your mom doing?"

"Not so good."

"Aw, hell."

"It's stage four uterine cancer, Andy. The

doctors can't do anything but try to make her comfortable."

Jennings shook his head sadly, then reached across the table and rested his hand on Mulligan's shoulder. "How long has she got?"

"A few months, maybe."

"I'm so sorry."

The two friends sat quietly, each lost in his own thoughts.

"You look like shit," Mulligan finally said.

"That's what working seventy-two hours straight will do to you."

"Think it's the same guy?"

"Oh, yeah. No question. A print we lifted from one of the murder weapons came back a match to the prints from the Medeiros case. But I knew as soon as I saw the bodies. The crime scenes are that similar."

"Why don't you start at the beginning," Mulligan said, "and tell me everything."

"I'll give you what I can, but I have to hold back a few details only the perp could know."

The evening before the murder, Connie Stuart and her twin sister, Mary O'Keefe, decided to go shopping. Mary picked Connie up and drove her to the Warwick Mall, where they bought new bathing suits and some shorts for the summer. Mary got the new Bon Jovi CD. Connie picked out a new set of kitchen knives.

On the way home, they talked about whether they should move in together now that it was clear that Connie's wayward husband wasn't coming back. Mary dropped her sister off at her house at nine forty-five P.M.

At eight the next morning, Mary called Connie, but she didn't answer. Three hours later, when Connie still wasn't picking up, Mary got a little worried, so she drove over. Connie didn't answer the door, but Mary had a copy of the house key. She let herself in.

The 911 call came in at 11:21 A.M. Saturday morning.

Help. Please help. There's blood everywhere. It's my sister. And her kids. Oh, God. They must be dead. So much blood.

Officers Peralta and Berube arrived first. They took a quick look inside the house, backed out, secured the scene, and called for detectives. Jennings and Mello got there just before noon.

Upstairs in the master bedroom, the detectives found a flowered sheet soaked crimson. It was draped over a lump centered neatly in the middle of a queen-size mattress. Jennings pulled the sheet aside, exposing Connie Stuart's naked body. Her arms and legs were arranged like the points of a star. On the floor at the foot of the bed, two more lumps lay beneath a chenille bedspread that had once been white. Beneath it, Mello found Sara, eight, and Emma, twelve, dressed in matching Little Mermaid pajamas. Blood had soaked through the mattress and pooled on the floor. The oak headboard, the walls, and the ceiling were splattered with it.

"The Stuart place backs up on a vacant lot, just like the Medeiros residence," Jennings said. "No trees, this time. Just a lot of scrub brush. The killer hid in a thicket a few yards from the back fence and spied on the family off and on for weeks."

"For weeks? How do you know that?"

"He made a little nest for himself in the leaves. And he left a dozen roaches behind."

"So he would have known that her husband moved out weeks ago," Mulligan said.

"That's the way I see it. Late Friday night or early Saturday morning, he came out of his hiding place and jumped the chain-link fence. He crossed the yard, pried the screen off an unlocked window, and slid it open.

Then he took his shoes off and climbed inside.

"He left a lot of physical evidence behind, just like last time. It tells a story, if you know how to read it."

The killer found Connie's new set of KitchenAid knives, still unopened, on the butcher-block kitchen counter. He ripped the top off the box and tore through the packaging, scattering cardboard and Styrofoam on the floor.

Carrying the four biggest knives, he crept up the carpeted stairs to the second floor and entered the dark bedroom where Connie was sleeping. He jumped on top of her and pounded her face with his fists. Then he used one of the knives to slice her nightgown from neckline to hem. He yanked it off her and tossed it over a bedpost. Then he went to work with the blades.

Sara and Emma must have heard their mother's screams. They leaped from their beds and ran into her room. There, the two children fought for their lives and the life of their mother, the killer's blades slicing their hands and arms as they tried to drive him off. But he was much too strong. When they fell to the floor, he continued to stab them, striking so hard that he broke off two blades in Emma's chest.

When he was done, he dropped the knives and padded down the hall to the upstairs bathroom, leaving a bloody trail of footprints on the hardwood floor.

At the bathroom sink, he flipped on the faucet and rinsed the blood from his face and hands. Perhaps it was then that he noticed he was bleeding. Somehow, he'd cut himself with one of the knives. Maybe his hand had slipped as he savagely plunged a blade into Connie. Or maybe it had happened as he struggled with the children.

He pulled a lilac towel from the rack and used it to stanch his wound. Then he rummaged through the medicine cabinet, knocking bottles of aspirin and cold tablets, a child's thermometer, and a box of tampons into the sink. He found a package of Band-Aids, tore it open, and slapped one on the cut. He dropped the crumpled bandage wrapper in the sink and the bloodstained towel on the bathroom floor. Testing proved the blood on the towel didn't come from his victims.

He returned to the bedroom, plucked souvenirs from Connie and her children, and covered their bodies. Then he carried his treasures down the stairs and exited the way he came, leaving fingerprints on the windowsill.

Outside, he pulled off his socks, put on his running shoes, and sprinted across the backyard, leaving size thirteen tracks in the soft ground. Before reaching the property line, he paused beside the swing set and vomited in the grass. Then he grabbed hold of a tree branch, stripping it of leaves as he hauled himself over the fence.

He peeled off his blood-soaked hoodie, threw it and his socks beneath some bushes in the vacant lot, and ran off.

"A few questions," Mulligan said.

"Shoot."

"How many times were they stabbed?"

Jennings flipped through his notebook. "Connie, twenty-two times. Sarah, her youngest, twelve times. And Emma, the twelve-year-old?" He closed the notebook slowly and locked eyes with Mulligan. "Fifty-two times."

Mulligan sat in stunned silence, willing the picture in his head to go away.

"Do you ever get used to it?" he finally asked.

"Haven't yet," Jennings said. "I hope the hell I never do."

"I wonder why he singled out Emma for special treatment."

"No idea."

"Why did he cover the bodies?"

"I don't know."

"What made him throw up?"

"Hard to say," Jennings said. "It wasn't because the gore turned his stomach, that's for sure. This guy *likes* the smell of blood."

"What did he take from the victims?"

"Some jewelry Connie's sister says they always wore. But that's one of the details we're holding back."

Mulligan reached for his cup of coffee and discovered it was cold. Jennings fetched another round.

"Got any suspects?" Mulligan asked.

"Not yet."

"So now what?"

"We're interviewing everybody who knew the Stuarts and the Medeiroses to see who might have had contact with both families."

"Neighbors, meter readers, trash collectors, landscapers?" Mulligan asked. "Gas station attendants, checkout clerks, hairdressers, teachers, PTA members?"

"All that and more."

"Sounds like a lot of people."

"Yeah, but I'm betting only one of them has a knife wound and size thirteen feet."

"Size thirteen?" Mulligan said. "Wait a minute. Didn't Becky Medeiros's killer wear size twelves?"

"So maybe he gained some weight. There's no doubt it's the same guy."

Mulligan shuddered and took a sip from his cup. "Why would someone do this?" he asked.

Jennings turned and looked out the window. It was nearly a minute before he turned back.

"Off the record?"

"Sure."

"Because I don't want to see this in the paper."

"Then you won't, Andy."

"This was a sex crime."

"They were *raped*?"

"Not exactly. After he killed them, he masturbated on the bodies."

Mulligan felt bile rise in his throat. "Did he jerk off over Becky Medeiros and her daughter, too?"

"He did."

"At least you've got his DNA."

"Yeah. From the blood on the towel, too. But with all the prints he left, no way we're gonna need it to convict him."

A couple of days after filing his story, Mulligan met his best friend at Hopes. This time, it wasn't just the men whose admiring eyes followed Rosie as she strode to her bar stool.

"How's your mom?" Rosie asked.

"Holding her own for now."

"I should go see her."

"She'd like that. She thinks the world of you, Rosie."

They ordered Buds, and Rosie dropped a twenty on the bar. Mulligan picked it up, pressed it into her palm, and told her to put it back in her purse.

"No way you're paying for anything tonight after what you did yesterday."

"In that case, I'll have champagne," Rosie said.

"The closest you can get to that here is Miller High Life, the champagne of bottled beers."

"Then I'll stick with Budweiser."

"Did Hardcastle get the story right?" Mulligan asked.

"Yeah, but I thought the headline was a bit much."

It had been the lead story on the metro page:

Heroic Lady Firefighter
Rescues Two Children
From Locust St. Blaze

"Tell me how it happened."

"Why? You already read about it."

"I want to hear you tell it."

"I will if you put out that cigar. It stinks."

So he did.

"When we rolled up, flames were jumping in one of the second-floor windows. Someone was screaming about two little boys trapped up there. Eddie Silvia and I pulled a ladder off the pumper and propped it under a window that didn't have flames in it yet. I was the first one up. I smashed the window and sash with a fire ax and climbed inside.

"Lucky for me, the kids were right there, choking on smoke that was seeping through the bottom of their bedroom door. I grabbed the nearest one and handed him to Eddie, who was right behind me at the top of the ladder. Then I grabbed the other one and carried him down. Nothing much to it, really."

"Tell that to their mother when she names her next born after you."

Rosie smiled at that.

"What was it like?" Mulligan asked.

"Better than the day I dropped thirty-two points on Tennessee."

"I'll bet. Think *I've* got what it takes to be a firefighter?"

"You serious?"

"Serious? . . . No, I guess not."

"What is it, then?"

"I'm starting to hate my job."

"What you're doing is important, Mulligan."

"Is it?"

"Of course it is. There's a serial killer on the loose, and the police are having a hard time catching him. People need to know about that."

"I guess. But it's such an ugly story, Rosie. I just wish I weren't the one telling them."

September 1991

The lock on the antique steamer trunk in his father's bedroom closet is easy to pick. Inside, the boy finds two dozen videotapes, each still in its original cardboard sleeve. He sorts through them, studying the glossy cover photos of naked women named Sheri St. Clair, Angel Kelley, Stacy Donovan, Christie Canyon, and Candie Evans. He stops when he comes to the one with a slim blonde named Ginger Lynn holding a large black penis in her small fist.

He returns the other tapes to the trunk, takes his selection downstairs to the living room, and slides it into the family VCR. Then he stretches out on the couch and unzips his fly. His parents are at work. His brother has football practice. His sister is at her dance lesson. The boy has the house to himself.

In the opening scene, the blonde strips and begins playing with the cocks of two scrawny white guys. The boy watches for a couple of minutes, then fast-forwards until he reaches the part with the brother. He has bulging biceps, six-pack abs, and a penis so huge that the blonde looks a little scared.

The boy reaches down and plays with himself. Nothing happens. After fifteen minutes of frustration, he gets up and pops the tape out of the VCR. He goes back upstairs and returns the video to the trunk. Then he enters his bedroom, fetches one of *his* tapes from the shoebox under his bed, and carries it downstairs.

When the movie reaches the part where Jason Voorhees stabs Alice in the head with an ice pick, the boy's dick is iron.

9

July 1994

"The chief's on a rampage," Jennings said. "If you don't watch your ass, you're gonna get hauled in."

"Hauled in?" Mulligan said. "What the hell for?"

"Interfering with a police investigation. Half the people we interview say they've already been questioned by you."

"That's gotta be an exaggeration. You've got thirty people working this. There's only one of me."

"Okay, so maybe it's just a quarter. That's not the point. What in God's name do you think you're doing, Mulligan? You're not a cop."

"Heck, Andy. I'm not even much of a reporter."

"So?"

"So I was thinking maybe I could help out a little. Some of the punks who talk to me would never spill anything to the cops."

Jennings fixed a hard eye on Mulligan, then took a sip from his cup of Dunkin'.

"I don't suppose you've learned anything useful, have you?"

"Not yet."

Jennings sighed, then rested his head in his hands. He was a lot grayer than when they'd first met two years ago. This case was tearing some life out of him.

"We're under a lot of pressure to solve this thing," the detective said. "The whole state's in a panic. Alarm systems are selling out. Folks who never considered owning a firearm before have stripped the local gun shops bare. People are installing dead bolts and outside floodlights."

"Some are even nailing their windows shut," Mulligan said.

"Really?"

"Yeah."

"I hadn't heard that."

They went back to their coffee, each adrift in his own thoughts.

"I take it you cleared Connie's ex," Mulligan finally said.

"Yeah. According to her twin sister, Carl Stuart made a big scene when he moved out. Claimed Connie had cheated on him with some guy she worked with at Johnson

& Wales. Mary insists it's not true, but we never did get to the bottom of it. And Carl has a sheet, an assault a couple of years ago for mixing it up with a drunk who hit on Connie at Lupo's."

"A jealous guy," Mulligan said.

"Looks like. But no way he's good for it. The stocking feet that tracked through the murder scenes could never have squeezed into his size nines. His prints are all over Connie's house, of course, but he's not a match for the ones we lifted from the knives, the medicine cabinet, and the windowsill. And as far as we can tell, he wouldn't have had any reason to kill Becky Medeiros."

"What about Peeping Tom complaints?" Mulligan asked. "We know the killer spied on Connie and Becky. Maybe he's been looking in lots of windows around the neighborhood."

"We've canvassed the neighbors," Jennings said, "but only a couple of them noticed a prowler, and none of them got a good look at him. They just heard rustling noises and saw some movement in the dark."

"So now what?"

"So far, we've interviewed more than three hundred people and gotten absolutely nowhere. All we can do is go back to the beginning and start over."

"The FBI been any help?"
Jennings raised an eyebrow.
"How'd you hear about that?"
"You're not the only person I talk to, Andy."
Jennings didn't say anything.
Mulligan gave him a moment to think about it, then said, "So?"
"This has gotta be off the record."
"Okay, let's hear it."
"The chief called the BSU last week and asked if they could give us a hand."
"The BSU?"
"The Behavioral Science Unit."
"What's that?"
"The part of the bureau that studies serial killers."
"And?"
"They sent a profiler named Peter Schutter up from Quantico. We gave him copies of our investigative files and walked him through both crime scenes."
"And he told you what?"
"Mostly stuff we'd figured out already."
"Such as?"
"That the same killer was responsible for both attacks. That he probably has a history of prowling, peeping, and animal cruelty. That the size of his footprints and the way he overpowered his victims indicates a large

male. That the sloppy crime scenes mean he's young and inexperienced. That the method of entry also tells us we're looking for a young guy, probably in his mid- to late twenties. Not that climbing through windows is that difficult, but an older man would have chosen a less strenuous way to get inside."

Jennings paused and drew a deep breath.

"And that he's going to kill again, probably after a cooling-off period of twelve to twenty-four months."

"And the clock is ticking," Mulligan said.

"Tell me about it."

"Think this guy Schutter would talk to me?"

"I suppose I could ask."

The following afternoon, Mulligan and Jennings met Schutter in his room at the Holiday Inn in downtown Providence. The agent's suitcase was on the bed, packed for his return trip to Washington.

"Detective Jennings tells me you've got some questions," Schutter said.

"I do," Mulligan said.

"A couple of ground rules first. Number one, anything I tell you must be attributed to an agent for the BSU. I do not want my name used. Number two, there are going to be things I *can't* tell you. Some details that only the killer could know must be withheld so the police can use them to rule out false confessions."

"I understand."

"Okay, then. Ask your questions."

"First off, I'm wondering why you agreed to talk to me."

"Our work at the BSU isn't well understood. Many police departments still are not availing themselves of our expertise. The director thinks the publicity could do some good. Besides, it appears that apprehending this killer will be difficult. The release of certain information might help members of the general public assist investigators with an identification. Detective Jennings says you are a person who can be trusted to keep your word and report on this responsibly."

"I'll do my best." Mulligan pulled out his notebook, where he'd written a short list of things that were puzzling him. "Can you explain why the killer covered the bodies?"

"His motivation isn't clear, but the *behavior* provides us with clues to his identity. Serial killers who murder strangers almost never cover the bodies. The perpetrator we are seeking not only knew his victims but lives within walking distance of the murder scenes. Killers who live farther away nearly always move the bodies and dump them."

"One of their *neighbors* did this?"

"There's a high level of probability."

"Why would he kill all these people?"

Schutter glanced at Jennings, who was shaking his head vigorously.

"I'm willing to discuss this," the agent said, "but only off the record. The families of the victims have been through enough. They don't need to be exposed to the worst of it."

"Off the record, then," Mulligan said.

"He kills because it's how he achieves sexual release."

"I already gathered that. But how does somebody get that way?"

"Sometime during preadolescence, probably when he was about ten years old, something happened that caused him to equate sex with violence. It could have been an event as simple as idly touching himself while watching slasher movies on TV. Psychologists call it 'imprinting.' It's the same thing that leads some males to associate sex with garter belts or women's shoes."

"Movies?" Mulligan said.

"I believe he is obsessed with them. Films like *Friday the Thirteenth* and *A Nightmare on Elm Street.* He sits in front of his TV and masturbates to them."

Mulligan raised an eyebrow and looked at Jennings.

"We checked all the video stores," the detective said. "Turns out half the people in town watch that stuff. And if he shoplifted them, there wouldn't be any purchase or rental records anyway."

"With slasher films as his inspiration," Schutter continued, "he built himself a fantasy world. At first, his fantasies would have been simple, but over time they grew more elaborate. At least a year before he killed for the first time, he was stabbing helpless women to death in Technicolor movies that played in a continuous loop inside his head. Eventually, the fantasies were no longer enough to satisfy him. That's when he made a conscious decision to cross the line between make-believe and murder."

Schutter paused to allow Mulligan to catch up with his note taking.

"You'd be shocked how many people are walking around with violent fantasies in their heads, imagining how delightful it would be to strangle you or stab you to death," the agent said. "What separates them from our killer is that most of them never decide to act on it."

"Good God," Mulligan said. "I wish you hadn't told me that. It gives me the creeps."

"Me too," Jennings said.

"Why the overkill?" Mulligan asked. "Why did he keep stabbing his victims after they were dead?"

"The females in the killer's fantasies always cower before his God-like power," the agent said. "They weep and beg him for mercy. Becky Medeiros didn't do that. She fought for her life."

"She spoiled his fantasy," Mulligan said.

"Yes, and that enraged him."

"What about the Stuarts?"

"The killer stabbed Connie Stuart twenty-two times and her eight-year-old daughter twelve times, but he plunged knives into the twelve-year-old fifty-two times. That tells us she was the one who fought him the hardest."

Mulligan felt like throwing up. That reminded him of his last question.

"Why did the killer vomit in the backyard?"

"For the same reason athletes do after running the Boston Marathon — low blood sugar and dehydration. That's how physically taxing the attack was."

January 1992

The boy fetches his father's hatchet from the garage, dashes back into the house, and skips up the stairs to the second floor. He stops in front of his sister's bedroom door and smirks at the "No Boys Allowed" sign. Then he turns the knob, steps inside, and pulls the door shut behind him.

The bed is covered with a frilly pink comforter and two matching satin pillows. A Michael Jackson poster hangs over the headboard. Beside the maple bureau, its top covered with jars of mysterious girly stuff, stands a bookshelf crammed with Barbie dolls.

Blond Barbies, brunette Barbies, redheaded Barbies. Barbies draped in prom gowns. Barbies stuffed into two-piece bathing suits. Barbies in tight tennis shorts. Barbies in revealing go-go outfits. Barbies in demure nurse's uniforms. Barbies in colorful summer dresses.

He selects a nurse Barbie, tears off her

uniform, and lays her naked on the floor. He studies her for a moment. Then, whack! He chops off her right leg.

He grins, pretending he can hear her scream.

Whack! Her other leg.

Whack! Her right arm.

Whack! Her left arm.

And finally, her head.

He does the same with bathing beauty Barbie.

Then a go-go Barbie.

Then another.

And another.

A half hour later, he sits there with his penis in his hand, surrounded by dismembered dolls in an imaginary pool of blood.

10

July 1994

On the twelfth day after the Stuart murders, Mulligan parked Citation on the street across from the murder house, got out, and started knocking on doors again. He figured he was wasting his time. The police had already talked to everyone in the neighborhood more than once. But he was haunted by what he'd learned from Schutter. He couldn't sit around doing nothing.

He'd just finished listening to a middle-aged woman prattle about the good-for-nothing police department when he spotted a black teenager riding a bicycle no hands down the middle of the street. It looked like the same kid he'd talked to outside the Medeiros house two years ago. What was his name? Oh, yeah. Kwame something.

"Hey, Kwame!"

The kid rolled up to the curb and braked.

"You're that reporter."

"That's right. Mulligan, from the *Dispatch.*"

"Are the cops ever gonna catch the guy or what?" Kwame asked. "My mom's really scared."

"They're doing the best they can," Mulligan said.

The kid had grown several inches since he'd last seen him. And he had a gauze bandage on his right thumb.

"So, Kwame. How'd you hurt your thumb?"

"A dog bit me."

"That right?"

"Uh-huh."

Mulligan reached for the hand. The kid jerked it back.

Mulligan grabbed for it again and ripped the bandage off. Underneath was a clean, two-inch cut closed by what appeared to be eight or ten stitches.

"That's no dog bite," Mulligan said.

"The hell it ain't." The boy threw him a defiant glare. "You're just hassling me 'cause I'm black."

"Look, kid. The cops think the person who killed your neighbors cut himself in the attack. If you hurt your hand breaking into a house or something, I don't give a shit. Just tell me the truth, okay?"

"I won't get in any trouble?"

"That's right."

Kwame looked up at the sky as if he were thinking it over — or maybe making something up.

"A week ago, when I was riding my bike, I saw this car that had a CD player sitting on the front seat. I been wanting one, you know. So I broke the car window with a rock and took it."

"And you cut your hand on the glass?"

"Yeah."

"What kind of car was it?"

"I don't know. I don't know nuthin' 'bout cars."

"Was it an old one?" Mulligan asked. Window glass in newer models would have shattered into harmless pellets.

"I don't remember."

"Where did this happen, exactly?"

"Corner of Gordon and Taplow over by Oakland Beach Elementary."

"Okay, then. That explains it."

"Can I go?"

"One last thing. What's your shoe size?"

"Ten," the kid said.

The reporter slid his foot next to the kid's. Mulligan's Reeboks were size eleven. Kwame's Nikes were bigger.

Mulligan watched the kid pedal down the

street. Then he strolled to his car, drove to Gordon and Taplow, and scanned the pavement for broken glass. He even got down on his knees to search.

He didn't find any.

Mulligan drove to the Warwick police station and checked the reports to see if someone had complained about a car being vandalized near the school. No one had.

He walked upstairs to the detective bureau and asked for Jennings.

"You think a *child* could have done this?"

"I think it's worth checking out."

"Come on, Mulligan. You heard the FBI profile. The guy we're looking for is in his mid- to late twenties. Besides, the kid you're talking about is black."

"Black? What's that got to do with anything?"

"Black serial killers are extremely rare. And they only kill other black people."

"I'm sure you're right, Andy, but would it hurt to run this by Schutter and see what he says?"

It took them ten minutes to make their way through the FBI phone tree and get the BSU agent on speakerphone.

"This kid is *how* old?" the agent asked.

"Fifteen," Jennings said.

"He would have been thirteen at the time of the Medeiros murder?"

"Uh-huh."

"Look, Detective. The bureau has compiled detailed files on hundreds of serial killers. The youngest one we ever encountered started killing at seventeen. Ninety-nine point nine percent of them were at least twenty-one, and the average age at first kill is twenty-eight and a half."

"Maybe so," Mulligan butted in, "but if Diggs isn't involved, why the lies about his shoe size and the cut on his hand?"

"He could be covering for something worse than breaking a car window," Schutter said. "Perhaps a housebreak or a robbery."

"Or murder," Mulligan said.

Schutter had nothing to say to that.

"Something else about the kid is nagging at me," Mulligan said. "The footprints in the Medeiros house were size twelve, but the ones at the Stuart house were size thirteen. Unless we're looking for two different guys, which you say we're not, our killer is still growing."

"I wouldn't put any stock in that," Schutter said. "Prints made by stocking feet can be deceptive."

"In what way?"

"They vary in size depending on whether the socks are loose or pulled on tight. No way this kid's your killer. Don't waste your time on him."

After they hung up, Mulligan pulled out a cigar and set fire to it.

"Not supposed to smoke in here," Jennings said. Then he shrugged, slipped a pack of Marlboros from his shirt pocket, and got one going.

"I still think it's worth looking into, Andy."

"Tell you what. After we finish recanvassing for the third friggin' time, I'll talk to the kid, see what he has to say. And Mulligan?"

"Yeah?"

"Stay the hell away from him and leave the investigation to the professionals."

"Whatever you say."

As he drove to work the next morning, Mulligan couldn't get Kwame Diggs out of his head. Before checking in at the sports desk, he decided to talk things over with the city editor.

"Schutter is full of shit," Lomax said.

"How so?"

"Ever heard of Tommy Knox?"

"Knox? Who's he?"

"Back in the 1960s, he was the starting fullback for the Tolman High School football team in Pawtucket. He was also a psychopath. He raped and murdered two women and badly injured a third; and he was the prime suspect in two other sex killings."

"How old was he?"

"Eighteen when they caught him, but when he killed his first victim, he was only fifteen years old."

"Where is he now?"

"He committed suicide in prison."

"The BSU didn't get started until the 1970s," Mulligan said.

"Yeah," Lomax said. "That's why Schutter never heard about this."

11

That afternoon, Mulligan braced teenage boys in Kwame Diggs's neighborhood, asking if they knew how he'd hurt his hand. He drew a blank until, around suppertime, he stumbled onto Eddie Hendricks.

He was fourteen. A friend of Kwame's. The two of them, he told Mulligan, liked to play touch football in the street.

"Any idea how he cut his thumb?"

"Naw."

"Look," Mulligan said, "I think he might be the one who killed your neighbors."

Eddie's eyes got wide.

"Better tell me what you know."

"I don't know nothin'."

"You can talk to me, or you can talk to the police," Mulligan bluffed. "You must have asked him about it. What did he say?"

The kid fell silent and studied his feet.

"Come on, Eddie. Out with it."

"He told me it was just a little cut," Eddie

finally said. "He didn't want to say how he got it. But this morning, he knocked on my door and said that if the cops came around asking about it, I should tell them he got hurt breaking into a car."

Mulligan took out his phone and called Jennings. "I've got something new on Kwame Diggs," he said.

"I thought I told you to stay away from this."

"Yeah, yeah. I know. But you really need to hear what I've got."

Next morning, Jennings and Mello drove to the Diggs house and knocked on the door. No one answered. They were just climbing back into their unmarked car when they saw a heavyset black teenager cruising down the street on his bicycle.

"Are you Kwame?" Jennings asked.

"Who's askin'?"

"I'm Detective Jennings and this is Detective Mello," the lead detective said, extending his right for a shake. Kwame hesitated, then took it. Jennings pretended not to notice the bandaged thumb.

"You the cops trying to figure out who killed all those people?"

"We are."

"What's the holdup, man? People around

here are crazy scared."

"Can I tell you a secret?" Jennings asked.

"Uh. I guess."

The detective leaned in close. "We don't have a clue who did this. Looks like the bastard's gonna get away with it."

"No shit?"

"No shit. We're just spinning our wheels now, reinterviewing people in the neighborhood who didn't know anything the first two times we talked to them."

"Damn."

"Okay if we ask *you* a few questions?"

"Me? I don't know nothin'."

"Sometimes people know more than they think, Kwame. You could have seen some little detail that might point us in the right direction."

As Jennings talked with Kwame, Mello opened the back door of the cruiser, pulled out two cans of Coke, and popped one open.

"Hot as hell out here," he said. "Want a Coke, partner?"

"Yeah, thanks."

Mello tossed him a can, and Jennings made a two-hand catch.

"Hey, got another one back there for Kwame?"

Mello fetched another Coke, careful to

handle only the top rim, and handed it to the boy. Kwame gripped it in his right and popped the tab with his left thumb.

"So, Kwame," Jennings said, "have you seen any unfamiliar vehicles around the neighborhood this summer?"

"Not really," he said, and gulped from the can.

"Seen any strangers lurking around?"

"I ain't seen nothin' like that." Another gulp.

"What about your friends?" Mello asked. "Any of them mention seeing something suspicious?"

"Nah," Kwame said, and drained the can.

Jennings waited for the kid to drop the empty into the gutter. He didn't.

"Well, thanks anyway," Jennings said. He and Mello got back into their car and watched Kwame pedal away down the street.

"Why didn't you take the can from him?" Mello asked.

"If we made him suspicious, he probably wouldn't give it up," Jennings said, "and wrestling it from him would smear the prints."

Kwame reached the corner, turned left, and tossed the empty into the street. It bounced, rolled, and teetered at the edge of a storm drain. The detectives waited until the boy was out of sight before driving to the corner. Mello pulled a latex glove onto his right hand, got out of the car, picked up the can by the rim, dropped it into an evidence bag, and climbed back into the passenger seat.

"Think we got lucky?" he asked.

"Maybe," Jennings said. "The kid gripped the can pretty tight, didn't move his hand around any that I could see, so I don't think he smudged the prints."

Two days later, the state crime lab matched Kwame Diggs's prints to the ones that had been lifted from the light bulb, front window, and kitchen windowsill at the Medeiros house. And to the knives, medicine cabinet, and downstairs windowsill in the Stuart house.

That evening, Jennings tracked down a Superior Court judge and got him to sign a warrant.

When police rapped on the door of the Diggs residence the following morning, the boy's parents were both at work. By law, that didn't matter. Warrant in hand, they could have kicked the door down and tossed the place. But they didn't have to. Kwame answered their knock and let the officers inside. Then he stretched out on the living room couch and turned on the TV.

As Jennings and Mello searched the house and grounds, two patrolmen, hands resting on the butts of their semiautos, watched the teenager munch Oreo Double Stuf cookies, swig Coke, and chuckle at a marathon telecast of *Voltron: Defender of the Universe,* a cartoon about a giant robot.

Upstairs, Jennings rummaged through Kwame's bedroom. In the closet, he found two pairs of size thirteen Nikes. Stuffed inside one shoe was a plastic bag containing what looked like a half ounce of marijuana. Then he rooted under the bed and pulled out a stash of slasher videos: *Prom Night, Friday the Thirteenth, Halloween,* and *A Nightmare on Elm Street.*

Outside, Mello combed through the backyard garden shed. Concealed inside a bag of potting soil, he discovered a Folgers coffee can. He pried off the plastic top, dumped the contents into a gloved hand, and let out a whoop.

He tugged an evidence bag out of his pocket and dropped Becky Medeiros's heart-shaped locket inside. Then he pulled out another bag for the earrings that had been torn from Connie Stuart and her daughters.

The detectives met in the kitchen to share what they'd found. Then they dragged Diggs up from the couch, cuffed him, read him his rights, and led him outside. At the curb, Mulligan stood beside a *Dispatch* photographer who captured the moment for the front page.

Jennings and Mello shoved their prisoner into the back of a patrol car. As it rolled away, the two exhausted detectives wrapped their arms around each other and wept with relief.

That evening, Jennings, Mello, and Mulligan were too keyed up to sleep, so they joined the department celebration at the FOP lodge. Word had spread about the kid reporter's role in the arrest. Everyone in the place wanted to buy him a drink.

By nine P.M., Mulligan was in an alcoholic fog. He drained his seventh bottle of Narragansett, slid off the bar stool, and staggered to the men's room to empty his bladder. And to get a moment alone with his thoughts.

He had no illusions about his role in the murder investigation. He knew the cops would have caught Diggs eventually. But would they have figured it out before he killed again?

Mulligan hated every minute he'd spent on this story. Until Kwame Diggs came along, he'd lived life just fine without getting this close to evil. He wondered if he'd ever get the stench of gore out of his dreams. But after a decade devoted to playing games and more than three years writing about others who played them, he'd done something that mattered. He understood, now, how Rosie felt — and it felt good. Maybe he *was* cut out for this kind of thing.

He'd heard that Vic Stanton was planning to resign from the *Dispatch*'s five-man investigative team to take a job at *The New York Times.* Would Lomax consider an inexperienced sportswriter for one of the most coveted jobs at the paper?

"I helped catch a serial killer," he told himself as he backed away from the urinal. "How many reporters can say that?"

He reclaimed his seat at the bar just as Malcolm Roberts, the state prosecutor assigned to the Diggs case, walked in and found everybody backslapping and offering toasts.

Roberts broke the mood.

"There's something you all need to know," he told the revelers. "Rhode Island's criminal codes haven't been updated in decades. When they were written, no one ever envisioned a child as twisted and dangerous as Kwame Diggs. The law says that juvenile offenders, no matter what their crimes, must be released and given a fresh start at age twenty-one. The attorney general is going to ask the legislature to rewrite the law so this won't happen again. But they can't change it retroactively.

"In six years, the bastard will get out and start killing all over again."

July 1994

The boy sprawls on his jail cell bunk and studies a spider. It's spinning a web on the ceiling. It has a plan. It knows exactly what it's doing.

Why didn't he wear gloves?

Why didn't he bring a hunting knife, something with a blade that wouldn't break off?

Why didn't he jerk off into a hand towel and take it away with him?

He'd been impulsive and reckless. He sees that now. Still, he might have gotten away with it if it weren't for that fucking reporter.

Then he smiles, knowing he'll be free again in half a dozen years. Even the public defender says so.

He pictures his trophies sealed in a plastic bag inside an evidence locker. He wishes he'd hidden them better so he could dream on them again when he gets out.

Next time, he'll think things through. Next time, he'll be like the spider.

He pulls himself to his feet, climbs onto the bunk, and plucks the bug from its web. He jumps to the floor, sits on the edge of the mattress, opens his palm, and gazes at the predator's swollen belly, its quivering legs.

Then he closes his fingers and crushes it in his big, strong hands.

Part II
Nobody's Right When Everybody's Wrong

12

March 2012

Larry Bird had been living in Mulligan's kitchen for less than a week, and already he'd become a big pain in the ass.

Every day, he shredded the newspaper he was supposed to shit on, kicked it through the bars of his cage, and watched it drop, shit and all, onto the scuffed linoleum floor. Every night, he let out two or three skull-piercing shrieks that made the veteran reporter bolt from his bed and grope for his gun. Larry knew only one English phrase, and he didn't squawk it often; but when he did, Mulligan had to fight the urge to strangle him.

Mulligan brushed his teeth, tugged on his jeans, pulled on a Boston Red Sox T-shirt with Jacoby Ellsbury's number 2 on the back, and was tying his black Reeboks when the fucker said it:

"Yankees win. Theeeeeeee Yankees win!"

Mulligan couldn't figure it. Why would a guy name a bird after one of the greatest sports heroes in New England history and then teach it to talk that crap? But there was no way to find out now, because the asshole responsible for this abomination was dead.

Mulligan would have preferred a dog — a big one that would jump all over him when he came home from work, curl up beside him when he rooted for the Sox on TV, and snore contentedly every night at the foot of his bed. After several recent disappointments, he'd come to believe that the love of a dog was preferable to the love of a woman. Dogs were unwaveringly faithful, and not a one had ever lied to him. But the landlord didn't allow dogs in this run-down tenement building in Providence's Federal Hill neighborhood; and with Mulligan's crazy hours, there was no way he could take care of one anyway.

The asshole, a small-time heroin dealer, had been sitting on the stoop outside his apartment in the Chad Brown housing project last Wednesday when a white Escalade rolled up, the passenger-side window slid down, and a dozen nine-millimeter slugs stuttered out. An hour later, Mulligan ducked under the yellow crime scene tape and yanked his reporter's notebook from his hip pocket. He doubted he'd need it, but he figured on being ready in case the investigating detective broke precedent and said something worth printing in *The Providence Dispatch.* They'd just started wrangling when a uniform lugged a big brass cage out of the apartment and set it down in the blood on the stoop.

"Oops," he said. "Sorry about that, Sarge."

"No biggie," the detective said.

"Really? Didn't I just compromise the physical evidence?"

"Compromise?" Mulligan said.

"It's what they're taught to say at the Police Academy," the detective said, "when what they really mean is 'fuck up.' "

"Oh, shit," the uniform said. "I can't believe I did that."

"Doesn't matter, kid," the detective said.

"It doesn't?"

"It might if we went to trial," the detective said, "but it's not like we're ever gonna ID the shooter."

Mulligan and the detective watched the uniform lift the cage from the stoop. A little metal sign clipped to the bars read: "Larry Bird." Inside the cage, a midnight-blue macaw squatted and took a dump.

"Looks like you've got a witness," Mulligan said.

"Yeah," the uniform said, "he must have heard the whole thing go down, but the shit-bird ain't talking. I don't think he likes cops."

"Birds of a feather," Mulligan said, and immediately regretted the cliché.

"You got that right," the detective said. He pointed at the fresh graffiti scrawled next to the apartment door: *If you see something, don't say anything.*

"Handsome bird," Mulligan said.

"If you want it, it's yours," the detective said.

"You serious?"

"Why not? The skel with all the holes in him won't be feeding it anymore, and I'd just as soon avoid dealing with the lazy pricks at Animal Control."

Which was how Larry Bird found a new home in Mulligan's kitchen and promptly dedicated himself to soiling it.

Mulligan finished tying his shoes, filled Larry's food tray, got pecked on the hand for his trouble, and told the bird to go fuck himself. Then he shrugged on his bomber jacket and went out the apartment door. He trotted down one flight of worn wooden stairs and stepped out into a cold morning rain.

■ ■ ■ ■

Gloria Costa unfurled her purple umbrella, stepped off the front stoop of her modest bungalow, landed in a puddle, and felt the water seep into her flats. A scream rose in her throat. She dashed for her little Ford Focus, stepped into a pothole, twisted her ankle, and nearly fell in the street. She regained her balance, unlocked the car door, closed the umbrella, and collapsed in the driver's seat.

She shut her eyes, took a deep breath, and repeated the mantra her psychologist had provided: "I am not having a heart attack. The tightness in my chest and the shortness of breath are symptoms of adrenaline overload. My hands are clammy and tingling because I am hyperventilating."

She opened her eyes, averted them from the rain-splattered windshield, and began the breathing exercise designed to ward off a panic attack. She took a deep breath, held it for ten seconds, and released it slowly through her nose.

The night it had happened, it was raining. A little thug in a black ski mask had forced his way into her car, punched her in the mouth, grabbed her keys, and driven her to a deserted street. There, he'd smashed her face into hash with his fists while chanting a mantra more powerful than the one her psychologist had given her: "I'm going to fuck your ass and slit your throat, you nosy picture-taking bitch." He'd yanked her sweatshirt over her breasts, ripped off her bra, put a Buck knife to her throat, and forced her to remove her jeans and panties. Somehow, she'd managed to pull away from his grasp, bolt from the car, and run bloody and naked through the storm.

"You beat him," her psychologist always told her; but to Gloria, that's not how it felt. The thug had never been caught. Whenever Gloria thought of him, which she tried mightily not to do, she pictured him lurking in the rain, waiting for another chance. Waiting just for her.

Gloria repeated the breathing exercise ten times until her heart rate slowed. Then she adjusted the rearview mirror and studied her face in it. This was something she disliked doing, because *he* had left his mark there. But how could a girl live without mirrors? She fixed her lipstick and ran a comb through her damp blond hair. Then she adjusted the pirate-style patch that covered her glass eye.

She liked to say that she wore the patch

because the glass eye made her look deranged, but the truth was that she couldn't stand looking at the gift he had given her. She remembered how Mulligan once told her the patch was sexy, and her lips curled in a tight little smile.

She stuck the key in the ignition, fired the engine, switched on the wipers, and suddenly realized she'd left her camera bag on the kitchen table. A news photographer was useless without a camera. There was nothing for it. She'd have to get out of the car and limp back to the house through the rain.

The classical music station was playing Rachmaninoff. Edward Anthony Mason III loved Rachmaninoff. If the composition had words, he would have sung along.

He gunned the engine, and the lovingly restored silver-blue 1967 Jaguar E-Type Series 1 coupe leapfrogged the rainy-morning traffic. He raced up an on-ramp and sped across the majestic Claiborne Pell Bridge that arced over Narragansett Bay's choppy east passage. The station was playing Dvořák now. Mason didn't care for Dvořák. He fiddled with the tuner, searching for another classical station. Finding only vapid soft rock, headache-inducing rap, smug Don Imus, and the Mike & Mike sports yakkers, he snapped the radio off.

Mason was glad it was finally Monday. The weekend had not been a pleasant one at the family manse in Newport, Rhode Island. All day Saturday his father, the publisher of *The Providence Dispatch,* had cloistered himself in the library and reviewed the paper's calamitous financials over and over again — as if he could somehow will them to change. But nothing — not even a series of buyouts and layoffs that had shuttered the paper's suburban bureaus and slashed its news staff from 340 to 80 over the last decade — had stanched the hemorrhaging.

Now there was little left to cut.

On Sunday, after returning from services at Trinity Episcopal Church, the old man had cracked open a bottle of twelve-year-old Glenmorangie single-malt Scotch and gotten uncharacteristically rip-roaring drunk.

This morning, as servants scurried about in the dining room, refilling coffee cups and clearing china sticky with half-eaten apple puff cakes, Mason's father had cleared his throat, clinked his spoon against his coffee cup to make sure he had his son's full attention, and made an announcement.

"It pains me greatly to say this, son, but

I'm going to talk to the board about putting the *Dispatch* on the market."

Probably too late for that, Mason thought. Mulligan had been proclaiming for years that the newspaper business had no future, although the veteran reporter did tend to express the idea in more colorful language. "Turning to shit," Mulligan used to say, and, more recently, "circling the fucking drain." At first Mason had disagreed, regurgitating the Pollyannaish prattle he'd been fed at the Columbia University Graduate School of Journalism about how the business was just going through "a difficult transition." But now the painful truth was too obvious to deny.

Dad, Mason thought, I doubt you can find a buyer stupid enough to take the *Dispatch*'s rotting corpse off our hands. But Mason had the courtesy, and the good sense, to keep the thought to himself.

Just twenty-eight years old, he was the scion of six inbred Rhode Island families that had owned the paper since the Civil War. He'd been working as a reporter for the last four years, learning the trade from the bottom up; but the plan had been for him to step up to the publisher's corner office once his father decided to step down. Now, as the Jag cruised north on Route 1 toward Providence, Mason wondered what he'd do with the rest of his life.

He wondered, too, how he would maintain the lifestyle to which he was accustomed now that his inheritance was shriveling. Not *all* of his trust fund was tied up in *Dispatch* stock, and for that he was grateful. But what about Mulligan and the rest of his friends at the paper? What would become of them?

Mason brooded on that for a while and then tried the radio again. Still finding nothing to his liking, he turned it off and started humming the nostalgic ragtime tune he'd composed at the family's Steinway. He'd already come up with a title: "Providence Rag." Now he was ready to write the words. The first stanza, an attempt to evoke the roar of the newspaper presses, was taking shape in his head when an unwelcome thought intruded.

One of these days, he might find himself driving a Prius.

Mason, who had the longest commute, arrived first. Gloria, who lived just fifteen minutes away in suburban Warwick, slipped in a half hour later, delayed by the ordeal of fetching her camera bag and repeating her breathing exercise. Mulligan, whose apartment was within walking distance, meandered in forty minutes after her.

One by one, the three journalists took the elevator to the third floor, stepped out into the newsroom, and walked past a slender, elderly black woman sitting in one of the white vinyl chairs set aside for visitors. She wore a red cloth coat and flat black shoes adorned with tiny red bows. Her red purse and matching umbrella rested on the floor beside her, and a soggy copy of the *Dispatch,* open to the metro page, lay in her lap. The woman lifted her chin and studied each of them as they passed her by. Mason gave her a curious glance and hurried on to his desk, but Gloria and Mulligan averted their eyes.

Unlike Mason, they knew who she was. They knew what she wanted.

Lomax, the sixty-two-year-old managing editor, checked the time on the newsroom wall clock and tossed Mulligan a dirty look. Mulligan didn't give a shit. He would never get paid for the overtime he'd put in on the Kessler story over the weekend, so he felt entitled to come and go as he pleased. He logged on to his computer and found a message from Lomax in his in-box:

Talk to her.

Mulligan pounded out a reply: *Give her to somebody else this time.*

Lomax: *It'll go quicker if you do it. She won't*

have to repeat her whole song and dance.

Mulligan muttered, "Aw, crap," rose from his ergonomically correct desk chair, and went to her.

"Good morning, Mrs. Diggs."

"Good morning, Mr. Mulligan." Her voice was even wearier than he remembered.

"Please come with me," he said.

He waited as she gathered her things and then led her to his cubicle. He fetched a desk chair, one of the dozens left over from when the *Dispatch*'s news staff was four times its current size, and invited her to sit.

"How may I help you today?" he asked.

Esther Diggs slapped the newspaper, still open to the metro front, on Mulligan's desk and pointed a skeletal finger at the story under his byline.

"This says Eric Kessler is getting out."

"Yes."

"But *my* boy is still in prison."

"Uh-huh."

"You think that's fair?"

"That Kessler is getting out, or that your son isn't?"

13

Eric Kessler had been a thirty-seven-year-old New England Telephone Company lineman in 1976, when his seven-year-old neighbor Brian Freeman went missing.

The soft-spoken father of two was among the scores of volunteers who had searched the Hope Valley section of rural Hopkinton for ten days until police finally called it off. The child's whereabouts remained a mystery until 1982, when Kessler was caught trying to strangle a nine-year-old Cub Scout. Detectives who searched his house, located less than a mile from the Freeman place, discovered the missing boy's skull in a gym bag under Kessler's bed.

He and Kwame Diggs were Rhode Island's most notorious killers.

Diggs's mother was gritting her teeth now and glaring at Mulligan.

"Both Kessler and your son," he told her, "should be drawn and quartered and have their heads impaled on pikes."

Mason, sitting in his adjoining cubicle, caught the gist and was stunned to hear Mulligan speak to the kindly-looking woman that way. He finished his regular morning call to the mayor's appointments secretary, hung up, and settled back to eavesdrop.

"My boy is innocent," Mrs. Diggs said.

"His prints were found all over the murder scenes," Mulligan said.

"A lie!"

"The cops found the locket he took from Becky Medeiros and the earrings he took from Connie Stuart and her daughters hidden in a coffee can in your garden shed."

"They were planted."

"He confessed."

"It was coerced."

"We've been over all of this many times before, Mrs. Diggs."

Her shoulders sagged.

Mulligan didn't have much patience left for this woman; but looking at her now, he found himself feeling sorry for her all over again. The ordeal had aged her. If he hadn't known she was sixty-six, he would have put her at eighty. Although she had moved out of state after the murders, she had continued to make the ninety-five-mile round trip from Brockton, Massachusetts, almost every week for the last eighteen years to visit her son at the state prison in Cranston. Her husband had died a few years after her son went to prison, and her two other children had moved far away. So she always made the trip alone.

She had never stopped believing in her son's innocence. Her belief was delusional, but there *was* something noble about it. Mulligan figured she deserved an explanation.

"Kessler pled guilty and was sentenced to forty years in prison," he said, "but Rhode Island law mandates that convicted felons, even murderers, get time off for good behavior; and Kessler has been a good boy inside. He has expressed remorse for his crimes, and he has followed prison rules to the letter. Nobody *wants* to let a child killer out ten years early. The state legislature is changing the law so this won't happen again. But they are going to have to release him at the end of May."

"I *know* that," she said. "I read your story."

"Your son," Mulligan said, "renounced his confession and was convicted of all five murders anyway. He continues to deny his guilt and has never expressed remorse for what he did. And he has not behaved himself inside. He's been caught with drugs in his cell. He assaulted two prison guards."

"He did *not.* Kwame was supposed to be set free twelve years ago. They faked those charges so they wouldn't have to let him out."

"You could be right."

"What are you going to do about it?"

"Nothing," Mulligan said.

She glared at him again, this time through tears. "Why are they doing this to my son and not to Kessler?"

"Kessler is seventy-three years old and has a bum ticker," Mulligan said. "He's no longer a threat to anyone. A Cub Scout could beat the crap out of him now."

"I think there's another reason."

"And what would that be?"

"Kessler is white, and my son is black."

Mulligan sighed and shook his head.

"I don't think that has anything to do with it."

Mrs. Diggs pulled a tissue from her coat, wiped the tears from her cheeks, gathered her purse and umbrella from the floor, and rose to leave. Then she turned back for a parting shot.

"Kessler cooked and ate that child," she said. "My Kwame never *ate* anybody."

Mulligan had heard the cannibalism rumor. Who hadn't? But because Kessler never stood trial, the details of his crime had never been made public. Mulligan briefly considered asking again for a look inside Kessler's private journal, which Hopkinton police chief Vincent Matea had kept under lock and key for thirty years. But what would be the point? The journal's contents, the chief always insisted, were too horrible to be revealed. If they were that terrible, Mulligan might not have the stomach to read them. And the *Dispatch,* which had withheld the most sordid details about the Diggs murders, would never print them anyway.

As Mrs. Diggs trudged toward the newsroom elevator, Mason sprang from his chair and followed her out.

14

Early next morning, Mason grabbed an empty chair, the same one Esther Diggs had sat in the day before, rolled it into Mulligan's cubicle, and plopped down beside him.

"I talked to Kwame Diggs's mother," Mason said.

"I kind of figured that."

"I think she has a point."

"About her son being innocent?"

"No, not that. After I talked with her, I spent a couple of hours in the news library reading your old stories about the case. No question he killed all those people."

"Then what?"

"That the state is faking new charges to keep him inside."

"Maybe so," Mulligan said.

"It's not right."

"Depends on how you look at it."

"They're breaking the law," Mason said.

"Name a Rhode Island public official who isn't."

"They're violating his civil rights."

"Far as I'm concerned, he doesn't have any."

"If they can do this to him," Mason said, "they can do it to anybody."

"But they don't."

"How do you know?"

Mulligan didn't have an answer for that.

"After I talked to Mrs. Diggs," Mason said, "I called Olivia Monteiro at the ACLU."

"So?"

"She was reluctant to talk about it at first. She kept saying nothing good could come from dredging up the whole story."

"She's right."

"I disagree."

"So you pressed her."

"I did. I couldn't get her to speak on the record; but off the record she thinks it's a conspiracy — that prison officials, prosecutors, and judges all know the charges they keep bringing against Diggs are bogus."

"Good for them," Mulligan said.

"She thinks even Diggs's lawyer may be in on it."

"Good for him, too."

Mason sadly shook his head. "I thought

you'd care about this."

"I don't. Monteiro isn't all that hot and bothered about it either. If she were, she'd file a civil rights suit on Diggs's behalf."

"So it's up to us," Mason said.

Mulligan stared at him. Subtract the Ivy League pedigree, the trust fund, and the Giorgio Armani suit worth more than *Dispatch* reporters made in a month, and the kid reminded him of himself — back when Mulligan was young and naïve, before two decades of working as a reporter had taught him how the world works.

"Look," Mulligan said, "I admit you've got a point. The law should apply equally to everybody. In a democracy, the authorities don't get to make up the rules as they go along."

"That's right."

"But what do you think would happen," Mulligan went on, "if you proved officials are falsifying charges against Diggs?"

"I'd be able to write a great abuse-of-power story."

"Yeah. But they'd also have to let Diggs out."

"I suppose they would."

"And if he gets out, he'll kill again."

"You don't know that."

"Yes, I do," Mulligan said. "Kwame Diggs

is a serial killer. Every night for the last eighteen years, he's been lying in his prison bunk, fantasizing about stabbing women and children to death."

"What makes you think that?"

"It's what monsters do."

Mason fell silent and thought about it for a while.

"I still think we have an obligation to look into it," he said.

"So who's stopping you?"

"I could use your help."

"No way," Mulligan said.

"Saying no to the publisher's son might not be a smart career move."

"When have I ever made a smart career move, Thanks-Dad?"

"Stop calling me that. I can't help it that my father is the publisher."

"Then why do you keep reminding me?"

They were both chuckling now, the momentary tension between them gone.

"What the hell," Mulligan said. "There's no future here anyway."

15

Gloria perched on the edge of her desk chair and squinted at the picture on the twenty-seven-inch iMac computer monitor with her one good eye.

The photo froze Kwame Diggs as he was being led inside the Superior Court building in Providence, his hands cuffed behind his back and his legs hobbled by a short steel chain. Two state cops held his bulging biceps in a tight grip. They were big men, but Diggs made them look like dwarfs. At six feet five and 330 pounds, he appeared fit enough to play nose tackle for Gloria's favorite team, the New England Patriots. Just behind him, two more state cops stood with shotguns at port arms.

Gloria clicked the mouse, zooming in for a closer look at the vacant expression on Diggs's concrete block of a face. She remembered exactly how she'd felt when she snapped the photo last year. She'd drawn the assignment to get a picture of Diggs as he was being taken to court to answer for his latest assault on a prison guard. She'd shot a lot of photos that day, but her hands had shaken so badly that this was the only one that wasn't a blurry mess.

Gloria closed the picture, searched the archives, and called up the file photo of Eric Kessler. A *Dispatch* photographer had taken it at the killer's last court appearance three decades ago. Kessler had been a big guy, too, but in his case, most of the weight was flab. She clicked the mouse again, zooming in on a face that looked as if it had been sculpted from a block of suet.

Kessler looked much creepier than Diggs, she thought, so why didn't his picture scare her as much? For a moment, she worried that it was because Kessler was white and Diggs was black. But no, that wasn't it. She'd never been one of those women who clutched her purse tighter when she passed a black man on the sidewalk. Then it came to her. Kessler's victims were boys, but Diggs had butchered three little girls and two women. Blond women who looked a lot like her. She remembered, then, how he had turned to leer at her as he was led up the courthouse steps. She called up Diggs's photo again. It made her shiver.

This morning, she'd caught wind of what Mason was up to. It was hard to keep secrets in the *Dispatch*'s newsroom.

What the hell was the publisher's son thinking?

16

Wednesday morning, Mulligan was summoned to Lomax's office. He slumped into a red leather chair, took a pull of coffee from a Styrofoam cup, and said, "What's up, boss?"

"We got ourselves a situation," Lomax said.

"And what would that be?"

"It's Mason."

"You're gonna have to be more specific."

"The kid's got a bug up his ass about Kwame Diggs."

"So I hear."

"I don't want any part of it," Lomax said.

"Me either."

"Then how come you're helping him?"

"I'm not."

"He says you are."

"Uh-uh. I told him no way."

"Guess he's not taking no for an answer," Lomax said.

"Looks like."

"I told him no, too," Lomax said. "Actually, I think I said, 'Fuck, no.' "

"And he reminded you that he's the publisher's son," Mulligan said.

"That he did. He also reminded me that if the *Dispatch* manages to stay afloat, he's going to be my boss someday."

"So the young pretender is starting to throw his weight around," Mulligan said.

"Oh hell, yeah."

"Meet the new boss, same as the old boss," Mulligan said.

"Huh?" The managing editor was not a Who fan.

Lomax took off his glasses and rubbed his eyes.

"You know," he said, "maybe you *should* help him."

"You've got to be kidding."

"That way you can keep an eye on him, let me know what he's up to."

"Is that an order?"

"Yeah. But Mulligan?"

"Um?"

"Don't help him too much."

Mulligan had been writing about crime and political corruption for nearly twenty years now. For more than a decade, he'd been a member of the paper's elite investigative team. After it was disbanded and three of its members laid off, he still eked out time for investigative work between routine assignments that used to be handled by reporters who were now collecting unemployment checks. Over the years, he'd learned a few things about serial killers. He knew, for example, that they have always walked among us.

In the fifteenth century, a wealthy Frenchman named Gilles de Rais kidnapped and slaughtered somewhere between one hundred and eight hundred peasant children. In the sixteenth century, a Hungarian aristocrat named Elizabeth Báthory tortured and murdered an estimated six hundred young girls. Herman Webster Mudgett, one of the first American serial killers, lured victims to his hundred-room World's Fair Hotel in Chicago in the 1890s, gassed them, and sold their skeletons to medical schools. Mudgett confessed to twenty-seven murders, but historians think there may have been two hundred and fifty. By those standards, Kwame Diggs was an underachiever.

A serial killer, by definition, is someone who commits at least three separate murders, each followed by a cooling-off period. Technically, Diggs didn't qualify because he was caught after his second attack. But Mulligan knew exactly what he was.

The day Mulligan's story about Kessler's pending release hit the paper, somebody opened a "Keep Eric Kessler Locked Up" page on Facebook. Within hours, it had more than six thousand followers. When word of what Mason is up to leaks out, Mulligan thought, the next protest won't be on a social-networking site.

It will be on the *Dispatch*'s doorstep.

17

Mason parked his vintage Jag in the lot outside 881 Eddy Street, sat behind the wheel, and mulled over what he'd learned when he Googled Marcus Aurelius Washington: Fifty-one years old. Boston College. New England School of Law. Ten years as a community organizer in the Roxbury section of Boston. Four terms in the Massachusetts legislature. Failed gubernatorial candidate. A half-dozen years as deputy director of the NAACP in Boston before moving fifty miles down I-95 last fall to run the organization's Providence branch.

This was going to be a waste of time, Mason told himself as he climbed out of the car. Washington probably hadn't been in Rhode Island long enough to have even *heard* of Kwame Diggs.

When Washington rose to greet him, Mason's first thought was that he knew this guy from somewhere. Then he realized it was only because he was a dead ringer for the right-wing clown whose campaign for the Republican presidential nomination had been derailed by a sex scandal. The Godfather's Pizza guy. What was his name? Oh, yeah. Herman Cain.

Mason settled into a brown leather visitor's chair across from the desk and took a quick survey of the framed wall photos: Washington posing with John Kerry, Jesse Jackson, Deval Patrick, Edward M. Kennedy, Barbara Jordan, and Eric Holder. He declined the obligatory offer of coffee or bottled water and explained what he had come for.

"I know all about Kwame Diggs," Washington said, his voice booming as if he were speaking from a pulpit. "His sweet mother was the first person at my door when I settled into this office. She's been quite persistent."

"How persistent?"

"She calls me every week."

"Do you think her son is a murderer?" Mason asked.

"Of course he is."

"I think so too."

"So why are you here?"

"Because I believe the state of Rhode Island may be violating his civil rights."

"Probably so," Washington said.

"What are you doing about that?"

"Not a thing."

They stared silently at each other. Mason fidgeted with his pen and notepad. Washington calmly clasped his hands on his desk blotter.

"I'm guessing your next question is, 'Why not?' " Washington said.

"It is."

The lawyer took a moment to compose his answer.

"Diggs was a big, scary-looking black kid who butchered five white females," he finally said. "Do you have any idea how much racial hatred that stirred up back in the nineties?"

"I don't. I was a kid myself back then."

"I didn't know either until I asked around about it."

"And?"

"And the answer is, 'Not all that much.' "

"Really?"

"Really. The day after Diggs's arrest, a local radio talk show host got a couple of on-air calls from morons who wanted to rant about the jigaboos. He cut them right off. It's a shame, he told his listeners, that the killer turned out to be a black kid, because it brought out the worst in some people.

After that, the subject of race never came up. Not publicly, anyway."

"Wow."

"Exactly. If this had happened in Boston, all you would have heard was nigger this and nigger that."

The word, spoken in Washington's resounding baritone, made Mason cringe.

"What about now?" Mason asked.

"How do you mean?"

"There's a big difference between the way the Diggs and Kessler cases are being handled. Mrs. Diggs thinks race has something to do with that."

"I suppose it's possible," Washington said, "but I don't really think so."

"Why not?"

"The two situations are quite different. Kessler committed an abominable act, but given his present age and condition, he's no longer a threat. He'll be standing before his Maker soon enough. Diggs is another story. When he turned twenty-one, it was obvious to everyone that he was too dangerous to be set free, no matter what the law said."

"So the authorities found creative ways to keep him locked up," Mason said.

"They did."

"Olivia Monteiro suspects that those creative ways violated the law."

"I haven't looked into that in any detail," Washington said, "but it may well be the case."

"Have you discussed this with her?"

"I have."

"And?"

"Officially, the ACLU has other priorities. Unofficially, Olivia is a young woman with two daughters."

"So *nobody* is investigating this?"

"Nobody but you, apparently."

Mason just shook his head.

"Look, Mr. Mason. You need to understand something here. The last thing the NAACP wants is a black serial killer on the loose in Rhode Island."

Mason got to his feet, shook Washington's hand, and thanked him for his time. Then he went out the door, strode through the parking lot, and froze. His ride was gone.

Mulligan had warned him more than once not to drive the Jaguar in Providence, the stolen car capital of New England. But the silver-blue coupe was a joy to drive. Mason took it everywhere. He pulled out his cell to report it stolen, but he figured it was already being dismantled in a nearby chop shop.

Mulligan, he thought, will probably get a good laugh out of this.

■ ■ ■ ■

Four days later, Mason drove his new car south on I-95, turned off at exit 13 in Warwick, and cruised toward a storefront lawyer's office located in a Post Road strip mall near T. F. Green Airport.

If he'd waited for the insurance money to come in, Mason would have had the cash for another vintage Jag; but given the precarious state of the paper's finances, it seemed prudent to economize. True, he had shelled out extra for the voice-activated touch-screen navigation system and splurged on a sound system with eight speakers, a four-disc CD changer, and MP3/WMA playback capability.

But this new car was no fun to drive. No fun at all.

Jerome Haggerty's legal secretary turned out to be a frumpy forty-something with a plunging neckline and long, straight hair that had been chemically tortured to the color and consistency of straw. No fun there, either. Haggerty apparently disagreed.

His first words to Mason: "Did you get a load of those tits?"

They were looking at each other now across Haggerty's obsessively neat desk, his reading glasses, a stapler, and a couple of ballpoint pens neatly arranged on the blotter and not photo or a scrap of paper in sight.

"As I told you on the telephone," Haggerty said, "I no longer represent Kwame Diggs."

"Since when?"

"Last week."

"Can you tell me why were you dismissed?"

Haggerty shook his head. Flakes of dandruff floated down to settle on his shoulder. "The client declined to say."

"I was hoping you still might be willing to answer a few questions about his case."

"Only if they do not intrude upon lawyer-client privilege."

"I understand."

Mason removed the cap from his Montblanc fountain pen and flipped open his notebook.

"By my count," he said, "the state has charged Diggs with four additional offenses since he was incarcerated for murder in 1994."

"I believe your numbers are correct."

"The first charge, filed two years after his murder convictions, was contempt of court for refusing to submit to a psychiatric evaluation?"

"It was."

"And he received the maximum sentence for that?"

"There's no maximum sentence for contempt," Haggerty said. "It is entirely at the discretion of the judge."

"Who gave him seven years," Mason said.

"Yes."

"Doesn't that seem excessive?"

"Let's just call it unusually stiff."

"Do you recall any other Rhode Island defendant getting such a lengthy sentence for contempt?"

"No."

"As I understand it," Mason said, "Diggs subsequently agreed to the evaluation."

"He did."

"Isn't a contempt sentence usually vacated when the offender agrees to comply?"

"In most instances, yes."

"But it wasn't in this case."

"No."

"Why was that?"

"The prosecutor presented evidence that Diggs's responses during the evaluation were evasive."

"Were they?"

"Off the record?"

"Sure."

"The prick lied his ass off."

"I see," Mason said, and scrawled something in his notebook. "While Diggs was serving the sentence for contempt, he didn't get into any additional trouble in prison, is that right?"

"Correct."

"But as that sentence was running out, he suddenly started smoking marijuana and assaulting prison guards?"

"Apparently so, yes."

"Why would he do that?"

"You'd have to ask him."

"So over the last nine years, he's been convicted of two assaults on prison guards and one count of possession of a controlled substance?"

"That is correct."

"And in each instance, he received the maximum?"

"He did."

"Together, those charges added more than forty years to his original sentence, is that right?"

"It is."

"Mr. Haggerty, do you have any reason to believe that the state concocted these charges to keep Mr. Diggs in prison?"

"I have seen no evidence to support such

an allegation."

"Have you looked for any?"

"Mr. Mason, do you have a law degree?"

"No."

"Are you trying to tell me how to do my job?"

"I'm just asking a question."

Haggerty narrowed his eyes and gave Mason a hard look. "I think we're done here."

"Before I go, would you mind providing me with the name of Diggs's new attorney?"

Haggerty shook his head again. More dandruff.

"That's something you can find out for yourself."

Mason exited Haggerty's office, pulled the door closed, approached the secretary, and waited patiently until she finished speaking on the telephone.

"Excuse me," he said. "I forgot to ask Mr. Haggerty one question, and I don't want to intrude on him again. Perhaps you could tell me who Kwame Diggs's new lawyer is."

"Felicia Freyer," the secretary said. She was actually smacking gum. "That was just her on the phone, asking us to send over our case files. Wait a sec and I'll give you her number."

"If you like," Mason said, "I'd be happy

to bring the files to her."

"Oh please," she said. "Do I look like I was born yesterday?"

Not even close, Mason thought.

She handed him a Post-it note with a phone number and a downtown Pawtucket address on it. He thanked her, tucked it in his shirt pocket, walked out into the parking lot, and found himself a tad disappointed that his new silver-metallic Prius was right where he'd left it.

Mason pegged Felicia Freyer at no more than thirty. She wore enormous horn-rimmed glasses, a boxy green dress that looked a half size too big, and, as best he could tell, absolutely no makeup. Her long blond hair, bound with a yellow scrunchie, was pulled back so tightly that her eyes lifted a little at the corners. She struck him as a woman who was working hard, and failing, to disguise her beauty.

"Thank you for seeing me on such short notice," he said.

"I had nothing better to do this afternoon. This is a new practice. I don't have many clients as yet."

"But one of them is Kwame Diggs," he said.

"Yes, that's correct."

There was a smokiness in her voice that Mason could get used to. It made "Yes, that's correct" sound like a jazz lyric. He glanced at her left hand. No ring.

"Do you mind telling me how you came to represent him?"

"His mother came to see me last month and begged me to take over his case."

"Last month? The way I heard it, he didn't dismiss Jerome Haggerty until last week."

"I needed some time to think it over. Defending such a notorious client is not something to be taken lightly."

"So why are you doing it?"

Freyer leaned back in her chair and slowly crossed her legs. Mason couldn't help taking it in.

"Have you met his mother?" she said.

"I have."

"Feel sorry for her?"

"Of course."

"Me too. So that's reason number one."

"What else?"

"The scuttlebutt around the courthouse is that the state has been fabricating charges to keep Kwame in prison."

"That's what I hear, too," Mason said. "A lot of people seem to think it's the right thing to do."

"They have a point," Freyer said.

"Maybe so."

"But it's still wrong," she said.

"Sure."

"If they can do it to him, they can do it to anybody."

"That's what I've been saying," Mason said.

"If prosecutors and prison officials have been conspiring to concoct phony charges, they are guilty of suborning perjury and obstructing justice," she said. "I think they should be held to account for it."

"So what are you going to do?"

"First I'm going to review all the case files. After that, I don't know. To pursue this properly, I need to hire a private investigator, but Mrs. Diggs can't afford it. That bastard Haggerty has been bleeding her dry for years."

"I'm an investigative reporter," Mason said. "Maybe not a real good one yet. I'm still learning. But I might be able to help."

Freyer gave him a searching look. Mason held her gaze and noticed that the eyes behind those glasses were a startling shade of green. They stared at each other until she blinked.

"Would you like to meet Kwame?" she said.

"I would."

"Okay," she said. "Give me a little time to set it up."

Cruising back down the interstate toward Providence, Mason couldn't get those green eyes out of his head.

Other women he'd met in Providence, fresh from boob jobs and collagen lip enhancements, offered themselves to him as trophies. He could almost feel their claws on his wallet. The Newport socialites introduced to him by family friends at art openings, museum galas, or country club functions were stiff and moneyed. They offered impeccable pedigrees, but no real-world intelligence. No fires burned anywhere near them. No jazz lurked in *their* voices.

So he'd focused on work, intent on wriggling out from under his father's shadow. Ending the day with a review of his notes and a tumbler of thirty-year-old single-malt had become his ritual. He'd been telling himself that a woman would just complicate things. That a woman would be a drain on his time and energy.

Felicia's green eyes made him realize how lonely he'd become.

Before he knew it, Mason was nearing his exit, the marble dome of the statehouse looming in his windshield. He swerved across two lanes and switched on the radio, hoping a blast of Mozart or Beethoven would drown out the smoky voice that looped like a wrong song inside his head. Getting involved with someone is a bad idea right now, he told himself. And a reporter getting involved with a source would be folly.

Halfway to Newport, the radio station faded to static. Mason flashed through the dial in search of more classical music. He was about to give up when he stumbled onto WTOP, where talk show host Iggy Rock was interviewing Chief Matea of the Hopkinton police. Matea was deflecting a question about Eric Kessler's secret journal when Iggy interrupted:

"Joining us now, just calling in, is Brian Freeman's father, Gordon. Mr. Freeman, you are on the air."

There was a moment of dead air. A cough. Then, "Chief?"

"Yes, Mr. Freeman. I'm here."

"Chief, I want to read that journal." Each word was stressed like the punch of a fist.

"As I've told you before, I can't let you do that, Mr. Freeman. It's been sealed by court order. Besides, what's in it is something no father should ever see."

"But I have to, Chief. Eric Kessler destroyed my family. He killed my wife too. She died of a broken heart. And I've been drinking since they found my boy." His voice quavered a little. "I need to know what that monster did to Brian, so when he gets out I can do the same thing to him."

"Damn!" Mason thought. Or maybe he said it out loud.

Until now, he hadn't considered how the families of *Diggs's* victims were going to feel when they found out his investigation could result in the killer's release from prison. The thought made him shudder.

18

Mulligan pushed open the door to Hopes and shrugged off his dripping raincoat. He draped it over a rickety bar stool, slid onto an adjoining one, and grabbed a handful of cocktail napkins to sop the rain from his hair.

It was a little after four in the afternoon, and the local press hangout was nearly deserted. Since Lee Dykas's death, the place had fallen into new hands, but otherwise it hadn't changed much since Mulligan and Rosie started drinking there more than twenty years ago.

Annie, the leggy Rhode Island School of Design teaching assistant who moonlighted as barmaid, was just starting her shift. She poured a club soda, plopped in a lemon wedge, and clunked the drink in front of Mulligan on the scarred mahogany bar.

"Thanks, but I was going to order Bushmills straight up and a bottle of Killian's

Irish Red."

"You sure about that?"

"I am."

"What about your ulcer?"

"Doc Israel says it's healed up good."

Annie dumped the glass and filled his order. Mulligan downed the shot and sipped from his beer. Then he slid an illegal Cuban out of his shirt pocket, clipped the end, and fired it up. Rhode Island prohibited smoking in public accommodations, but nobody at the local press hangout gave a shit about the nanny-state law. Tobacco-phobes had plenty of other places to drink.

Mulligan was on his second beer, watching Boston Bruins highlights on the TV over the bar, when Gloria came through the door and unfurled her umbrella. She stripped off her raincoat, laid it on top of his, and climbed onto a bar stool. He studied her reflection in the mirror as she did her breathing exercise, thinking she must have had a pressing reason to walk all the way over here through the rain. She was still at it when Annie swung by and dropped Gloria's usual, a bottle of Bud, on the bar.

Gloria opened her eyes, turned to Mulligan, and said, "You're drinking again."

"Thanks to God, I am."

"In defiance of doctor's orders?"

"Not this time, no. He cleared me to get back in the game."

"You should probably still go easy."

"I'll try," Mulligan said.

Gloria's breathing had not yet completely calmed. Mulligan fought the urge to pull her into a bear hug and tell her everything was all right. The platitude would sound empty, and he wasn't sure how much he believed it with people like Kwame Diggs in the world. Besides, he knew how much Gloria hated being coddled, how determined she was not to let dread rule her life. Except for his old friend Rosie, she was the most fearless woman he knew. That was just one of the reasons he admired her. She was a fine news photographer, too — better than any of the paper's two-eyed shooters.

"So, Gloria," he said, "what brings you out on this godforsaken afternoon?"

"I needed to talk to you, but I never saw you come in today. I thought I might find you here."

"I was out working on something."

"What?"

"A follow on Kessler."

"Are they going to find a way to keep him in prison?"

"Doesn't look like it." He swigged from

his longneck and asked, "So what's on your mind?"

"Mason," she said.

"What about him?"

"Did you hear what he's working on?"

"He told me."

"What the hell is he thinking?"

"He's thinking that a whole bunch of our public servants have been conspiring to break the law."

"If he can prove it, will they have to let Diggs out, too?"

"Probably."

She squeezed her eyes shut.

"Jesus."

"Don't worry about it, Gloria. Mason's not that good."

"He may be better than you think. He learned a lot working with you on that pornography investigation."

"Um."

"Can't you talk him out of this?"

"I tried. Lomax tried, too."

Gloria picked up her beer and took a long swallow.

"We've got to do something," she said.

"I already have."

"What?"

"Mason asked me to help him."

"And?"

"And he thinks that I am."

Gloria smiled at that.

"What did you do?"

"I suggested he go through all the transcripts of Diggs's trials, find the names of the witnesses who testified about the drug charge and the prison assaults, and interview them."

"Ha! When he talks to them, they aren't going to tell him anything, are they?"

"They'll swear that their lies were the truth, the whole truth, and nothing but the truth."

"So help them God," Gloria said.

"You bet."

"That should slow him down," she said, "but it probably won't stop him."

"Maybe he'll get discouraged and give up."

"Does he strike you as the kind who gives up?"

"No," Mulligan said.

Gloria shook her head, then pushed damp strands of hair back from her good eye.

"We've got to make sure Diggs doesn't get out," she said.

"We?"

"Uh-huh."

"You're a *photographer,* Gloria."

"I'm a *journalist.* Mostly I use a camera;

but I know how to ask questions, and I know how to take notes."

Mulligan gave her a searching look.

"Don't take this wrong," he said, "but after what you've been through, I don't think it's a good idea for you to get involved in this."

"It's because of what I've been through that I *have* to get involved in this."

Mulligan puffed on his cigar, drained his beer, and asked Annie for another.

"Okay, Gloria," he said. "What do you have in mind?"

February 2000

The worst thing is the boredom, every day the same as the last.

Wake up at seven A.M. Three tasteless meals a day shoved through the bars. A half hour of exercise in the yard every afternoon. Lights out at ten P.M. The asshole in the next cell howling the same off-key Motown song, "Papa Was a Rollin' Stone," for what seems like an hour every night. The Mob hit man three cells down screaming at him to shut the fuck up.

It's so bad that he actually looks forward to the weekly visits from his mother, even though the only thing she ever talks about is Jesus.

He pulls the thin blanket up to his chin, rolls over to face the cinder-block wall, and closes his eyes. Tonight, he chooses *A Nightmare on Elm Street,* the opening scene playing on the inside of his eyelids.

But in his version, Freddy Krueger isn't the

one flashing the knife-bladed finger-glove. In his version, all of his victims are blondes.

19

April 2012

It had taken three weeks for the Superior Court clerk to print out all the trial transcripts, nearly eight thousand pages counting legal briefs. No way Lomax was going to approve the seven-hundred-and-eighty-five-dollar processing fee. Even if he'd agreed with what Mason was doing, he'd have trouble squeezing the payment out of the dwindling newsroom budget. Mason didn't even ask. He just shelled out the money himself.

He began by reading the transcripts of the two murder trials. The physical evidence tying Diggs to the killings was overwhelming, but Mason found it curious that the prosecution had never established a motive. Then he quickly read through Diggs's contempt, drug, and assault cases. His first run through all the documents consumed the best part of a week.

Setting aside the murder cases, he combed through the other four transcripts again, underlining key points and jotting down the names of every judge, lawyer, and witness. He saw right off that there was no point in interviewing them. At least not yet. Not until he came up with something to challenge their stories.

Come on, Mulligan, Mason said to himself, did you really think I'd fall for that? But there had to be somebody out there who would tell him the truth.

Mason dropped the transcripts in his file drawer, locked it, pulled his iPhone from his jacket pocket, and called the new source he was developing. A guy who moonlighted at an automobile dealership to supplement his meager wages as a clerk for the State Department of Corrections.

"Bristol Toyota. How may we serve you?"

"Don Sockol, please."

"May I tell him who is calling?"

"Edward Mason."

"One moment, please. . . ."

"Hi, Edward! How are you enjoying the Prius?"

"I love it," Mason lied.

"So how can I help you today?"

"I was hoping you could do me a favor."

"Anything for a great customer."

"I'd like to get a list of the guards who worked at the Department of Corrections between 1994 and 2011."

"Oh, jeez. That would be a lot of people. Can you narrow it down any?"

"I'm looking for guards who would have had contact with Kwame Diggs."

"Okay, then. That would be guys who worked Supermax. Probably still be a few hundred names, though. We have a lot of turnover."

"That's fine."

"So you're workin' on a story about Diggs, huh?"

"That's right."

"Great. I'm happy to do anything that will help keep that crazy sonovabitch locked up."

Mason thought it best not to straighten him out.

"Just keep my name out of it, okay?" Sockol said. "I don't want to get in any trouble."

"I will. You have my word."

20

Mulligan and Gloria circled the statehouse in Secretariat, his pet name for his battered old Ford Bronco. All of the parking spaces, even the illegal ones, were taken, so they shelled out a few bucks to park in the garage at the Providence Place Mall and walked up the hill to the noon rally.

The forecast was for rain, but that hadn't discouraged the turnout. Thousands had gathered on the long slope of the statehouse lawn, ringed by dozens of uniformed state cops and a squadron of mounted Providence police. Most of the crowd was in shirtsleeves, thanks to global warming. The ninety-eight-degree temperature was an all-time Providence record for April.

As they passed through the crowd, Gloria snapped photos of people waving hand-lettered signs:

Justice for Brian Freeman.

What Are You Thinking?

And dozens bearing an old photo of Eric Kessler and a single word: *Monster.*

Gloria spotted a little boy, no more than six, standing beside his parents. He held a sign containing a photo of Brian Freeman and a message he'd apparently written himself:

This Could of Bin Me.

"That one," Gloria said, "will end up on page one."

Monsignor Ignatius Buffone stood at a lectern that had been placed at the top of the statehouse steps, raised his hand for silence, and spoke into the microphone.

"Dear Lord, bless the Freeman family and all of the good people of Rhode Island who have gathered here on this day. We pray that you will give our public servants the wisdom to protect us from those who would do evil to our children. And Lord, please stay your rain just a little while longer. Blessed be God in his angels and in his saints."

Then Providence's hottest radio host, Iggy Rock, stepped forward, adjusted the microphone, and shouted, "Good morning, Row Dyelin!"

Iggy's birth name, Mulligan knew, was Armen Bardakjian. He'd grown up in the Providence neighborhood of Fox Point; flunked out of Rhode Island College, which was no easy thing to do; washed out as a Yugo salesman, Dunkin' Donuts store manager, and Amway distributor; and failed to make the grade as a wife beater. After he slapped his wife for the third time, she drove him to the emergency room to get his bruised testicles and broken nose treated.

Now, as Iggy Rock, he had reinvented himself as a right-wing radio howler, his shtick a cross between Laura Ingraham–style moralizing and Rush Limbaugh–style liberal bashing. At first, he had called himself Igneous Rock, but he'd recently shortened it to Iggy after realizing few of his listeners knew what igneous meant.

"Thank you all for answering my call to gather here today," Iggy was saying. "Look at the size of this crowd. This is democracy in action. Your voices *will* be heard!"

He thrust both hands in the air as if signaling a touchdown, and the crowd erupted with cheers and applause.

"I am honored to be your host for these proceedings," he said. "Without further ado, I want to introduce a true Row Dyelin hero, Chief Vincent Matea of the Hopkinton Police Department."

Matea, looking stiff in his dress police uniform, stepped forward, removed his cap, and placed it on the lectern.

"Thank you, Iggy," he said, "but I'm no hero. I'm just a country policeman who tries to do an honest job."

That drew a smattering of appreciative applause.

"Back in 1982, when I was a sergeant, I arrested Eric Kessler for the murder of Brian Freeman."

The crowd roared its approval.

"In the years since," Matea continued, "I have been the custodian of Kessler's private journal. It depicts his bizarre fantasy world and graphically describes the unspeakable things he did to that innocent little boy. It still gives me nightmares, but this is a burden I must bear alone. A court order and simple human decency prevent me from sharing its contents with you.

"What I can tell you with certainty," he continued, "is that Eric Kessler does not deserve his freedom. If it were up to me, he would remain in a prison cell until he rots. That's all I am prepared to say, so let me introduce you to the man you have come here to see: Brian's courageous father, Mr. Gordon Freeman."

The crowd clapped politely as the tall, gaunt man stepped to the microphone. Iggy rushed to his side, grabbed his hand, and thrust it in the air.

"Let's have a huge Little Rhody welcome for Mr. Freeman!"

The applause swelled.

"I can't *hear* you!" Iggy shouted.

The crowd responded with a roar.

Before it subsided, Freeman began to weep.

"Thank you for coming," he said, his deep voice trembling. He sounded like a man who had gone one day without drinking and now wished he hadn't. "Thank you all for remembering Brian. My son was a beautiful little boy, and Eric Kessler took him from me. It is unthinkable that this monster would ever be set free, but the unthinkable is about to happen."

He paused, swiped the tears away with his palm, and continued, his voice stronger now.

"Nothing will ever bring my boy back, but I promise that this madman will never enjoy a single day of freedom. If Eric Kessler gets out of prison, I'm going to kill him."

That sounded like an applause line to Mulligan, but it stunned the crowed into silence.

"Still," Freeman said, "I'd rather not get locked up myself. So I have come here to ask, to *demand,* that the folks with the power to stop this do the right thing. They say the law requires that Kessler be released.

I say there is a higher law that says he must not be."

This time, the applause line did its job.

"Attorney General Roberts is here with us this morning," Freeman said. "I'd like him to come to the microphone now and tell us what he's going to do about this."

The crowd booed and hooted as the patrician, silver-haired politician, who had first come to public attention as the lead prosecutor at Kwame Diggs's murder trials, stepped to the lectern.

Iggy elbowed him aside and shouted, "What? I still can't *hear* you. Show him how you really feel."

Visibly irritated, Roberts stiff-armed Iggy away from the microphone.

"Two days ago," Roberts said, "Eric Kessler was observed flushing paper towels down the toilet in his cell. That is a violation of prison rules. For this offense, corrections officials were able to shave thirty days from the good time he earned during his years of incarceration. This fortunate turn of events has provided us with additional time to find a resolution to our dilemma."

That provoked angry shouts.

"That's *it*?"

"That's all you've got?"

"Impeach Roberts!"

The crowed took up the chant: "Impeach Roberts! Impeach Roberts!" The attorney general's expression never changed. He waited for the chants to subside before continuing.

"We are attempting to persuade Mr. Kessler that it would be in his best interest to agree to voluntary commitment in a secure psychiatric hospital upon his release."

That provoked a scattering of applause.

"If he refuses, we could ask a judge to order his involuntary commitment," Roberts said. "However, I don't want to mislead you. As a rule, the courts are very reluctant to issue such orders."

With that, the crowd howled in protest. Roberts shrugged and stepped back. Iggy took his place at the microphone and led the crowd in the chant: "Impeach Roberts! Impeach Roberts! Impeach Roberts!"

After a few minutes of this, Iggy raised his hand to silence the crowd, urged everyone to flood the attorney general and the governor with letters and e-mails, and thanked everyone for coming.

"They sure were pissed," Gloria said as she and Mulligan headed back to the newspaper to file the story.

"You really can't blame them," Mulligan

said. "They've got a lot of things to be angry about."

"You think this is about more than Kessler?"

"Oh, sure. Rhode Island's unemployment rate is the second highest in the country. Half the home mortgages in the state are underwater. Most of our cities and towns can't afford to pay the pensions they've promised to teachers, cops, and firemen. Central Falls is in bankruptcy, Pawtucket is on the brink of it, and Woonsocket is in such a mess that it's begging the state to take over its school system."

"And don't forget Curt Schilling," Gloria said. The former Red Sox World Series hero's video game business was in so much trouble that the state was on the verge of losing the entire seventy-five million it had loaned him to lure the company to Providence.

"That's right," Mulligan said. "All Iggy Rock has done is gather all that fear and anger and focus it on Kessler. When he's finished with that, he'll get people worked up about something else. It's what he does."

"He's good at it," Gloria said. "You gotta give him that."

"He is," Mulligan said. "Imagine what he'll do with the Diggs case when he finds out what Thanks-Dad is up to."

Back in the newsroom, Mulligan called Providence police headquarters and asked the desk sergeant for the official crowd estimate.

"Six thousand," he was told.

Mulligan thanked him and hung up.

Crowd estimates, Mulligan knew, were the product of a dishonest, age-old game between cops and journalists. Cops knew journalists were going to ask for them, so they just pulled numbers out of their asses. Journalists then published the figures even though they knew they were bullshit.

It was a lesson Mulligan had learned back in 2004 when he covered the Boston parade celebrating the Red Sox's World Series victory over the St. Louis Cardinals. When he wrote the story, he left out the official crowd estimate.

"Why isn't it in here?" the city editor had demanded.

"Because it's three point two million," Mulligan had said.

"So?"

"The population of Boston is six hundred thousand. If every man, woman, and child in the city, including those who don't give a rat's ass about baseball, had actually shown up, another two point six million people would have had to drive in from out of town. No way that happened. If it had, they'd still be looking for parking spaces."

The city editor had ordered him to put the number in the story anyway.

It was a fight Mulligan couldn't win. He dutifully dropped the inflated six thousand figure into his story about the statehouse rally for Tuesday morning's paper.

21

Gloria was seated alone at a table in back, working on her second Thursday afternoon Bud, when Mulligan walked into Hopes with a bulging shopping bag under each arm.

"That all of it?" she asked.

"It is."

"How long did it take you to print all this out?"

"Nine hours."

"I believe it. You look like you didn't get much sleep."

"I don't want Mason to know what we're up to," Mulligan said, "so I had to wait until he went home last night."

"What time was that?"

"After ten."

"He's dedicated," Gloria said.

"Yeah, but so are we."

Mulligan dumped the bags, and computer printouts of every crime story and police log the paper had published about Diggs's hometown of Warwick between 1988 and 1994 spilled onto the table. Back then, before the paper started to retrench, there was a five-person news bureau in Warwick; and every police report, from murders to dogs hit by cars, ended up in the *Dispatch*'s West Bay edition.

"You take 1988 through 1990," he said. "I'll take the rest."

"What am I looking for?"

"Serial killers start with small cruelties and gradually work their way up to murder. Look for unsolved cases of Peeping Toms, animal torture, arson, and assaults on women and children. He was just a kid back then, not old enough to drive, so focus on addresses within a mile or two of his house."

"And what are you looking for?"

"Unsolved assaults, murders, or attempted murders between 1991, the year before he killed Becky Medeiros and her daughter, and 1994, when he slaughtered the Stuart family."

22

The official name of the bunkerlike, reinforced concrete building off Interstate 95 in Cranston is the High Security Center, but no one in Rhode Island calls it that. To the locals, it's Supermax, and it warehouses the state's most violent criminals.

It was built in 1981, when a glad-handing former beer salesman named J. Joseph Garrahy was governor. He made sure it was big enough to house 138 men. But now, only 84 of Rhode Island's 3,311 inmates were considered badass enough to be locked up there.

It was costing the state a hundred and fifty-seven thousand dollars per convict annually to run the facility, nearly four times the average for the state's other prisons. Taxpayers didn't complain. This was a rare case of them getting what they paid for. No one had ever escaped from Supermax.

Inside, a dozen sad-faced women sat on

two rows of molded plastic chairs that were bolted to the waiting room floor. Three of the women were attempting to shush their unruly children, who seemed to think this was a playdate. The rest of the women didn't look as if they had the energy to make the effort. Mason, the only man in the room, stood in a corner with Felicia Freyer, Diggs's new lawyer, and tried to stay clear of the mayhem. He thought she looked like a polished diamond among the slope-shouldered women.

After what seemed like a long wait, a single prison guard dressed in a gray uniform with black piping on the pants legs stepped into the room and passed out sign-in forms. Mason hurriedly filled his in, not marking the box you were supposed to check if you had ever been convicted of a felony.

Then another guard entered, holding a drug-sniffing German shepherd by a short leash.

"Do not attempt to pet the dog," he shouted.

The pooch meandered through the narrow room, failed to alert, and was led away.

The first guard collected the paperwork. Then he muttered something into a radio fastened to his left shoulder, and a steel door rolled open. The guard led Mason and Freyer through it, the three of them stepping into a claustrophobic steel compartment about the size of a small elevator. The door rolled shut behind them, and Mason heard the lock clank. Fifteen seconds later, a similar door in front of them buzzed and slid open.

Mason and Freyer stepped out into a long, narrow room lined with twelve cramped booths. Each was furnished with a single blue plastic chair. Mason pulled one out for Freyer and stood beside her, peering through a thick Plexiglas partition smeared with greasy handprints and no telling how many years' worth of dried tears. Beyond the partition another steel door slid open, and Kwame Diggs lumbered in, his big hands cuffed in front. He wore leg chains and an orange jumpsuit. A tan patch on his chest held his six-digit prison number: 694287.

When he was arrested at the age of fifteen, Diggs had been a five-foot-ten, 250-pound behemoth with close-cropped naps, a mild case of acne, and lips that snarled for the camera. In prison, he'd grown into a giant with a shiny shaved skull and a neatly trimmed goatee. His face, Mason thought, looked disconcertingly jolly.

Diggs approached the partition, his gait part grizzly bear and part furniture mover, and dropped into a plastic chair that looked too frail to hold his weight. He raised his big cuffed paws and picked up a black telephone receiver. Freyer already held its twin to her ear.

Behind her, women and children were filing in and taking their places in the other booths. A guard hollered, "You've got thirty minutes."

"How are you today, Kwame?" Freyer asked. She paused for his clipped response. "Well, hang in there. This is Edward Mason, the reporter I told you about. Will you talk to him?"

Diggs nodded.

"Good," she said, "but first let me give you a rundown on what I've been doing on your case." As she talked, Mason kept checking his watch, the half hour they were allotted ticking away. Finally, Freyer handed Mason the phone. It crackled with static, like a long-distance call to Rwanda.

" 'Sup, cuz?"

Mason was surprised by Diggs's voice. It still had a trace of child in it.

"I'd like to ask you some questions if that's all right."

"Sure, no biggie. If I don't like 'em, I'll

just rip this partition down and twist your fuckin' head off."

Mason reeled back from the glass. Diggs threw back his head and howled.

"Man, you shoulda seen your face just then. Just kidding, cuz. No way anybody can break through this glass. Folks done tried it, believe me."

"We don't have much time," Mason said, "so can we get to it?"

"Shoot."

"Back in 1996, you were convicted of contempt for refusing a psych evaluation."

"Yeah."

"Why did you refuse?"

"Lawyer told me to."

"Haggerty?"

"Yeah, him."

"Why didn't he want you to take it?"

"He said they'd use the answers to get me locked up in the crazy house."

"But after you were sentenced to seven years for contempt, you changed your mind?"

"Hell, yeah. Wouldn't you?"

"They say you were evasive during the evaluation."

"The dude in the white coat kept asking why I killed all those people. I told him I didn't."

"But you did, didn't you?"

"Same answer, cuz."

"What else did they ask you?" Mason said, although he already knew from reading the case files. There had been a lot of questions about why Diggs was so angry. He'd insisted that he wasn't.

"It was a long time ago," Diggs said. "How the hell am I supposed to remember that shit?"

"Fair enough," Mason said. "Let's talk about the time you were convicted of having drugs in your cell."

"Weed," Diggs said. "The screws be sayin' they found weed under my mattress."

"And did they?"

"Come on, man. I'm jonesin' for a joint right now, straight up. But you seen the security in this place, right? No way I can get any drugs in here."

"So you're saying it was planted."

"Not exactly."

"What, then?"

"They didn't even bother to hide the shit in my cell. Probably just grabbed a baggie from an evidence locker so they could wave it around at the trial."

"What about the two assaults on prison guards?"

"Never happened."

"No?"
"No."
"You never got mad and hit somebody?"
"Be wanting to, sure. Plenty of times."
"And why would that be?"
"The screws are always fuckin' with me. Tossin' my cell. Blaggin' my burn. Tearin' up the family pictures my mama sends me. Spittin' in my food. Every day calling me names. *Child killer. Pervert. Nigger.* Anything to get me to take a swing at 'em."
"Blagging your burn?"
"Stealing my cigarettes. Which they did all the time before the fuckin' warden banned smoking in here."
"When they mess with you, what do you do?"
"I laugh at 'em, cuz. Just laugh and give 'em a big ol' pickaninny grin. Back when I was on the street, I used to get hot about shit like that. Some kid called me *nigger* in the school yard, I'd whup his ass and rub his face in the dirt. But I've had a lot of time to work on my self-control in here. Believe me, I'm way too smart to give them bastards what they want."
"So they made it all up?"
"Yeah."
Mason asked Diggs for the names of prison guards he might talk to. All Diggs

knew were a few last names.

Glancing at his watch, Mason saw that his time was nearly gone. "I'd like to come back and see you again. Would that be okay?"

"Sure. Ain't like I got anything better to do. Meanwhile, can you do me a favor?"

"What?"

"Send me somethin' to read."

"What do you like?"

"Black history," Diggs said. "I already read all they got on that in the prison library. I been askin' my moms for more, but she don't get me nothin' 'cept shit about Jesus."

"Time's up," the guard hollered. "Phones down. Form a line at the door."

23

Gloria sipped from her can of Coca-Cola and peered into the cage in Mulligan's kitchen.

"Is it a boy or a girl?" she asked.

"No idea."

"Does it talk?"

"It does."

"Polly want a cracker?" Gloria said.

And Larry Bird said, "Theeeeeeee Yankees win!"

"Damn!" she said.

"Yeah."

With Ellsbury, Crawford, Kalish, Bailey, Lackey, and Matsuzaka all on injured reserve, the Sox's season was already doomed. Why did Larry have to keep rubbing it in?

"Does it say anything else?" Gloria asked.

"No. I've been trying to teach it to say, 'Yankees suck,' but its loyalty to the Evil Empire is unshakable."

"Pretty bird, though."

"If you want it, you can have it."

"I don't think so," she said. "I don't allow that kind of profanity in *my* house."

Mulligan jiggled the cage door open and filled Larry's feed tray, the bird stabbing its bill at the oven mitt the reporter had taken to wearing for protection. Then he tore open a package of paper plates and dropped two of them beside the Caserta Pizzeria box on his maple yard-sale table by the kitchen window.

"Hope pepperoni's okay."

"Are you kidding?" Gloria said. "Caserta could whip up a pie with bird-seed topping, and it would probably be good."

She sat in one of the vinyl kitchen chairs and dug in. Outside, the day was fading, so Mulligan snapped on the overhead light. Then he fetched two bottles of Killian's from the wheezing fridge, dropped into the chair across from Gloria, and snagged a slice.

"So what did you come up with?" Mulligan asked.

Gloria reached into her purse and extracted the pad she'd filled with notes on what she'd found in the news library computer printouts.

"For starters, five reports of Peeping Toms," she said.

"From Diggs's neighbors?"

"All within eight blocks. The first two in 1988, when Diggs would have been, what, ten years old?"

"Yeah."

"Then two more in 1989 and one in 1990. And Mulligan?"

"Um?"

"One of the complainants was Becky Medeiros."

"Anybody get a description?"

"One in '89 thought it might have been a black kid, but she wasn't sure. The others, no."

"The Diggses were the only black family in that neighborhood back then," Mulligan said.

"Yeah, I know."

"What else you got?"

"A dozen unsolved housebreaks," Gloria said. "In most of them, the perp made off with TVs, VCRs, jewelry, stuff like that. But in two, the only thing taken was bras and panties."

"Could have been our guy," Mulligan said. "Making dry runs before he escalated."

"That's what I was thinking."

"Anything else?"

"Two reports of animal cruelty. In January of 1990, a dog was mutilated and dumped in the trash can behind Diggs's next-door neighbor's house. Nine months later, somebody bound a dog and cat together with twine, doused them with lighter fluid, and set them on fire behind the neighborhood elementary school."

"That it?"

"It is. How about you?"

"Between the Medeiros murders in '92 and the Stuart murders in '94, Diggs's neighbors made three complaints about prowlers and one about a Peeping Tom, but none of them saw enough to provide a description."

Gloria shook her head, making her blond hair bounce. "We're not getting anywhere. This is all penny-ante stuff. The cops wouldn't have put much effort into it, so there's not going to be evidence tying any of this to Diggs."

"Yeah. And the statute of limitations has run out on it, too," Mulligan said. "But I found something else."

"Spill."

"In 1991, a year before the Medeiros murder, somebody broke into a house on Inez Avenue about three miles from Diggs's neighborhood."

"Three miles?"

"Uh-huh. Might have been him, though.

He could have ridden his bike there, no problem."

"So what happened?"

"The intruder found an open window, ripped the screen off, and climbed inside. Found a twenty-six-year-old woman named Susan Ashcroft asleep in her bed, grabbed the clock radio off the nightstand, and whacked her in the head with it. Knocked her out cold. Then he went into the kitchen, took a serrated steak knife from a drawer, and went to work on her."

"Oh God!" Gloria felt her stomach drop.

"About three in the morning, the woman came to in bed, blood all over her. She lived alone, no one there to help her, but she had the strength to grab the phone from the nightstand and call the cops. She had five stab wounds, three in her breasts and two more in her abdomen. Three of the wounds were superficial. Hesitation wounds, the police called them. But the other two were deep."

"Like he wasn't quite sure he could go through with it at first?"

"What it sounds like."

"Did she survive?"

"She did."

"Was she a blonde like the others?"

"I don't know, Gloria. The story doesn't say."

"Did the police ever try tying this to Diggs?"

"I don't know that either. I never heard about this until now."

"B and E and attempted murder," she said. "It could be enough to put Diggs away for a long time."

"Yeah. There's no statute of limitations on either charge in Rhode Island," Mulligan said. "If we can find evidence that he did this, he could be prosecuted as an adult now."

"Even though he was a kid when it happened?"

"That's right."

They spent a few minutes plotting their next move. Then Mulligan carried the portable TV out of the bedroom, set it on the kitchen counter, and plugged it in. He grabbed two more Killian's from the fridge and handed one to Gloria.

"Planning on having me stay for a while?" she said.

"I was hoping you'd want to keep me company."

"Okay," she said. "But no cop shows."

Mulligan flicked through the channels with the remote and stopped on the Bruins–

Canadiens game. The announcer was giving a medical update on Nathan Horton, the Bruins' high-scoring right-winger, who was still woozy from a concussion he'd suffered when he was blindsided by a Philadelphia Flyers forward several months earlier. Mulligan made a mental note to see his bookie and bet against the team repeating as Stanley Cup champions.

"I *love* hockey," Gloria said.

"Really?"

"Yes!"

"Will you marry me?"

"Not today."

A few years back Gloria had a thing for Mulligan, but he was seeing somebody then, so nothing came of it. Since the attack, she'd been on a couple of dates with a handsome Textron executive and discovered she couldn't stand being touched.

Maybe someday, she hoped, she'd get over it.

24

First thing next morning, Mulligan draped a towel over Larry Bird's cage, carried it down the stairs, and packed it in the back of Secretariat. He drove across town to Hope Street and parked in front of Zerilli's Market.

Leaving the bird in the car, he walked into the place and strolled down a narrow grocery aisle, passing racks of Twinkies and Ding Dongs and coolers filled with cheap American beer. When he reached the back of the store, he climbed a short staircase and knocked on a windowless steel door. When the electric lock buzzed, he turned the knob and stepped inside.

Dominic "Whoosh" Zerilli was slumped in a wooden chair behind his keyhole desk, an unfiltered Camel cigarette dangling from his lower lip and a phone pressed to his ear. He was dressed in a white shirt, loud tie, suit coat, and undershorts, the pants draped over a hanger on his clothes rack to preserve the crease. His big mutt, Shortstop, was sprawled in front of the minifridge. A huge thighbone looked like a toothpick in the dog's jaws.

"Two hundred on the Bruins to repeat. Got it, Vince," Zerilli said.

He hung up, jotted the bet down on a piece of flash paper, and dropped it into a washtub at his feet. If the cops ever raided the place, he'd drop his cigarette into the tub and, *whoosh!* Good-bye, evidence. Which was how the seventy-seven-year-old bookie had gotten his nickname. But the cops, content with their payoffs, hadn't bothered him in years.

"How are you, Whoosh?"

"Rheumatism's been acting up again, and my fuckin' prostate's the size of a softball. Takes me ten minutes just to take a piss."

"Sorry to hear that."

"Maggie's been buggin' me to turn the book over to my no-good nephew and move us into one of them gated retirement communities down in Florida. I told her no way. Them fuckin' places are full of *old* people."

Zerilli got up, opened the door to his storeroom, and disappeared inside. A minute later, he reappeared with a box of illegal Cubans and handed it to Mulligan.

The reporter pried it open, took out a Partagás Presidente, snipped the end with his cigar cutter, and stuck it in his mouth. Zerilli leaned over to give him a light.

It was their ritual: Zerilli presenting Mulligan with cigars and asking him to swear that he'd never tell anyone what went on inside the bookie's inner sanctum. Mulligan swearing and getting a cigar going. About a year ago, the bookie finally dispensed with administering the oath, but they both understood it was implied.

"So what odds are you giving on the Bruins surviving the first round?" Mulligan asked.

"They're three to two favorites."

"Give me a hundred on the Capitals."

"You sure? I mean, no way Boston's going all the way again, but Washington ain't that good."

"I'm sure."

"Okay. Your funeral."

"So listen," Mulligan said. "This time, I brought *you* a present. Something that might help draw customers into the store."

"I don't see nothin' in your hands."

"I left it in the car."

Together they walked outside and fetched the cage from the Bronco. Mulligan carried it inside, set it on the candy counter, and pulled off the towel.

"Now ain't that a fine-lookin' specimen," Zerilli said.

"It is."

"He got a name?"

"Larry Bird."

"Does it talk?"

"Doesn't say much, but maybe you can teach him."

"Thanks, Mulligan. I'm gonna leave it right here so folks will see it right off when they come in."

"You're welcome."

"Come on back to the office," Zerilli said. "Got something I need to tell you."

As they stepped back through the steel door, Shortstop growled. A low rumble.

"Easy, boy," Zerilli said. "Mulligan doesn't want your fuckin' bone."

"So what's up?" Mulligan asked.

"Gordon Freeman was in here the other day."

"That right?"

"Yeah."

"What did he want?"

"A gun."

"Aw, hell. You didn't sell him one, did you?"

Zerilli shrugged. "He woulda just bought one off somebody else."

"What kind of gun?"

"A piece-of-shit twenty-five-cal. Raven."

"He'll be lucky if it doesn't blow up in his hand," Mulligan said.

"If he fires it a lot, yeah, but I get the feelin' he's only planning to use it once."

"I don't give a shit about the guy he's planning to shoot," Mulligan said, "but I'd hate to see the old guy get in trouble."

"Me too, but there's no way I can go to the fuckin' cops. Figured maybe this was something you could handle."

"I'm on it," Mulligan said. He rose, opened the door, and then turned back. "I don't suppose he bought anything else when he was in here."

"Just a few groceries."

"Do you remember what exactly?"

"Four cans of Hormel chili, some eggplant, and a bottle of olive oil."

Chili? It was probably nothing, Mulligan told himself. But on the drive back to the office, he couldn't help wondering.

Fifteen minutes later, Mulligan dropped into his chair in the newsroom, called the Hopkinton Police Department, and asked for Chief Matea.

"What is it, Mulligan? We're pretty busy here."

"Really? Did somebody shoplift a Snickers bar from the 7-Eleven? Some kids leaving burning bags of dog poop on doorsteps again?"

"Screw you."

"Sorry. Sometimes I can't help myself."

"So why the call?"

"I was hoping you could tell me what Hormel chili, eggplant, and olive oil mean to you."

Matea's stony silence told Mulligan he was on to something.

"It's Eric Kessler's recipe, isn't it?"

"Don't take this as confirmation, but where in hell did you hear that?"

"Can't say, but I think you should see if you're missing something."

"Just a second."

It was five minutes before the chief came back on the line.

"Sonovabitch."

"The journal's gone?"

"Yeah. Did you take it?"

"Of course not."

"Better tell me what you know."

"I know that Gordon Freeman went shopping the other day with Kessler's grocery list. I also know he bought a handgun."

"Oh, shit. You know what kind?"

"A Raven 25."

"And you know this how?"
"I can't tell you that."
"Jesus Christ."
"Did you find tool marks on the drawer you had the journal in?"
"Yeah."
"How could he have gotten inside your office?"
"No idea."
"Still just one guy manning the station overnight?"
"Yeah."
"Think he dozes on the job?"
"I think maybe I should have a word with him. And I guess I better bring the old man in."
"What if he doesn't cooperate?"
"Probably won't."
"Can you search his place?"
"Not without a warrant."
"What I told you isn't enough to get one?"
"Not even close."
"Okay," Mulligan said. "Let's talk about what we *can* do."

25

According to the telephone directories, there were three Susan Ashcrofts living in Rhode Island. Gloria picked up her desk phone and placed some calls.

"Hello." A man's voice.

"Hi. My name is Gloria Costa. I'm a newsperson at the *Dispatch.*"

"Yes?"

"I'm trying to locate a woman named Susan Ashcroft who lived on Inez Avenue in Warwick back in 1991."

"I'm sorry, but you've reached the wrong party. We moved here from Connecticut three years ago. My wife grew up in New Jersey. She never lived in Warwick."

"I see. Could the person I'm looking for be a relative?"

"No. I'm sorry I can't be helpful."

"Okay, then. Thank you for your time."

That was strike three.

Gloria hung up, grabbed her camera bag,

tugged on her leather jacket, and headed for the elevator.

"Where you off to?" the picture editor called to her. "The council meeting doesn't start till seven."

"It might go long," Gloria said. "I thought I'd grab a burger first."

"Okay, then."

She'd drawn the assignment to shoot the Warwick City Council, where the first reading of an ordinance to slash the pensions of city workers was on the agenda. If she hurried, she could get there before the town offices closed for the day.

Twenty minutes later, she stood at the counter in the city clerk's office, peering at a marriage certificate. Susan Ashcroft of 66 Inez Avenue, Warwick, had married Timothy Zucchi of 22 Sunapee Ct., Coventry, and she'd taken his name. The ceremony was held at Norwood Baptist Church, just down the road on Budlong Avenue, on May 3, 1996.

Just five years after the woman was attacked. Maybe there's hope for me yet, Gloria thought.

Shortly before eight the following evening, Gloria parked her Ford Focus in front of a raised ranch on a suburban street in Coventry, walked up a brick, tulip-lined front walk, and rang the Zucchis' doorbell. The door was opened by a tall, silver-haired man in a tobacco-colored cardigan sweater.

"Ms. Costa?"

"Yes."

"Please come in. My wife is expecting you."

He led her down a short flight of stairs to a cozy family room, where a slim woman was seated beside a calico cat on a dark blue floral sofa. The woman had a Kate Atkinson paperback in her lap and what might have been a gin and tonic in her hand, but the first thing Gloria noticed about her was that her long, straight hair was a lustrous shade of dark brown.

The woman shooed the cat and patted the sofa cushion next to her, inviting Gloria to sit.

"Can I get you anything?" the woman's husband asked. "A gin and tonic, perhaps?"

"Nothing, thanks," Gloria said.

"Well then, I'll leave you two alone."

Gloria picked up a framed photograph from the end table. In it, a teenage girl and two somewhat younger boys mugged for the camera.

"Your children, Mrs. Zucchi?" she asked.

"Call me Sue," the woman said. "That

picture is of me and my brothers. My two children are in the big photo over the fireplace."

"Handsome boys."

"Smart, too." Gloria looked again at the photo in her hands. "You were blond," she said.

"I used to be."

"When did you color it?"

"In 1994. Right after Kwame Diggs was arrested for killing the Stuart woman and her two little girls."

"Because all of his victims were blond?"

"Yes. For some reason, I've never been able to go back to my natural color."

"Do you think Diggs is the one who attacked you?"

"I think it must have been."

"What makes you think so? Was it something you saw that night?"

"No. I never got a look at him. He knocked me out, and by the time I came out of it he was gone."

"What, then?"

"About a week after Diggs was finally caught, a Warwick police detective came by to tell me the person who'd stabbed me had been arrested. He said they didn't have evidence to charge him with attacking me, but that they had enough to put him away for things he did to other people."

"Did he say it was Diggs?"

"No, and I didn't ask. I wasn't in any condition to talk about this back then."

"But you assumed he meant Diggs?"

"Oh, yes. Before he left, the detective told me I didn't have to be afraid anymore. But I was. For a long time."

"I understand," Gloria said.

Susan Zucchi gave Gloria a searching look. "For some reason, I get the feeling you're one of the few people who does."

"Yes," Gloria said.

The two women sat quietly for a moment. The cat wandered over and rubbed against Mrs. Zucchi's leg.

"Can you tell me," the woman said, "why you are asking about this after all these years?"

"We're researching a story about Diggs."

"Why? They aren't going to let him out, are they?"

"I don't think so," Gloria said, not wanting to frighten the woman. "We just want to remind people why they never should."

Gloria said her good-byes and trotted up the stairs, where Mr. Zucchi materialized to show her out.

She got into her car and cranked the ignition. Then she tilted the rearview to look at herself in the mirror. If Diggs ever did get out, maybe she'd color *her* hair, too.

26

"Corrections Department library. Paul Delvecchio speaking."

"Hello. My name is Edward Mason. An inmate at Supermax tells me he has read all of the books on black history in your collection and has asked me to send him additional titles. I'm wondering if you have Taylor Branch's Martin Luther King trilogy."

"One moment please. . . . No, sir, we don't. The only book we have by Taylor Branch is *The Cartel,* a book about college sports."

"Okay, then."

"But sir?"

"Yes?"

"You will not be permitted to bring books to the prison, and they will be returned if you mail them yourself. They can be delivered to an inmate only if they are shipped directly from a major bookseller."

Mason thanked him, hung up, and logged on to Amazon.com. He placed an order for *Parting the Waters, Pillar of Fire,* and *At Canaan's Edge* and arranged for them to be mailed to Diggs at Supermax.

As Mason logged off, a copyboy dropped the morning mail on his desk. Mason sorted through it and found a manila envelope from Don Sockol, his Corrections Department source. Inside was the list he'd been waiting for. It contained 184 names. Beside each was a mailing address. The list also indicated which of the men were still employed as guards at Supermax and which ones had quit, retired, or been transferred to other units.

Mason figured those no longer employed by the Corrections Department might be more willing to talk. He flipped through the list and marked them with a yellow highlighter. Blacks might be more sympathetic to Diggs than whites, Mason thought, so he searched the highlighted names and circled fifteen probables.

It was a place to start.

Wyclef Jefferson lived on the top floor of a three-story tenement house in the Elmwood section of Providence. A few quick questions established that he was thirty-six years old, had worked at Supermax for eleven years until he burned out, and had quit in January to take a job as a security guard at the Providence Place Mall.

He was seated now in a maple rocker, a bowl of unshelled peanuts in his lap and a pile of broken shells on the bare wood floor by his stocking feet. Mason sat across from him on a matching sofa, his notepad open in his lap.

"Have some," Jefferson said, extending the bowl toward Mason.

"No thanks."

Jefferson's wife, Jada, swooped in with a bottle of Red Stripe in each hand. She dropped one on the end table next to her husband's chair and offered the other to Mason.

"Thanks, but I'm fine," he said.

"Don't trust a man that won't drink with me," Jefferson said.

"Well then," Mason said, and extended his hand for the beer.

"And honey?" Jefferson said.

"Yes, baby?"

"Tell the kids to turn down that damned rap music."

"I will."

"Prefer jazz myself," Jefferson said as his wife darted from the room. "Miles, Dizzy,

Coltrane, Charlie Parker."

"The giants," Mason said.

"Damned straight."

"So tell me," Mason said. "How well did you know Kwame Diggs?"

"Not well. You don't exactly make friends in Supermax."

"He ever give you any trouble?"

"Mouthed off to me sometimes."

"He ever take a swing at you?"

"If he had, the fucker would still be walkin' with a limp."

Yeah, right, Mason said to himself. If Diggs had wanted to, he could have torn Jefferson's arms and legs off and entertained the cell block by juggling them. But Mason swallowed the thought and moved on.

"According to court records," he said, "Diggs assaulted a guard named Robert Araujo on March 12, 2005. Do you remember the incident?"

"No. That was my day off."

"Really?"

"Yeah."

"You remember what days you had off seven years ago?"

Jefferson glared.

"When you returned to work that week, did you happen to notice if Araujo had any visible injuries?"

"I don't recall."

"I see. I also understand that Diggs assaulted a guard again last year, and that on another occasion a bag of marijuana was found in his cell. Do you remember any of that?"

"I musta been off on those days, too."

This wasn't getting Mason anywhere, so he decided to come at it from another angle. "I hear security is pretty tight at Supermax."

"Yeah, it is."

"That makes me wonder. How could someone smuggle a bag of marijuana in there?"

"You'd be surprised," Jefferson said. "Inmates got all kinds of tricks."

"Such as?"

"Like sometimes one of their bitches will stick a plastic bag in her mouth and pass it to her man when they kiss in the visitors' room."

Mason just stared at him.

"What?" Jefferson said.

"I've been in the visitors' room. Assuming they could fool the drug-sniffing dog, just how would they manage to kiss through that thick sheet of plate glass?"

"Fuck you. Finish your beer and get the hell out."

Mason set the half-full Red Stripe on the

floor, went out the door, tramped down the stairs, and pointed his Prius toward the next name on his list.

June 2006

Except for his waking dreams, books are the only thing that sustain him.

In the dim overhead light, he squints at the final page of *Africans in America: America's Journey through Slavery,* written by a brother named Charles Johnson and a sister named Patricia Smith. He wonders idly if the two of them are fucking.

He had read the book swiftly, lingering only over the chapters about Denmark Vesey, Gabriel Prosser, and Nat Turner, ferocious brothers who led bloody rebellions against their white masters.

He closes the book, drops it on the floor beside his cot, and picks up a paperback from the prison library. *Soul on Ice,* by Eldridge Cleaver. On the first page, a dateline: Folsom Prison, Jan. 25, 1968. He smiles at that.

And he *loves* the brother's last name.

27

May 2012

Mulligan grabbed his desk phone and started to dial. Then he thought better of it. He hung up, stood, and peeked over the top of his cubicle. Mason was just a few feet away, bending over several sheets of paper that were spread across his desktop.

"Whatcha got there?" Mulligan asked.

"A list of guards and former guards at Supermax. You probably know some of these guys. Maybe you can point out the ones who are straight shooters."

"Sure thing," Mulligan said.

Mason gathered up the sheets of paper and handed them over the top of the cubicle.

Mulligan flipped through the names, recognizing about thirty of them. He picked up a red marker and made checks beside the ones who would lie to a reporter about the weather.

"Here you go, Thanks-Dad," he said, handing the list back. "Try the twelve I marked first."

"Thanks, Mulligan."

"You're welcome."

Mulligan tugged on his jeans jacket and headed for the elevator. Mason watched him go. Then he glanced at the names Mulligan had checked. One of them was Wyclef Jefferson. It didn't surprise him any. He figured his colleague could be counted on to weed out the guards who wouldn't tell him anything.

Mulligan took the elevator down, stood on the sidewalk, fired up a Partagás, and placed the call from his cell.

"Warwick Police Department."

"Andrew Jennings, please."

"Lieutenant Jennings retired from the force last November."

That was news to Mulligan. He and his old friend had lost touch a couple of years back.

"He's an old pal of mine. Do you know how I can reach him?"

"I'm not permitted to give out his phone number, but you can find him at the FOP lodge on Tanner Avenue most afternoons."

When Mulligan pulled up to the lodge a

half hour later, there were only four cars in the parking lot. He found Jennings alone at the bar, the former cop's right arm curled around a bottle of Narragansett and a whiskey back. His forearms were still roped with muscle, but his hair had thinned, and he seemed smaller than Mulligan remembered. He looked gaunt, as if something more than the job had drained out of him.

Mulligan took the adjoining stool, tapped him on the shoulder, and said, "How you doing, Andy?"

"Mulligan? Long time." His voice still rumbled like a muscle car. "I'm doin' jess fine. And you?"

"About the same."

"Really? Cuz from what I been hearin', things aren't too good at the paper."

"We've had a lot of layoffs, but I'm still hanging on."

"I ever tell you I was a paperboy when I was a kid?" Jennings asked.

"I don't think you ever did."

"In those days, the *Dispatch* was so fat I could only carry ten at a time. Now it looks like a fuckin' pamphlet."

The bartender wandered over, wiped a wet spot with a bar rag, and gave Mulligan the once-over.

"Don't remember seeing you in here

before," he said. "You on the job?"

"I'm not."

"It's members only here, buddy."

"He's a friend of mine, Rico," Jennings said.

"Then the first one's on the house. What's your poison?"

"Whatever Andy's having. And bring him a reload on me."

"Thanks, pal," Jennings said.

"You're welcome, Andy. So tell me, how's Mary?"

"She's good."

"Still teaching at the high school?"

"She is."

"I hear *you* finally turned in the badge."

"Yeah. It was time." But the look in his eyes said he wasn't so sure.

Rico delivered their order, moseyed toward the other end of the bar, and gazed up at a television tuned to a Fox News show hosted by a blond airhead named Megyn Kelly.

Mulligan swallowed his shot of bourbon and took a swig of beer. He was eager to get to the point, but he knew Jennings liked to chat about this and that before getting down to business.

"So," Mulligan asked, "what are you doing with yourself these days?"

"Mornings I putter around the house. Most afternoons I drop in here to play a little pool and shoot the shit with old friends. 'Course, I'll have to find another job if the Republicans on the city council get their way. They're tryin' to slice all the city pensions in half."

"Already happened in Central Falls," Mulligan said. "From what I hear, Providence and Pawtucket could be next."

"Hard times," Jennings said.

"Unless you're on Wall Street."

"Jesus, don't get me started. They keep shipping jobs overseas and the whole country's gonna be outta work. One of these days, you'll dial 911 and find yourself talking to some moron in Bangladesh."

They sipped their beers, Mulligan hoping they'd chatted enough.

"So," Jennings said. "Workin' on anything interesting?"

"I am. I was thinking you might be able to help."

"Let's hear it."

"Twenty-one years ago, somebody broke into a house on Inez Avenue and attacked a woman with a knife."

"Sue Ashcroft," Jennings said.

"You remember this?"

"Oh yeah. It was maybe my third or fourth

case after I made chief of detectives."

"Her name's Susan Zucchi now," Mulligan said. "One of my colleagues tracked her down through her marriage license. Found her living in a nice house in Coventry."

"That so?"

"Yeah."

"How is she?"

"She's good. Got herself an attentive husband, a couple of fine sons."

"Glad to hear it. But why would the *Dispatch* go looking for her now, after all these years?"

"To ask her about Kwame Diggs."

"Diggs? Shoulda shot that fucker full of holes when I had the chance." He picked up his shot and sipped. "So what did she have to say?"

"That she's always believed he was the one who attacked her."

"Most likely was," Jennings said.

"Really? He would have been just twelve years old."

"He was only thirteen when Becky Medeiros was butchered, and we know for sure he did that."

"Why didn't I hear anything about this back then?" Mulligan asked.

"Chief's orders. Folks were in a panic over the Medeiros and Stuart murders. He didn't see any point in making things worse."

"Was there any evidence tying Diggs to Ashcroft?"

"Nothing hard. Just circumstantial."

"No prints?"

"A couple of bloody palm prints in the bedroom, but they were smeared. Not good enough to make a comparison."

"No DNA?"

"Not enough of anything you could test. At least not back then. Folks who believe what they see on them *CSI* shows think there's always hair, saliva, skin cells, or some other damned thing the lab rats can use to finger the perp. Most times it ain't that easy."

"What about the circumstantial evidence?"

Jennings raised his right hand and ticked it off one finger at a time: "Ashcroft was young and blond, just like Diggs's other victims. In all three attacks, the perp pried the screen off an unlocked rear window and climbed inside. All three times, he didn't bring a weapon with him. Just grabbed what he could find in the victims' kitchens. All three times, the victims had multiple stab wounds."

"Nowhere near the same amount of rage, though," Mulligan said. "Sue Ashcroft was stabbed only five times."

"We figured he was escalating."

"You took Diggs's confession, right?"

"Yeah. Me and Mello."

"He confessed to the Medeiros and Stuart murders, but not the attack on Ashcroft?"

"That's right."

"Why?"

"We got the feeling he was embarrassed about that one because he didn't finish her off."

"No shit?"

"That's how it seemed, yeah."

"Tell me about the confession."

"What do you want to know?"

"What was his demeanor?"

"Boastful."

"Run it down for me."

"We put him in an interrogation room, chained him to a table, and asked him again if he wanted a lawyer. He said he didn't."

"A teenager can make that decision for himself?"

"Long as he understands his rights when they're explained to him, yeah."

"Then what?"

"We asked if he wanted his parents present. He said no way. He actually *begged* us not to call his mother. We did anyway, of course. Got to notify the parents when you arrest a juvenile. But between you and me, we took our sweet time about it."

"You interrogated him before they got there?"

"We don't like to question a teenager with the parents in the room if we can avoid it. The kid usually clams up in front of Mom and Dad. And a lot of times, when we ask the kid a question, the parents answer it. So, yeah, we did."

"You can do that?"

"Back then, yeah. There's still no *law* against it, but now it would be a violation of the state's judicial guidelines unless the parents agree to it. That's how it is in most states now."

"So what happened?"

"I told Diggs we had him dead to rights. Fingerprints at the two murder scenes. Trophies from the victims in his garden shed. No way he was gonna talk his way out of it. Mello told him that if he came clean about what he'd done, the judge might go easier on him at sentencing."

"Which was a lie?"

"Oh, hell yeah. . . . Diggs stared at us for a minute, thinking it over. Then he nodded and started talking. He told us how he stalked his victims. How he broke into their houses. Where he found the knives in their kitchens. How he broke knife blades off inside of Becky Medeiros and one of the Stuart kids. And Mulligan?"

"Yeah?"

"The fucker was smiling the whole time, like he enjoyed reliving it. Couple of times he even laughed. Spilled details for nearly two hours before his parents showed up."

"They bring a lawyer?"

"Not then, no."

"Did he say why he killed those people?"

"We were about to get into that when his mother and father stormed in."

"So then what happened?"

"Soon as they barreled through the door, he started bawlin'. Told them he'd never hurt anyone. I got the feeling he was more afraid of his mother than he was of us. He claimed the only reason we'd arrested him was that he was black. Accused us of calling him *nigger* and beating him with a phone book to make him confess."

"Did you?"

"Call him *nigger*? Of course not. Beat him? We wanted to, believe you me. Would have loved to kick the smile off that murdering sonovabitch's face. But we didn't. We were completely professional. No way we were gonna risk screwing up *this* interrogation."

"But you did," Mulligan said. The trial judge had thrown out the confession on a technicality the reporter had never fully understood.

"Not really," Jennings said. "The judge knew the confession was good, but he concocted a bullshit reason to toss it."

"Why would he do that?"

"The physical evidence was more than we needed to convict, so he didn't want to risk having some bleeding-heart liberal appeals court overturn the verdict by ruling that the kid hadn't understood his rights or some such bullshit."

"Where'd you hear that?" Mulligan asked.

"From the prosecutor."

"Roberts?"

"Yeah. He said the judge explained it to him in confidence, so you can't put that part in the paper."

So no one but the judge, the police, the prosecutor, and Diggs's trial lawyer, Mulligan realized, had ever heard Diggs's confession.

"The interrogation was videotaped?"

"It was."

"Any way I can get a look at it?"

"I'll have to think about that."

"You have a copy?"

"I do. Made copies of the murder books too. Took it all with me when I left the force."

"Anything in them that didn't come out at the trials?"

"Oh, yeah. Lots of ugly, perverted stuff. Since the fingerprints and the trophies he kept from his victims were all we needed for a conviction, the prosecutor left out some of the sordid details to spare the victims' families. I had it in the back of my mind that I might write a book about the case someday, but I'm thinking now that's never gonna happen."

"Why not?"

"Mary doesn't want me reliving it all over again. I gotta admit she has a point."

"May as well give everything to me, then."

"You'd have to give me a real good reason."

Mulligan sipped his beer and thought about how he should put this.

"I'm worried," he said, "that Diggs is going to get out."

"You've gotta be shittin' me."

"Wish I were."

"What the fuck's going on, Mulligan?"

"You've heard the rumors about the state faking charges to keep Diggs inside?"

"Yeah. Of course I have."

"It's probably true. And now somebody's looking into it."

"*What?* Who?"

"I'm not prepared to say."

"It's the goddamned ACLU, isn't it?"

"Sorry, but I can't get into that."

"Those sons of bitches."

Mulligan didn't say anything. He figured it was best not to straighten Jennings out.

"So you're looking for a legal way to keep Diggs locked up?"

"I am."

"Well, okay, then. I doubt I have anything that will help, but if you come over to the house for lunch Saturday, I'll walk you through what I've got."

"Not till Saturday?"

"Mary's leaving town Friday night," Jennings said. "Gonna spend the weekend with her brother in Nashua. I don't want her listening in on our conversation."

Mary was Connie Stuart's twin sister. Andy had grown close to her during the murder investigation, and he'd married the younger woman three years after Diggs was sent to prison.

It was Mary, Mulligan remembered, who had discovered her sister's body.

28

Mulligan was on his way back to Providence when the theme from *The Godfather,* his ring tone for Zerilli, started playing in his shirt pocket.

"Mulligan."

"Get your ass over here right fuckin' now."

"Is there a problem?"

"There sure in hell is."

"Okay. I'll be right over."

Twenty minutes later, he pushed through the door and found the bookie, scowling and arms crossed, standing by the candy counter.

"I give you the finest fuckin' cigars in the world, no charge, and *this* is the thanks I get?"

"What are you talking about, Whoosh?"

"What am *I* talking about? What this goddam *buzzard's* talkin' about is the problem."

Right on cue, Larry Bird said it. "Theeeeee Yankees win!"

"Oh, that."

"Forgot to mention this when you pawned the shitbag off on me, did you?"

"Guess I did."

"You got any fuckin' idea how many customers I lost the last week because of you? Just this afternoon Marty Kelley and his wife came in, heard the bird squawk his bullshit, turned around, and walked right the hell out."

"I'm sorry, Whoosh."

"*Sorry?* That's all you got to say?"

"I'm very, very sorry."

"Goddammit, Mulligan. Get this muthafucking Yankees lover out of my store right now."

"Okay, okay. . . . But first, can I collect what I won on the Bruins?"

Zerilli grimaced, pulled a thick wad from his pocket, and peeled off three fifty-dollar bills.

"And before you go, you can clean up the bird shit he kicked all over the fuckin' counter."

29

Mason pushed through the front door of Ward's Public House on Post Road in Warwick and scanned the room. The bar stools were empty. Five booths were occupied by families, the fathers dining on burgers, the women picking at salads, and the kids wolfing something that looked like chicken nuggets. A guy with Twisted Sister hair sat alone in another booth, a black guitar case by his side and a bottle of Heineken in his fist.

None of them looked as though they could be Tyrone Robinson, so Mason took a seat at the bar. He ordered a Red Stripe, which he was developing a taste for, and settled down to wait. After the beer was delivered, he slid his notebook from his jacket pocket and flipped through his notes, not that there was anything worthwhile in them. So far, he'd talked to nine former prison guards and gotten nothing useful. Reviewing the notes was just something to do.

"Hey, man," someone called out. "You the reporter dude?"

Mason turned and saw Twisted Sister waving at him. He grabbed his beer, walked over, and slid into the booth.

"Tyrone Robinson, I presume."

"Presumed otherwise when you came in."

"That's true."

"I get that a lot."

"I'll bet."

"Tyrone's a family name," he said. "My grandma was a big fan of some old-timey movie dude."

"Tyrone Power?"

"Yeah, him. She slapped the name on my old man, and he passed it down to me. I don't use it, though. I go by 'Ty.' "

"Ready for another beer?" Mason asked.

"You buyin'?"

"Sure."

"Hey, Donnie," Ty called out. "Bring us another round."

"So," Mason said, "what can you tell me about Kwame Diggs?"

"He's a righteous brother," Ty said.

"How so?"

"Never makes trouble. Keeps to himself. Mostly just sits in his cell and reads books."

"Really? According to court records, he assaulted two guards."

Before Ty could answer, his cell phone rang. He dug it out of his shirt pocket, checked the number on the screen, and said: "Hey, Chuckie. Thanks for calling me back. . . . Yeah, yeah. I'll be on time for the gig if you tell me where the hell it is. . . . But what's the name of the place, dude? . . . I *know* it's your brother's pub. You said that ten times already. . . . Ohhhhh," he said, and then he chuckled. "See you at eight thirty sharp."

He clicked off and shoved the phone back in his pocket.

"Turns out the name of the place *is* My Brother's Pub," he told Mason. "For a while there, I thought I was in that Three Stooges routine. You know. 'Who's on First'?"

"Abbott and Costello," Mason said.

"Huh?"

"It wasn't Three Stooges. It was Abbott and Costello."

"Whatever, dude."

"So is this how you're making a living now? As a musician?"

"Yeah. Our band's got a regular Thursday night gig at Lupo's Heartbreak Hotel in Providence, and we get booked all over on weekends. Westerly. Pawtucket. Newport. Fall River. Even opened for Roomful of Blues in Boston a couple of times. I play lead guitar. The bass player's a former Supermax guard, too, so we call ourselves the Screws."

"Catchy," Mason said. "What kind of music do you play?"

"Heavy metal. You dig it?"

"I prefer classical music," Mason said.

"Awesome. The Stones. Led Zeppelin. Steppenwolf. *Love* that retro shit, man."

Mason started to laugh, then swallowed it when he realized Ty wasn't joking. "So," he said, "can we get back to Diggs now?"

"Shoot."

"Tell me about the assaults."

"Never happened," Ty said.

"No?"

"No way."

"How do you know?"

"It's an open secret. Everybody knows they're just fuckin' with the dude."

"Can you prove it?"

"How do you prove a negative, man?"

Mason had been wondering the same thing.

"According to court records," he said, "Diggs assaulted a guard named Robert Araujo on March twelve, 2005. What do you know about that?"

"The asshole made it up."

"Why would he do that?"

"Because the warden asked him to."

"You know this how?"

"Heard Araujo talkin' about it in the break room one time."

"What did he say?"

"That the warden wanted to make sure Diggs stayed locked up. Araujo said he faked the assault charge to help out."

"Do you remember his exact words?"

"Hell, no. It was seven years ago, dude."

"Who else was there?"

Ty thought about it a moment.

"I don't remember, but I *do* remember they were acting like Araujo was a big fuckin' hero. High-fiving him, patting him on the back, and shit."

"Close your eyes," Mason said. "It will help your recall."

"You're shittin' me, right?"

"Just try it. Close your eyes and visualize the break room. Araujo is there, bragging about what he'd done. Others are patting him on the back. Who are they?"

"Chuckie Shaad," Ty said. "Oh, and Frank Horrocks."

"Anybody else?"

"Yeah, but I don't remember who."

"Look around the room," Mason said. "Who do you see?"

"Uh. The new guy, John Pugliese, is playing cards at a table by the vending machines. I can't see who with, though."

"Now look at Araujo. Does he have any sort of visible injury?"

"No."

"Okay," Mason said, and Ty opened his eyes.

"Damn," he said. "That actually works, huh?"

"Sometimes," Mason said.

"Think it would help me remember the words to 'Symphony of Destruction'?"

"What's that?"

"Only Megadeth's biggest hit ever, dude."

"You'd probably be better off writing them on your wrist," Mason said. "Diggs was also charged with assaulting a guard named Joseph Galloway last fall. What can you tell me about that?"

"I was out of there by then."

"Oh. Right. So you never saw Diggs hit anybody?"

"Never. And they gave him plenty of reason to, believe me."

"Tell me about that."

"The guards were always trying to provoke him into doin' something. Trashing his cell. Calling him names. Nigger, nigger, nigger, whenever he was close enough to hear."

"And what did Diggs do?"

"Didn't do nothing. Just turned the other cheek. He's a goddamned political prisoner, dude."

"How do you mean?"

"They wouldn't be doing none of this if he was white."

"Why do you think that?"

"Come on. It's *sooo* obvious. I mean, you don't see them fuckin' with Eric Kessler this way, do you?"

"I see your point," Mason said, and jotted the quote in his notebook. "So, you worked as a guard for six years, is that right?"

"About that, yeah."

"Why did you quit?"

"I didn't. They fired me, man."

"Why?"

"They said I was coming to work stoned."

"Were you?"

"It was just a couple of times. They coulda let it slide. But no. They had to make a big fuckin' deal out of it."

"Stoned on what?"

"Cocaine."

Mason hadn't asked Ty about the drugs supposedly found in Diggs's cell, but he saw no point in going into that now. A guard who had been fired for drug use had zero credibility.

30

Charlie, the fry cook at Mulligan's favorite diner, had the radio tuned to Iggy Rock's drive-time talk show on WTOP. The only thing the callers wanted to talk about was Eric Kessler's looming release from Supermax. Most of them sounded angry. Iggy assured them that they should be.

Mulligan listened for a few minutes, then tuned it out and folded the *Dispatch* to the opinion page. The lead editorial demanded that the state find a way to keep Kessler in prison. Just how this was to be done, the writer didn't say. The op-ed page was filled with letters to the editor, all of them about Kessler. They sounded pretty much like the radio callers. The Kessler story was heating up.

Charlie turned from the grill to top off Mulligan's coffee.

"What the fuck are they going to do about this?" he said. There was no need to define "this." It was all anyone was talking about.

"I don't know, Charlie."

"Well, then maybe you oughta find out," the fry cook said.

Mulligan nodded, sipped his coffee, and scanned the sports section, finding nothing but bad news about his favorite teams. Then he flipped to the metro page, spotted the headline on Billy Hardcastle's metro column, and gasped. Everybody already knew that Providence's fifteen city councilmen never paid their parking tickets, so why did *this* jerk find it necessary to write about it? It didn't qualify as news. According to the column, every councilman had at least forty outstanding tickets. Shirley Iannuzzo, who represented the seventh ward, was in first place with 246.

Printing this, Mulligan figured, was asking for trouble.

He finished his eggs, drained his mug dry, strolled two blocks to the paper, and saw that he was right. The Providence police were out in force, slapping Denver boots on the cars parked at the fifteen-minute parking meters in front of the newspaper building. Most of them belonged to reporters and copy editors who never paid *their* parking tickets either. Mulligan was glad he'd walked to work today. The tab for *his* unpaid tickets was more than Secretariat was worth.

He took the elevator to the third floor, settled into his desk chair, checked his computer messages, and found one from Lomax: *See me.* So he strolled into the managing editor's glass-walled office, dropped into a leather chair, and said, "What's up, boss?"

"Give me an update on Mason."

"He's hiding his cards, not telling me much."

"How do you *think* he's doing?"

"Far as I can tell, he's not getting anywhere."

"I hear he's been interviewing prison guards," Lomax said.

"Yeah. I've been steering him to the ones I know aren't going to tell him anything."

"Good. Think he's getting discouraged?"

"I don't know."

"I hear *you've* been poking into the Diggs case, too," Lomax said.

"Where'd you hear that?"

"From an ex-cop I know."

Mulligan wasn't all that surprised. It was hard to keep secrets in a state as small as Rhode Island.

"So, what are you after?" Lomax asked.

"I'm hoping to tie Diggs to something that

can keep him locked up legally."

"Getting anywhere?"

"Not yet."

"I don't like it when you go off the reservation, Mulligan. Why didn't you tell me about this before?"

"I've been working it on my own time. Didn't want to bother you with it unless I came up with something."

"Gonna stay on it?"

"I am."

"Fine, but it will still have to be on your own time. We're too short-staffed for me to spare you while you're off tilting at windmills."

"I understand. Something else you should know. Gloria Costa's been giving me a hand with it."

"What? After everything she's been through?"

"I tried to talk her out of it, but she was insistent. The whole thing was her idea, actually."

Lomax sighed and shook his head.

"Look," Mulligan said. "She's a journalist. A darned good one. We can't keep protecting her."

"Okay, Mulligan. But can I count on you to keep a close eye on her?"

"I promise."

"Meanwhile, we've still got a daily paper to put out. I need you to do another follow on Kessler today."

"Far as I know," Mulligan said, "there's nothing new to write about that."

"Come up with something. That story is selling papers. I want to keep it on the front page."

"Any suggestions?"

"How about talking to the governor? You're old friends, right? Maybe she'll spill something we can use."

"I'll see what I can do."

Mulligan walked back to his cubicle and stared at his desk phone. He and Fiona McNerney *had* been close once. A quarter of a century ago, they'd been high school classmates, sometimes studying together and often partying at Hopes, where the bartenders rarely bothered to glance at their fake IDs. Later, when Fiona agonized over whether to take her vows as a Little Sisters of the Poor nun, it was Mulligan she'd poured her heart out to. For decades, they'd remained friends; and she'd been one of his best sources during her one term as state attorney general. It was then that a *Dispatch* headline writer, impressed by her tenacity, had dubbed her "Attila the Nun," and she'd reveled in the name. When the Vatican finally demanded she choose between politics and the church, she'd given Mulligan the scoop that she would stick with politics and run for governor.

But shortly after that, she'd betrayed him, leaking something he'd told her in confidence. And the leak had gotten somebody killed. The somebody deserved it, Mulligan had to admit. Still, he wasn't ready to forgive.

He picked up the phone, called her office, and waited on hold for five minutes before he was put through.

"Hi, Mulligan."

"Hello, Governor."

"Long time," she said.

"More than a year."

"I've missed you."

He'd missed her, too, but he wasn't about to admit it.

"The reason I'm calling," he said. "Lomax is bugging me for a follow on Kessler. Wants to keep the story alive in the paper. I was hoping you could give me something that will get him off my back."

"I can do that."

"Let's hear it."

"I'm a little busy right now. Why don't we get together later at the Trinity Brewhouse?"

"Not Hopes?"

"I don't go there anymore. My press secretary says the governor should patronize a better class of gin joint."

"The Brewhouse can get loud," Mulligan said. "It's not the best place for a conversation."

"Happy hour starts at four. If we get there at three, we'll have the place pretty much to ourselves."

So when Mulligan walked through the door ten minutes early, Fiona was already there, sitting alone by a window overlooking the Providence Public Library. She was a small woman whose chopped-short hair had gone prematurely gray. A pint of amber microbrew sat on the table in front of her. On the street outside the window, the governor's official limo idled at the curb, a state trooper behind the wheel.

Before Mulligan could seat himself on the stool across from her, Fiona sprang up and gave him an awkward hug.

A waitress materialized and said, "Menu?"

"No thanks," Mulligan said. "Just bring me some chips and salsa and a glass of Tommy's Red."

Fiona and Mulligan sat uncomfortably for a moment, eyes averted, each hoping the other would speak first.

"It's good to see you," she finally said.

"Wish I could say the same."

"You're not going to make this easy, are you."

"Guess not. We Irish know how to hold a grudge."

"Better than anybody," Fiona said.

"You're looking well," Mulligan said. He decided not to mention the new lines at the corners of her eyes. "Running the state must agree with you."

"Since the election, it's been one disaster after another," she said. "The state pension system is collapsing. Tax revenues have plummeted. Unemployment is over ten percent. Half our cities and towns are on the brink of bankruptcy. And we might have to set a child killer loose. And you know what?"

"What?"

"I fuckin' love it."

Not the choice of words you'd expect from a governor, let alone a former nun, but Fiona had always been herself around Mulligan.

"So what about you?" she said.

"What *about* me?"

"Judging from all your page-one bylines, I gather the job is going well."

"I'm doing okay."

"Seeing anybody?"

"No."

"Cooled off on that hot lawyer, did you?"

"She cooled off on me," Mulligan said.

"Oh. Too bad."

"I'll get over it."

"Meaning you haven't yet?"

"Can we talk about something else?"

"Sure. Think the Red Sox have a shot at the playoffs?"

"No."

"*No?* That's all you've got to say about that?"

"It is."

She scowled.

"I probably should tell you to go to hell and walk out the door," she said. "But I'm not going to do that. I'm still your friend, even if you don't want to think so. So I'm going to give you what you came for."

"Shoot," Mulligan said, and slid a notebook from his jacket pocket.

31

Mason sat at the dining room table, sipped his morning coffee, and listened patiently to his father.

"The older members of the board are not eager to sell," the old man said. "They have always valued the influence the newspaper gives them in the affairs of the community, and they are willing to preserve that influence, even at a substantial financial loss."

"Meaning Uncle Arthur, Aunt Charlotte, and Aunt Mildred?"

"And my brother Bradford as well."

"How very noblesse oblige of them," Mason said.

"Quite so," his father said.

"And the younger members?"

"Except for Cameron, who sided with his father, all of your cousins voted to sell."

"So that's it, then," Mason said.

"Yes, I'm afraid so. I've been directed to engage the services of Dirks, Van Essen &

Murray, the leading brokerage firm for newspaper mergers and acquisitions, to negotiate the sale of the *Dispatch.*"

"To whom?"

"The board would prefer to reach an agreement with one of the respectable newspaper groups: Belo, Media General. The New York Times Company, perhaps."

"And if they're not interested?"

"Over the last couple of years, we've had several inquiries from General Communications Holdings International," his father said. "If no alternatives present themselves, we might be compelled to work something out with them."

Mason was familiar with that company's track record. For a decade, it had been buying up struggling newspapers and television stations at rock-bottom prices, stripping their newsrooms bare of staff, filling their news holes with wire copy, running them into the ground, and then selling off their equipment and real estate.

For *The Providence Dispatch,* one of the finest small-city newspapers in America for 150 years, it would be an ignoble end.

Mason nodded, indicating that he understood.

"Why don't we drive in together this morning?" his father said. "We can talk about this some more on the way."

"I'd like that," Mason said, "but I'm not going straight in. I have an interview scheduled this morning."

After his father left, Mason asked the maid to refill his coffee. He lingered over it as he read the morning paper, starting with Mulligan's front-page update on the Kessler case. State officials were scheduled to appear before Superior Court judge Clifford Needham on Thursday to ask that Kessler be ordered to submit to a psychiatric evaluation, which he had declined to take voluntarily.

"It is our position," Governor McNerney was quoted as saying, "that Eric Kessler is suffering from a severe mental disorder that would make him an imminent danger to the public if he were to be released, as scheduled, next week. If this can be confirmed by a mental health professional, we will then ask the court to order that he be confined indefinitely in a secure facility until such time as his condition no longer presents a serious risk to the community."

Kessler's court-appointed defense attorney, Austin Donahue, declared that he would oppose the petition.

"This is a naked attempt to subvert the law and violate my client's rights," he was quoted as saying. "He has paid his debt to society, and under the laws of our state, he is entitled to his freedom."

Mulligan had given the governor the last word: "Kessler's debt to society is not something that can ever be repaid."

Huh, Mason thought. Maybe Mulligan and Fiona have finally made up.

An hour later, Mason sat in a cubicle at Supermax and watched Diggs drop into the chair on the other side of the thick glass partition.

Diggs's lawyer hadn't come along this time, but she'd arranged for Mason's name to be placed on the inmate's approved visitors list. Mason should have been pleased to have Diggs all to himself. But he wasn't. He missed Felicia.

Since they'd met, his nighttime ritual of reviewing his notes and sipping his whiskey had taken a disturbing turn. He'd been imagining *her* there, curled up beside him on the Belgravia leather sofa, intent on her legal work. Every once in a while, still engrossed, she'd reach out and touch his arm. Mason was amazed, and a little flustered, about how that imaginary contact made him feel.

The killer plucked the telephone receiver

from the wall and said, " 'Sup, cuz?"

"Did you get the books I sent you?" Mason asked.

"Yeah. I'm already a hundred pages into the first one. Didn't realize there was so much stuff I didn't know about Dr. King."

"You're welcome."

"So what we be talkin' about today, cuz?"

Not the phony charges that had been brought against him, Mason decided. Their first conversation had convinced him that Diggs didn't have much light to shed on that. But in his eighteen years of incarceration, Diggs had never been interviewed by a reporter. If Mason could coax him into talking about his life, he could write a kick-ass profile of the killer. Mason envisioned the page-one headline: KWAME DIGGS IN HIS OWN WORDS. It would be a solid scoop — enough to justify the time he'd been putting in, even if his investigation of the bogus charges flamed out.

As it happened, getting Diggs to talk about himself was not difficult. He was his favorite subject.

"How old were you," Mason asked, "when your family moved to Warwick?"

"I was seven."

"Before that, you lived in Providence?"

"Yeah. In an apartment on Willard Avenue."

"Where did you go to school?"

"Flynn Elementary."

"That's on Blackstone Street, right?"

"Yeah. Right around the corner."

"Did you like it there?"

"It was cool. Lots of neighborhood shorties to hang with. Stickball games in the street every afternoon. My moms worked the overnight at Miriam Hospital, so she was always there when I got home from school."

"Who took care of you at night?"

"My dad, when he wasn't workin' a double shift."

"And when he was?"

"My sister," Diggs said. "She's two years older than me."

"When you were seven, she was only nine, Kwame."

"Yeah, but our nana lived right upstairs."

"Why did you move?"

"It was a bad neighborhood, cuz. Rundown houses. Gangs. Rats big enough to saddle up and ride. I didn't realize how shitty it was when we was livin' there 'cause I didn't have nothin' to compare it to. But my moms, she hated it. Always talkin' about how she wanted her kids to grow up in the

’burbs. Told me later she was scared Amina, Sekou, and me would end up smokin’ crack or hooked on skag if she didn’t get us the hell outta there.” And then he laughed. “I mean, shit. Like there’s no fuckin’ drugs in Warwick.”

“How did you feel about moving?”

“I was happy at first. When I saw that new house, it was like a dream, cuz. Our own flower garden out front. Big backyard to play in. Trees to climb. A swing set with a slide. I even got my own room.”

Diggs fell quiet for a moment, giving Mason time to catch up with his notes. A guard had confiscated the reporter’s tape recorder at the door, informing him that electronic devices were not permitted.

“My papa,” Diggs finally said. “He worked a lot of overtime at the Narragansett bottling plant to save the down payment for that place.”

“He’s gone now?” Mason asked.

“Yeah. Died of a bad heart five years after I hit the bin. Moms still blames it on my conviction. She says Papa never got over it. Bastards wouldn’t even let me out for the funeral.”

“Hit the bin?”

“Went to prison.”

“You said you were happy about the move

at first. Did something change after a while?"

"Yeah."

"What was that?"

"I looked around the neighborhood and saw it was full of nothin' but white folks."

"No other black kids?"

"Just me and my brother and sister."

"What was that like for you?"

"What the fuck do you think it's like when there ain't nobody else looks like you?"

"I don't know," Mason said. "Tell me."

Diggs took a deep breath and let it out slowly through his nose. "Lonely. You're an outsider. You don't belong there. Everybody be burnin' you off all the time."

"Burning you off?"

"Giving you the eye."

"That's how your neighbors treated you? Like an outsider?"

"Most of 'em, yeah. Lookin' down their noses at us. Callin' us *nigger* behind our backs. Tellin' their kids not to play with the porch monkeys."

"How did that make you feel?"

Diggs focused on the ceiling, as if the answer were written up there.

"Maya Angelou said, 'Bitterness is like cancer. It eats upon the host. But anger is like fire. It burns it all clean.' "

"So you were angry."
"What the fuck do you think?"
"What about school? Any black kids there?"
"Just a handful. We always sat together in the lunchroom. Hung out in a group near the school steps at recess."
"Why?"
"Self-defense, cuz."
"Because the white kids picked on you?"
"Hell, yeah, they did. Catch one of us alone and they'd whack us up."
"That ever happen to you?"
"A couple of times, sure."
"Tell me about that."
"One time five or six of 'em caught me walkin' home from school alone. Snatched the *Indiana Jones* lunch box my moms had just bought me and threw it down a storm drain. Socked me in the grill, knocked me down in the street, and whupped my natural ass. It was a serious bang-out, cuz. When they got done with me, I limped home cryin'."
"Were you hurt bad?"
"Split lip. Bloody nose. Black eye. My damn ribs ached for a month."
"What did your parents do?"
"Told me to turn the other cheek like Jesus said."

"What *did* you do?" Mason asked.

"Time's up," the guard hollered. "Phones down. Form a line at the door."

"Didn't do nothin' at first," Diggs said as he rose to leave. "I was just a scared little kid. But then, the next year, I got bigger."

32

Chief Angelo Ricci stepped in front of a squadron of uniformed Providence police guarding the doors to the Superior Court building on Benefit Street and spoke calmly into his bullhorn.

"Your attention for a moment, please," he said. "I want you to know that we're on your side. We agree with what's written on your picket signs. We agree with everything you've been saying. Just remain orderly, okay? We don't want to have to arrest anyone today."

Below him, protesters carrying signs with Kessler's picture on them swarmed over the wide courthouse steps. Gloria mingled with them, snapping photos with her Nikon. Mulligan stood near the cops on the top step and did a rough count, putting the crowd at just over a hundred.

Attorney General Roberts arrived shortly before ten A.M., trailed by an entourage of assistant prosecutors lugging briefcases. The crowd greeted them with chants and boos but parted so they could climb the stairs and enter the building.

Gloria joined Mulligan on the top step and snapped a few wide-angle shots. Then Mulligan squeezed through the police line, pushed through the doors, and made his way through the metal detectors.

The spectator benches in Judge Needham's third-floor courtroom were jammed. Gordon Freeman was seated in the first row, just behind the prosecutor's table. Eric Kessler, Mulligan noted, was absent, his presence apparently not required. Mulligan walked down the center aisle to the jury box, which had been reserved for press, and took a seat just in time for the bailiff's cry:

"Hear ye, hear ye. The Superior Court of Rhode Island and Providence Plantations, County of Providence, is now in session, the Honorable Judge Clifford H. Needham presiding. Please rise."

The rotund little judge, nicknamed "Taxi" because of his resemblance to the star of a 1980s sitcom, bustled in. He climbed onto the booster seat, which he needed to see and be seen over the top of the judicial bench, and asked everyone to be seated.

"I am aware that emotions are running high today," he said, "but I will not tolerate outbursts of any kind. Anyone attempting to disrupt these proceedings will be removed. There will be no second chances. Do I make myself clear?"

He swept the courtroom with a stern gaze and then said, "Are the attorneys present?"

"Attorney General Malcolm Roberts for the People, Your Honor."

"Austin Donahue representing Eric Kessler, Your Honor."

"Very well. Mr. Roberts, you may proceed."

The attorney general rose to address the court: "Your Honor, the State of Rhode Island hereby withdraws its petition that the court order Eric Kessler to be examined by a psychiatrist."

Donahue spun, cocked an eyebrow, and stared at Roberts. Spectators gasped and grumbled. Then several of them began to shout.

"No!"

"What the hell are you doing?"

Then three men in the back row picked up the familiar chant: "Impeach Roberts! Impeach Roberts!"

"Order!" the judge bellowed, slamming his gavel on the bench. "Bailiff, please escort those gentlemen in the back row from my courtroom."

It took ten minutes before decorum was restored.

"Mr. Roberts, please continue."

"Your Honor, Eric Kessler has been suffering from a heart condition for several years. Late last night, he suffered a severe cardiac episode and was transported to the intensive care unit of Rhode Island Hospital. According to the chief cardiologist, his condition is grave."

"I see," the judge said. "What is his prognosis?"

"I am told that he could linger for six months or so, but he is not expected to recover. Therefore, the State has decided that justice would be served if Mr. Kessler were to be released from custody as scheduled on Friday. He will remain at Rhode Island Hospital until his condition stabilizes and then be transferred to a skilled nursing facility."

"Very well. Mr. Donohue, do you have anything to add?"

"No, Your Honor."

"Case dismissed."

May 2012

The man sprawls on his back in his prison bunk and curses to himself. The old fantasies aren't working.

For eighteen years, all he had to do to get a raging hard-on was close his eyes and pretend he was climbing through a bathroom window. Imagine a knife in his hand and he could come without touching himself.

Some nights, he'd relive one of his murders. Other times, he'd pretend he was Freddy Krueger or Jason Voorhees. Tonight he tries it all, but his cock remains flaccid. Perhaps it's because his release from prison seems close now. He hungers for a new victim.

He thinks about the blondes he has known: Jenny, the skinny bitch who thought she could play football with the boys. Mrs. Montgomery, the eighth-grade math teacher who taunted him with her short skirts. Connie Stuart's twin sister, Mary, who glared at him through wet eyes at his trial. Susan Ashcroft, the one that got away. Maybe, if he gets out, he could track her down and finish her off.

He pictures them naked one at a time, then in a group, cowering before his godlike power. The sheet rises, his penis a tent pole.

33

June 2012

Mulligan parked Secretariat at the curb in front of Jennings's barn-red ranch-style house in Warwick and watched the ex-cop trot down the sidewalk with his two Irish wolfhound–size mutts, Smith and Wesson.

"Just got back from our daily constitutional," Jennings said as the dogs sat on their haunches so Mulligan could pet them. "Hope you weren't waiting long."

"No problem," Mulligan said. "I just got here."

The four of them went through the gate to the small, sun-drenched backyard, where Jennings had a charcoal grill and a well-stocked cooler on the flagstone patio. Jennings tied on a "Taste My Meat" barbecue apron and got the charcoal going while Mulligan played fetch with Smith and Wesson. Man, he wished he could get a dog of his own. Larry Bird didn't fetch anything but trouble.

When the cheeseburgers and foot-longs were ready, the two men settled into red vinyl lawn chairs with heaping paper plates in their laps and bottles of Narragansett in their fists. The dogs sat at their feet and gazed wistfully at the meat.

"Don't give 'em nothin'," Jennings said. "I fed 'em before their walk. I never give 'em scraps when I eat. It would just teach 'em to beg."

After the meal, the men dropped their grease-soaked plates into a trash can, lingered over their second beers, and talked about the sorry state of the Red Sox. Later, Mulligan roughhoused with the dogs while Jennings scrubbed the grill clean and bragged about how his son from his first marriage was doing.

"Jerry's an expert on the locomotion of early hominids," Jennings was saying. "Spent the last five years studying ankle-bones. Can you imagine that? I don't understand much of it, but it's paying off for him big-time."

"How so?" Mulligan asked.

"He's one of the scientists studying a couple of two-million-year-old skeletons some kid stumbled over in a cave in South Africa. The way he tells it, the discovery is going to rewrite the story of human evolution."

"No kidding?"

"Yeah. The kid just got tenured at Boston University. He's making quite a name for himself."

"Good for him," Mulligan said.

Jennings finished with the grill, rinsed his hands with the garden hose, wiped them on the apron, and took it off. Then he handed Mulligan another beer and led him through a sliding glass door to the family room. There he plucked a videotape from a bookshelf, slid it into the DVD/VCR combo, and pressed play.

"If you don't mind, I'm gonna go back outside with the dogs while you look at this," Jennings said. "I don't need to see it again."

Mulligan stretched out in a leather recliner that Smith and Wesson had gnawed through to the stuffing in several places, nursed the beer, and watched for nearly two hours without taking notes. Over the years, he'd seen video of other killers confessing their crimes — three times at murder trials and once in the media room at state police headquarters. Two of the killers had wept. Two had showed no emotion. But never before had he seen a killer's eyes light up like this. Never before had he heard one giggle.

The confession was just as Jennings had described it, so Mulligan should have been prepared. Still, it shocked him. What disturbed him most was what happened just before Diggs's parents entered the room.

Jennings, momentarily losing his composure, called Diggs a sonovabitch and told him he'd be spending the rest of his life in prison.

"Wrong, asshole," Diggs said. "I'm a kid. They'll have to let me out on my twenty-first birthday. The most I'm gonna do is six years in juvie."

"Bullshit," Jennings said. "You don't know what you're talking about."

The kid must have researched the state's antiquated juvenile justice statutes before he committed his crimes. He knew the law better than the detective did.

Mulligan turned off the VCR, walked to the door, and watched Jennings work with Smith and Wesson. The ex-cop was teaching them to play dead.

34

"When we left off last time," Mason said, "you were telling me about getting beaten up by white kids in the neighborhood."

"I remember," Diggs said.

"And then you got bigger, you said."

"Uh-huh. Shot up crazy when I turned twelve. Grew four inches over the summer."

"They didn't pick on you after that?"

"They didn't dare."

"Did you do something to get even?"

"Damn straight."

"Tell me about that."

Diggs cracked a grin. "Jimmy O'Keefe. He was the main one. Pig-eyed white boy who liked to act tough. After I got bigger, he was still near as tall as me. But he was a coward, cuz. Even when I was little he never tried nothin' 'less his peeps was around. First day of school, eighth grade, I caught him alone on the playground and beat the shit out of him. Smashed his nose. Blacked both his eyes. Whacked his arm against the pole that held up the basketball hoop. Heard his fuckin' wrist snap, cuz. It was beautiful."

"Did you get in trouble for this?"

"Not really. The principal? Mr. Hennessey? He suspended me for a month. Like he thought *not* goin' to school was some badass punishment. The man was a fool."

"What about the police?"

"They didn't do nothin'. Held me in a cell for a couple of hours. Then let me go with a lecture about keepin' my nose clean."

"Why would they do that?"

"I don't know, cuz. Maybe they had better things to do than bust kids for brawlin'."

"After that, you weren't afraid of the white kids anymore?"

"Never again, cuz. Like Stokely Carmichael said, 'All the scared niggers are dead.' From then on, the white kids were afraid of *me*."

"Your brother and sister, did they get picked on too?"

"Amina, she just got called names. But Sekou? He got messed with somethin' awful. Till I told everybody they'd get what Jimmy O'Keefe got if they didn't stop messin' with him. Gotta look after your little brother."

"So things got better after that?"

"With the kids, yeah. But the grown-ups? They still disrespected me, dog."

"How?"

"Whenever I'd go into the Cumberland Farms to pick up milk or a carton of Kools for my moms? The fuckin' clerk would follow me around like he thought I was gonna steal something. Every time a cop saw me riding my bike down the street? He'd stop me and ask who I swiped it from."

"It must have been frustrating, not being able to do anything about any of that."

"What makes you think I didn't?"

"What did you do, Kwame?"

"A bunch of stuff."

"Give me an example."

"One time, I was riding my bike by this white bitch's house. She gave me the eye and said something under her breath. Probably figured I couldn't hear her, but I read her lips, cuz. *Nigger.* That's what she said. Got so mad I started to cry. Tears just ran down my face. I didn't say nothin', though. Just rode my bike on home. But that night, once it got dark, I came back."

He paused, wanting Mason to beg for the rest of it.

"What happened then, Kwame?"

"I broke her car window with a baseball

bat, squirted lighter fluid on the seats, and tossed in a match. Hid in the bushes and watched it burn till the fire truck showed up."

"How'd that make you feel?"

"I was fuckin' happy, cuz."

"Did you get caught?"

"Uh-uh. I got clean away."

"What was the woman's name?"

"Medeiros," Diggs said. "Becky Medeiros."

Mason froze. Diggs grinned.

"A few months later, when they found the bitch dead, everybody else was real sad. Me? I laughed my ass off."

Back in the newsroom, Mason logged on to his computer, looked up Rhode Island's criminal laws online, and learned that there was no statute of limitations on arson.

At first, he was excited. If he could prove that the charges prison officials had brought against Diggs were false, the killer still might not get out of jail. He could be charged with torching Medeiros's car.

But as he dug further, his mood turned somber. Torching a car was only fourth-degree arson, punishable by no more than three years in prison. Still, he told himself, it was better than nothing.

35

Jimmy Cagney screeched from Mulligan's cell phone: "You'll never take me alive, copper!" The line from the 1931 movie *The Public Enemy* was his ring tone for law enforcement sources.

"Mulligan."

"He's on the move," Chief Matea said.

"Heading north?"

"Yeah. He just took the I-95 turnoff onto Route 295."

"Sounds like this could be it. I'll meet you there."

Twenty minutes later, Mulligan and the Hopkinton police chief sat together at Eric Kessler's bedside on the second floor of the Woonasquatucket Convalescent Center in the little town of Greenville. From the look of him, Kessler wasn't exactly convalescing. The room reeked of antiseptic, rancid breath, and urine. Mulligan chewed on an unlit cigar, the *Dispatch* sports page open on his lap. Matea sipped from a can of Mountain Dew and studied the door.

Mulligan was halfway through a preview of the upcoming Summer Olympics when Matea hissed, *"Shhhhhh,"* and dropped his right hand to the heel of his semiauto. Seconds later the door swung open, and Gordon Freeman stepped into the room.

"Afternoon, Gordon," Matea said. "Nice of you to drop by."

Freeman froze. For several seconds, the only sound in the room was the beeping of Kessler's heart monitor.

"Turn around, please," Matea said, "and put your hands against the wall."

Freeman's eyes shifted to the door. For a moment, Mulligan thought he was going to bolt. Instead, he turned and did as he'd been told.

Matea calmly got out of his chair, lifted Freeman's shirttail, and yanked the .25-caliber Raven from his waistband. The chief unloaded the little pistol and slipped it into the inside pocket of his suit jacket.

"Flowers would have been more appropriate, don't you think?" he asked.

"I'm not saying anything without a lawyer."

"Now, Gordon, why would you need a lawyer? Have you done something illegal? I didn't notice anything. How about you, Mulligan?"

"All I see," the reporter said, "is a man visiting a sick neighbor."

"I'm not under arrest?"

"You can put your hands down now, Gordon."

Mulligan pulled himself out of his chair.

"Mr. Freeman," he said, "please step over to the bed."

Eric Kessler lay on his back, a sheet and a sky-blue blanket pulled up to his chin. An oxygen tube ran into his nose. His face was ashen. Mulligan grabbed the sheet and blanket and whipped them off.

The child killer's ankles were bloated with fluid, but the withered arms poking out of his hospital johnny looked like month-old road kill. His eyelids fluttered open. Then he startled. His unfocused eyes darted about the room before settling on Freeman.

"You," he said, his voice a hoarse whisper. That was all he could manage before he drifted away again.

Mulligan put a hand on Freeman's shoulder. "Tell me," he said, "have you ever watched a man die of congestive heart failure?"

"Can't say that I have."

"A lot of his heart muscle is dead," Mulligan said. "The organ can't pump enough blood to keep his body working. His kidneys are failing. Fluid is building up in his lungs. He needs to cough it up, but he can't. He's too weak. Eric Kessler is slowly drowning in his own fluid. It's a rotten way to die."

"You make it sound like shooting him would be doing him a favor," Freeman said.

"It would," Matea said. "Go on home now, Gordon."

"Just a second," Mulligan said. "I was wondering. What were you planning to do with all that chili, eggplant, and olive oil?"

Freeman's eyes widened in surprise. He dropped into one of the visitor's chairs, looking tired and defeated.

"Before he had his latest heart attack, I was planning to snatch him off the street," he said. "I was gonna tie him up and stick him down my cellar. I figured on cutting out a chunk of his thigh and make him watch me cook it before I killed him."

Mulligan and Matea stared at him.

"Hey, no way I was gonna *eat* it, guys," Freman said. "I'm not like *him,* for chrissake."

With that, Freeman rose and shuffled toward the door.

"One last thing, Gordon," Matea said.

The old man looked back over his shoulder.

"Tomorrow morning, come by the station and return that journal you borrowed."

36

The slender sixty-six-year-old black woman walked briskly along the sidewalk toward city hall, her head tilted down as if she were depressed, or lost in thought, or perhaps trying to avoid catching anyone's eye. Although it was early June, the noon temperature seventy-eight degrees by the digital thermometer that hung outside the Bank of America building, she was still wearing that red cloth coat.

Gloria had just photographed some kids flying a kite in Burnside Park when she spotted the woman and decided, on impulse, to follow her. The woman continued past city hall, climbed the three steps to Charlie's greasy spoon, and slipped inside.

Gloria stopped on the sidewalk outside the diner and asked herself what the hell she was doing. She and Mulligan were supposed to be partners on the Diggs investigation, but he'd excluded her from his conversations with Jennings, claiming the ex-cop might not talk freely in the presence of someone he didn't know. She suspected he was just shielding her from the grizzly details of the old murders. She was sick of him treating her like an invalid. And she was eager to do something useful on her own.

Would talking to Kwame Diggs's mother be useful? Probably not, but Gloria couldn't be sure.

Inside, the counter, stools, and booths were all occupied by the lunch crowd, most of them regulars from the paper, city hall, and the surrounding office buildings. Esther Diggs was seated alone by a window overlooking the park, her coat now removed, folded neatly, and placed beside her on the booth's cracked vinyl seat.

"Excuse me," Gloria said. "All of the other seats are taken. Would you mind if I join you?"

The woman raised her eyes from the menu, looked Gloria up and down, and frowned. "Well . . . I suppose it would be all right."

"Thank you so much," Gloria said. She slid into the other side of the booth and placed her camera bag on the table.

"Are you a photographer?"

"Yes, I am."

"I hope you're not planning to take my picture."

"No. I was shooting pictures in the park. I just came in to grab a bite."

"You work for the paper?"

"For the *Dispatch,* yes," Gloria said.

"Because I don't want my picture in that rag," the woman said, her tone suddenly snappish. Then she smiled apologetically and added, "Not when my hair is such a mess."

"I think you look very nice," Gloria said.

Charlie wandered over to take their orders — a bacon cheeseburger, fries, and a Coke for Gloria and a garden salad, light Italian dressing on the side, and a glass of water for Mrs. Diggs. The older woman reached into her purse, pulled out her wallet, and looked inside, perhaps checking to be sure she had enough cash to pay for her meal.

"Are those your grandchildren?" Gloria asked.

"No," Mrs. Diggs said, turning the open wallet toward Gloria. "Those are my children, Amina and Sekou. Of course, they're all grown now."

"Are they your only kids?"

"Yes, they are."

"Do they live nearby?"

"No. Amina's out in Oakland, California. Got herself a fine husband, two sweet little girls, and a good job as a software developer for a computer company. Sekou lives in Tuscaloosa. He's still single, but not for much longer, God willing. If you watch college football, you can see him sometimes on the TV. He's the defensive backs coach at the University of Alabama."

"You must be proud of them."

"Oh, yes."

"I imagine you don't get to see them often."

"Not as much as I'd like to, but they call their mother most every week, thank the Lord."

"Amina and Sekou. Are those African names?"

"Why, yes, they are. Most people these days think they're Muslim names, but that's not so. *Amina* is Swahili. It means 'truthful.' *Sekou* is Guinean. It means 'wise.' "

"I'm curious," Gloria said. "You're obviously a Christian woman."

"Yes, I am, but how did you know?"

"You've mentioned God a couple of times, and you're wearing a gold cross around your neck."

The woman smiled and caressed the cross with her right hand.

"So I was wondering," Gloria said. "Why didn't you give your children biblical names like yours?" That was a slip. Gloria knew it the moment it escaped her lips.

Mrs. Diggs's smile vanished. "You know who I am, don't you."

"I do."

"How?"

"I saw you a couple of months ago when you came to the newsroom."

"You tricked me."

"I didn't mean to," Gloria lied.

"What do you want?"

"Nothing, really. I was just making conversation."

"Are you tape-recording this?"

"No, of course not."

"Are you going to put what I've told you in the newspaper?"

"Do you think you have said anything newsworthy, Mrs. Diggs?"

She thought about it for a moment.

"No, I don't suppose I have."

"Well, all right, then," Gloria said. "We're just a couple of girls making small talk, okay?"

The older woman frowned, thinking it over, and then startled Gloria by saying, "I apologize."

"Whatever for?" Gloria said.

"For telling a lie."

"About not having any other children?"

"Yes."

"That's all right, Mrs. Diggs. I understand why you might not want to talk about Kwame."

The woman ate a forkful of her salad, took a sip of water, and looked out the window.

"Did you just come from visiting him?" Gloria asked.

"Yes. We had one of our nice little talks." Then the frail old woman simply sat there, eyes fixed on the world outside, her tiny hand circling the water glass. Gloria was afraid Esther Diggs was signaling an end to their conversation until she suddenly said, "Kwame's an African name too. It comes from Ghana and means 'born on a Saturday,' although he wasn't. We just liked the way it sounds, or rather my late husband, John, did."

"Didn't you?"

"I would have named our daughter Hannah and our sons Aaron and Daniel, but John called them slave names. According to him, Diggs is a slave name, too. He always wanted to change it to Mandela or Mobutu, but you have to hire a lawyer and go to court for that, and we never could spare the money for such foolishness."

She finished her salad and pushed the plate to the side.

"If you work at the *Dispatch,* you must know that reporter Mulligan."

"I do."

"He's a terrible man."

"He certainly can be sometimes," Gloria said.

"You must know Edward Mason, too."

"Of course."

"Edward is a respectful young fellow. He's the only person I've met in years who cares about what happens to Kwame. He told me he's trying to help him, but I don't think he's getting anywhere."

"Don't give up, Mrs. Diggs," Gloria said, although she hoped the woman was right. "Edward is a very good reporter, and he's just getting started. These things take time."

Mrs. Diggs nodded uncertainly.

Charlie cleared away the plates and dropped a single check on the table. Mrs. Diggs opened her purse, but Gloria picked up the bill and handed the proprietor her MasterCard.

"No, no, no," Mrs. Diggs said. "I can pay my own way."

She counted out ten one-dollar bills and slid them across the tabletop to Gloria. Gloria slid them back.

"Well, at least let me leave the tip," Mrs. Diggs said, returning six bills to her purse and leaving the other four on the table. "You're a nice young woman, even though you work for that newspaper. God bless. I've enjoyed our little talk."

"Perhaps we can do it again sometime," Gloria said.

Mrs. Diggs didn't reply. She slipped on her coat, clutched her purse, and tottered out of the diner.

Psychologists used to blame serial killers on uncaring or abusive mothers. Some still espouse the theory, but it has largely fallen out of favor. It would be folly to draw conclusions about the household Kwame Diggs grew up in from this one conversation. Gloria knew that. Still, she felt certain that Esther Diggs was exactly the loving, churchgoing woman she appeared to be.

Gloria looked out the window and watched the woman cross the street, her head tilted toward the pavement as if looking for lost change.

37

"Frank Horrocks, please."

"May I tell him who is calling?" A woman's voice.

"Edward Mason. I'm a reporter for the *Dispatch.*"

"The newspaper?"

"Yes."

"What's this about?"

"I've got a few questions for a story I'm working on."

"A story about what?"

"The state prison."

"My husband doesn't work there anymore."

"Yes, I know."

"And you still want to talk to him?"

"I do."

"Why?"

"I'm sure he'll tell you all about it after you put him on the phone."

"Is he in some kind of trouble?"

"Not that I am aware of."

"Well, all right," she said. "Hold on and I'll get him."

Mason listened to dead air for a couple of minutes, thinking the best thing about calling people at home is that you don't get put on hold and have Muzak piped into your ear.

"Hello."

"Mr. Horrocks?"

"Yeah."

"My name is Mason. I'm a reporter for the *Dispatch.*"

"Well, la-de-fuckin'-da."

"I was hoping you'd be willing to meet with me and answer some questions."

"I don't think so, pal. I'm too busy."

"You are? I heard that you're out of work."

"Go fuck yourself."

"I promise I won't take up much of your time, sir. I could really use your help for a story I'm working on."

"What kind of story?"

"It's about some things that happened at Supermax when you worked there."

"I ain't got nothin' to say about any of that," he said, and hung up.

That went well, Mason said to himself. So much for the first guy the cokehead, Ty Robinson, had seen in the break room that day. Fortunately, there were two left to try.

Charles "Chuckie" Shaad, the next one on the list, told Mason that he was waiting for callbacks from a couple of places where he'd applied for jobs.

"So you understand why I can't talk right now," he said. "I don't want to tie up the phone."

Doesn't everybody have call waiting now? Mason thought, but what he said was, "Perhaps we could meet later at a place of your convenience."

"Yeah, okay. Let's say half-past eight at Galway Bay."

"What's that?"

"An Irish pub."

"Do you know the address?"

"It's right behind McCoy Stadium, left-field side. I'll be the big galoot in the M & D Truckers cap. Sorry, gotta go."

The old stadium, built with taxpayer money during the tail end of the Great Depression, was the crowning boondoggle of one of Rhode Island's legendary political bosses, Pawtucket mayor Thomas P. McCoy. He had personally selected the site, a swamp known locally as Hammond's Pond. A construction crew spent months draining and excavating it over and over again, battling mountains of muck that kept sliding back into the work area.

The original lowball estimate for the project was six hundred thousand dollars, but by the time it was completed in 1942, the bill had escalated to 1.2 million. That was more than it had cost to build the seventy-thousand-seat Yale Bowl in New Haven three decades earlier. McCoy Stadium seated only fifty-eight hundred fans when it was completed, although it had since been expanded to hold ten thousand.

For decades, McCoy Stadium was notorious for a playing surface so hard that batted balls ricocheted from it as if they had been launched by bazookas. According to local legend, construction workers had filled the swampy site with thousands of bags of cement purchased at an exorbitant rate from one of the mayor's cronies.

Mason had never been to McCoy, home of the minor league Pawtucket Red Sox, so he left early in case he had trouble locating the pub. He found it right off, spotting a massive Guinness sign nailed to the side of a three-story commercial building that looked as if it had been thrown together between the two world wars. The inside was a pleasant surprise of gleaming circular bars, polished brass fixtures, and a menu that made him regret he'd already eaten. They didn't carry Red Stripe, so he ordered a Smithwick's and nursed it for twenty minutes until Shaad shambled in.

The ex–prison guard looked the place over, saw Mason give him a wave, greeted him with a hearty handshake, and asked the bartender for a pint. It was apparent he was a regular because he didn't have to specify the brand. He dipped his gray mustache in the foam head of his Guinness and then turned back to Mason.

"So what's this all about?"

Mason ducked the question, saying, "What's with the hat? Are you a trucker now?"

"I drove for M & D for a couple of years before I got laid off last month. Probably just as well, 'cause I didn't like it much. Too many nights on the road away from family. I'm tryin' to catch on with a rent-a-cop company now, but it ain't easy thanks to the assholes in Washington. George Bush wrecked the economy, and Obama and the Republicans in Congress can't stop pissing on each other long enough to do anything about it."

"Why'd you leave the prison job?"

"Wasn't like I had a choice. I was one of the ten Supermax corrections officers let go in 2010 when the department's budget got slashed. Our union raised hell about it. Said fewer guards would make the job more dangerous. But the governor didn't give a shit."

"I see," Mason said, and jotted something in his notebook.

"Why the personal questions?" Shaad said. "Ain't nothin' newsworthy about me, is there?"

"No, nothing like that," Mason said. "I want to ask you about Kwame Diggs, but I like to know who I'm talking to first." He had skipped that step with Ty Robinson, but the young reporter was a quick study.

Shaad froze, his glass in the air.

"Diggs? What about him?"

"Was he difficult to handle inside?"

"Why do you want to know?" The ex-guard's shoulders stiffened, his whole body on alert.

"I've been visiting him," Mason said. "It's the first time he's ever opened up to a reporter."

"So?"

"So I think I've got the makings of a pretty good story, but I need to verify what he's been telling me. I don't want to take his word for everything."

Shaad's shoulders relaxed.

"I'll bet," he said.

"So did he make much trouble for you?"

Shaad took off his cap, laid it on the table next to his beer, and looked up at the ceiling, thinking over his answer, maybe, or pondering whether he should say anything at all.

"No," he finally said. "Not really."

Shaad sipped his beer. Mason looked at him expectantly. It was a trick he'd learned from Mulligan. Just sit quietly and the person you are interviewing may feel compelled to fill the silence.

"When I was a rookie," Shaad said, "some of the veteran corrections officers told me Diggs used to be a real handful. Always bitching about the food, stealing smokes from other inmates, making a fuss when the guards tossed his cell. He was such a big guy that sometimes it took four or five guards to get him under control. But he was just a kid back then, you know? Still learning how to behave on the inside. By the time I came on board in 2001, he'd calmed down a lot."

"Ever see him assault anybody?"

"No. Nothing like that. He pretty much kept to himself. Spent a lot of time reading in his cell. Never bothered anybody, and nobody bothered him. Inmates don't much like child killers, so most of 'em have a rough time inside. But Diggs? He was way too big to mess with. Truth be told, I think even the gangbangers were afraid of him."

"What about his interactions with the guards?"

"He was real polite with us. With Diggs, it was always 'Yes, sir,' this and 'Yes, sir,' that. Once in a while he'd crack wise and say, 'Yes, massa,' but he always smiled when he said it."

"Do you remember a guard named Robert Araujo?"

"Bobby? Oh, sure."

"Back in 2005, Diggs assaulted him. At least, that's what the court records say."

"Yeah, I heard something about that."

"What did you hear?"

"Just that Diggs took exception to something Bobby said and got into it with him a little bit."

"What did Araujo say to set him off?"

"No idea. I wasn't there."

"Diggs tells me some of the guards called him names to provoke him."

"I used to hear some of that, yeah."

"Pervert?"

"Sure."

"Child killer?"

"Uh-huh."

"Nigger?"

"Well . . . maybe sometimes."

"Were you one of them?"

"Uh-uh. The job is dangerous enough without going around looking for trouble."

"But Araujo did?"

"I couldn't say."

"The day after the alleged assault, Araujo talked about it with other guards in the break room."

"That so?"

"You should know. You were there."

"Says who?"

"Others who were present," Mason said, exaggerating a little because his only source for this was the cokehead.

"Maybe I was."

"What do you remember about that?"

"Not much."

"The way the others who were there tell it, Araujo admitted the assault never happened. He said he faked it on orders of the warden, isn't that right?"

"Look," Shaad said, "I don't know what you're up to, but I don't want any part of it."

"*You* look," Mason said. "Diggs is a bad guy. We both know that. But if prison officials are faking charges against him, they're bad guys too. They laid you off, Chuck. It's not like you owe them anything."

Shaad didn't reply. He picked up his Guinness and drained it. Mason figured he was about to leave. Instead, the ex-guard hailed the barkeep and ordered another.

"Okay," Mason said. "Let's talk about something else."

"And what would that be?"

"The time Diggs was charged with having marijuana in his cell."

"What about it?"

"I think it's bullshit," Mason said.

"Because?"

"Because I've seen the security at Supermax. I don't see any way he could get marijuana in there."

Shaad studied the head on his beer for a moment, then said, "Neither do I."

"There are no drugs in the state prison?"

"The other units are loaded with them. Weed. Coke. Meth. Oxy. But Supermax? No way."

"So the drug charges must have been faked, then, huh?"

"I wouldn't know anything about that."

"Okay," Mason said. "Let's go back to that day in the break room."

"Let's not."

"You already told me you were there," Mason said. "So were Frank Horrocks, Ty

Robinson, and John Pugliese. They all heard Araujo admit the assault charge was faked."

Mason hadn't talked to Pugliese yet, and Horrocks had refused to talk to him, but Shaad didn't know that.

"If those guys already told you about this, why are you asking me?"

"I'm just being thorough."

Shaad took another sip of his beer, stalling for time.

"I don't want my name in the paper," he finally said.

"Not for attribution, then," Mason said.

"What does that mean?"

"It means that when I write the story, I'll identify you as a former Supermax guard but won't use your name."

"How can I be sure of that?"

"Because you have my word."

Shaad studied Mason for a moment.

"You know," he finally said, "I'm surprised Horrocks and Pugliese told you about this."

"Why is that?"

"Because they thought Araujo was some big fuckin' hero."

He paused, and once again Mason waited for the ex-guard to fill the silence between them.

"It was supposed to be me," Shaad said.

"How do you mean?"

"Warden Matos came to me first. He wanted me to swear out an assault complaint against Diggs. I told him I wouldn't do it."

"What did he say to that?"

"He tried to talk me into it. Said I'd be performing a public service. I told him I didn't want Diggs running around loose, either. He shoulda got the needle for killing all those people. Three of 'em were just little girls, for chrissake. But no way I was gonna go to court and lie."

"What did the warden do then?"

"He said not to worry about it. Told me he'd find somebody else. Oh, and he asked me to keep my mouth shut about our conversation."

"And the somebody else was Araujo?"

"I guess so, yeah."

"Tell me about that day in the break room."

"Araujo was sitting at one of the tables when I came in. Some of the other guards were shaking his hand, patting him on the back. I thought maybe he'd just had a baby or hit the lottery or something, so I asked what was up. And he told me."

"Told you what, exactly?"

"That he'd sworn out a phony complaint about Diggs. Seemed real proud of himself, like he'd just hit a grand slam to win the World Series."

"Do you remember his exact words?"

"No."

"Who else was there that day?"

"Other than the guys you already talked to?"

"Uh-huh."

"Let me think . . . I'm pretty sure Paul Delvecchio was there, too."

Mason had heard that name before, but at first he couldn't place it.

"Delvecchio?" he finally said. "Doesn't he work in the prison library now?"

38

Felicia Freyer wore her blond hair down today. She'd applied lipstick the color of pink carnations and just a hint of eyeliner and mascara. Diggs gave her an appraising look as she picked up the phone to talk to him through the glass. Mason saw the look and felt a brief flicker of anger.

"We're making some progress, Kwame. It's not enough to get you out yet, but we have reason to be hopeful. . . . Yes, I understand you're frustrated, but these things take time. . . . Why don't I let Mason tell you what he's found out so far?"

She reached up and handed the phone to Mason, who was standing beside her chair.

"So, cuz," Diggs said, "you fuckin' her yet?"

"Excuse me?"

"Come on. You can tell *me.*"

"Why would you ask me that?"

"Because she's totally sweatin' you, cuz. I

mean, the bitch never put on makeup for me, so it's gotta be for you, right?"

He smirked and arched his left eyebrow.

"I don't think so," Mason said, although the thought *had* crossed his mind.

From anyone else, Mason would have passed this off as crude but harmless banter, but Diggs was giving him the creeps.

"You want to know what I've got so far or not?" the reporter asked.

"Shoot," Diggs said.

"First off, you're right about the drugs. I don't see any way of getting a bag of marijuana through all this security."

"I already told you *that,* cuz. What else you got?"

"I found two former guards who overheard Araujo admit he faked one of the assault charges against you."

"No shit?"

"Yeah, but the problem is one of them got fired for coming to work high, so he doesn't have any credibility. And the other one won't let me use his name. It's not anywhere near enough to get you released. It's not even enough to put in the paper."

"Oh."

"I'm still working on it, though. I got a lead on a couple more guards who might know the truth about the assault charges."

"You're giving me hope, cuz. That's all I got to live for in here."

"Tell me, Kwame. What do you think you'd do if you got out?"

"I dunno. Wouldn't go back to the old neighborhood, that's for *damn* sure. If I did, I'd probably get lynched. I guess I'd have to change my name and move out of state. Maybe find a place in Brockton near my moms. Or go down to Alabama so I could be close to my brother."

"How would you make a living?"

"Been thinking about that for a while. At first, I figured I could learn about computers. So I could fix 'em, maybe, or work someplace that makes 'em. But then I decided what I really want to do is go back to school and get a degree so I can teach black history to kids."

Was Diggs's grasp on reality that tenuous? Mason considered explaining why someone convicted of murdering two kids wasn't ever going to get hired to teach them, but he decided to let Diggs find that out for himself.

"Do you think you'd ever hurt anybody again, Kwame?"

Felicia glanced up at Mason, frustrated that she could hear only his side of the conversation. Diggs rubbed his face and studied the ceiling, where he always looked for the answers to difficult questions.

"Tell me, cuz," the prisoner finally said. "*You* ever think about killing somebody?"

"No."

"What about fucking somebody up. Ever want to do that?"

"A few times, I guess."

"Why?"

"Because they were giving me a hard time."

"About what?"

"Let's see. . . . Last winter, I was in a bar in Newport, and a couple of drunks started making crude remarks to my date. When I asked them to stop, one of them pushed me."

"I bet you wanted to shove a beer bottle up his ass. Am I right?"

"Not quite, but I did have an urge to punch him in the nose."

"Did you?"

"No."

"Why not?"

"I was afraid he and his buddy would gang up on me and beat me up. And I didn't want to get arrested."

"You controlled your anger and considered the consequences," Diggs said, sounding like a parent administering a lesson.

"That's right."

"When I was a kid, I didn't know how to do that. Whenever somebody disrespected me, I'd feel this rage boil up inside, and it wouldn't go away until I hurt them back. But I'm a grown man now, cuz. I still get mad sometimes, but I've learned to control it. I understand now that there are better ways than killing to get even with the racists."

"Like what?"

"Like educating people about black history, and voting for Obama, and giving money to the NAACP. When I was a kid, I thought like a young Malcolm X. Brother Malcolm said, 'If someone puts his hand on you, send him to the cemetery.' He also said, 'When you drop violence on me, then you've made me go insane; and I'm not responsible for what I do.' Now I'm down with Dr. King, who said, 'Nonviolence is a powerful and just weapon, which cuts without wounding and ennobles the man who wields it.' That was in one of them books you got me. When I get angry now, I just listen to those words inside my head."

"What are you angry about now, Kwame?"

"I'm angry that the state of Rhode Island thinks it's okay to make up shit to keep a black man locked up. If they was following the law, I'd have got out when I was twenty-one. I coulda had a life. A job. An education. Maybe a wife and kids. But when justice is perverted, tyranny prevails."

Mason marveled that the same man who called him "cuz" could say things like "tyranny prevails." He figured it was something else Diggs had read in one of his books.

"What the state is doing to you is illegal," Mason said, "but if you'd gotten out at twenty-one, you would have done only six years for killing five people. Does *that* sound like justice to you?"

"Time's up," the guard shouted. "Phones down. Form a line at the door."

Diggs fixed Mason with an angry glare, but it quickly vanished. His mouth curled into a sly smile.

"The bitch wants you, cuz. I been watching the way she keeps eyein' you. If I was you, I would be *so* hitting that."

In the prison parking lot, Felicia touched Mason on the arm and said, "Want to go for coffee?"

The touch, maddeningly brief, was better than the ones he'd imagined.

"Mason? Coffee?" Her hand brushed his arm again.

"I'd love to," he said, hoping he hadn't answered with an exclamation point.

"Caffe-Bon-Ami on Park Avenue?"

"Sounds good."

"Meet me there in ten minutes, and you can fill me in on Diggs's side of the conversation."

Mason climbed in behind the wheel of the Prius and watched Felicia walk away in a black skirt that swung and swept her knees. When she disappeared around a corner, he flipped the visor down and checked his hair in the vanity mirror.

Then he opened his notebook and flipped to a page he'd starred in his notes: "I understand now that there are better ways than killing to get even with the racists."

A slip of the tongue? A confession with an explanation? Next time, Mason thought, he'd have to ask Diggs about it.

At the coffee shop, Mason knew he was supposed to talk to Felicia about Diggs, but he was distracted by her perfume, a blend of wildflowers and spice. Every time she moved, the scent rose from her skin. And it had his name on it.

After they ordered — she liked her coffee sweet and black, the same way he did — Felicia reached across the booth and touched his arm again.

"Mason, what do you do when you're not working?"

"I think about working."

Felicia laughed.

"Oh, God, I'm the same way. Lately, I . . ." She hesitated, sipped from her cup. "You're going to think this is really weird."

"What?"

"I've caught myself pacing around my condo having full-fledged conversations about work . . . with myself . . . out loud."

Mason chuckled.

"I'm not sure this is funny," Felicia said. "It *can't* be healthy."

"In that case, I'm *really* in trouble," Mason said. "I've been having late night conversations with another person . . . who's not there."

They were both laughing now.

"I hope it's at least someone interesting. Bill Gates? Andrew Sullivan, maybe? Michelle Obama?"

"Actually, it's you."

She looked down and ran her fingers around the edge of her coffee cup.

"Mason?"

"Um?"

"That's what I was hoping you were going to say."

She raised her eyes and tossed a look that caused a warm glow to wash over him, a glow he hadn't felt since Darcy Ames, the prettiest girl in the ninth grade, asked him to the Sadie Hawkins dance.

"So what now?" she asked.

"I don't know. I've been telling myself that I don't have time for a woman in my life right now. I've tried to stop thinking about you. But I can't. I love how sensational you look when you dress down and don't bother with makeup. I obsess about your green eyes and that ski-slope nose and that long neck I've been wanting to kiss. I love the way you sneak a look at me when you don't think I notice. And the way my arm tingles when you touch me. Like you're doing right now."

Felicia leaned in, and they locked eyes.

"But we can't get involved right now," she said.

"No, we can't. Not until Kwame's situation is resolved. It would be a conflict of interest."

"For both of us," Felicia said.

Mason drew a deep breath and then sighed audibly.

"If you're going to keep me at arm's length," he said, "I advise you never to wear that perfume again."

She laughed and squeezed his arm, trying

to make him smile. Mason just stared and stared.

39

Mulligan parked Secretariat beside Andy Jennings's Ford pickup in the Warwick police station parking lot. He found the ex-cop waiting for him on the front steps. They entered the building together, passed through the metal detector, and tromped upstairs for their morning appointment with Chief Oscar Hernandez.

The first thing Mulligan noticed as Hernandez rose to greet them was that he'd grown a potbelly since his promotion to chief last year. The second thing Mulligan noticed was a ten-by-twelve-inch color photo of Joe Arpaio, the jowly sheriff of Maricopa County, Arizona, who was notorious for his harassment of Mexican immigrants. It was pinned to a bulletin board with thumbtacks, and it had several dozen small holes in it. Mulligan guessed they were made by the five darts that rested beside the blotter on Hernandez's big mahogany desk.

"How's retirement treating you, Andy?" the chief asked.

"I miss the action," Jennings said. "Some days I don't know what to do with myself."

"Maybe you need a hobby."

"Yeah, right. Like I could get into scrap-booking or collecting stamps."

"How's Mary?"

"She's good, Oscar. I'll tell her you asked after her."

"Mulligan, I see you've survived the lay-offs."

"So far, but one of these days my luck's gonna run out."

The looming truth of that led to an uncomfortable pause. Finally, Hernandez cleared his throat.

"So what can I do for you gentlemen this morning?"

"You can give us access to the evidence from a cold case," Jennings said.

"What case?"

"The Susan Ashcroft stabbing."

Hernandez folded his hands on his desk blotter, looked Jennings in the eye, and said, "What for?"

"We want to take another run at nailing Kwame Diggs for it."

"And by we, you mean you and Mulligan?"

"Yup."

Hernandez shook his head vigorously.

"Last time I checked, newspaper reporters were not considered law enforcement officers in the state of Rhode Island. And you don't carry a badge anymore, Andy. When I said you need a hobby, this isn't what I had in mind."

"You owe me this, Oscar," Jennings said. "If I hadn't insisted on promoting you to detective twelve years ago, when Chief Bennett thought Hispanics weren't fit for anything but patrol . . ."

"I might still be riding shotgun in a squad car," Hernandez said.

He clasped his hands on his blotter and studied the two men for a moment.

"I can see this is important to both of you," he said. "What is it you're not telling me?"

"We're worried that Diggs is going to get out," Jennings said.

"You kidding me?"

" 'Fraid not."

"What the hell makes you think that?"

"The charges the state has brought against him since he turned twenty-one were all concocted," Mulligan said.

"So I've heard," Hernandez said.

"Now somebody's poking into that, and if they can prove it, he'll have to be released."

"You must be shitting me."

"Wish I were," Mulligan said.

"Who the hell would want to do that?"

"He's got an aggressive new lawyer," Mulligan said. "I hear she's good, and she's getting some outside help."

"From whom?"

"Sorry, but I can't get into that."

"Do *you* know?" the chief asked, turning his eyes on Jennings.

"Mulligan won't tell me either," he said, "but it smells like the ACLU."

"*¡Santa Madre de Dios!*" He leaned back in his chair and studied the ceiling. "You know, it was years before I stopped having nightmares about what I saw inside the Medeiros house."

"I still get 'em sometimes," Jennings said.

"If I give you access to the evidence," the chief said, "what do you hope to find?"

"Back in 1991, DNA testing wasn't as sophisticated as it is now," Jennings said. "We're thinking Diggs might have shed something — a drop of blood, a few hairs, some skin cells — that could still be tested."

"It's a long shot," the chief said. "A lot of old evidence has been lost or tossed. Even if we can find it, chances are the DNA has been degraded or contaminated."

"I know," Jennings said, "but it's the only shot we've got."

"Okay," the chief said, "I'll have our property clerk look for the evidence boxes. If he finds them, you can observe him as he goes through the contents; but I don't want you touching or removing anything. We have to preserve chain of custody. If you see something that might be worth testing, I'll have him hand-deliver it to the state crime lab. The lab has a huge backlog. I'm talking hundreds of cases going back years. But Diggs is the magic word, so I might be able to get them to fast-track this."

"When can we start?" Jennings asked.

"I'll call DeMaso in Property this morning and get him started. If he finds the boxes, I'll be in touch."

40

"I wasn't there," John Pugliese said.

"Two former guards I spoke with said you were," Mason told him.

"They're mistaken."

"They seemed pretty sure."

"Hell, I wasn't even *at* Supermax in 2005. When Diggs was charged with assaulting Araujo, I was working medium security. I didn't get transferred to Supermax till 2007."

"Oh."

They were sitting across from each other in a booth at the diner near Providence City Hall. Pugliese, swarthy and well muscled, chomped on one of Charlie's lard-slicked bacon-and-egg sandwiches. Mason, who'd enjoyed a breakfast of mascarpone-stuffed French toast with peaches at home, nursed a cup of sweetened black coffee.

"What about the assault on Joseph Galloway last fall?" Mason asked.

"Oh, I know all about that one."

"Tell me about it."

"Why should I?"

"Why shouldn't you? You don't have anything to hide, right?"

"He doesn't," someone said, "but he still has to work there."

Mason turned toward the voice, saw Mulligan standing behind his left shoulder, greeted him with a thin smile, and slid over to make room for him in the booth.

"How have you been, John?" Mulligan asked.

"I'm hanging in there," Pugliese said.

"Really? Last time we spoke, you'd gotten your nose broken for the second time and were dying to get the hell out of that madhouse."

"I still am, but there's no jobs out there, Mulligan."

"The Crips still got a hard-on for you?"

"Yeah. It's more than a year since I broke Stanley Turner's arm in the exercise yard, but the gang has a long memory."

"Why not quit and collect unemployment for a while, John? Better that than a shiv in the ribs."

"I just might," Pugliese said. "Then again, maybe I'll join the army. See if I can get into one of those training programs they've got for electrical engineering or heating and cooling mechanics."

"Aren't you too old for that?" Mason chimed in.

"Not quite. The maximum enlistment age is thirty-five. I looked it up."

To Mason, John Pugliese looked like somebody who'd seen thirty-five a decade ago.

Charlie wandered over, plunked a cup of coffee in front of Mulligan, and took his order of bacon and scrambled eggs.

"The army's not a bad idea," Mulligan said, "now that Iraq is over and Afghanistan is winding down."

"That's what I'm thinking," Pugliese said.

"Then again, we might end up in a shooting war with Iran," Mason said, trying not to show his irritation at the way Mulligan had usurped the interview.

"Or Pakistan," Mulligan said.

"Or North Korea," Pugliese said. "Then I'd have more than shivs to worry about."

They were still kicking the sorry state of the world around when Charlie slapped Mulligan's order on the table and topped off his coffee.

"If you're serious about quitting," Mason said, "why not talk to me about Galloway? I mean, what do you have to lose?"

"What do I have to gain?" Pugliese said.

"Not a thing," Mulligan put in.

"I wouldn't say that," Mason said.

"No?" Pugliese said.

"You'd have the satisfaction of helping me expose officials who are perverting the criminal justice system," Mason said. "I think that's worth something."

"Not much," Pugliese said. "Besides, if you succeed, they'd have to release Diggs. When he killed again, it would be on me."

"Maybe he wouldn't," Mason said.

"He would," Mulligan put in. "And it wouldn't just be on Pugliese. It would be on you, too, Mason."

Mason let out a long sigh. "I've thought a lot about this in the last few weeks," he said. "The way I see it, my first obligation as a journalist is to the truth."

"Regardless of the consequences?" Mulligan said.

"No," Mason said. "But what about the consequences of letting them get away with this? If they can frame Diggs, what's to stop them from doing the same thing to the next guy who comes along? Maybe somebody whose crime isn't as serious. Maybe somebody who isn't guilty of anything at all. Our public officials are supposed to uphold the law, not break it."

"You do realize we are in Rhode Island, right?" Mulligan said.

"Yeah, yeah. I know all about our sordid history," Mason said. "Crooked politicians, corrupt judges, dirty cops. It's been that way for as long as anybody can remember. Hell, it's been that way for three hundred years. But for the last hundred and fifty of them, the *Dispatch* has crusaded against it. Sure, we don't catch them all. Not even close. But we nail enough to make the rest of them think twice.

"Now the paper is dying," he continued. "Who's going to investigate public corruption when we're gone? Bloggers? The bobbleheads on TV? Don't make me laugh. When we know public officials are corrupting the criminal justice system, it's our *job* to do something about it. If we don't, the First Amendment is just words on paper. And this could be one of our last chances to set something right."

"Nice speech," Mulligan said.

"It was," Pugliese said. "Did anyone else hear the music playing?"

"One of our last chances?" Mulligan said.

"That's right," Mason said.

"Something going on that I should know?" Mulligan asked. "Is the paper closing down?"

"Not in front of Pugliese," Mason said. "We'll talk about it later."

That was a conversation stopper. The three men sat for a while and sipped their coffee.

"You know, Mulligan," Pugliese finally said, "I remember you giving me that same speech one time — minus the part about the newspaper dying."

"When was that?"

"About six years ago when you wanted me to spill my guts about no-show jobs at medium security."

"Oh, yeah," Mulligan said. "I remember now. I tried to snow you with that First Amendment crap, but you didn't tell me shit."

"Did the speech work any better this time?" Mason asked.

"I'm thinking about it," Pugliese said.

"According to court records," Mason said, "Galloway and another guard had just taken Diggs out of his cell for his exercise period when a scuffle broke out."

"So I've heard."

"Diggs supposedly got mad for no apparent reason, charged into Galloway, cracked his head against the hallway wall, and then headbutted him."

"Uh-huh."

"Earlier, you said you know all about it. What do you know?"

Pugliese slid his eyes off Mason and looked at Mulligan.

"Up to you, John," Mulligan said. "I wouldn't, but it's your ass."

The guard stared at the tabletop and rubbed his chin. Then he moved his eyes back to Mason.

"I was there," Pugliese said.

"You were?" Mason said. "According to the court records, the other guard was named Quinn."

"Eddie Quinn. That's right."

"So what were you doing there?"

"Normal procedure," Pugliese said, "is for two guards to escort a prisoner to the exercise yard, but Diggs was so big that three were always assigned to him."

"And that day, you were the third?"

"I was."

"So you were a witness. Why didn't you testify at the trial?"

"The warden asked me to, but I refused."

"Why?"

"Because I didn't want to commit perjury."

Mason and Mulligan both stared at Pugliese, knowing that whatever he said next could change everything.

"So what really happened in that hallway, John?" Mason asked.

"Not a fucking thing. We led Diggs out of his cell, and he walked quietly to the yard. He didn't give us any trouble at all."

After Pugliese left, the first thing Mulligan said was, "Are you going to quote him by name?"

"Why shouldn't I? He never said it was off the record."

"Better give him a heads-up before the story runs, then."

"I will once I have enough to get it in print."

"Are you close?"

"I think so, yes."

"On just the Galloway case, or the Araujo assault too?"

"Both," Mason said. "And the drug charges as well."

"Prison guards are your sources for all this?"

"For most of it, yeah."

He picked up his mug, discovered that the coffee had gone cold, and waved Charlie over for a refill.

"Tell me what more you need," Mulligan said, "and maybe I can help."

"The same way you've been helping so far?"

"I culled that list of guards for you."

"That *was* a help," Mason said. "I crossed the ones you recommended right off my list. Saved me a lot of time." And then he laughed.

Mulligan stared at him and shook his head.

"How long have you known?"

"Right from the start," Mason said.

"You're getting pretty good at this, aren't you."

"Not as good as you."

"Of course not," Mulligan said, and they both chuckled.

"Still friends?" Mulligan asked.

"Always," Mason said.

"So what's going on with the paper that you couldn't talk about in front of Pugliese?"

"I'm not supposed to talk about it at all," Mason said. "Can I trust you not to repeat this?"

"I promise, Thanks-Dad."

"Will you *please* stop calling me that?"

"Sorry, Thanks-Dad, but some habits are hard to break."

Mason shot Mulligan an annoyed look, then said, "The board has decided to put the paper on the market. They're hoping to get an offer from one of the major chains like Belo or Media General."

"They won't."

"Probably not, but General Communications Holdings International has expressed interest."

"Who the hell is that?"

"Not anybody either of us would want to work for, even if they didn't lay us off, which I'm pretty sure they would."

"Guess I need to start looking for another line of work," Mulligan said.

"Yeah," Mason said. "Me too."

41

By the time Mulligan left the diner, the sky was dark. A quarter moon hung low over the city.

It was months since his last talk with Rosie. He used to visit her once or twice a week, but lately he'd fallen out of the habit. Tonight, he needed his best friend.

He climbed into Secretariat, crossed the bridge over the Providence River, stopped at Gilmore's Flower Shop in East Providence, and sprang for a bunch of cut daffodils. Then he cruised back across the river, drove to Swan Point Cemetery, rolled slowly through the gate, and parked at the edge of the grass.

He rummaged through the Bronco's storage compartment for his flashlight but couldn't find it. It didn't matter. Off to his left, the silhouette of Pastor's Rest Monument, marking the final resting place of Providence's leading nineteenth-century ministers, stood pitch black against a charcoal sky. With the obelisk as his guide, he would have no trouble finding his way.

He clutched the daffodils in his right fist, tucked an autographed Manny Ramirez Red Sox jersey under his left arm, and trudged blindly through the vast graveyard. He was nearly there when he cracked his knee against a grave marker that leaped at him out of the darkness.

Over the decades, he and Rosie had told each other almost everything. That's what best friends forever were for. He knelt in the damp grass beside her granite gravestone and ran his fingers over the words he knew by heart:

Rosella Isabelle Morelli. First Woman Battalion Chief of the Providence Fire Department. Beloved Daughter. Faithful Friend. True Hero. February 12, 1968 — August 27, 2008.

She'd been racing to a house fire on a foggy night when her command car crashed and burned. The fire had been deliberately set. The arsonist had never been caught. Mulligan had never stopped hunting for the bastard.

After clearing away some withered flowers, he placed the fresh ones on her grave. Then he draped the jersey over the shoulders of her tombstone, just as he did every time he came.

Manny Ramirez had been Rosie's favorite player. She was gone before he started bitching about his paltry hundred-and-sixty-million-dollar contract, before he knocked the team's sixty-four-year-old traveling secretary to the ground, before the Sox traded him to the Dodgers, before he was suspended for using performance-enhancing drugs. Mulligan figured she didn't need to hear about all that. He wrapped his arms around the granite and gave her a hug.

"It's a beautiful night, Rosie. A sliver of moon is hanging over the Seekonk River, and I can hear the Canada geese honking as they forage in the grass. . . . No, I'm not seeing anyone just now. . . . Last I heard, Yolanda was planning to marry that Brown chemistry professor. After her, nobody seems to measure up."

They sat together in silence, peering up at stars barely visible through the spill of the city's lights. Somewhere up there, an American spaceship was carrying a rover named *Curiosity* on a 350-million-mile journey to the surface of Mars. Mulligan hoped Rosie could see it as it sped through the firmament.

"Rosie, I'm confused. All my working life, I've lived by a simple code: The truth will set you free. But lately I've been trying to conceal it. . . . Why? Because if the truth comes out, a serial killer will be set free. . . . Yeah, I remember that old song. 'There's something happening here. What it is ain't exactly clear.'

"Tonight, Thanks-Dad said some things that made me wonder if maybe I'm on the wrong side of this thing. He talked about the First Amendment and what being a reporter is all about. Fact is, he sounded an awful lot like I used to, Rosie. . . . Yes, I remember that part of the song, too. 'Nobody's right if everybody's wrong.' "

He imagined he could hear her singing that old Buffalo Springfield tune, her crystal voice drifting on the muggy night air.

42

The morning mail was light — a couple of press releases, a subscription renewal form for the *American Journalism Review,* a funds solicitation from the Columbia University alumni office, and a single legal-size white envelope with Mason's name and the newspaper's address hand-printed in neat block letters. There was no return address.

Mason didn't like the look of it, so he walked the envelope over to the newsroom's east-facing windows and held it up to the sunlight. As far as he could tell, it contained only a piece of paper with something written on it. He returned to his desk, slit the top of the envelope with a letter opener, and slid out a sheet of typing paper. On it were two lines hand-printed in the same block letters:

WE KNOW WHAT YOUR DOING,
RICHIE RICH.

IF YOU KNOW WHATS GOOD FOR YOU, YOU'LL STOP.

Mason stood and handed the threat and the envelope it came in over the top of the cubicle divider.

"Hey, Mulligan," he said. "What do you make of this?"

Mulligan checked the postmark on the envelope, looked the letter over, and handed it back. "Well, it's got two grammatical errors," he said, "so it's probably not from a copy editor."

"I think we can rule out English teachers, too," Mason said.

"The paper is cheap stock you can buy anywhere," Mulligan said. "Other than that, all we know is that it was mailed yesterday from the 02886-7157 ZIP code. Hold on a sec."

He logged on to the USPS ZIP code finder and typed the number in.

"That's the post office on Post Road in Warwick, the one near the airport."

"How worried do you think I should be?"

"Not very."

"I guess word of what I'm working on is starting to get around."

"How many people have you interviewed so far?"

"Let's see. There's Diggs's former lawyer, his new one, the heads of the ACLU and the NAACP, and more than two dozen guards and former guards."

"And all of them probably told their husbands and wives, who told their friends, who then passed it on to *their* friends," Mulligan said.

"So you're saying this could have come from anybody."

"Yeah, but most likely it's from someone with something to lose."

"One of the guards who lied in court?" Mason said.

"Or a family member of one of Diggs's victims," Mulligan added.

"It's a bit unsettling. I've never been threatened like this before."

"Get used to it. It goes with the job. The more the word spreads, the more people are going to be pissed off at you. And some of them are going to find creative ways to let you know about it."

Mason fretted about the threat all afternoon as he tried to line up more interviews with former prison guards. Most of them hung up on him, but a couple agreed to meet. By the time he was done for the day, he'd finally stopped thinking about the letter.

He stepped out of the *Dispatch*'s front door, crossed the street to the parking lot where he'd left his car, and stopped dead. On the driver's-side door of the Prius, someone had left him a message in red, yellow, blue, and green refrigerator magnets.

B SMART MASON
WE C U

43

Mulligan and Mason sat in the red leather chairs across from their boss's desk and waited for him to explain why they'd been summoned.

"Iggy Rock called this morning," Lomax said. "He informed me that he's got three sources telling him our publisher's son here is trying to get Kwame Diggs sprung from prison."

"Aw, hell," Mulligan said.

"It was bound to leak out eventually," Lomax said.

"Yeah," Mulligan said, "but you can count on Iggy to put the worst possible spin on it."

"Who are his sources?" Mason asked.

"He declined to say," Lomax said.

"Probably some of the guards I've been talking to," Mason said.

"Most likely," Lomax said. "He wanted me to send you over to WTOP tomorrow morning to answer questions on the air. I said no way. Then he asked if *I* would do it. I said no to that too."

"You probably need to release a statement," Mulligan said.

"Already have."

Lomax snatched a sheet of paper from his desk and read from it.

"At any one time, *The Providence Dispatch* is working on dozens of stories, some of which never advance to the point of meeting our high standards for publication. It is our policy, therefore, never to comment on work in progress. I can assure you, however, that the editors of this newspaper have no desire to see Kwame Diggs released from prison."

"Sounds about right," Mason said.

"To Iggy," Mulligan said, "it will smell like red meat."

"All right, then," Lomax said. "Time for you both to put your cards on the table. Mason, while you've been trying to prove that Diggs was framed, Mulligan and Gloria Costa have been trying to connect him to something that could keep him in prison legally."

"Good," Mason said. He turned to Mulligan and asked, "What progress have you made?"

"You first, Edward," Lomax said. "What have you got so far?"

"First off, it's obvious the drug charge against Diggs was bogus."

"How do you know that?"

"There's no way a visitor could have smuggled marijuana past Supermax security," Mason said, giving a quick rundown on the guards, the thick glass, and the drug-sniffing dog.

"Was the security that tight back in 2005, when the drug charge was filed?" Lomax asked.

"It was. I checked. The guards I talked to all say sneaking drugs in there would have been impossible."

"Bullshit," Mulligan said.

"What do you mean?"

"A guard easily could have done it."

"Oh," Mason said. "I should have thought of that."

"So your case that Diggs was innocent of the drug charge completely falls apart," Lomax said.

"Maybe not," Mason said. "I did some research and learned that Diggs is the only prisoner in the history of Supermax who has ever been charged with having drugs in his cell. That's pretty odd, don't you think?"

"Odd, yes," Lomax said. "But it doesn't

prove anything."

"I suppose not."

"What about the assaults on the guards?" Lomax asked. "What are your sources telling you about that?"

"That they were both faked."

"Let's start with the assault on Galloway," Mulligan said. "How many sources have you got on that?"

"Just Pugliese."

Mulligan smirked.

"You believe him, don't you?" Mason said.

"I do. He's a straight shooter. But I'm not the one you have to convince."

"You're saying I need another source?" Mason said.

"Of course you do," Lomax said.

"But who is that going to be?" Mulligan asked. "There were only two other witnesses, Quinn and Galloway himself, and they both swore under oath that the assault happened."

"Maybe they bragged to their friends about setting Diggs up," Mason said. "That's what Araujo did after he faked the 2005 assault charge."

"Tell me about that," Lomax said.

"A day after the charge was filed, Araujo talked about it with other guards in their break room. He said the warden had asked him to file a false complaint to keep Diggs in prison. The other guards treated him like a hero, backslaps and fist bumps all around."

"Who are your sources for this?" Lomax asked.

"Two former guards, Chuckie Shaad and Tyrone Robinson. The warden came to Shaad first and asked him to file a false complaint against Diggs. Shaad told me he thought Diggs deserved to stay in prison forever but that he wasn't willing to lie in court to make it happen."

"Did he and Robinson both go on the record?" Lomax asked.

"Robinson did, but I don't think I can quote him."

"Why not?"

"The warden fired him for coming to work high on cocaine."

"You're right. You can't," Lomax said. "What about Shaad?"

"I can use what he gave me, but he doesn't want to be named."

"Okay," Lomax said. "What else have you got?"

"Robinson and Shaad both said guards were always trying to provoke Diggs into taking a swing at them."

"How?"

"By calling him names. Pervert, child killer, the n-word."

"Did they tell you how Diggs reacted?"

"They said he just smiled at them. Diggs told me the same thing. He claims he's too smart to give them what they want."

"You've been talking to *Diggs*?" Lomax asked.

"I have. His new lawyer set it up. I've interviewed him three times already, and I'm going back again Wednesday."

"You should have told me about this before, Edward," Lomax said.

"I suppose I should have."

"What else has Diggs been saying?"

"He insists the drug and assault charges were fabricated, but he hasn't been any help proving it."

"So why are you going to see him again?"

"I've been interviewing him about his life. Moving to Warwick when he was seven, how hard it was being the only black kid in the neighborhood, his interest in black history. Stuff like that."

"Sounds boring as shit," Lomax said.

"It's not, actually," Mason said. "I was thinking that if my investigation washed out, I could always write a profile."

"Have you asked him about the murders?" Mulligan asked.

"I have. He still says he's innocent. . . . So, do you think I have enough to write the abuse of power story yet?"

"If I understood you correctly," Lomax said, "you've got one on-the-record source for the Galloway case and one not-for-attribution source for the Araujo assault."

"Yes, sir."

"Then you're not even close."

Mason's shoulders slumped. That profile might be the only thing he'd be able to get in print after all.

"Your turn, Mulligan," Lomax said. "Rundown what you've got."

"A year before the Medeiros murders," Mulligan said, "somebody broke into a house three miles from where Diggs lived and stabbed a woman named Susan Ashcroft."

He quickly ran through the details of the crime, the circumstantial evidence linking Diggs to it, and his hope that the killer's DNA might still be found on something stored away in the evidence boxes.

"How long since you asked the Warwick cops to look for them?" Lomax asked.

"A week."

"And they still haven't located them?"

"Not yet. Chief Hernandez says a lot of evidence from old cases has been lost or thrown out."

"If this doesn't pan out," Mason butted in, "I might have something that could keep Diggs locked up for a while."

"Out with it," Lomax said.

"A few months before Becky Medeiros was killed, Diggs torched her car. It's only fourth-degree arson, though. The most he could get for it is three years."

"Where'd you get that?" Lomax asked.

"Diggs told me about it."

"Did he say *why* he torched her car?"

"He said she called him the n-word, and it made him mad."

"Why the hell would he tell you this?" Mulligan asked.

"We were talking about how angry he used to get when people disrespected him. That was one of the examples he gave me."

"Interesting," Mulligan said. "One problem with it, though."

"What's that?"

"It never happened."

"What makes you say that?"

"Gloria and I searched the news archives for all the crimes that occurred in Diggs's neighborhood around the time of the murders. The *Dispatch* printed every police incident in the West Bay edition back then, and there was no mention of this."

"Maybe the reporter missed it," Mason said. "Or maybe the item was cut for space."

"I suppose that's possible," Mulligan said. "But I've also been talking to a retired cop who was the lead detective on the murders. If it had happened, he would have known about it. But he never mentioned it either."

"Maybe it slipped his mind," Mason said. "Or maybe he didn't think it was important."

Mulligan pulled the cell phone from his shirt pocket and made a call.

"Andy? It's Mulligan. . . . No, I haven't heard anything from Hernandez yet either. Listen, someone just told me that Becky's car was torched a few months before the murder. . . .You sure? . . . Okay, thanks."

Mulligan ended the call and glared at Mason.

"Like I said. It never happened. That should make you wonder what else Diggs has been lying to you about."

"It does. I'll try to be more careful."

"See that you do," Lomax said. "And Edward?"

"Yes, sir?"

"Next time you talk to Diggs, ask him about Susan Ashcroft. Now get the hell out of my office. . . . Not you, Mulligan. We need to talk."

As soon as Mason left, Lomax asked Mulligan to close the office door.

"So what do you think?"

"Thanks-Dad wants this story so bad that it's blinded him to some things," Mulligan said. "But the kid's a hell of a reporter. A lot better than I thought. He's just a couple of sources shy of nailing it."

"You taught him too damn well," Lomax said.

"So this is *my* fault?"

"I didn't mean it like that." Lomax removed his glasses, wiped them clean on his shirtsleeve, put them back on, and said, "Aw, shit."

"You don't have to print it," Mulligan said.

"Crossing the publisher's son might not be the best thing for my job security."

"Hell, Ed," Mulligan said, "the way things are going, none of us will be working here much longer."

Lomax leaned back in his chair and plunked his feet on his desk.

"Three more years is all I need," he said. "After that, I'm putting in for my pension. Doris has it all figured out. Says we're gonna sell the house in Cumberland, buy a used RV, and spend our golden years touring the country."

Mulligan knew Lomax wasn't going to get

those three years. The veteran reporter was sorely tempted to spill what Mason had told him in confidence. Lomax deserved to know.

But all Mulligan said was, “Nice plan.”

“What will *you* do, Mulligan, when the paper finally goes under?”

“Oh, I don’t know. Maybe I’ll invest my meager life savings in a case of Bushmills, hole up somewhere, and try to write the Great American Novel.”

“In other words, you got no fuckin’ idea.”

44

"Citizens of the state of Rhode Island and Providence Plantations, the hour is nigh. Truth, courage, honor, justice, and the American Way have returned once again to the public airwaves. Stay with us now for the singular voice that makes godless liberals and America-hating socialists pee their pants. The voice that makes God-fearing patriots stand up and cheer."

"Hey, Charlie," Mulligan said, "would you mind turning the radio up?"

"Really?" the fry cook said. He turned from the grill to glance first at Mulligan and then at Mason, seated side by side at the lunch counter. "You two pinkos care what Iggy has to say?"

"Not usually," Mulligan said, "but he's going to be talking about the *Dispatch* this morning."

Iggy Rock's theme music was playing now, a medley that began with a few bars of "Also

Sprach Zarathustra," segued to Jimmy Cagney's rendition of "You're a Grand Old Flag," and concluded with the last verse of Lee Greenwood's "God Bless the USA."

To Mulligan, that always seemed like enough of an introduction, but Iggy apparently didn't think so.

"Ladies and gentlemen and children of all ages, hold on to your hats and buckle your seat belts. Get ready for a rollicking three hours of news and commentary from the prince of pundits, the champion of liberty, the voice of conservatism, and the defender of the Republic. The one! The only! *Iggy Rock!*"

But still no Iggy. First, listeners were treated to Ronan Tynan singing the first verse of "God Bless America," followed by the opening trumpet blast of the theme from *Rocky.* Only then did Iggy's voice boom from the radio speakers.

"Good morning, Row Dyelin! This is your host, Iggy Rock. Today, we'll expose what the bloodsucking teachers union is doing to bankrupt our cities and towns. But first, a WTOP exclusive report on a shocking plan by the liberal-loving *Providence Dispatch* to spring serial killer Kwame Diggs from his rightful place in the state prison.

"You remember Diggs, don't you? In the

1990s, he terrorized the city of Warwick, brutally murdering two young women and three little girls. Since then, he's been caught with marijuana in his cell and been convicted of beating two prison guards.

"But now, I have learned from unimpeachable sources, the *Dispatch* is attempting to prove that the state of Rhode Island framed Diggs on those drug and assault charges. For the last several months, the newspaper has been interviewing prison guards, and perhaps others as well, in an irresponsible attempt to impeach the testimony of witnesses who testified for the prosecution in those cases.

"My sources tell me the *Dispatch* may be only days away from publishing its report. And if the newspaper succeeds in throwing doubt on Diggs's convictions, Rhode Island could be forced to set this monster loose to roam free among us.

"I know what's going through your minds. What in the name of God are the editors of the *Dispatch* thinking? To find out, I invited the newspaper's managing editor, Ed Lomax, to appear on the show this morning to answer your questions.

"The editor of a newspaper that expects other people to answer *its* questions ought to be willing to come here and answer a few himself, don't you think? After all, refusing would be the epitome of hypocrisy. Well, it turns out that Ed Lomax *is* a hypocrite. He flatly refused to appear on this program. Instead, he sent over this three-sentence prepared statement," Iggy said, and then read the text.

"So what do you make of that?" he asked. "Yeah, I know. Sounds like bullshit to me, too. So why don't we give him a call and see if we can drag a little more out of him."

The touch-tone sound of a telephone being dialed, and then: "*Providence Dispatch,* Ed Lomax speaking."

"This is Iggy Rock at WTOP, and you are on the air. The people of Row Dyelin are deeply concerned about your plan to help Kwame Diggs get out of prison so that he can kill again, and we demand that you answer our questions."

"You have my statement on this matter, Mr. Bardakjian. I have nothing further to say at this time," Lomax said. And then he hung up.

"Well, there you have it," Iggy said. "Once again, *The Providence Dispatch* demonstrates that it has nothing but contempt for the people of Row Dyelin. The board is lit up like a Christmas tree, so let's take some calls. Sal from North Providence, you are on the air."

"This is freaking nuts, Iggy. If Diggs gets released, the editors of the *Dispatch* should be charged with conspiracy to commit murder. Soon as I hang up, I'm calling them up and canceling my subscription."

"Great idea, Sal. Let's everybody do that. Show them that we mean business! Natalie from Pawtucket, you are on the air."

Mulligan finished his coffee, turned to Mason, and said, "Well, that could have gone worse."

"How do you mean?"

"At least he didn't give Sal from North Providence and Natalie from Pawtucket your name."

"Why do you suppose he didn't?"

"Maybe he didn't want to put a target on your back," Mulligan said.

"He didn't mind putting one on Lomax. Not that it makes much difference, I guess. I've got a target on my back already. Here, take a look at this."

He handed Mulligan his iPhone. On the screen was a photo of a car door with a message written in what appeared to be alphabet refrigerator magnets.

STOP NOW
OR ELZE

"Else with a *z*?" Mulligan said. "Nobody's spelling is that bad. Looks like your correspondent ran out of the letter *s*."

"That's how I figure it."

"This was left on your car?"

"It was."

"When?"

"Last night. There was another one, too. Scroll back to the previous picture."

"How the hell do I do that?"

"Give it here," Mason said.

He took the phone from Mulligan, flicked a finger across the screen, and handed it back to him. This time, the message on the car door read:

B SMART MASON
WE C U

"That one's from a week ago," Mason said.

Mulligan took a minute to think it over. In his mind, he compared it with the threatening note Mason had gotten in the mail:

WE KNOW WHAT YOUR DOING, RICHIE RICH.

IF YOU KNOW WHATS GOOD FOR YOU, YOU'LL STOP.

"Any more threatening letters?" he asked.

"A couple more, yes."

"What did they say?"

"Pretty much the same thing as the first one."

"Somebody obviously wants you to stop *something,*" Mulligan said. "Do the messages ever say what?"

"I just assumed it was the Diggs story," Mason said. "I mean, what else could it be?"

"I don't know, Thanks-Dad. You tell me."

"I can't think of anything."

"Not screwing somebody's wife, are you?"

"Of course not."

"Ripping somebody off in some sort of business deal?"

"No. Nothing like that."

"Okay, then," Mulligan said. "Let me poke into this. See what I can find out."

As he walked back to the newspaper, Mulligan puzzled over the threats. Refrigerator magnets were an awfully polite way of leaving threatening messages. Why weren't they just scratched into the paint? The more he thought about it, the more it felt as though those brightly colored magnets were something a woman would use.

Mulligan had just stepped off the elevator when "Confused" by a San Francisco punk band called the Nuns began playing in his shirt pocket. His ring tone for the governor.

"Mulligan."

"Is it true?"

"Just between us?"

"Yes."

"Can I actually *trust* you this time, Fiona?"

"I promise."

"The story's not nailed down yet, but it's in the works."

"Who's reporting this? Is it you?"

"Hell, no."

"The *Dispatch* would actually *print* it?"

"The publisher's son is the one working on it, so I gotta think yes."

"Holy Mother of God."

"My feeling exactly, although I'd be prone to use more colorful language."

"When is the story likely to break?"

"Hard to say. Maybe in a couple of weeks. Maybe never. Thanks-Dad doesn't have enough sources yet."

"How likely is it that he'll pull this off?"

"If I were a betting man, I'd put the odds at fifty-fifty."

"You *are* a betting man."

"Oh, yeah. I forgot."

"Is my name going to surface in this?"

"You were the A.G. when Diggs was prosecuted for Galloway, so your fingerprints are all over it. I doubt Thanks-Dad will be able to prove it, though. The kid's good, but he's not that good. He's close to nailing the warden for subornation of perjury and obstruction of justice, but I doubt he'll be able to take it any higher."

"If he does, will you give me a heads-up?"

"Maybe. No guarantees."

"I know I promised to keep this confidential, Mulligan, but I'm going to have to share it with the attorney general."

"Fiona . . ."

"I'll keep your name out of it, but I have to do something. I can't stand by and allow Kwame Diggs to be released from prison."

"Of course you can't."

"If he gets out, innocent people are going to die."

"And it would be fatal to your political career."

"That's the last thing on my mind right now."

"Like hell."

They both fell quiet for a moment.

"Attorney General Roberts and I are going to have to put our heads together," Fiona said. "See if we can come up with a contingency plan."

"Like what?"

"Maybe we can persuade a judge to order

a psychiatric exam. If we can get Diggs declared a dangerous psychopath, we could get him locked away in a mental hospital."

"You'll have to do some serious judge shopping to pull *that* off," Mulligan said.

That evening Mulligan had a few brews at Hopes, watched the Sox fall to the Athletics on the West Coast, and played a couple of games of pinball.

Shortly after two A.M., he returned to the newsroom. The lights were dim. The overnight cops reporter was snoozing in his cubicle. The rest of the desks were empty.

Mulligan padded to Gloria's cubicle, sat in her chair, opened the shallow drawer under the desktop, and rummaged through the contents. Cheap ballpoint pens, paper clips, an unopened pack of Post-it notes, three tubes of lipstick, a small brass key, spare media cards, a flash drive, and an old roll of Kodak film nobody had use for anymore. He slid the drawer closed and pulled the handles on the two-drawer file cabinet under the right side of the desk. It was locked. He reopened the shallow drawer, removed a small brass key, and inserted it in the file drawer lock.

The top file drawer contained, of all things, files. The bottom drawer was a jumble of battery chargers, cables, camera lenses, filters, and flash attachments. Stuffed all the way in the back, concealed under an empty camera case, he found two Ziploc bags. One contained what appeared to be about a quarter ounce of marijuana. The other held a handful of candy colored alphabet refrigerator magnets. He dumped them on the desktop, sorted through them, and couldn't find an "s."

Mulligan drove home and swept up the shredded, shit-streaked newspapers Larry Bird had kicked onto his kitchen floor. He pulled on an oven mitt, lined the bottom of the cage with the arts section of the *Dispatch,* and filled the bird's water tube and food tray.

Then he fetched a Killian's from the fridge, flopped onto his mattress, pulled his cell phone from the pocket of his jeans, and punched in a number.

"Hello?" The voice was groggy, as if the call had woken her.

"Sorry about calling in the middle of the night, Gloria, but I have to ask you for a favor."

"Mulligan?"

"Yeah."

"What time is it?"

"Nearly three."

"This better be important."

"It is. I need you to stop leaving threatening messages on Mason's car."

Dead air. And then, "How'd you know?"

"I'm an investigative reporter, Gloria. I know all kinds of stuff."

"Does Mason know?"

"He doesn't."

"Are you going to tell him?"

"No."

"Okay, then."

"And Gloria?"

"Yeah?"

"Don't mail him any more threatening letters, either."

"*What?* I never did that."

"You sure?"

"Of course I'm sure."

"Okay, I believe you. Good night, Gloria," Mulligan said. Then he hung up and growled, "Aw, crap."

45

Saturday breakfast at the Mason family manse in Newport was hotcakes topped with cream and fresh strawberries. The old man waited until the plates were cleared before broaching the subject.

"Son, Ed Lomax tells me you are the one working on the story that's got Iggy Rock all fired up."

"I am."

"He also told me he asked you not to."

"That's true."

"Would you mind telling me why you made the decision to proceed?"

Mason took several minutes to explain his reasoning and to run through what he'd learned so far.

"Why didn't you tell me about this before?" his father asked.

"I was afraid you might tell me to stop."

"I probably would have. This is causing us a good deal of trouble, son. Since Iggy Rock broke the news, more than three thousand readers have canceled their subscriptions. That's nearly four percent of our circulation."

"I know."

"Did you also know that because of this, Media General and Belo have withdrawn their inquiries about acquiring the *Dispatch*?"

"Sorry, Dad."

"Frankly, I'm not sure how serious their interest was in the first place, but now they're saying they feel compelled to wait until they know how much permanent damage has been done."

"I see."

"I'm also receiving concerned inquiries from the board of directors."

"What are you going to tell them?"

"I haven't decided."

"If I get the story, are we going to publish it?"

"I can't say just yet. Let's see what you come up with first." Mason was awash with conflicting emotions. Regret at the damage he'd done to the newspaper. Pride that his father understood what he was doing — and maybe even approved of it, if only a little.

After breakfast, he brooded over one last cup of coffee. Then he wandered into the music room and sat at the piano. He plunked out the tune to "Providence Rag," his work in progress, jotted two lines of lyrics on a page of sheet music, studied what he'd written, and crossed it out. He had too much on his mind to concentrate.

He sat quietly and let his mind drift to Felicia. Dropping his hands to the keys, he began to play Debussy's "Clair de Lune," the most romantic piece of classical music he knew by heart.

He wondered. When they were finally done with Kwame, would she let him take her to Paris? But he was getting ahead of himself. Probably he ought to kiss her first. They'd both been so ambitious, spending their lives working toward something they couldn't touch — and that couldn't touch them back. It scared and thrilled him now, the way he wanted to fill those hollow spaces with Felicia. The way he wanted time to fly.

46

"So what's the topic for today, cuz?"

"Susan Ashcroft."

"Who the hell is that?" Kwame asked.

"You don't remember her?"

"No."

"A year before Becky Medeiros was murdered, someone broke into her house in Warwick, bashed her in the head with a clock radio, and stabbed her five times."

"That sucks, E, but why tell me?"

"Aren't you the one who did it?"

"Fuck, no. I already told you. I ain't never stabbed nobody."

"Do you know anything about what happened to her?"

"This is the first I ever heard about it."

Mason peered at Kwame through the smeared Plexiglas and spoke again into the crackling visitors' room telephone.

"Okay, then, Kwame. Let's talk some more about your childhood."

And so they did. A half hour later, Mason had all he needed to write his profile.

"So does that mean you're not coming back?" Kwame asked.

"I'm still looking into the assault charges," Mason said. "I'll be back to talk to you again soon."

"I'm keeping the faith, cuz. Malcolm X said, 'Truth is on the side of the oppressed.' " And then he cracked a smile. "So tell me. You pumpin' my fine-ass lawyer yet?"

"That's really none of your business, Kwame."

"Come on, cuz. Does she get all wet and shit when you play with her titties?"

Before he could stop himself, Mason flashed on a vision of Felicia nude from the waist up. Diggs sniggered. Mason squashed a sudden urge to punch the glass as hard as he could, to shatter it and wipe that smirk off the killer's face.

Ten minutes later, heading for his car in the prison visitors' lot, Mason was still feeling unnerved. He realized that whenever he thought of Kwame's victims, they were just that — victims. He felt sorry for them, but he had to strain to remember all of their names. He wished Kwame had never met Felicia. He didn't want him to look at her face. He didn't want him to ever speak *her* name.

He stepped around a rusted Dodge van, spotted his car, and saw that someone had smashed the headlights and taillights.

47

Two cardboard boxes, each the size of a mini fridge, had been placed on a long metal worktable in the basement of the Warwick police station. Judging by the scrawls on the orange evidence seals, they hadn't been opened since 1996.

"Is this everything?" Mulligan asked.

"No," said Sergeant Mario DeMaso, the department evidence clerk. "According to the logs, there should have been three boxes. There's no record of anyone checking one out, but I've looked everywhere. The damn thing's just gone."

"How can that be?" Mulligan asked.

Jennings, standing beside him, shrugged. "Mulligan," he said, "this happens more often than you'd like to think."

DeMaso broke the seals with a fingernail and removed the lids. Mulligan and Jennings crowded around, bending to the boxes. Inside were evidence bags, some made of clear plastic and others of brown paper. Each had a label listing its contents, where and when it was collected, and the name of the officer who had bagged it. Each also included a chain of custody record that documented every instance in which the evidence had been removed for examination.

DeMaso carefully emptied the boxes, placing the evidence bags on the table. The men didn't open them. They just read the labels. The largest bags held Susan Ashcroft's pillowcase, her sheets, her blanket, and a stuffed bear. Smaller ones held a water glass and a blood-splattered paperback book collected from her nightstand. A dozen envelopes contained hairs, fibers, and other small bits of dubious value that had been plucked from the bedding and from the bedroom carpet.

"Where's the clock radio the vic was struck with?" Jennings asked.

"Must have been in the missing box," DeMaso said. "The kitchen knife she was stabbed with doesn't seem to be here, either."

"So what do you think?" Mulligan asked.

"I'd say your best bet for DNA is the bedsheet and the hairs," DeMaso said. "But I'd also have the pillowcase and blanket examined again to see if the fucker shed anything on them."

"Sounds right," Jennings said.

"Okay," DeMaso said. "I'll drive it over to the crime lab this afternoon."

48

"Today, I want to ask you about your confession," Mason said.

"I already told you it was coerced," Diggs said. "The fuckers beat me and then told me what to say."

"I'm not talking about *that* confession. I'm talking about the one you made to *me.*"

"What the fuck you talkin' about?"

"When we were discussing how you used to get angry, you told me this." Mason flipped open his notebook and read from a page: " 'I understand now that there are better ways than killing to get even with racists.' "

Diggs didn't say anything. Mason sat silently and stared at him through the Plexiglas.

"Shit," Diggs finally said. "You took that out of . . . what the fuck's the word?"

"Context?"

"Yeah. Out of context."

"I don't think so."

"I thought you was on my side," Diggs said.

"I'm on the side of the truth," Mason said.

They stared at each other some more. After thirty seconds, Diggs averted his eyes.

"Look, Kwame. I don't understand why you keep denying that you killed those people. Everybody knows you did it. Admitting it can't do you any harm now. You've already done your time for it. And who knows? Showing remorse might even do you some good."

Diggs sat silently, his eyes lowered. When he finally spoke, his voice was soft and raspy.

"Don't know why I let you in, cuz. Don't know why I tell you shit."

Another moment passed before he lifted his eyes to meet Mason's and whispered, "It's 'cause of my moms."

"Your what? I didn't quite catch that."

"My moms. How do you tell your mother that you stabbed five people to death? How do you look into the eyes of the woman who gave birth to you and say that shit? You can't, cuz. You just can't fuckin' do that. So all these years I been telling her I'm innocent. And she believes me, cuz. She really does."

"What exactly have you been telling her?"

Diggs closed his eyes and rubbed them with the backs of his cuffed hands. For the first time, Mason noticed a scar on Diggs's right thumb. He wondered if it was from when he cut himself with the knife he used to murder the Stuart family.

"When I was thirteen," Diggs said, "I started hanging on the streets. Got in with some older kids who liked to break into houses and steal shit. Some nights, they'd ask me to come along as a lookout. My moms didn't know about the break-ins, but she knew those kids were trouble. She always told me to stay away from them. So I figured I could blame everything on them. I told my moms I was there the nights of the murders but never went inside — that I didn't even know anybody got killed until the police came around asking questions."

"Why didn't she go to the police with that story?"

"Cuz she knew I'd get arrested anyway, as an accessory to murder."

"How'd you explain your fingerprints at the crime scenes and the trophies in your garden shed?"

"I told her the police planted all that stuff."

Mason took a deep breath.

"Why did you kill those people, Kwame?"

"Cuz they hated black folks."

"Not just Becky Medeiros? The Stuarts, too?"

"Oh, yeah. Connie Stuart and them little girls would stand on their front stoop and point at me when I rode my bike in the street. They'd say, 'There goes the porch monkey,' and then they'd laugh at me. Made me so fuckin' mad I couldn't think straight.

"James Baldwin said, 'To be a Negro in this country and to be relatively conscious is to be in a rage almost all the time.' " He spoke the line in a monotone, as if he were giving a grade school oral report. "I was in a rage, cuz. All I could think of was kill, kill, kill. The anger didn't go away until they were all dead."

Mason stared at Diggs through the glass.

"Kwame," he said, "how do you feel now about what you did?"

"I got blood on my hands I can't wash off. I took the lives of five human beings. I see them in my sleep. I'm sorry every single day."

"What about Susan Ashcroft? Are you ready to admit you attacked her, too?"

"I don't know nothing about no Susan Ashcroft."

Mason sadly shook his head.

"Be real, cuz," Diggs said. "No way I can come clean on that. You and me, we both know the law. I could be charged as an adult, and then I'd never get out of here."

As Mason walked to his car in the prison parking lot, he found himself believing that Diggs was sorry, but he figured the only person he was sorry *for* was himself.

When he reached the Prius, he found the lights he'd had repaired were broken again. And this time, the windshield was smashed, too.

49

"Mason turned in his profile of Diggs this morning," Lomax said.

"How's it look?" Mulligan asked.

"The writing needs some punching up, but it's going to make news. Diggs spilled his guts."

"Um."

"I figure on stripping it across page one on Sunday, but I thought you ought to look it over first." Lomax lifted a stack of paper from his laser printer, stapled the pages together, and handed them across the desk to Mulligan. "You know more about Diggs than I do, so I'm counting on you to make sure there are no problems with this."

Mulligan scanned the first two paragraphs:

> Kwame Diggs, the notorious killer who stabbed two women and three children to death in their Warwick homes in the 1990s, has at long last acknowledged his guilt. In

a series of exclusive jailhouse interviews with *The Providence Dispatch,* he also disclosed — for the first time — *why* he killed.

Diggs explained that he committed the murders in the throes of a rage he felt powerless to control, furious at white neighbors who taunted him with racial epithets.

"I'll need some time with this," Mulligan said, "but I can already tell you I'm going to have issues."

He left Lomax's office, used the Xerox machine to make a second copy, dropped it on Gloria's desk, and asked her to join him at his place for dinner.

By nine that evening, they'd both read Mason's story twice, filling the margins with notes and staining the pages with grease from still another Caserta Pizzeria pie.

"You don't buy the black rage excuse, do you?" Gloria asked.

"Of course not," Mulligan said. He was about to elaborate when Larry Bird interrupted with a squawk.

"Theee Yankees win!" The bird glared smugly.

"Can't you teach him not to say that?"

Gloria asked.

"I'm still trying."

"So," Gloria asked, "how do you want to break this up?"

"See if you can get Diggs's family to talk to you," Mulligan said. "I'll talk to Jennings and to Diggs's old middle school principal."

"What about that FBI agent who profiled Diggs back in the nineties?" Gloria said.

"Good idea," Mulligan said. "I'll see if I can track him down."

Esther Diggs lived alone in a one-story cottage on Ruth Road in Brockton, Massachusetts, just a couple of blocks from Cardinal Spellman High School. A well-tended bed of petunias and pansies lined her cracked concrete front walk, and a pot of pink geraniums hung beside the door.

Inside, Gloria and Mrs. Diggs sat together in the living room on a faded pink-and-green floral sofa, both sipping hot tea from dainty porcelain cups.

"I see that you like elephants," Gloria said.

Pachyderms trailed one another across the fireplace mantel, lounged on the end tables, and crowded trunk to tail on the shelves of a floor-to-ceiling bookcase that also held a few romance novels, several self-help tomes, and half a dozen spiritual guides by

T. D. Jakes, Joyce Meyer, and Joel Osteen. The herd numbered at least a hundred, mostly ceramic but a few of carved wood, blown glass, or molded plastic.

"May I tell you a secret?"

"Certainly, Mrs. Diggs."

"I really *don't* like elephants."

"Then why in the world do you have so many?"

The woman chuckled and slowly shook her head.

"When Kwame was eight years old, he bought me an elephant figurine for my birthday. That one right there," she said, pointing to the coffee table where a white, eight-inch-tall ceramic elephant with red lips and rouged cheeks reared on its hind legs. It seemed poised to stomp on a *People* magazine with a photo of Kim Kardashian on the cover.

"Hideous, isn't it?"

"It is," Gloria said. She felt the same way about the Kardashians.

"But of course, I gushed over it. I told Kwame it was the most wonderful gift I had ever received. So naturally the kids bought me more elephants for Christmas. And for my next birthday. And the one after that. And the one after that. Before long, visitors noticed them. Neighbors. Cousins. Aunts and uncles. So they started bringing me elephants, too, trinkets they picked up for fifty cents or a dollar at tag sales and secondhand shops. I didn't have the heart to tell folks I didn't like them, and one thing just led to another."

Mrs. Diggs's bottom lip quivered, and Gloria was afraid she was about to cry. Instead, the two women burst out laughing.

"But I don't imagine you're here to talk about elephants," Mrs. Diggs said.

"No," Gloria said. "I'm helping Mason out on his story about Kwame, and I wanted to ask a few questions about his childhood."

"I guess that would be all right."

"Was he a happy child?"

"It seemed to me that he was. He loved video games, playing ball with his friends, riding his bike around the neighborhood. He really loved that Schwinn of his. He'd ride fast, no hands, right down the middle of the street. I'd holler, 'Kwame, put your hands on the handlebars before you fall and crack your head!' And he would. But as soon as he thought I wasn't looking, he'd be riding no hands again."

"Did he have many friends?"

"Oh, my goodness, yes. The neighborhood was full of kids, a lot of them Kwame's age. They were always hanging out together, playing card games, listening to music, playing football in the street."

"I understand you were the only black family in the neighborhood back then."

"That's true."

"How did Kwame feel about that?"

"That was never an issue with Kwame. He didn't think much about color back then, as far as I could tell, and he fit right in with the white boys his age. Of course, there *were* a few black kids in his school. He made friends with them, too, and sometimes they'd sleep over at our house. But so did some of the white boys."

"How about your white neighbors? Did they treat your family well?"

"Why, yes, they did. I was worried about that when we first moved in, seeing as we were the first black family and all. But on thc very first day, that nice Mrs. Bigsby who lived next door came by to welcome us to the neighborhood and bring us one of her homemade cherry pies. Connie Stuart, God bless her soul, took the trouble to bring us a tuna casserole even though she was pregnant at the time. Over the years, we were invited to lots of backyard barbecues and kids' birthday parties and such. People couldn't have been nicer. Until after Kwame was arrested, of course. Then everyone stopped talking to us."

"Was *everybody* nice before that?"

"Not everybody, no. There were a couple of people who shunned us. When we said hello, they'd just turn their heads. But they were the exception. Most everybody was very neighborly."

"Including Becky Medeiros?"

"We didn't get to know her very well, but she always smiled and greeted us whenever we passed by her house on one of our walks. Kwame said that when he'd ride by her house on his bicycle, she'd flag him down and give him cookies sometimes. Not homemade. The store-bought kind. Oreos or Fig Newtons."

"So none of your neighbors ever called your kids racist names, then?"

"Lord, no. Some of the *black* boys called each other nigger. I caught Kwame doing it once, and I took his bike away for a week. I told him, 'Young man, I don't ever want to hear that filthy word come out of your mouth again.' "

"What about at school? Did he and his brother fit in well there?"

"Yes, they did. It was hard to get Kwame to study or do his homework, but we didn't get on him about it because he got mostly B's anyway. And he always got an A in history. Sekou and Amina were more studious, and Sekou was very good at sports."

"Did the white kids ever pick on them?"

"Not that I ever heard."

"Kwame never got in any school-yard fights, then?"

"Goodness, no."

"He never came home from school with a split lip or black eye or maybe a bloody nose?"

"He got a bloody nose a couple of times playing football, I do recall that. But fights? No. If that had happened, I'm sure I'd remember."

"Mrs. Diggs, I want to be honest with you here. Kwame has been telling Mason a lot of things that just aren't true."

The woman folded her hands, rested them on her knees, and studied them for a moment. Gradually, her gaze turned to steel.

"If Kwame did that," she said, "I'm sure he must have had his reasons."

50

"I hope you've got something else you can put on page one on Sunday," Mulligan said.

"Problems?" Lomax said.

"Oh, yeah. Big-time."

"Anything that can't be fixed in the next forty-eight hours?"

Mulligan thought about it for a moment. "Depends on how fast Mason can rewrite this piece of shit. But what's your hurry?"

"Tuesday morning, I sent the story down to promotion," Lomax said. "Asked them to work up a radio promo so it would be ready once we had the piece set to go. The dumb bastards didn't just *write* the promo. They sent it out. It started running on WTOP and WPRO last night."

"Aw fuck," Mulligan said.

"Yeah," Lomax said. "If you run a promo and then don't run the story, you look like a fool."

"What's the promo say?"

Lomax picked up a sheet of paper from his desk and read aloud: " 'Coming this Sunday: Rhode Island's most notorious killer in his own words. Kwame Diggs breaks his silence to explain why he killed. And you'll find it only in *The Providence Dispatch.*' "

"That all of it?"

"It is."

"Nothing about black rage, then?"

"No."

"Thank God," Mulligan said. "Diggs lied his ass off to Mason about that."

"Guess we better get the kid in here," Lomax said.

"Yeah. And we'll need Gloria, too."

Mulligan and Gloria had already claimed the leather visitors' chairs opposite Lomax's desk, so Mason rolled in a spare desk chair from the copy desk.

"Edward," Lomax began, "earlier this week I asked Mulligan to look over your Diggs profile, and he recruited Gloria to help him with the task. Today, they came back with some concerns that need to be addressed before the story can be published."

"I see," Mason said. "What are they and what do I need to do to fix them?"

"Your story portrays Diggs as a young man who killed in a blind rage because his neighbors called him racist names. Mulligan and Gloria believe he lied to you about that. They say it's simply not true."

Mason blanched visibly. He'd expected nitpicks about a few details. Instead, the central premise of a story he'd invested weeks in was being challenged. He felt cornered and ganged up on. His first instinct was to argue.

"So I suppose you geniuses think you know the real reason he killed," he said, surprised to find that he'd balled his fists at his sides.

"Yeah, we do, Thanks-Dad," Mulligan said. "Diggs is a psychosexual serial killer. He stabbed women and little girls to death because he got off on it."

Mason drew a deep breath and told himself to calm down.

"Okay," he said. "Perhaps you know some things I don't. Why don't you lay it out for me?"

Gloria took the lead, describing what Esther Diggs had told her about how kind and welcoming their neighbors had been.

"I asked her specifically about Connie Stuart and Becky Medeiros," Gloria said. "She told me that on the day they moved in, Stuart brought them a tuna casserole. And she said Becky Medeiros used to give Kwame cookies.

"After I talked with Mrs. Diggs, I called Kwame's sister, Amina, in Oakland and his brother, Sekou, in Tuscaloosa. They told pretty much the same story about the neighbors. Sekou didn't want to say much about Kwame. He said the last thing he needed was for folks in Alabama to know he was the brother of a serial killer. But Amina said Kwame was a very strange kid. When he was twelve or thirteen years old, he chopped the arms, legs, and heads off all of her Barbie dolls. And she thinks he killed her cat. Her mother never wanted to believe anything bad about Kwame, but Amina spent most of her childhood scared to death of him. She said he never actually hurt her, but she put a bolt latch on her door to stop him from creeping into her bedroom at night.

"Oh, and Marcus Washington checked his records for me and found that before she was killed, Becky Medeiros was contributing two hundred dollars a year to the NAACP."

"I see," Mason said, hating how disappointed he sounded. "Is there anything else?"

"The story Kwame told you about breaking a racist bully's arm in a school-yard brawl?" Mulligan said. "I tracked down Craig Hennessey, who was the school principal at the time. He said it never happened."

"He must be pretty old now," Mason said. "Maybe he forgot."

"I doubt he'd forget something like that," Mulligan said. "Besides, Andy Jennings, the lead detective on the Medeiros and Stuart murders, says the same thing. Back in '96, he did a lot of digging into Kwame's background. If it had happened, he would have found out about it. Just to be sure, I asked him to check the old police files. He confirmed there's no record of it."

"I see," Mason said, feeling smaller by the moment. He was glad Felicia couldn't see him now.

"I also tracked down Peter Schutter, a retired FBI agent who did a psychological profile of Diggs back in the nineties. He says Diggs's race rage excuse is laughable. If that had been his motive, why didn't he kill any men or boys? How come all of his victims were women and little girls?

"The evidence that these were sex murders is overwhelming," Mulligan continued. "I won't bother you with all the details, but how about this? Diggs masturbated on the dead bodies."

"What?" Mason said. "I didn't see anything about that in the trial transcripts."

"That's because family members of the victims attended the trial," Mulligan explained. "Prosecutors didn't want them to have to sit there and listen to all the sordid details. They had more than enough evidence to convict without dragging that stuff up."

"There was nothing about it in your old *Dispatch* clippings either," Mason said.

"I knew about it, but I didn't use it," Mulligan said. "At the time, it seemed like the decent thing to do."

Lomax raised an eyebrow.

"It was all off the record," Mulligan said. "My sources wouldn't even let me tell my editors about it."

Mason put his head in his hands.

"I guess I really fucked up." He rarely used the f-word, but it felt appropriate to the occasion.

"Yeah, you did," Lomax said.

"I'm sorry, Mr. Lomax. You'll have my resignation on your desk in the morning."

Lomax shook his head.

"It won't be accepted, Edward. The mistake you made is one a lot of aggressive young reporters make early in their careers. You fell in love with your story."

"I don't understand."

"What Diggs told you made for good copy," Lomax said. "You got excited about it. So excited that you lost perspective. You *wanted* his story to be true, so you convinced yourself that it was. As a result, you neglected to check it out properly."

Mason looked Mulligan in the eye. "Did *you* ever make a mistake like that?"

Before he could reply, Lomax cut him off. "Yeah, he did. But only once. More than once and he wouldn't still be here."

Mason looked ashen.

"Edward, you've still got the makings of a fine profile here," Lomax said, his eyes softening a little. "It's just going to be a different story from the one you thought you had. What you've got is the story of a killer who finally admits what he did but tries to excuse it by making up lies about his victims. I'll give you exactly sixty seconds to get over feeling sorry for yourself. Then I need you to sit down with Mulligan and Gloria and rewrite this thing from top to bottom."

He shot his cuff and checked his watch.

"I'll need the copy on my desk no later than forty-seven hours from right now."

51

Monday morning, the three friends gathered for breakfast at the diner in Kennedy Plaza. Outside the grease-flecked windows, the street was still wet from last night's rain.

Charlie clunked plates of bacon and eggs in front of Mulligan and Gloria. Mason, who had breakfasted on apple puff pancakes at home, sipped his second cup of the fry cook's strong coffee.

"You sure you don't want anything else, kid?" Charlie asked. "That was one hell of a story Sunday. Whatever you want is on the house."

"Thanks, Charlie, but I think I'll just stick with coffee."

The cook nodded and turned back to the grill. Mason swiveled on his stool to face Mulligan and Gloria.

"In the rush to get the story in shape to print, I never did properly thank you two for saving my butt."

"You're welcome," Mulligan said.

"I still think it should have had your bylines on it," Mason said.

"Nah," Mulligan said. "It was your story, Thanks-Dad. You're the one who got Diggs to talk." He shoveled a forkful of eggs into his mouth, checked his watch, and said, "Hey, Charlie, would you mind tuning the radio to WTOP?"

"What a scumbag Kwame Diggs is," Iggy Rock was saying. "How *dare* he play the race card? I'm gonna give credit where credit is due here and say *The Providence Dispatch* did a great job exposing Diggs for the lying pervert that he truly is.

"But before any of you start regretting that you canceled your subscriptions, there's something you need to know. According to my sources, the newspaper is continuing its investigation into the drug and assault charges that have kept Diggs behind bars. How the *Dispatch* could persist in this after what it published Sunday is beyond me. I have again invited Ed Lomax, the paper's managing editor, to come on this show and explain, but once again he has refused to face our questions.

"The phone board is all lit up, so let's take some calls. Marcie from Johnston, you are on the air."

"Hi, Iggy. Longtime listener, first-time caller. I just want to say that the editors and reporters at the *Dispatch* are a bunch of commie nigger lovers who —"

"Marcie from Johnston, you are *off* the air. Let's not have any more of that, people. Kwame Diggs killed because he is a vicious sexual predator. The fact that he's black had nothing to do with it, okay? If you want to know the truth, most serial killers are white. Paulie from Pawtucket, you are on the air."

"Good morning, Iggy. What the hell is . . ."

52

"Okay, let's try it this way," Mason said. "I'll tell you what I already know, and you straighten me out if you think I've got something wrong."

"I'm listening," Paul Delvecchio said.

"On the morning of March thirteen, 2005, you were among a group of guards hanging out in the Supermax break room. Bob Araujo, Chuckie Shaad, Ty Robinson, Frank Horrocks, and maybe one or two others. Most of them were drinking coffee and making small talk. A couple of them were playing cards."

"I'm supposed to remember where I was seven years ago?"

"You'll remember this, all right," Mason said. "It was the morning after Araujo was supposedly assaulted by Kwame Diggs, and he was telling everybody who'd listen what really happened."

"And what was that?" Delvecchio asked.

He took a sip of his coffee and sank his teeth into a leaking jelly doughnut.

"The way Araujo told it, he faked the assault charge on Warden Matos's orders so they'd have an excuse to keep Diggs locked up. The other guards gave Araujo the hero treatment, shaking his hand and slapping him on the back."

"Not the way *I* remember it," Delvecchio said.

"So you *do* recall that morning."

The prison guard slammed his fist on the counter.

"Here's what *you* better remember, asshole. You better remember what happened to your fucking car. You know what kind of people drive a Prius? Tree huggers, socialists, and faggots. I got you pegged as all three. Keep this up and it won't be your windshield that gets busted next time. It'll be your fuckin' skull."

With that, Delvecchio got up and stomped out of Dunkin' Donuts.

53

Diggs put the visitors' room phone to his ear and scowled.

"What the fuck you doin' to me, cuz? Why'd you put all that shit in the paper?"

"You get the paper in here?"

"The prison library gets it, yeah."

"I put in all the things you told me, Kwame."

"Yeah, but you also put in a bunch of crap that made me look like a liar."

"Some of the things you told me weren't true."

"You played me, cuz. When I get out of here, I'm gonna fuckin' *wreck* you."

"That so?"

"Count on it," he said, and slammed his cuffed hands against the Plexiglas.

Two guards roused themselves from the wall they'd been leaning on, gunfighter-strutted up to Diggs, and grabbed him roughly by the shoulders.

"Calm the fuck down, asshole," Mason heard one of them yell, the words faint through the thick Plexiglas. The guards then talked quietly to Diggs for a few seconds. When the tension fell from his shoulders, they sauntered back to their post along the wall. But they kept their eyes locked on him.

"Tell me something, Kwame," Mason said. "Do you think I'm going to keep looking into the charges against you if you threaten me like that?"

Diggs didn't speak.

"How do you suppose you're going to get out of here without my help?"

"Sheee-it. You ain't been any help so far."

"I've found out enough to convince me that you were framed on the drug and assault charges, Kwame. I just don't have enough evidence to prove it yet."

"Of course I was framed. Did you see the fuckin' video?"

"Video? What video?"

"Exactly, cuz."

"What are you trying to tell me?"

"Everything that happens in here is on video. There's cameras all over the fuckin' place. So how come they didn't show no video of me whacking out guards at my trials, huh? Can you explain *that*?"

■ ■ ■ ■

That evening, as Mason headed home for the night, his newly repaired Prius was running rough. As he dipped off the Claiborne Pell Bridge and rolled into Newport, flames shot from the hood.

Firemen arrived in minutes and smothered the engine fire with extinguishers. A city cop arranged a tow and gave Mason a lift home.

54

"Bristol Toyota. How may we serve you?"

"Don Sockol, please."

"May I tell him who is calling?"

"Edward Mason."

"One moment, please. . . ."

"Good morning, Edward. How's the Prius treating you?"

"Fine and dandy," Mason lied.

"So how may I help you today?"

"I'm working on another story about Kwame Diggs, and I could use your help again."

"Man, that story in the Sunday paper really tore him a new one," Sockol said.

"It did," Mason said.

"Was the information I sent you any help?"

"It sure was. Thanks so much."

"That's great. But what's this I been hearing about the *Dispatch* trying to get Diggs sprung?"

"Don't believe everything you hear on the radio," Mason said. "That's just Iggy Rock trying to stir up trouble."

"That's what I figured. I gotta tell you, though. A lot of the guards believe that shit. Some of them are pretty worked up about it, so you better watch your back."

"Thanks. I will."

"So what do you need now?"

"Is it true that everything that happens in Supermax is caught on surveillance cameras?"

"Not everything, no."

"What's covered?"

"The corridors, the exercise yard, the visitors' room . . . all the common areas. No cameras in the cells, though. Got to give the skels their privacy."

"The guards' break room?"

"No."

"How long do they keep the tapes?"

"There aren't any tapes. It's all digital nowadays. The video files are stored on hard drives. We're supposed to delete the old stuff every five years, but we don't always get around to it, to tell you the truth."

"Do you have access to the files?"

"Yeah. The hard drives are kept in my office."

Careful, Mason told himself. If Sockol

figures out what you're after, you're sunk.

"I don't suppose there's any interesting video of Diggs."

"Actually, there is, although it's not from the surveillance cameras. Last summer, the warden brought in some lame poet from Providence College to run a writing workshop. The idea was to help the inmates get in touch with their feelings or some such bullshit. We record all our education programs, so we've got video and sound of the whole thing."

"Diggs was there?"

"Yeah. The inmates were supposed to write poems and read them out loud. Most of them just sat on their asses for an hour and laughed at the guy, but a few of them actually wrote something."

"Including Diggs?"

"Uh-huh. The other guys wrote about their mothers or their dogs or how much they missed their kids. But Diggs? He wrote some rap lyrics about fucking blondes."

"No kidding?"

"Yeah. Afterwards, all the guards were talking about it, so I cued the video in my office and watched it. Diggs was doing this bouncy little dance while he rapped about all the places he wanted to put his dick. Creepy as all hell."

"Any chance *I* could see that video?"

"Uh . . . you can't come to my office to watch it. That would get me in a world of trouble."

"I understand," Mason said, making his voice thick with disappointment. Don't suggest the solution, he thought to himself. Let Sockol work it out.

The Corrections Department clerk thought it over, then said, "What if I made you a copy?"

"Could you? That would be great."

"I could download it onto a portable hard drive and drop it in the mail. Long as you don't tell anybody how you got it."

"I promise."

"Anything else you need?"

"There is. A source tells me there might be surveillance footage of Diggs acting freaky a couple of other times."

"Where and when?"

"March twelve, 2005, and October twenty of last year," Mason said. "Both times as he was being led from his cell to the exercise yard."

"Prisoners can be taken to the yard any time between eight A.M. and four P.M. Can you narrow down the time any?"

Mason could. Testimony at the two assault trials had established the exact times of both alleged attacks. But what he said was, "Sorry, but I can't." The less Sockol knew, the better.

"Okay, then," Sockol said. "Diggs's cell is about sixty yards or so from the yard, so that means video from a half-dozen cameras. With eight hours of video from each camera, that's . . . uh . . . forty-eight hours for each day. No way I've got time to wade through all that. I'll have to download it all for you if that's okay."

"That would be fine."

"The stuff from 2005 might have been deleted, but I'll look to be sure. The other date is no problem. Just give me a day or two, okay?"

In 1989, *The New Yorker* published "The Journalist and the Murderer," a two-part series by Janet Malcolm. In it, the author painted a cynical portrait of the journalist. "He is a kind of confidence man," she wrote, "preying on people's vanity, ignorance, or loneliness, gaining their trust, and betraying them without remorse."

Four years ago, Mason's journalism ethics professor at Columbia had made the infamous article required reading, and it ignited a spirited in-class debate. Mason disputed Malcolm's point, arguing that it probably said more about the kind of journalist *she* was than it did about journalists in general. But now, he found himself rethinking his position.

Malcolm was dead-on, he decided. Except for one thing. She got the lack of remorse part wrong.

"Edward Mason, *Providence Dispatch.*"

"Hello, Mr. Mason. This is Detective Sergeant Christopher Sullivan of the Newport PD."

"Yes?"

"Can you tell me, sir, if you have been having trouble with anyone? Have you received threats of any kind?"

"Can you tell me why you are asking?"

"After you answer my question."

"Some people are unhappy about a story I've been working on for the *Dispatch.*"

"What kind of story?"

"One involving the State Department of Corrections."

"Can you be more specific?"

"I'd rather not do that on the telephone."

"I see. Can you tell me, then, how this unhappiness has been expressed?"

"I've received several threatening notes in the mail, a couple of messages were left on my Prius, and the car was vandalized twice in the state prison parking lot."

"I see. Did you file police reports about the vandalism?"

"I did, with the Cranston police."

"And do you still have the threatening messages?"

"I still have the ones that came in the mail. The others were in the form of alphabet refrigerator magnets placed on my car door, but I took photos of them with my phone."

"Could you stop by and bring the letters and the photos with you?"

"Certainly. Can you tell me what this is about now?"

"Sir, your car fire earlier this week was not an accident. Someone tampered with the vehicle."

"Tampered how?"

"Someone poured nitromethane into your gas tank."

"Nitro-*what*?"

"Nitromethane. It's an organic compound commonly used in industrial applications."

"What kind of applications?"

"The way it was explained to me, it's used in the manufacture of pesticides, explosives, and coatings, and is also widely used as a cleaning solvent."

"What did it do to my car?"

"Again, as it was explained to me, the

compound makes an automobile engine run very hot. As you probably know, sir, your Prius runs on electric power only until it reaches forty miles per hour. At higher speeds, the gasoline engine kicks in."

"And when it did, it ran so hot that it caught fire?"

"That is correct."

"What time do you get in tomorrow morning, Detective?"

"I'll be at my desk by eight."

"I'll see you then."

"Fine. And in the meantime, sir, I suggest that you take precautions."

Ten minutes after Mason signed off, the phone rang again. This time it was his insurance agent calling to tell him that his automobile policy had been canceled. Great. To get back on the road, he was going to have to find an insurer with a high-risk pool and pay three times the normal rate.

55

"What's in the package, Thanks–Dad?" Mulligan asked.

"Some video."

"Of what?"

"Of Diggs inside Supermax."

"*What?* How the hell did you get that?"

"A source."

"What's on it?"

"Come along," Mason said, "and we'll have a look."

Three small conference rooms, each equipped with a computer, were located just off the main newsroom. The reporters entered one of them, and Mason ripped open the package. Inside was a portable hard drive. Mason fired up the computer, connected the hard drive, and found seven video files. One was dated August 5, 2011, the date of the prison poetry workshop. The other six were dated October 20, 2011, the day Diggs allegedly assaulted a guard named

Joseph Galloway. There was nothing from the date of the alleged assault in 2005. Apparently, that video had been deleted from the Corrections Department's records.

Mason opened the August file first and discovered that it was in color and included audio.

A dozen prisoners sat in molded plastic chairs arranged in a half circle. Mason pointed his finger at the screen, indicating where Diggs slouched. His long legs stretched out in front of him, and his eyes were closed.

The speaker was prattling about how the prisoners could explore their deepest feelings through poetry. All they had to do, he said, was discover something he called "your second throat."

"Quite true," Mason said. Mulligan didn't say anything. To him, it sounded like psychobabble. As the poet droned on, Diggs never stirred. His eyes remained closed.

After five minutes of this, Mason hit the fast-forward button, stopping several times to check on Diggs. Each time he was the same. There was no hint that he was paying attention.

Mason clicked the fast-forward button again, slowing the video when the poet distributed notebooks and urged the prisoners to write. Most ignored him, but a few started scribbling. Diggs appeared to be asleep.

Fast-forwarding again, Mason found the part where the first prisoner, a skinny dude with a shaved skull and a swastika neck tattoo, rose to read his poem to the group.

My moms, she was an angel. I was her baby boy.
She loved me unconditionally. She thought I'd bring her joy.
But I became a gangster, seduced by the streets.
Now I cool my heels in Supermax
While my moms sits home and weeps.

"Good Christ!" Mulligan said. "I can't take much of this."

"Look at Diggs," Mason said. The big man was hunched over a pad of paper now, scribbling furiously.

Mason hit the fast-forward button again, stopping just as Diggs pulled himself to his feet.

"Can a brother get a beat?" he said.

Half the prisoners responded, and Diggs bounced to the rhythm of their beatboxing.

Some blondes they come from bottles.

Some come from DNA.
But you can't tell the difference till you tear their clothes away.
The fake ones aren't so bad, 'cause they still have all the parts.
They get wet in the right places, and they know the loving arts.
But real blondes are the best of all. Their pubes are smooth as silk.
I love it when they suck my dick and drink my manly milk.

As Diggs continued to recite, the beatboxing dribbled to a halt.

I like 'em young and tender, I like 'em with long legs.
I like 'em when they spread real wide. I love it when they begs.
Blondes hunger for the black man, their most forbidden fruit.
They cry like they don't want it, but they shiver when I shoot.
Inside I only dream of them, lying on my bunk.
But when I'm free, I'll fuck them all and fill them full of spunk.

As Diggs returned to his seat, his fellow inmates stared at him in stunned silence.

"Loved the beat, hated the lyrics," Mulligan said. "I give it a six out of ten."

"Why would he do that?" Mason said. "Didn't he know how it would look?"

"He probably never thought it would go public," Mulligan said. "Or more likely, he didn't think at all."

"It's *not* going public," Mason said. "I mean, we'd never post something like this on our Web site, would we?"

"Probably not," Mulligan said. "But if the wrong person gets a hold of this, it'll get ten million hits on YouTube."

"Let's check the rest of the files," Mason said, opening the first one. It was a standard surveillance video. Black-and-white, no audio.

An empty corridor lined with cells appeared on the computer screen. The light was dim. Nothing stirred. The time-and-date stamp in the lower right corner said, "October 20, 2011, 12:01 A.M."

"Isn't that the day Diggs allegedly assaulted Galloway?" Mulligan asked.

"It is," Mason said. "According to court testimony, the assault occurred just after two P.M." The reporters sat in silence as Mason fast-forwarded fourteen hours.

Three guards strutted down the corridor and approached one of the cells.

"Recognize them?" Mulligan asked.

"The one with the Schwarzenegger muscles is Galloway. The tall, lean one is Quinn. And of course you know Pugliese."

A pair of big hands reached through a slot in the cell door, and Galloway slapped handcuffs on them. Then the door slid open, and Diggs lumbered out. Galloway scowled and appeared to say something. Diggs responded with a grin.

"Wish we could hear what they're saying," Mason said.

The guards led Diggs down the corridor beyond the range of the camera.

Mason clicked the video off, opened the next file, and fast-forwarded to two P.M. again. A few seconds later, Diggs and the guards appeared, walking calmly down the corridor and out of sight. Mason repeated the process with the remaining four files until Diggs and his escort reached the exit to the exercise yard. There, Galloway uncuffed him. Then he and Quinn roughly shoved him out of sight through the door.

"Holy shit," Mulligan said.

"This proves the assault never happened," Mason said.

"That's what I meant by 'Holy shit.' I wonder why nobody ever deleted this."

"They probably just forgot about it," Mason said. "They had no reason to think it would get out."

"Is there any video from the 2005 assault?" Mulligan asked.

"Apparently not. My source told me they usually delete the video files after five years."

"Doesn't really matter," Mulligan said. "You've made your case."

"I'm going to look at all the rest of the video," Mason said. "Just to make sure there isn't anything else interesting on it. After that, I'll write my story."

"It might be better if you didn't."

"I disagree."

"Think Lomax will publish it?"

"We'll know soon enough."

56

"Aw, shit," Lomax said.

"Yeah," Mulligan said.

"Any chance the kid got it wrong?"

"No. He's done a brilliant job on this."

Lomax removed his glasses and rubbed his eyes with the back of his hand.

"Guess I've got a big decision to make."

"You do."

"If I kill the story, the publisher might back me up," Lomax said. "He's never second-guessed me before, so I doubt he'll start now. Not even for his son."

"So kill it," Mulligan said.

"Maybe."

"*Maybe?* Jesus. You want to be responsible for Diggs getting out?"

"Of course not. But I'm not keen on being responsible for covering up perjury and obstruction of justice, either."

Mulligan took a deep breath and slowly let it out through his nose.

"Yeah," he said. "I get what you're going through. As a journalist, your gut tells you to publish. But as a husband and father . . . I'm just glad I'm not the one who has to make the call. So what are you going to do?"

"First I'm going to read the story. Then I'm going to look at the video myself and make Mason show me all of his notes. After that, we'll see. If I don't kill it, I'll have to walk it upstairs and talk things over with the old man. This one is above my pay grade. There's a lot at stake here, Mulligan. If we publish, Iggy Rock will have a field day, we'll lose a few thousand more subscribers, and we'll probably have a horde of angry protesters at our door."

They looked at each other for a moment.

"Any chance you're going to bail me out?" Lomax asked. "What's the word on those DNA tests you've been waiting for?"

"Nothing yet," Mulligan said, "but it shouldn't be long now."

57

Two days later, Mulligan checked his phone messages and found one from Jennings asking him to call right away.

"Hi, Andy. What's up?"

"I just heard from Chief Hernandez, and the news ain't good. The crime lab couldn't find any viable DNA."

"Aw, crap."

"All the samples were either contaminated or degraded because of improper storage."

"So that's it, then," Mulligan said. "We've got no way to connect Diggs to the attack on Susan Ashcroft."

" 'Fraid so."

"I've got some bad news, too."

"What's that?"

"At least one of the assault charges against Diggs was definitely faked, and there's a chance the news is gonna go public soon."

"Jesus!"

"Yeah."

"Goddamn ACLU! I *hate* those bastards."

"Yeah . . . about that . . . I haven't been entirely straight with you."

"What are you talking about?"

"It's not the ACLU that's been digging into it," Mulligan said. "It's another *Dispatch* reporter."

"Iggy Rock was telling the *truth*?"

"There's a first time for everything," Mulligan said, and then gave Jennings the rest of it.

"Why didn't you tell me this before?"

"I was hoping the kid would flame out, so I've been trying to keep a lid on it."

"The *Dispatch* is gonna *publish* this shit?"

"I don't know. The brass hasn't made up its mind yet."

"We've gotta do something," Jennings said.

"Yeah, but what?"

"No fuckin' idea. Why don't you come on over tonight and we'll brainstorm over a few brews."

Jennings answered the door with a Narragansett in each hand.

"Evenin', Mulligan. Didn't know you were bringing a date."

"Andy, this is Gloria Costa, a photographer at the *Dispatch.* She's been helping me out on the Diggs story."

"What do we need a photographer for?"

"She's not here to take pictures, Andy. She's damned smart, and she knows the story inside and out."

"Humph," Jennings said. He handed each of his guests a brew, told them to make themselves at home, and trudged into the kitchen for another beer.

"Where's Mary?" Mulligan called to him.

"I'm right here," she said, walking in from the kitchen with a plate of oatmeal cookies. She placed it on the coffee table beside her husband's murder books.

"Is it really true?" she asked. "Are they going to have to let Diggs out?"

She was still bending over the table, not letting go of the plate of cookies. She was holding her breath.

"It's possible," Mulligan said.

She stood slowly and said, almost to herself, "He killed my twin sister."

"I know."

"What if he comes after me?"

"Then I'll shoot him dead," Jennings said as he walked back into the living room. "I'll fill him full of lead and dance on his fucking corpse."

"Andy, you know I don't like that kind of talk," she said. "But I know I can count on my big handsome lug to keep me safe." She turned and hugged him hard and quick. "I'll leave the three of you alone now. What you'll be talking about is something I don't want to hear."

After she left, Jennings sat on the sofa between the two journalists. Together they paged slowly through the detective's murder books on the Medeiros and Stuart cases, looking for something, anything, they might have overlooked. It was an hour before any of them spoke.

"You know what's bothering me?" Gloria finally said.

"What?" the men said in unison.

"The gap."

"What gap?" Jennings asked.

"The two years between the Medeiros and Stuart murders."

"That bothers you why?" Mulligan asked.

"We think he attacked Ashcroft first, right?"

"We're sure of it," Jennings said. "Just can't prove it."

"And that happened just a year before he killed Becky Medeiros, right?"

"That's right."

"Don't serial killers usually escalate?" Gloria asked.

"They do," Jennings said.

"So why did Diggs wait so long before his second attack?"

"I've always wondered the same thing," Jennings said.

"What I'm thinking," Gloria said, "is that maybe he didn't."

58

"Are the attorneys present?" Judge Needham asked.

"Felicia Freyer representing Kwame Diggs, Your Honor."

"Attorney General Malcolm Roberts for the State, Your Honor."

"Then let's proceed. Miss Freyer, I bclieve you have a motion."

"I do, Your Honor. I respectfully ask that this hearing be closed to the press on the grounds that —"

"Did I miss some big news this morning, Miss Freyer?"

"Your Honor?"

"Has the First Amendment been repealed?"

"No, Your Honor."

"Then your motion is denied."

"I would appreciate a chance to argue it, Your Honor."

"That would be a waste of the court's

time, Miss Freyer."

"Then I would ask at least that the television pool camera be removed."

"On what grounds?"

"As Your Honor is aware, this matter is highly controversial. The presence of cameras can only serve to further inflame the public, to the detriment of my client."

"Miss Freyer," the judge said, making the name sound like something he'd found stuck to the bottom of his shoe, "are you concerned that pretrial publicity could prejudice the jury pool?"

Freyer stood there, speechless.

"Perhaps I should remind you that this is not a trial and that there will be no jury."

"I understand that, Your Honor, but —"

Needham cut her off in midsentence.

"This issue will be decided by the presiding judge, Miss Freyer. Are you suggesting that the presence of cameras will somehow prejudice my ruling?"

"Certainly not, Your Honor," Freyer fibbed. The diminutive judge was notorious for playing to the cameras.

"Well then, this motion is also denied. Do you have anything further?"

"Not at this time, Your Honor."

"Very well. Mr. Roberts, you may proceed."

The attorney general rose to address the court: "Your Honor, the People of Rhode Island come before you to request that Kwame Diggs, currently an inmate in the High Security Center of the State Department of Corrections, be ordered to submit to a psychiatric evaluation to determine whether —"

"I have read your petition and supporting briefs, Mr. Roberts," the judge said. He turned from the attorney general and faced the camera. "Do you have anything new to add, or are you also determined to waste the court's time?"

"Nothing further, Your Honor," Robert said, and sat back down.

"Miss Freyer?"

"Yes, Your Honor?"

"I have read your submission as well. Do *you* have anything to add?"

"I do, Your Honor. I would ask that my client be allowed to address the court on this matter."

"For what purpose, Miss Freyer?"

"Surely Your Honor will want the opportunity to hear from Mr. Diggs himself before deciding whether the State's order should be granted."

"Miss Freyer, are you under the misapprehension that I have a degree in psychiatry?"

"No, Your Honor."

"Psychology, perhaps?"

"Not that I am aware of, Your Honor."

"So I ask you again. What purpose would your request serve?"

"I withdraw it, Your Honor."

Needham turned again to the cameras.

"You will have my ruling by early next week. Court is adjourned."

59

The publisher's fourth-floor corner office was paneled in solid Ecuadorian mahogany. A bank of high windows looked out over a parking lot, a McDonald's, and a neon-splashed strip club called the Sportsman's Inn. The office was furnished with calfskin chairs and an antique cherry desk big enough to hold a map of Rhode Island its actual size. In the center of the desk, a video was playing on a twenty-seven-inch Apple monitor.

"Okay, Ed," the publisher said. "Turn that contraption off. I've seen enough."

"So what do you think?" Lomax asked.

"I think my son is turning into a damn fine newsman."

"Yes, sir. He surely is."

The old man opened his humidor, drew out two fifty-five-dollar Opus X cigars, clipped the ends, and handed one to Lomax. He set fire to his with a gold S. T. Dupont butane lighter and leaned over to give his managing editor a light. Then he rose from his desk chair, crossed an expanse of Persian rug, and stared out the window. For a long minute, he smoked in silence while red and blue lights from the strip club licked his face clean. With his back still to Lomax, he finally spoke.

"I need your best judgment on this, Ed."

"Well," Lomax said, "it's a tough call."

"That's what I pay you for, Ed. To make the tough ones."

Lomax drew hard on his cigar and blew a slipstream across the desk.

"It's an important story, sir, but publishing it will have serious consequences."

The old man spun on his heels and thrust a bony finger at Lomax.

"Don't tell me what I already know. Tell me why you believe we should run this."

"Sir?"

"I know you think we should, Ed. Otherwise you would have killed it already, and we wouldn't be having this conversation."

Lomax dragged himself up from the plush leather visitor's chair and joined his boss at the windows.

"Here's how I see it," he said. "If we suppress a story about perjury and obstruction of justice, the First Amendment purists on the staff will be outraged. One of them will leak it, and we'll be crucified in the *Columbia Journalism Review* and every journalism blog on the Internet. But if we run the story and it leads to Diggs's release, the criticism will be far worse. More readers will cancel their subscriptions, and we'll probably lose some advertisers to boot."

"And if Diggs gets out and kills somebody else?" the old man said.

"We'll have a hard time living with ourselves."

"What's your bottom line, Ed?"

They both puffed again, blue cigar smoke mingling in front of their faces.

"For a hundred and fifty years, the *Dispatch* has been fearless in its pursuit of official corruption," Lomax said. "Sometimes our stories have been applauded. Sometimes they've been met with howls. But we have never given in to pressure from readers or advertisers. We've always given the public the facts and let the chips fall where they may."

"Things are different, now, Ed. The paper is in more financial trouble than even you know. The board is increasingly apprehensive about the losses. It has directed me to put the *Dispatch* up for sale."

"I see."

"Our recent circulation losses have already made several potential buyers shy away," the old man said. "We can't afford to lose any more readers."

"I understand," Lomax said. "Shall I kill the story, then?"

The old man blew three perfect smoke rings.

"Walk with me," he said.

They stepped out of the office and strolled down a corridor lined with framed photographs of historic *Dispatch* front pages: The assassination of Abraham Lincoln. The annihilation of Custer's Seventh Cavalry. The Battle of the Somme. The 1929 stock market crash. Pearl Harbor. The Kennedy assassination. The moon landing. The *Challenger* explosion. The election of the first black president.

The publisher opened the door to the boardroom and snapped on the lights, illuminating a meeting table surrounded by two dozen antique leather chairs. The table was big enough to land a Boeing 747. On one wall, a huge glass case was crammed with plaques, medals, and trophies.

"See that medal right there?" the old man said. "It's the Pulitzer Prize George Boyle won in 1919 for exposing corrupt military contractors during World War One. It was just the third year the Pulitzer was awarded. That one up there? It's the Pulitzer Mulligan won twelve years ago for blowing the lid off bribery in the state court system. That's the last Pulitzer Prize the paper won. Probably the last we ever will win."

They smoked in silence and peered into the case, their eyes moving across three more Pulitzer medals and scores of plaques, trophies, and framed certificates for excellence in feature writing, beat reporting, hard news coverage, photography, and investigative reporting. Polk, Hillman, Livingston, National Headliner, Overseas Press Club, Ernie Pyle, and Robert F. Kennedy Awards. Goldsmith Prizes. Batten Medals . . .

"A grand legacy," Lomax said.

"And a lot to live up to," the old man said. "If *The Providence Dispatch* is to pass into history, I will not have it cowardly slink into the darkness. Run that baby, Ed. Page one, with a second-coming headline."

"Yes, sir. I'll have it ready to go for Sunday."

"Make it a week from Sunday," the publisher said. "I've got some arrangements to make first."

"Yes, sir."

"And, Ed? Be sure to post the videos on our Web site."

"All of them, sir?"

"All of them. The one with Diggs's poem should be accompanied by a sensitive-content warning. I trust you to handle that with the appropriate discretion."

July 2012

Freedom is tantalizingly close now. He stares at the bars of his prison cell and imagines them dissolving, sees himself strutting out of the prison gate. No cuffs binding his hands. No leg chains hobbling his gait.

He pictures himself shopping for his murder kit. Rubber gloves. A glass cutter. Condoms. A Buck knife. In his mind, he caresses each of the items, then carefully packs them in a small black valise.

His lawyer says he shouldn't get his hopes too high. Legal hurdles remain. A judge might order him to take a psychiatric evaluation. But he beat the headshrinkers once before. He can do it again. The hot little ho is probably screwing that reporter right now. He imagines catching them in the act, a knife singing in his hand.

He thinks about the other blessings freedom could bring. Finding Susan Ashcroft and finishing the job. Plunging his blade into Connie Stuart's twin sister, a thrilling way to reenact his finest moment. Walking down a city sidewalk stinking with blondes, picking one out, and following her home. So many honey-haired bitches to choose from.

His thoughts drift to the one-eyed photographer, the way she shivered when she took his picture last fall. He knows her name. It was right there, under the photo in the newspaper he read in the prison library. Gloria Costa.

He wonders if she can still weep out of both eyes.

60

Mulligan worked the phones all morning, trying to flesh out an advance about Judge Needham's pending ruling on a psychiatric evaluation for Diggs.

The sheriff's department confirmed that in the last five days, sixteen bomb threats had been called in to the Providence Superior Court building. Felicia Freyer reported that someone had slashed the tires on her Acura MDX. And Needham's secretary said the judge had received thousands of e-mails and a bulk mail bag full of letters in the last week. Some of them urged the judge to "do the right thing." Others threatened him with dismemberment or death if he didn't.

No, the secretary hadn't sorted through them all. No, she couldn't read any of the letters or e-mails to Mulligan. She had turned them all over to the police, who had asked her not to release anything to the press for fear that publicity would "bring more squirrels out of the woodwork." That was a bizarre way to put it, but Mulligan decided to use the quote. He figured readers would know exactly what she meant.

The Boston Globe, The New York Times, The Associated Press, and four national TV news organizations were planning coverage of Needham's ruling, and both Greta Van Susteren and Nancy Grace, who Mulligan doubted had ever even *been* to Rhode Island, were already tweeting about the case.

A "Keep Kwame Diggs Locked Up" Facebook page now had 53,612 followers — not nearly as many as the Texas hold 'em poker, *Family Guy,* or Vin Diesel fan pages, but still impressive.

Two years ago, Lomax had ordered the whole news staff to sign up with Facebook and Twitter to keep track of stuff like that. Mulligan had reluctantly complied, but his Facebook profile was nearly devoid of personal information. Under Religion, he had typed, "None of your business." Under Politics, he had listed, "Disgusted." And under Favorite Quotes, he'd posted: " 'Fuck this yuppie journalism shit' — the late Will McDonough, a reporter's reporter." He'd left everything else blank.

Because he'd never uploaded a profile picture, and never would, its place was held by a head-and-shoulders silhouette that reminded him of a pistol-range target. He'd never once posted a message on either Twitter or Facebook; and when others — mostly old acquaintances he hadn't missed, old girlfriends he'd been glad to be rid of, and people he'd never met — tried to "friend" him, he always clicked the "not now" button because there wasn't one that said "fuck off."

Mulligan had nearly finished writing the advance when a courthouse tipster phoned with the perfect tidbit for a kicker. Judge Needham had already made his decision but was dithering with the draft because he was waiting for a custom-made, boy's-size judicial robe — one with stylish yellow lightning bolts on the sleeves — to be shipped from Academic Apparel in Chatsworth, California.

The judge wanted to look pretty for the camera.

Nancy Grace and Greta Van Susteren had both been leaked advance word of Judge Needham's ruling — or so they claimed. Grace, the CNN court reporter and failed *Dancing with the Stars* contestant, was reporting that Needham had approved the state's request and that Diggs would be examined by a committee of experts at the

Harvard University Department of Psychiatry. Van Susteren, the Fox News harpy, was reporting that Needham had denied the state's request, and she was howling for his removal, branding him "a liberal activist judge who is way out of the mainstream."

Mulligan figured both of them were talking out of their asses.

On Thursday morning, the protesters on the Superior Court building steps numbered three hundred by Mulligan's rough count. He bobbed and weaved through them, made his way to Needham's third-floor courtroom, and settled into a seat in the jury box between a reporter for the *National Law Journal* and a stringer for *The New York Times.*

Needham's new robe was a wonder to behold, the lightning bolts on the sleeves reminding Mulligan of the design on the San Diego Chargers' football helmets. The judge again cautioned the packed benches that he would not tolerate any outbursts, swiveled on his booster seat to face the TV camera, and read from his decision.

"In the matter of *The State of Rhode Island and Providence Plantations versus Kwame Diggs . . .*"

He began by noting that in 1994, Diggs

had been examined by a psychiatrist and found competent to stand trial on five counts of first-degree murder.

"During his eighteen years of incarceration," the judge said, "Mr. Diggs has never been diagnosed as mentally ill by the prison medical staff, and he has received no psychiatric treatment. It is conceivable, however, that he could be suffering from a mental illness that the Corrections Department negligently failed to diagnose despite having many years in which to do so.

"But if that is the case, in what way is it relevant to the issue at hand? The State has offered no evidence that the mentally ill are more dangerous, per se, than other members of the public. In point of fact, they are not. Statistics show that as a group, they are much more likely to be victims of violent crimes than to commit them.

"Given these facts, which are not in dispute, it is reasonable to conclude that the State's insistence on a psychiatric examination at this time is nothing more than subterfuge to deprive Mr. Diggs of his civil liberties."

Needham then digressed to review the shameful history of involuntary psychiatric commitments in the United States. For the best part of two centuries, he said, thousands of citizens who had committed no crimes were declared "deviant," "socially aberrant," or "morally insane" and locked away in lunatic asylums, often for life. Their so-called deviant behaviors, he explained, had included masturbation, extramarital sex, homosexuality, and denying the existence of God.

"In some cases," he said, "husbands had their wives involuntarily committed just to get rid of them."

He then turned to recent reports that some political dissidents in China had been declared "politically insane," forced into psychiatric hospitals, and subjected to electroshock therapy.

"Such abuses should offend the sensibilities of every civilized person," the judge said. "And yet now, the attorney general of the state of Rhode Island seeks to have Kwame Diggs declared mentally ill on the grounds that he *might* pose a danger to others at some indeterminate date in the future."

Mulligan stole a glance at Attorney General Roberts, who was squirming in his chair at the defense table.

"The court is cognizant of what is at stake in this case," the judge said. "It is common knowledge that both Attorney Freyer and

The Providence Dispatch have been making inquiries about the drug and assault convictions that have kept Mr. Diggs incarcerated since his original sentence expired in 2001. The prospect that Mr. Diggs could be released as a result of these inquiries has engendered widespread fears — fears that have been stoked by an irresponsible member of the media.

"Of course, there is no guarantee that *any* prisoner will become a law-abiding citizen upon release. The recidivism rate is sixty percent. If the legal standard was a guarantee, we would never release anyone. It is worth noting, however, that the recidivism rate for murder is less than two percent within three years of release.

"Nevertheless, the murders for which Mr. Diggs was originally incarcerated were particularly heinous and brutal. The people of the state of Rhode Island are entitled to receive some degree of assurance that he would not pose an intolerable threat to public safety if he were ever to be released from state custody.

"The bar the State must meet in cases such as this has been set high. According to a large body of case law, a finding that Mr. Diggs is mentally ill would not be enough to justify continuing his confinement. Nor would a finding that he might pose a danger at some point in the future be sufficient. Rather, the State can commit Mr. Diggs to a secure psychiatric facility against his will only if it presents clear and convincing evidence that his release would pose an imminent threat to himself or others.

"Imminent does not mean three years from now," the judge said. "It does not mean six months from now. It means that Mr. Diggs must be declared so deranged and violent that he would pose a mortal threat to society on the day that he steps out of the prison gates.

"To determine whether Mr. Diggs would, in fact, pose such a threat, the court hereby orders him to submit to a psychiatric evaluation by a qualified professional to be selected by the State of Rhode Island.

"Court is adjourned."

As the judge scrambled down from his booster seat, spectators filed out. Mulligan made his way over to the prosecution table and tapped the attorney general on the shoulder.

"Is it true that you plan to have Diggs examined by Harvard psychiatrists?" he asked.

"No," Roberts said.

"Who will be performing the examination?"

"We have yet to determine that."

Back in the newsroom, Mulligan called the director of Eleanor Slater Hospital, the state mental hospital in Cranston; the chief psychiatrist at Butler Hospital, a private mental hospital in Providence; the head of the Department of Psychiatry at Rhode Island Hospital in Providence; and the chairman of the Department of Psychiatry and Human Behavior at Brown University. All four said they had been contacted by Roberts's office. All four said Roberts was shopping for a psychiatrist who would not be reluctant to authorize an involuntary commitment.

All four wished him good luck with that.

61

"Believe me," Jennings said, "after we arrested Diggs for the Medeiros and Stuart murders, we spent weeks trying to connect him to unsolved crimes. There's nothing there."

"Just in Warwick?" Gloria asked. "What about the rest of the state?"

"He was a kid back then," Mulligan said. "He wasn't even old enough to drive. He couldn't have gone far by himself."

"Maybe he had a friend who took him somewhere," Gloria said.

"The state police gave us a hand looking into that," Jennings said. "They came up dry."

"Did his parents take him out of state for a vacation?" Gloria asked. "Maybe Disney World or something?"

"We asked them about that," Jennings said. "They said they didn't. We asked the neighbors, too. None of them could remember the family being away for any length of time between the two murders."

Jennings walked into his kitchen and came back with three Narragansetts.

"I want to watch Diggs's confession," Gloria said.

"Why?"

"I have my reasons."

"I'm not sure it's something you should see, Gloria," Mulligan said.

She wheeled on him and glared.

"Okay, fine," Mulligan said. "Go ahead and show it to her, Andy."

Jennings turned on the TV and slid the tape into the VCR. Then he and Mulligan took their beers into the backyard to play with Smith and Wesson.

Two hours later, Gloria turned the video off, ejected the tape, and dropped it into her purse. She helped herself to another beer from the refrigerator and went outside to join the men.

"I need to borrow the tape for a few days, Andy."

"What for?"

"I've got an idea."

"Thank you for agreeing to see me again, Mrs. Diggs."

"You're welcome, dear. Can I get you

something?"

"I'm fine, thank you."

"I'm going to have some lemonade. I squeezed it fresh just before you arrived."

"In that case, I'd love a glass."

"Make yourself at home, Gloria. I'll be back in a jiffy."

Gloria sat on the faded pink-and-green floral sofa beside an enormous black-and-white tomcat. The cat was sleeping. Gloria reached down and massaged him behind his ears.

"What's his name?" Gloria asked as Mrs. Diggs returned with two moisture-beaded glasses on a hammered-aluminum tray.

"Justice."

"A fine name," Gloria said as the woman seated herself primly on the other side of the cat.

"On the phone, you said that you have some news for me," the woman said.

"I do," Gloria said. "Mason wanted me to tell you he has found proof that your son was framed for last year's assault charge."

"Thank the Lord!"

"The paper will be running the story soon."

"Does this mean Kwame will be getting out?"

"That will be up to the courts," Gloria

said, "but it *is* possible."

"That would be the answer to all of my prayers," Mrs. Diggs said. "My baby might be coming home." She plucked a tissue from the sleeve of her yellow housedress and dabbed at her tears. "Thank you for coming all the way up here to tell me. You could have just given me the news on the telephone, you know."

"It's not the only reason I came," Gloria said.

"It isn't?"

"No. I wanted to ask if you still think your son is innocent of all those murders."

"Of course I do."

"Even after reading Mason's last story? The one in which Kwame admitted his guilt?"

"Oh, yes. Kwame told me why he had to say that."

"What did he tell you?"

"He said his lawyer and Mr. Mason convinced him that an expression of remorse would help his case, even though he never killed anyone."

"I see. Tell me, Mrs. Diggs. Did you ever see the video of Kwame's original confession to the Warwick police?"

"Heavens, no. Years ago, Kwame's first lawyer, Mr. Haggerty, asked me if I wanted to watch it, but I said no, thank you. Kwame told me how the police beat it out of him. I couldn't never bear to watch my boy being abused. Or listen to those awful lies."

Gloria opened her purse and slid out the videotape.

"I'd like you to watch it now, Mrs. Diggs."

"Whatever for?"

"Because it's important that you do."

"No! I won't. Can't you understand? This is my *son*!"

Gloria rose from the couch and turned on the thirty-two-inch television.

"Stop it! Turn that off right this minute."

Gloria slid the tape into the VCR.

"Nooooo!" Mrs. Diggs howled. "You can't make me do this."

Gloria pushed play.

The woman screamed. She snatched the ceramic elephant with red lips and rouged cheeks from the coffee table and hurled it. It struck the edge of the TV stand and shattered.

The interrogation room appeared on the screen. Two police officers, seen from behind, were seated in metal chairs on one side of a battered metal table that was bolted to the floor. On the other side, a teenage Kwame slouched in a matching chair, his cuffed hands resting on his chest.

He was grinning.

"Get out!" Mrs. Diggs screamed. "Get out of my house and don't ever come back!"

She turned toward the end table and grabbed another elephant.

Gloria bolted for the door. As she pulled it open, she glanced back at the old woman. Mrs. Diggs was rooted beside the snoozing cat, a ceramic elephant in her right fist, her arm cocked. She looked even older now, her eyes leaking and her mouth wide as if she were preparing another scream.

The video continued playing. As Gloria stepped outside and pulled the door closed, she heard Kwame giggle.

62

The type on the printing plates ran upside down and backwards. Once the presses were turned on, the plates would be inked and the images transferred first to the blanket cylinders and then, in mirror image, to the rolls of newsprint coursing through the huge machines.

Lomax had long ago taught himself to read the backwards-flowing type. Just before midnight, he climbed up on a press and squinted at the page-one plate, making sure the last minute fixes he'd sent to the composing room had been made in time for the first-edition press run. Then he returned to the newsroom and checked the final edits on the videos before hitting the computer button to post them, along with Mason's story, on the newspaper's Web site.

The six videos proving that Diggs had assaulted no one on October 20, 2011, had been edited into a single four-minute segment. The ninety-second video of Diggs's poem about blondes, included to supplement the story's assessment of his character, was preceded by a warning about "violent and sexual content."

Earlier that day, Lomax sat down with Mason to explain the decisions he'd made when he edited the story.

"I left in the stuff about how the 2005 assault might have been fabricated," he said. "Your reporting on that isn't conclusive, but it's strong enough to suggest a pattern of official misconduct."

"Good," Mason said.

"But I cut out the stuff about how Diggs may have been framed for the drug charge. You're probably right about that, too, but the reporting isn't strong enough to hold up."

"I disagree," Mason said.

"I don't care what you think," Lomax snapped.

"You're the boss," Mason said.

"Look," Lomax said, softening a little. "Mulligan is right about this. A guard could have circumvented security and brought Diggs the drugs. You know what's at stake here, Mason. We can't afford to get anything wrong. You should be happy we're printing any of this at all."

"Okay."

"And Mason? It would be best if you don't come in tomorrow. A lot of people are going to be furious at us. With your byline on the story, it might not be safe."

At one A.M., Lomax felt the newsroom floor shudder as the presses roared to life. He took the elevator down to the mailroom and snatched one of the first copies to roll off the press. The ink on the seventy-two-point, second-coming headline was still wet.

Diggs Framed on Assault Charge

Beneath the headline, a smaller subhead:

Official Misconduct Could Force Killer's Release

The managing editor tucked the Sunday newspaper under his left arm, made his way to the lobby, and strode out the *Dispatch*'s front door. There, three square-jawed behemoths, each squeezed into a blue uniform that looked a size too small, stood watch. Five more Wackenhut security guards, hired by the publisher for the occasion, were stationed at other points around the building. Each was equipped with pepper spray and a billy club.

Lomax drove home, cracked open a fresh

bottle of Scotch, and sipped from it all night, too agitated to sleep.

63

At seven o'clock on Monday morning, Mulligan grabbed a breakfast sandwich and coffee to go at Charlie's diner and ambled past the old Biltmore Hotel toward the *Dispatch.* When he reached Fountain Street, he saw that the newspaper's windows had been reinforced with masking tape.

He stopped to watch two Providence cops order Iggy Rock to move WTOP's mobile broadcast van from an illegal parking spot across from the newspaper's front door. The van swung around Burnside Park and claimed two metered spaces next to Union Station, a 114-year-old yellow-brick train station that had been converted to house an array of offices, pubs, and retail shops. From there, Iggy had a good view of the street in front of the newspaper.

As Mulligan reached the *Dispatch*'s front door, he saw Gloria trotting down the sidewalk. He waited for her, and together they flashed their newspaper IDs at the Wackenhut guards. They entered the lobby and took the elevator upstairs to the newsroom. There they found Lomax already at his desk, two empty newsroom vending machine coffee cups in front of him and a fresh one in his hand.

"Mulligan," Lomax said, "you'll be writing the protest story. That means monitoring Iggy Rock's broadcast, checking with the circulation department on cancellations, and watching the street activity from the roof."

"The roof? I should be on the street."

"No way. This means you, too, Gloria. You can get all the photos we need from there. The story's not worth either of you getting hurt."

"Okay, boss," she said.

"And keep away from the windows today," Lomax added.

By seven thirty, the telephones in the circulation department were ringing off the hook. Mulligan spent a half hour listening to a dozen clerks try to talk angry readers out of canceling the paper. He asked a few of them what the callers were saying and got a bunch of quotes, most of them unprintable. Then he returned to his desk, snapped on a radio Lomax had placed there, and listened to Iggy rant about the "criminal-loving left-wing extremist *Dispatch.*" The host urged his listeners to mass in front of the paper for the day's protest.

At nine A.M., Mulligan joined Gloria on the flat, tar-paper roof. The crowd on the sidewalk across the street had swelled to about four hundred people, some carrying signs reading "Screw the *Dispatch*" and "Cancel Your Subscription." As the crowd spilled into the roadway, Providence police cruisers blocked off Fountain Street. A hundred yards to the north, thirty cops massed Burnside Park.

By noon, the crowd reached a peak of eight hundred people by Mulligan's estimate. They had been chanting off and on all morning. Sometimes, "Screw the *Dispatch.*" Sometimes, "What are you thinking?" A few tossed eggs that broke against the newspaper's red-brick walls and splattered the uniforms of the Wackenhuts.

"They're so *angry,*" Gloria said.

"And scared," Mulligan said.

The day was hot and humid, the tar paper sticky under Mulligan's Reeboks. Gloria's arms were turning red. She dropped the camera, letting it hang by its strap from her neck, and smeared on some sunscreen.

Shortly after one P.M., two young men

broke from the crowd, crow-hopped toward the building, and threw baseball-size rocks. One caromed off the brick, bounced off the sidewalk, and clipped the thigh of a woman protester. From the roof, Mulligan and Gloria heard her shriek. The other rock must have hit a window, because they heard glass shatter.

Five Wackenhuts bolted from the front steps and charged the rock throwers, two of the guards firing cans of pepper spray and one swinging his billy. The rock throwers fell to the pavement. The crowd surged forward, driving the guards back. The police stood fast in the park, perhaps realizing their intervention would only make things worse. Gloria's shutter clicked, capturing a bird's-eye view.

By two o'clock, storm clouds gathered over the harbor. Gloria looked at the sky and shivered. Thunder boomed, and a bolt of lightning struck the Sportsman's Inn's neon sign. It exploded in a shower of sparks as the rain came down hard and heavy.

Gloria's shoulders shook. She closed her eyes and began her breathing exercise.

"Give me the camera," Mulligan said. "I've got this."

"I'm okay."

"Get your pretty butt inside. The show's

about over for today, anyway."

Gloria surrendered her camera and headed for the stairwell.

Below, the crowd was breaking up. Soon only a dozen stragglers remained, some of them holding umbrellas. Mulligan raised the camera and took a few shots of a nearly deserted street littered with abandoned, rain-soaked protest signs.

64

The city's old retail district, squeezed into four compact blocks between Pine and Fountain Streets, had been crumbling since the 1960s; and after Waterplace Park and the Providence Place Mall were built in the 1990s, all of the action had shifted several blocks north. The early-twentieth-century storefronts that were left behind — the ones that hadn't been torn down to make way for Johnson & Wales University dormitories — now housed discount liquor stores, bucket-of-blood bars, secondhand shops, palm readers, unlicensed massage parlors, or nothing at all. The governor's limousine, a state trooper behind the wheel, idled at the curb in front of Hopes on Washington Street, as out of place as a debutante in a sweatshop.

Mulligan pushed through the front door and found Fiona waiting for him at a table in back. He grabbed a Killian's at the bar, wandered over, and dropped into the seat across from her.

"Thought you weren't supposed to hang out here anymore," he said.

"So my press secretary kept telling me," she said. "According to him, cheap bottle beer, restrooms with condom dispensers on the walls, and a warped linoleum floor that gets mopped once a week are not in keeping with the image a governor needs to cultivate. This morning, I reminded him that, despite our downtown renaissance, our little city-state is still a working-class bastion, and that this is *exactly* the image a governor who wants to be reelected should cultivate."

"You did?"

"Yes. Just before I fired him."

"You fired him for *that*?"

"Not *just* for that, no."

Mulligan whipped out his notepad and said, "Tell me more."

When she finished enumerating her former staffer's deficiencies, Mulligan asked, "Have you named a replacement yet?"

"I was hoping you might take the job."

"Thanks, but no thanks."

"It pays twice what you make now — and a lot more than nothing, which is what you'll be making when the *Dispatch* goes under."

Mulligan held his longneck up to the ceiling light and studied its contents through the amber glass. "If I was going to flack for anybody, it would be you, Fiona, but it's just not in me to tell lies for a living."

"I prefer to think of it as spin."

"Same thing. This why you wanted to see me? To offer me a job?"

"There's more," she said, and slid a nine-by-twelve-inch manila envelope across the table. "I thought you might want a look at the psychiatric evaluation of Diggs before Judge Needham's hearing tomorrow."

"What's the headline?"

"That he's fucking nuts."

"Crazy enough to be involuntarily committed?"

"That depends," Fiona said.

"On what?"

"On what Needham cares about more — the legal niceties or his personal safety."

Reginald Baer, deputy chief of psychiatry at Butler Hospital, sat stiffly in the witness chair, his posture that of a man in need of disk surgery. He wore a navy-and-white polka-dot bow tie and clutched a copy of his report in both hands. Attorney General

Roberts paced in front of him, a duplicate rolled in his left fist.

"If you would," Roberts was saying, "please tell the court where and when you conducted your psychiatric evaluation of Kwame Diggs."

"On July twenty-six, twenty-seven, and thirty at the Corrections Department's High Security Center in Cranston, Rhode Island."

"And how long were these sessions?"

"Approximately two hours each, for a total of six hours."

"Did the inmate cooperate? Did he answer all of your questions willingly?"

"He did."

"Since the court has already had the opportunity to review your written evaluation, I'd like to skip ahead to your conclusions."

"Fine."

"Did you find that Mr. Diggs is suffering from a mental illness?"

"I did."

"And what is your diagnosis?"

"Mr. Diggs suffers from bipolar disorder."

"And how long has he been bipolar?"

"It is impossible to say with certainty, but given the answers he provided about his childhood, the onset was probably in his early teens."

"Please explain in laymen's terms what

bipolar disorder entails."

"Bipolar disorder is often referred to in the vernacular as manic depression. It is characterized by extreme mood swings that range from severe depression to feelings of euphoria. An example many people would be familiar with is John Nash, the Princeton University graduate student portrayed by Russell Crowe in the film *A Beautiful Mind.*"

From his seat in the jury box, set aside once again for press, Mulligan saw Roberts wince. In the film, John Nash was a sympathetic figure.

"Are some bipolar patients more debilitated than others?" Roberts asked.

"Most certainly."

"Please tell us how it has affected Mr. Diggs's ability to function."

"In his case, the condition was accompanied by an inability to develop genuine friendships and intense feelings of resentment toward society. His isolation led him to construct a fantasy world, which, over time, became more real to him than the world the rest of us live in."

"Did Mr. Diggs describe this fantasy world to you?"

"He did. It involved violent daydreams, sometimes accompanied by compulsive masturbation."

"Are individuals such as Mr. Diggs likely to cross the line between fantasy and reality and act out their daydreams?"

"Only rarely."

"But in this case, he did?"

"Yes."

"Excuse me," the judge broke in. "Dr. Baer, you are referring to the murders that Mr. Diggs committed more than a decade ago, is that right?"

"Yes, Your Honor."

"And he has not acted out his daydreams on any occasion since that time, is that correct?"

"It is, Your Honor, but in prison, he would have had no opportunity to do so."

"Thank you. Mr. Roberts, you may proceed."

"Dr. Baer," the attorney general said, "did you find that Mr. Diggs is suffering from any other mental problem?"

"I did."

"And that would be?"

"Antisocial personality disorder, or ASPD."

"Please explain that condition to the court."

"Persons with severe ASPD are malignant narcissists. They lack empathy and are typically deceitful, impulsive, manipulative, and incapable of feeling guilt."

"In layman's terms, someone with ASPD would be considered a psychopath, isn't that correct?"

"Objection," Diggs's lawyer, Felicia Freyer, broke in. "Mr. Roberts is leading the witness."

"This is not a criminal trial, Miss Freyer," the judge said. "Please refrain from unnecessary objections that waste the court's time. Dr. Baer, you may answer."

"Psychopath is not a term I care to use, but it would be the layman's term, yes."

"There are degrees of ASPD, are there not?" Roberts asked, continuing his incessant pacing.

"There are."

"Is there a test for measuring its severity?"

"Several. I prefer the Hare Psychopathy Checklist, a group of twenty criteria that measure a person's antisocial behavior on a scale of one to forty."

"Did you perform this test on Mr. Diggs?"

"I did."

"And what did you find?"

"He scored a twenty-six."

"I see. And what would be an average score in the general population?"

"Four."

"So Kwame Diggs's score was nearly seven times normal?"

"Six point five times, to be precise."

From the jury box, Mulligan saw that Freyer was furiously scribbling notes.

"In your opinion, Doctor," Roberts said, "is Mr. Diggs in need of inpatient psychiatric care?"

"Yes."

"And in your opinion, would he be a danger to himself or others if he were to be released without such treatment?"

"In my medical opinion, he would be, yes."

"Thank you, Dr. Baer," Roberts said. He stopped pacing and took his seat at the prosecution table.

"Miss Freyer," the judge said, "do you wish to question the witness?"

"I certainly do, Your Honor."

Her huge glasses were gone today, and her blond hair had been sheared to a gentle swirl that barely brushed her shoulders. She had hoped to hire her own psychiatric expert, but Mrs. Diggs couldn't afford it. Nevertheless, the young lawyer appeared confident as she rose to address the witness.

"Dr. Baer, are you saying that my client is a psychopath?"

"I never used that term."

"Forgive me, Doctor. I believe you prefer to call it antisocial personality disorder, is that correct?"

"It is."

"And according to your testimony, my client scored a twenty-six on the Hare test used to diagnose this condition, is that also correct?"

"Yes."

"Are you aware, Doctor, that according to Kent Kiehl and Joshua Buckholtz, who wrote about this condition for *Scientific American,* a patient is not considered a psychopath unless he scores at least thirty on the test?"

"Again, I must object to the term *psychopath,* but I am aware of their work, yes."

"Are Kiehl and Buckholtz recognized experts in this area of study?"

"They are widely considered to be, yes."

"Do you agree with their conclusion?"

The witness hesitated and began fussing with his bow tie.

"Dr. Baer?"

"I suppose so, yes."

"Is there some reason your report failed to mention that Kwame Diggs's score on the Hare test was too low for him to be diagnosed — if I may be excused for repeating the term — as a psychopath?"

"I can only assume that it was omitted in error."

"In *error*?" Freyer said, putting all the incredulity she could muster into the question.

"Yes."

Freyer smirked, shook her head in mock dismay, and consulted her notes.

"During your evaluation, Doctor, did Mr. Diggs express sympathy for the victims of his crimes?"

"He did."

"On six separate occasions, isn't that correct?"

"I would need to review my report to be sure, but that is approximately correct, yes."

"Were his expressions of remorse sincere?"

Again with the bow tie.

"They appeared to be so, but it is impossible for me to say with certainty."

"If my client were a *true* psychopath, would he be capable of feeling remorse?"

"He would not."

"So if I understand your testimony, then, Doctor, my client is *not* a psychopath. Isn't *that* correct?"

"Well . . ." Once again, the witness's hands flew to his bow tie. "You must understand that it's not that simple."

"Then please explain it to us."

"Antisocial personality disorder isn't an infectious disease like rabies or influenza. It's not something that you either have or do not have. It consists of a series of traits and behaviors that are prevalent in the general population to varying degrees. Mr. Diggs is unique . . . well, not unique, but quite unusual — in that he exhibits them to a much greater degree than is the norm."

"But not great enough to be diagnosed as a psychopath."

"That would be correct," Dr. Baer said.

"Doctor, how many individuals do you suppose are in the courtroom today?"

"I would estimate about two hundred."

"In your professional opinion, Doctor, what are the odds that any of *them* are psychopaths?"

"Objection, Your Honor," Roberts shouted.

"Overruled," the judge said. "I want to hear this."

"Most studies," the witness said, "indicate that three point six percent of the general population meet the criteria for that diagnosis."

"So if my math is right," Freyer said, "the odds are that seven of the people present today have this condition, is that right?"

"If the people in this courtroom are

representative of the general population, which is not something we can know with any degree of certainty, that would be correct, yes."

"And how likely is it, Dr. Baer, that any of those seven people are going to leave here today and go out and murder someone?"

"I couldn't say."

"Well, do you consider it likely?"

"No."

"It is, in fact, extremely unlikely, is it not?"

"I suppose so, yes."

"Now then," Freyer said, "let's turn to your testimony that Kwame Diggs is also bipolar. Are bipolar patients typically dangerous?"

"No."

"Are they more likely than the average person to commit violent crimes?"

"I am aware of no evidence that they are." Again with the bow tie.

"Can bipolar disorder be controlled with medication?"

"In most cases, yes."

"Is my client currently taking such medication?"

"He is now, on my recommendation."

"Has his condition improved since he began taking the medication?"

"I have no firsthand knowledge of this."

"Have you spoken to the Corrections Department medical staff about how he is doing on the medication?"

"I have."

"And what have they told you?"

"Objection. Hearsay," Roberts bellowed.

"Must I remind you, Mr. Roberts, that this is not a criminal trial?" the judge said. "Objection overruled. The witness may answer."

"They say that he is improving."

"Is there any reason to believe that Kwame Diggs would not continue to do well if he is released?"

"That depends on whether he continues to take his medication."

"Do you have any reason to believe that he wouldn't?"

"No, but I have no reason to believe that he would, either."

"So you can't be sure either way."

"That is correct."

"Your Honor," Freyer said, "I have no further questions at this time."

"Mr. Roberts," Judge Needham said, "would you care to reexamine?"

"Yes, Your Honor." He rose and approached the witness.

"And Mr. Roberts?" the judge said. "Please refrain from that infernal pacing."

"I'll try, Your Honor. Dr. Baer, you testified that patients suffering from antisocial personality disorder are deceitful, manipulative, and incapable of remorse, is that correct?"

"It is."

"So when Mr. Diggs expressed remorse for his crimes, he was probably lying, isn't that correct?"

"He may have been. There is no way to be sure."

"And if he promises to continue his medication for bipolar disorder, that could also be a lie, isn't that right?"

"It could be, yes."

"Can his antisocial personality disorder also be controlled with medication?"

"There are no medications available to treat that condition."

"Thank you, Doctor," Roberts said, and returned to his seat.

Visibly relieved, Dr. Baer rose and stepped from the witness chair.

"One moment, Doctor," Judge Needham said. "I have a few questions of my own."

"Yes, Your Honor," the psychiatrist said. He sighed audibly and settled back into the witness chair.

"If Kwame Diggs were to be released from custody, do you think he would immediately seek to commit another murder?"

"It is conceivable that he would do so."

"Doctor, it is *conceivable* that any of us might do so. What I need to know is how *likely* it is."

Again with the bow tie.

"If you are asking me to give you odds," the witness said, "I cannot provide a medical answer."

"You're saying you don't know?"

"That is correct."

"I have nothing further," Judge Needham said. "The witness is excused. Mr. Roberts, would you like to be heard at this time?"

"Yes, Your Honor," he said, rising to address the court. "The State has presented incontrovertible medical evidence that Kwame Diggs is suffering from not one but two serious mental disorders. Our expert witness has testified that if he were ever to be released, he would pose a danger to himself and others. We ask the court to order that he be remanded to a secure mental hospital once his current sentence for assaulting a prison guard expires — or in the event that said sentence should be vacated. The State asks that he remain confined until such time as his condition no longer poses a risk to himself and to the people of Rhode Island."

"Miss Freyer?" the judge said.

"Your Honor, the State has failed to meet its burden to prove that Kwame Diggs poses an immediate threat to himself or others. We ask that the State's request be denied."

Needham swiveled in his chair and faced the TV pool camera, a troubled expression on his face.

"The court is mindful of the horrific nature of the crimes for which Kwame Diggs was convicted," he said. "I am also aware that the prospect of his release has produced an atmosphere of fear and anger such as I have never seen in my twenty years on the bench. As a grandfather of six, five of them girls, I understand those emotions, and to a degree I share them. However, the court must follow the law without respect to the vagaries of public opinion."

As the judge paused for a deep breath, Mulligan noticed that a woman in one of the spectator benches was surreptitiously thumbing a text message on her smart-phone.

"The evidence is clear that Kwame Diggs is suffering from two serious mental disabilities," the judge continued. "What is not clear is the degree to which his release would pose an imminent danger, and that is the standard on which this case must be decided. I shall require a day or two to study the evidence and review the case law again before making my decision. I ask for your patience . . . and your prayers.

"Meanwhile, I have been informed by the bailiff that a large and disorderly crowd has formed on the courthouse steps. In the interest of safety, I urge the attorneys and the witness to exit the building through the north-side door, where you will be provided with a police escort to your vehicles. Spectators and members of the press who wish to avoid the tumult are also invited to depart by the side door.

"This court is adjourned."

Mulligan shoved through the front door of the courthouse and found a skirmish line of uniformed Providence cops standing on the front step. They were edgy this time. Five of them had drawn batons from their Sam Browne belts and were slapping the shafts against their palms.

Standing behind Chief Angelo Ricci, Mulligan did a rough count. About nine hundred, he figured, many of them waving protest signs and all of them looking angry. They spilled down the steps, onto the sidewalk, and out into Benefit Street, where they were obstructing traffic.

A half-dozen TV reporters, accompanied by cameramen, were working the crowd, shoving their microphones into the faces of protesters for quotes that would pad their evening reports. Mulligan looked around for Gloria. He knew she was out there somewhere, snapping pictures.

At the curb across the street, Iggy Rock was broadcasting live from the back of WTOP's mobile van, his words lashing the crowd from a pair of loudspeakers.

"According to our source inside the courtroom, Judge Needham claims he needs, and I quote, *some time,* unquote, to make his ruling," Iggy was saying. The source, Mulligan figured, was the woman he'd seen texting. "He needs *time*?" Iggy snarled. "Really? What for? Time to get out of town before he sets a monster loose to prey on our wives, sisters, and daughters?"

The crowd hooted and shook their signs.

"Because that's what he's going to do," Iggy shouted. "He telegraphed his decision by what he said at the conclusion of the hearing. He said, and again I quote, 'What is not clear is the degree to which his release would pose an imminent danger, and that is the standard on which this case must be decided.' "

The crowd howled.

Not the most responsible thing for Iggy to be doing, Mulligan thought, but at least he hadn't passed along the word that the principals in the case were leaving by the side door.

The first egg landed with a splat on Chief Ricci's visor. Suddenly, the air was thick with them. Mulligan remained behind the chief, using him for cover.

Two of the uniforms raised their batons and stepped forward.

"Steady," Ricci commanded, and the officers froze in place.

Ricci raised a megaphone to his lips. "Let's keep it peaceful, people," he shouted. "We don't want anyone to get hurt today. The show's over now. Time to go home."

More hoots. More eggs.

Then someone threw a rock. It sailed over the chief's head and cracked one of the courthouse's glass doors.

The chief lowered the megaphone.

"Okay, then," he said. "Let's move them out."

The cops raised their batons and waded into the crowd. Ricci watched them go and sadly shook his head.

And then he ducked.

Mulligan regained consciousness in the

Rhode Island Hospital emergency room with a throbbing headache and a gauze bandage on his left temple. To his right, he heard a commotion. He turned his head on the pillow and saw stocking feet protruding from the cuffs of a Providence police uniform, the rest of the prone figure obscured by a partially closed curtain.

A TV mounted on the wall was tuned to the news. After a couple of minutes, Mulligan caught the gist. Three police officers, a dozen protesters, and a journalist had been taken to the hospital with an assortment of gashes, bruises, and broken bones.

65

"Mrs. Diggs?"

"Yes?"

"It's Gloria."

"I have nothing to say to you." Her voice was so cold and bitter that it made Gloria shiver.

"Did you watch the confession?"

Esther Diggs was silent for a moment. Then she hung up.

66

WTOP's mobile broadcasting van claimed a spot on Benefit Street across from the Superior Court building shortly before eight thirty A.M. Minutes later, police chased it off.

At nine, an hour before Judge Needham was expected to take the bench, protesters began to gather again on the courthouse steps. Outside his courtroom's swinging double doors, sheriffs ordered spectators to drop their cell phones into a cardboard box. The authorities were not about to let Iggy Rock stir up trouble again today.

It was ten forty-five before Needham emerged from his chambers and climbed onto his booster seat behind the bench.

"I have made a decision in this case," he said. "I shall not read it in full at this time; but immediately after we adjourn, the attorneys and representatives of the press may obtain copies in the clerk's office. Afterwards, I suggest you all again exit the building by the side door."

He paused and looked directly into the pool camera.

"The State has failed to offer convincing evidence that Kwame Diggs poses an immediate threat to himself and others," he said. "Therefore, the petition that he be involuntarily committed to a psychiatric facility upon completion of his sentence is regrettably denied."

Howls rose from the spectator benches.

From his seat in the jury box, Mulligan saw Attorney General Roberts slump at the prosecution table, his head in his hands. Needham climbed down from the bench, scurried out of the courtroom, and, Mulligan figured, headed right out of town.

The crowd outside the courthouse was the largest one yet, but today it was oddly subdued. Perhaps because the judge's ruling had broken its spirit. Perhaps because the Providence police were out in force, at least forty officers bunched on the courthouse steps and a dozen mounted officers patrolling the perimeter.

Mulligan walked among the protesters, collecting a few bitter quotes for his story. As he was about to leave, someone shouted,

"Impeach Needham!"

The crowed picked up the chant.

67

"You've been busy," Mason said.

"I have."

It was a balmy evening, so they'd taken a sidewalk table at Andino's Italian Ristorante on Atwells Avenue, the main thoroughfare through the city's Italian neighborhood of Federal Hill.

Felicia tossed Mason an inviting smile and offered him a bite of her lobster ravioli. He nibbled the creamy pasta from her fork, closed his eyes, and sighed. Then he dipped his fork into his plate of veal saltimbocca and raised it to her lips.

"I take it you were served," she said. Mason didn't want to talk about Diggs, but his specter was at the table with them.

"I was," he said.

"And?"

"The paper's attorney will fight the subpoena for my notes," he said. "No way we're ever going to give them up."

"But will you testify?"

"Only to what's in the story," Mason said. "Nothing more."

"What about the video?"

"Did you subpoena the Corrections Department for it?"

"I did, but I'm afraid they might claim it's been discarded. The bastards could be erasing it as we speak."

"If you can't get the tape from another source," Mason said, "we'll surrender our copy."

"With your testimony, that should be enough."

"The hearing is still scheduled for Wednesday?"

"It is. Judge Needham will be presiding again."

"Think he'll rule in your favor?"

"It's a slam dunk."

"When will Diggs be released?"

"That depends on whether Roberts appeals the decision — and on how long the state Supreme Court drags its feet before admitting there are no grounds to overturn it."

"So it's almost over," Mason said.

There was a life waiting on the other side of the ugliness they'd been surrounded by for so long. Looking at Felicia, her hair glistening in the candlelight, he decided it was time to cross the line.

"How's October in Paris sound?" he asked, and then immediately regretted it. He hadn't just crossed a line. He'd hurdled the Atlantic.

She laughed as if she thought he was kidding.

"Don't be so fast to spoil me. I'm thinking October in Rhode Island. The crisp air will smell of dead leaves, decaying shellfish, and a hint of petroleum. And there'll be carved pumpkins on every stoop. It's a great time to cuddle up in front of a fire. Let's see how that works out and then take it from there, okay?"

The robe with the yellow lightning bolts was not in evidence on Wednesday. Judge Needham had reverted to classic black for the occasion.

The hearing on Freyer's petition — including Mason's testimony and a viewing of surveillance video reluctantly provided by the Corrections Department — took less than an hour.

"Do you have anything further, Mr. Roberts?" the judge asked.

"No, Your Honor," the attorney general said.

"And you, Miss Freyer?"

"Nothing further, Your Honor."

"Sit tight," the judge said. "You'll have my ruling in a half hour."

"All rise," the bailiff boomed as the judge slid down from his booster seat and scurried to his chambers.

"A half hour? Really?" said Nancy Grace, the CNN court analyst, who was seated beside Mulligan in the crowded jury box.

"I think the judge is in a hurry to get out of town," Mulligan said.

As they waited, Grace and reporters for *The New York Times, The Boston Globe,* and the Associated Press peppered Mulligan with questions: Why did the *Dispatch* run Mason's story? Did the decision cause internal dissension in the newsroom? How many readers had canceled their subscriptions?

Ten thousand and counting, Mulligan knew, but he kept it to himself.

"If I've learned anything in my twenty years in the news business, it's this," he told Grace. "*Never* talk to a reporter."

"All rise," the bailiff shouted.

The judge hustled back into the courtroom, scrambled onto his booster seat, and turned to face the pool TV camera. He'd been gone less than twenty minutes.

"Kwame Diggs is a cold-blooded killer," Needham said. "There is nothing to suggest that he has been rehabilitated in prison, and I shudder to think what he might do upon his release. If it were in my power, he would remain locked up until the day he dies. However, the law and the facts in this case are clear.

"Because of a loophole in Rhode Island's criminal statutes, Diggs's original sentence was nowhere near severe enough to fit his crimes. He long ago served out that sentence. Since then, he has been held against his will for offenses allegedly committed during his incarceration. He is currently serving a sentence for assaulting a prison guard. Evidence presented here today proves conclusively that this charge was fabricated by the alleged victim, Joseph R. Galloway, and his fellow guard, Edward A. Quinn. It is clear to the court that they did so under the direction of Warden Alphonse J. Matos. We have also heard compelling evidence that Diggs's prior conviction for assaulting another guard was obtained with perjured testimony.

"These convictions are hereby vacated, and I order the State to release Mr. Diggs forthwith."

Howls rose from the packed spectator seats.

"Fuck, no!"

"Goddamn you!"

"How can you do this?"

"Criminal-loving prick!"

"Order!" Needham shouted, slamming his gavel on the bench. "Bailiff, clear the courtroom."

It was ten minutes before the bailiff and three sheriffs were able to herd the snarling spectators through the swinging courtroom doors, leaving only the lawyers and members of the press inside.

"Let's proceed," the judge said. "I am directing the attorney general to order the arrests of Mr. Galloway and Mr. Quinn on charges of perjury and conspiracy to obstruct justice and Warden Matos on charges of conspiracy and subornation of perjury. I further direct the attorney general to commence an investigation to determine whether others, including prosecutors in his department, were complicit in this affair.

"When those sworn to uphold the law conspire to subvert it, no matter how justified they believe their cause may be, they undermine the very fabric of our justice system. Such police state actions reek of despotism and cannot be tolerated in a democratic society.

"Court is dismissed."

Reporters raced from the courtroom to file their reports. Mulligan watched them go and then sidled up to Roberts, who was gathering his papers at the prosecution table.

"Will you appeal?" he asked.

"Of course."

"What are your chances?"

"About the same as my chances of getting reelected — slim and none."

"Do you have reason to believe that any of your prosecutors were involved in obstruction of justice?"

"Off the record?" Roberts asked.

"No," Mulligan said.

The attorney general stuffed his papers in his briefcase and trudged toward the door.

Outside the courthouse, it was chaos. Some protesters chanted. Others screamed epithets. A few threw eggs. Several wept. An effigy of Judge Needham — a pink balloon for a head and a straw-stuffed black raincoat for a body — was set ablaze. Mounted police tried vainly to disperse the crowd, which Mulligan estimated at nearly a thousand.

When the first rock was thrown, he

grabbed Gloria by the arm and dragged her inside the courthouse.

"Hey!" she said. "Knock it off."

"You knock it off," he said. "You've got enough pictures."

On her way home from work that evening, Gloria stopped off at the CVS on Post Road and went directly to the hair care aisle. She ran a pink nail along the row of hair-coloring products and selected a box of Clairol Nice 'n Easy.

Ten minutes later she pulled into her driveway, raced inside, stripped off her clothes, and stepped into the shower. After thoroughly soaking her blond hair, she stepped out, squeezed it dry, and rubbed it roughly with a terrycloth towel. Then she tore open the Clairol package, removed the plastic gloves, and pulled them on.

She twisted the tops off the activator cream and hair-coloring containers and mixed them in the applicator bottle, shaking vigorously as directed. After parting her hair into small sections with a rat-tail comb, she applied the mixture, starting at the roots and working her way to the tips.

When she was done, she wrapped a towel around her head and walked naked into the living room. There she picked up her iPod, stuck the earbuds in her ears, and spent ten minutes listening to Adele. Then she returned to the bathroom, stepped back into the shower, and rinsed the excess dye from her hair.

After toweling off, she stood over the sink, squeezed out a nickel-size dot of Clairol color-conditioning treatment, and worked it into her hair with her fingers. Then she returned to the living room and listened to one more Adele song, "Take It All." It was her favorite.

When it ended, she got back into the shower and rinsed out the conditioner. Then she stood in front of the mirror and blow-dried her dark brown hair.

Mulligan used to tell her she looked like a young Sharon Stone. She wondered what he'd think now.

68

"Maybe you should go see her."

"She probably won't let me in," Gloria said.

"Just ring her bell and say you need her to return the videotape," Mulligan said. "That might get her to open the door."

"And then what?"

"Once you get your foot inside, try to get her talking."

Which was when Larry Bird changed the subject by shrieking, "Theeeee Yankees win!"

"You're so right, Larry," Gloria said. "If you've been reading the sports section before you poop on it, you know they've been kicking our ass all summer."

She turned back to Mulligan and said, "I guess maybe it's worth a try."

"When are you going?"

"Soon as I finish my beer."

"Shouldn't you phone first to make sure

she's home?"

"She's not answering my calls."

"Want me to come along?"

"No thanks. It will probably go better if it's just us girls."

Gloria drained the beer and headed for the door.

"Hey, Gloria?"

"Yeah?"

"The new look is seriously hot."

The light was draining from the sky as Gloria's Ford Focus coasted to a stop in front of the white, one-story cottage on Ruth Road in Brockton. She climbed out and scurried up the concrete front walk past the bed of pansies and petunias. As she stepped under the green awning that covered the front stoop, a soft rain began to fall. Resisting the urge to bolt for her car, she rang the bell.

She heard footfalls, then sensed someone staring at her through the peephole.

"Yes? Who is it?"

"It's Gloria . . . Gloria Costa . . . from the *Dispatch.*"

"You're not Gloria."

"Yes, I am, Mrs. Diggs. You can see my eye patch, can't you? I changed my hair is all."

"Oh . . . I didn't recognize you at first."

"Are you going to let me in?"

"No, I don't think I will. Not after what you made me do. Besides, I'm not dressed for company."

"I need to talk to you."

"I don't believe we have anything to say to each other."

There was not a trace of light in her voice.

"Can you at least give me back the videotape I left here? I need to return it to the person I borrowed it from."

"Well, all right," she said. "I'll just be a minute."

In less than that, she cracked open the door and handed Gloria the tape, which she had placed in a small brown paper bag. Gloria saw that she was wearing a white terrycloth bathrobe and pale blue slippers. She'd been beautiful once, Gloria thought, but time and heartbreak had withered her.

Mrs. Diggs began to push the door closed.

"I didn't see you at the courthouse Wednesday," Gloria said.

"I decided not to go. Too many people. All those cameras."

"You heard what the judge decided?"

There was tension on both sides of the door, each woman pushing lightly against it.

"Oh, yes. Kwame's lawyer called me right away with the news."

"If he's released, will he be staying with you?"

"At first, yes. Until he gets a job."

She thinks someone will *hire* him? Gloria thought.

"My baby might be coming home," Mrs. Diggs said. A tear slid down her left cheek. "After all these years."

Gloria thought she looked more apprehensive than happy. The rain was stronger now. The old woman pushed harder against the door. Gloria needed to keep her talking.

"Mrs. Diggs," she said, "how come you've never asked me about my eye? I mean, you must have wondered."

"Yes . . . but it's none of my business. If you wanted to talk about it, you would have."

"I'd like to talk about it now," Gloria said, her lower lip quivering. "It was raining the night it happened. Now I'm terrified of the rain. Please let me in."

"If this is another one of your tricks . . ."

"It's not. I swear."

"Oh, you poor thing," Mrs. Diggs said, opening the door wide. The bitterness slid from her shoulders, revealing the gentle, churchgoing soul beneath. "Can I get you anything? Do you need to sit down?"

"Just let me stand here for a moment and do my breathing exercise," Gloria said.

Mrs. Diggs watched curiously until Gloria was finished.

"Does that help?" the old woman asked.

"It does."

"Sit down, and I'll bring you something," she said, and walked out of the room. Gloria heard her fussing in the kitchen.

A few minutes later they were seated on the faded couch, cups of hot tea nestled in saucers on their laps.

"I'd just opened my car door when it happened," Gloria said. "Out of nowhere, a man slammed into my back. . . ."

Gloria felt guilty about manipulating this kindly woman; but the more she talked about the terror and humiliation of that night, the better it felt to tell the story to someone who was not being paid to listen. Mrs. Diggs sat silently, taking an occasional sip of tea.

When Gloria was finished, the woman took her hand.

"Good Lord!" she said. "You poor child."

"It was awful," Gloria said, "but not nearly as horrible as it was for the women and children your son killed."

Mrs. Diggs glared at Gloria, then lowered

her eyes.

"Did you watch the confession?" Gloria asked.

The woman's head twitched, an almost imperceptible nod.

"Did you see anyone beating Kwame?"

She hunched her shoulders, then slowly shook her head.

"Did you see the way his eyes lit up when he talked about killing?"

Mrs. Diggs began to weep, her thin body racked with sobs. After a minute, maybe two, she wiped her eyes with the back of her hand, then mumbled something.

"What was that? I couldn't hear you."

"The worst part," the woman said, her voice a hoarse whisper. "The worst part was the way he laughed about it."

Gloria took the teacup from the woman's quaking hand and set it on the coffee table. Mrs. Diggs was sobbing again, her chest heaving. The robe parted, revealing a shriveled breast. Gloria averted her eyes and waited for the worst to pass.

"Mrs. Diggs? Are you all right?"

"Of course I'm not all right."

"Neither am I," Gloria said. "I'm scared."

"Of my son?"

"Yes."

"Is that why you dyed your hair?"

"It is."

The woman fell quiet again, then whispered, "Maybe they won't let him out."

"They'll have to unless they discover something else to charge him with. Do you know of anything like that, Mrs. Diggs?"

The woman shook her head no.

"The police tried to connect him with unsolved crimes in Rhode Island and couldn't find anything," Gloria said. "Did you ever take him out of state? For a vacation, maybe?"

Another head shake. Then Mrs. Diggs began to cry again. Gloria quietly let herself out.

69

The streetlight outside Mulligan's tenement had burned out months ago. From his kitchen window, he could barely make out the activity on the street.

He'd been drawn to the window by the pounding bass line of an overamped car radio. Some rap song he couldn't identify. A white Escalade was rolling slowly down America Street, as if the driver were looking for an unfamiliar address. It pulled to a stop, the doors flew open, and four figures stepped out. Moments later, feet pounded on the stairwell leading to Mulligan's second-floor apartment.

Mulligan didn't like the feel of it. He went to the bedroom, opened his bedside table drawer, and pulled out his Colt .45.

The pistol was a family heirloom, his maternal grandfather's sidearm when he served in the Providence Police Department. For years, it had resided in a shadow box mounted in a place of honor on Mulligan's wall. But a few years ago, after his stories about a Mount Hope arson spree had led to death threats, he'd gotten a permit to carry. The only place he'd ever fired it was at the range at the Providence Revolver Club.

The visitors were pounding on his door now, a door not sturdy enough to keep them out if they were determined to get in. He tucked the gun into the waistband at the small of his back, went to the door, and opened it.

Four black teenagers swaggered in. They wore matching black-and-white Oakland Raiders sweatshirts and loose jeans that sagged low on their hips. Tattoos on their necks identified them as members of the Goonies, the city's newest street gang.

"Where is it, muthafucka?" the shortest one said.

"Tell me," Mulligan said. "Where did you guys get the name Goonies, anyway? Was it inspired by your favorite movie, or is it just an endearing form of goon?"

The short one raised an eyebrow and cracked a smile. "Shit," he said, "I don't muthafuckin' know."

Which was when Larry Bird decided to

join the conversation: “Theeee Yankees win!”

“*There’s* the muthafucka!” the tallest one said.

“So,” the shortest one said, “why’d you steal our muthafuckin’ bird?”

“I didn’t,” Mulligan said. “After the shooting at Chad Brown, the cops didn’t want to be bothered with it, so they gave it to me.”

“You’ve been taking care of the muthafucka?” the short one said.

“I have,” Mulligan said.

“Feeding it and cleaning the cage and shit?”

“Yup.”

“That’s cool,” the short one said. “But we want the muthafucka back.”

“Can you prove it’s yours?”

“It belonged to my muthafuckin’ cousin,” the tall one said.

“The guy who got shot?”

“Yeah.”

The guys who shot him were also driving a white Escalade, Mulligan remembered, but he figured it best not to bring that up.

“How’d you find me?” Mulligan asked.

“We been askin’ around,” the short one said.

Mulligan raised an eyebrow. The short one did not elaborate.

"You gonna give us trouble, muthafucka?" the tall one asked.

"Muthafucka!" Larry Bird said. "Muthafucka! Muthafucka! Muthafucka!"

"It's all yours," Mulligan said. "And you may as well take the package of bird feed on the counter."

The tall one grabbed the cage, the short one snatched the seed, and the four young hoodlums swaggered out the door and pounded down the stairs.

Mulligan watched them go. Then he pushed the door closed, locked it, and said, "Good riddance, muthafucka."

70

Protesters gathered in front of the newspaper every day now; but they seldom numbered more than twenty, and there were no more rock-throwing incidents. Still, two weeks after Mason's story was printed, the publisher thought it best to keep the Wackenhut guards at their posts.

On Wednesday morning, Mulligan took the elevator to the third floor, stepped out into the newsroom, and walked by a slender, sixty-six-year-old black woman sitting in one of the white vinyl chairs set aside for visitors. She wore a yellow summer dress and flat white shoes. Her white vinyl purse rested in her lap. She looked up at Mulligan and scowled.

Two minutes later, Mason walked in and spotted her.

"May I help you, Mrs. Diggs?" he asked.

"No, thank you, Mr. Mason. I'm waiting for Gloria Costa."

When Gloria arrived five minutes later, the woman rose to meet her.

"I have something I need to tell you," she said.

From their desks, Mulligan and Mason watched Gloria lead the woman to one of the small meeting rooms and close the door.

"Please sit down, Mrs. Diggs," Gloria said, and then pulled a chair over to sit next to her. "I've been worried about you. Are you okay?"

"No," the woman said. "I don't think I ever will be again."

Gloria waited in silence, letting the woman get to it in her own time.

"In the summer of 1993, when Kwame was fourteen, we sent him to a sleepover camp. It was the first time he'd ever been away from home."

That was the year between the Warwick murders, Gloria knew.

"What was the name of the camp?" she asked.

"I can't remember. It was a long time ago."

"Do you remember where it was?"

"In the Catskills."

"What town?"

"Big Indian."

"How long was he gone?"

"Just three days. Then the camp sent all the children home."

"Why did they do that, Mrs. Diggs?"

"Because something happened."

"What was it?"

The old woman lowered her eyes and spoke in a whisper.

"One of the camp counselors was murdered."

71

"I was a cub reporter back in '93," said Dan Hurley, city editor of *The Poughkeepsie Journal.* "It was the first time I covered a murder. Big Indian is a little out of our coverage area, but the victim was from New Paltz, just across the Hudson, so it was a big story for us."

"Tell me what you remember," Mulligan said.

"Her name was Allison Foley. Just turned eighteen. Would have been a freshman at Stony Brook University in the fall."

"How did she die?"

"Brutally. She was stabbed a dozen times in the chest with a jackknife. When the killer figured out the blade wasn't long enough to pierce her heart, he stabbed her in the neck and then strangled her with her belt."

"Where did this happen?"

"In the woods about eighty yards from a cabin she shared with three other camp counselors."

"Was the knife recovered?"

"Yeah. Tossed in the bushes about twenty yards from the body."

"Prints?"

"Nothing usable."

"Footprints around the body?"

"No. When she went missing, counselors and campers searched the woods for her and tromped all over the scene."

"Any physical evidence at all?"

"Yeah. The killer masturbated on her body."

"Suspects?"

"Detectives focused on a known sex offender who lived in a shack few miles away in Shandaken. He didn't have an alibi, and he had the same blood type as the killer."

"They knew that how?"

"They tested the semen for blood type, and it matched the information in his police jacket. That gave them enough for a warrant to test his DNA, but when they went to pick him up, he was gone. One of the state cops, a detective named Forrest, never did stop searching for him, but the guy was a ghost."

"What did the victim look like?"

"Tall. Athletic. A real pretty girl."

"What color was her hair?"

"Blond," Hurley said. "So how about telling me why you're asking about this now."

"Think I know who killed her," Mulligan said.

Jennings rode shotgun in Secretariat as Mulligan cruised south on I-95 toward Connecticut.

"How come you didn't bring Gloria along?" Jennings asked. "She earned the right."

"She did, but Lomax said he couldn't spare both of us."

"That why you brought the camera?"

"Uh-huh."

Jennings cracked open a Narragansett and handed it to Mulligan, who shook his head no. The ex-cop shrugged and took a pull from the can.

"Doesn't seem fair," he said.

"It isn't."

"She must be pissed."

"Oh hell, yeah."

At New Haven, Mulligan swung north toward Waterbury, then picked up I-84 west. At Danbury, he pulled off the highway for coffee at McDonald's. A few minutes later, he crossed the New York State line and took the Taconic Parkway heading north. Just west of the little town of Lagrangeville, he slipped off the parkway and took country roads the rest of the way to Poughkeepsie.

Shortly after one P.M., nearly five hours after they'd left Providence, he pulled into the parking lot of the Coyote Grill, a pub on South Road, where they found two men in T-shirts and Yankees caps waiting for them at the bar.

"Mulligan?"

"Yeah."

"Don't you know you can get shot wearing a Red Sox cap in these parts?"

"I figured I'd risk it. You must be Dan Hurley."

"I am. And this is Carter Forrest, the retired New York State cop I told you about."

Mulligan shook their hands and introduced them to Jennings. Moments later, the four men were seated in a booth, waiting for their burgers.

"You really think a *fourteen*-year-old camper could have done this?" Forrest was saying.

"He stabbed two women and three little girls to death in my town by the time he was fifteen," Jennings said. "So, yeah. He definitely could have done this."

"And here's the worst part," Mulligan said, taking a few minutes to run down

Diggs's legal status. "If we can't nail him for Foley, they're going to have to turn him loose."

"You've *got* to be shitting me," Forrest said.

" 'Fraid not," Jennings said.

"Okay, then," Forrest said. "Let's get to work." He opened his briefcase and slid out a loose-leaf binder — his copy of the Allison Foley murder book.

"And you'll be wanting this," Jennings said, passing Forrest copies of the Medeiros and Stuart murder books. The two ex-cops started paging through them. Thirty minutes later, after the burgers and beer had been consumed, they were still at it.

"Why don't you two save that for later," Hurley said. "Mulligan wants to visit the scene while it's still daylight."

"Nothing worth seeing up there after all those years," Forrest said.

"For a cop, sure," Hurley said. "But for a journalist who wants to write about the case, it's solid gold."

They piled into Forrest's Jeep Wrangler, leaving the Bronco in the pub parking lot. They crossed the Mid-Hudson Bridge, bisected the little city of New Paltz, and swung north on a two-lane that passed through a series of small towns and then skirted a large reservoir. As the road wound up into the Catskills, following the course of the swift Esopus Creek, the towns were fewer and the forest thicker, oak and maple gradually giving way to red spruce, hemlock, and balsam fir.

An hour after they'd started, they reached the village of Big Indian and turned right on Fire House Road. Five minutes later, Forrest braked and pulled onto a weed-choked gravel road past a faded wooden sign: "Little Indian Summer Camp."

Mulligan slid down the car window and photographed the sign.

The Wrangler rolled past athletic fields overgrown with saplings, milkweed, and poison ivy. Off to the right were two large log buildings. One was black with fire damage. The other had a spindly young spruce growing through the middle of its collapsed roof.

"The administration building and the crafts building," Hurley said as Mulligan snapped a few more photos. "In the nineties, Frank Hudson and his wife, Julie, ran the place. Before the murder, they were just barely hanging on. Afterwards, they had a lot of trouble attracting customers. Finally, they just pulled up stakes and moved away."

Weeds scraped the bottom of the Wrangler

as it climbed the gravel trail into the mountains. As they gained elevation, balsam fir and red spruce gave way to beech and birch. A quarter mile in, ramshackle cabins dotted the woods on both sides of the road. The windows were broken, the stoops crumbling, the rotting shiplap siding green with algae and moss.

"The campers' cabins," Forrest said, and kept driving. He continued on for another sixty yards, then pulled over beside a cluster of six somewhat larger cabins.

"The counselors' quarters," he said, and they all climbed out. "Watch out for the poison ivy."

He led the way through the weeds to a cabin with a faded "31" painted beside the entrance.

"Allison Foley slept here," he said, "with three other young women."

The windows were broken, and the door and front stoop were missing. Hurley gave Mulligan a boost, and he climbed inside.

"Careful," the editor said. "The floor might be rotted out."

Mulligan stood in the doorway, a musty smell filling his nostrils, as he waited for his eyes to adjust. To his right and left, two sets of bunk beds, the mattresses covered with animal droppings. Ahead of him, an open door. Behind it, a yellowed toilet with the seat missing.

Mulligan took a step. The floor felt spongy under his feet. He stepped back into the doorway. The floor of the cabin was littered with empty beer cans and Thunderbird wine bottles.

"Looks like somebody had a party in here," he shouted.

"Figures," Hurley said. "Vagrants have taken to camping out in the abandoned cabins. The local cops used to chase them off, but now they just leave them be."

Mulligan raised his camera and took a few flash photos. In the corner to his left, something hissed. He wheeled and saw a large opossum rear on its hind legs, eyes glowing red.

"There's one in here now," Mulligan said. "The four-legged kind."

"Raccoon?" Hurley asked.

"Opossum," Mulligan said.

"Careful," Forrest said. "A lot of them are rabid."

Mulligan turned and jumped down into the late afternoon sunlight. He backed off a few yards and snapped exterior shots of the cabin while Hurley and Jennings climbed inside for a quick look.

"Stand by the door so I can get you in the

shot," Mulligan told Forrest.

"I'd rather not," Forrest said.

"You've chased this case for nineteen years," Mulligan said. "Like it or not, you're a big part of the story."

Forrest doffed his Yankees cap, exposing a thick crop of steel-gray hair, smiled sheepishly, and reluctantly complied.

Then he led the men into the stillness of the trees through a thick undergrowth of brambles and giant purple hyssop in full bloom. Briars clutched at their jeans, the thorns biting through and raking their skin. Eighty yards in, they stopped at the base of a large birch.

"This is where they found her," Forrest said.

Mulligan snapped a photo of the retired trooper standing beside the tree. There was nothing more to see.

That evening, Mulligan and Jenkins checked into the Days Inn near Vassar College in Poughkeepsie, then met Forrest and Hurley for a late dinner at the Coyote Grill.

Over steaks and beer, Forrest flipped through his murder book, running down the fine points of the Foley case. Then Jennings did the same with the Diggs cases.

"So if the DNA from the Ashcroft case

hadn't been contaminated, you would have nailed the bastard," Forrest said.

"Yeah," Jennings said. "Think the DNA from the semen he spilled on Foley might still be good?"

"I doubt it," Forrest said. "It's been a long time. I'm not sure it's even still in storage. But it doesn't matter."

"It doesn't?"

"No. The state crime lab ran a DNA test on it back in '93. A copy of the result is in the back of the Foley murder book. Get your lab to compare it to a sample from Diggs. If it's a match, New York will charge him with murder, and he'll spend the rest of his sorry-ass life getting corn-holed in Attica."

"Fantastic," Jennings said. "My old boss at the Warwick PD can get our state crime lab to expedite this. We should have our answer in a few weeks."

Early next morning, Mulligan and Jennings were on their way back to Providence when the opening licks of Paul Simon's "Kodachrome" streamed from Mulligan's shirt pocket. His ring tone for Gloria.

"Mulligan."

"How's it going?"

"Good. I think we've got him."

"Better hurry."

"Why's that?"

"The state Supreme Court just turned down Roberts' appeal without a hearing. Diggs is going to be released next week."

"Aw, shit. Do you have the date and time?"

"No. The authorities are keeping a tight lid on that. They want to avoid a media circus."

"I'll bet," Mulligan said.

72

"Good morning, Governor."

"Mulligan? Calling me at home on a Saturday? Must be a social call."

"It's not."

"Oh. Too bad."

"You *know* why I'm calling, Fiona."

"You want to know when he's being released."

"I do."

"We're keeping it under wraps. The less publicity the better. No way we want Iggy Rock and his mob waiting for Diggs in the prison parking lot."

"You know we'll handle it the right way."

"Just you and a photographer?"

"Not me. Mason and Gloria."

"Noon on Monday," she said. "His mother will pick him up and take him home."

"Thanks."

"You're welcome."

"Anybody going to keep tabs on him?"

"We'll give him a police escort to the state line. After that, he's Massachusetts' problem."

"The authorities there have been informed?"

"We've alerted Brockton PD and the Massachusetts State Police. They'll keep an eye on him, drop in on him from time to time. That's all they can do."

"Until he kills again."

"Yeah. Until then."

"Still having fun playing governor?"

"Right now, not so much."

Monday, there were only a half-dozen cars in the Supermax visitors' lot. Only one of them, a gray 2002 Chevrolet Malibu, had Massachusetts plates. Gloria pulled her Ford Focus into the space next to it. A moment later, Felicia drove into the lot.

At five past noon, Kwame Diggs strode out of the prison gate, his arm around his mother. Esther Diggs looked incredibly small. She glanced up at her son as if she were looking at a stranger. Kwame closed his eyes, tilted his face up to the sun, rolled his shoulders, and grinned. Gloria's shutter clicked.

Diggs turned and stared at her. She got the impression he was trying to figure out where he'd seen her before. She was very glad, then, that she'd colored her hair.

"How's it feel to be out, Kwame?" Freyer asked. She didn't sound as though she really wanted to know.

"Great," he said. " 'Free at last, free at last.' Dr. King said that."

"What are you going to do first?" Mason asked.

"I'm heading to McDonald's for three Double Quarter Pounders with Cheese and a McFlurry with M&M's. Then I'm gonna go home with my moms."

"Then what?"

"Hell, I don't know." He turned to his lawyer. "Thanks so much, Miss Freyer. I owe you my life."

"Mason did most of the work," she said.

"I know. Thanks, Mason. I owe you big-time."

He extended his hand. Mason hesitated, then shook it.

"Know how you can repay me?" Mason asked.

"How?"

"Don't kill anybody else."

Diggs's eyes flashed cold, but his mouth cracked into a grin. His mother got into her car without speaking and cranked the ignition. Diggs opened the passenger-side door, slid the seat all the way back, and wedged himself inside.

"Felicia," he said, "you looking *hot* today, girl. See you around sometime." Then he started to close the car door.

"Hey, Kwame," Mason said.

"What?"

" 'People pay for what they do, and still more for what they have allowed themselves to become.' James Baldwin said that."

Diggs scowled and jerked the door shut.

Mason, Gloria, and Freyer stood in the parking lot and watched a state police car, lights flashing, lead the Malibu out of the parking lot. A second cruiser tagged along behind.

"How did his mother look to you?" Mason asked.

"Scared," Freyer said. "Jesus! What the hell have we done?"

Part III
Predation

73

Gloria, Mason, and Mulligan gathered around a speakerphone in a private office off the main newsroom.

"What are they using for a DNA sample?" asked Peter Schutter, the retired FBI profiler.

"His old toothbrush and some other toiletry items from his prison cell," Mulligan said.

"How long before the test results come back?"

"They're expediting it," Mulligan said, "but it's going to be at least a couple of weeks."

"And he's going to be running around loose until then?"

"He is."

"Jesus Christ!"

"He's moved into his mother's place in Brockton, Massachusetts," Gloria put in. "Do you think she's in any danger?"

"My guess is no, but I can't say for sure."

"What do you think he'll do?" Mason asked.

"Stalk women and stab them to death."

"How much time do you think we have?" Mulligan said.

"Hard to say."

"What's your best guess?"

The retired agent sighed heavily into the receiver.

"When Diggs went to prison he was just a kid — an inexperienced, disorganized killer. His crimes had been reckless and poorly planned, leaving evidence all over the place. For the last eighteen years, he's been reliving the murders over and over in his mind, thinking about all the mistakes he made. He'll tell himself to be careful now — watchful and methodical. He'll try to take his time selecting his next victim. He'll try to plan his crimes carefully. That *could* slow him down."

"But it might not?" Mulligan asked.

"That's right," Schutter said. "Diggs is obsessed with killing women. It's what he lives for. Assuming you're right about the Foley homicide, he had a one-year cooling-off period between his murders. He's been waiting for eighteen years now. The desire and frustration bottled up inside of him must be overwhelming. No matter how much his mind tells him to be careful, he could simply explode at the first victim of opportunity. Best-case scenario? I'd say you've got a month, maybe two. But don't be surprised if he kills tonight."

"Any way to know how he'll select his victims?" Gloria asked.

"They'll be blond and vulnerable, of course. Other than that . . ." Schutter paused in thought for a moment. "Is there any particular blonde he could be obsessing about? A woman he remembers from his past, perhaps?"

"Mary Jennings," Mulligan said.

"Who's that?" Schutter asked.

"Connie Stuart's twin sister."

"He would have seen her at his trial?"

"Yeah."

"She'd be about fifty now," Schutter said. "Diggs always liked them young, so she's no longer his type." He paused again, then said, "But in his warped mind, he might still picture her as a young woman. You should warn her to take precautions."

"What about Susan Ashcroft?" Gloria asked.

"Another older woman," Schutter said. "But she's the one who got away, so he probably still fantasizes about her. Anybody else?"

"Diggs's lawyer is a pretty thirty-year-old blonde," Mason said. The dread was like a stone in his chest. He'd had vivid, horrifying dreams about Kwame's hands on her. "She visited him at least a dozen times in the last few months. Sometimes we went together, and I didn't like the way he looked at her."

"Tell me about that," Schutter said.

"He looked her up and down. Commented on her hair and makeup. A couple of times, when I visited him by myself, he said she liked me and asked if I was, as he put it, 'getting any.' He pressed for details. Kept saying, 'Come on, you can tell me.' "

"I don't like the sound of that," Schutter said.

Mason didn't either. He wondered if he should have challenged Kwame, warned him to stay away from Felicia. Instantly, he realized why he hadn't. Because Kwame had threatened him, too.

"Freyer was there when Diggs got out," Gloria said. "He told her she looked hot and said something about seeing her around sometime."

"I *really* don't like the sound of that," Schutter said.

And I didn't say anything, Mason thought. Out loud he said, "Jesus!"

"Let's not overreact," Mulligan said. "Diggs was fifteen when he went to prison. He's never driven a car. How would he even get back to Rhode Island?"

"He could hitch a ride or take public transportation," Schutter said, "but he probably won't. He's a marked man in Rhode Island. Besides, he's got plenty of blondes to choose from in Brockton."

The agent paused, then said, "What about you, Gloria?"

"He's only seen me a couple of times. Last year when I took his picture outside the courthouse and this week when I photographed his release. I don't think he even knows my name."

74

A late summer bug hit the newsroom hard. Mulligan spent the next two weeks working nights on the copy desk, filling in for a sick-in-bed slot man whose respiratory infection had turned into pneumonia. Mulligan wrote headlines, edited city hall and state-house copy, and did whatever else was necessary to get the daily paper out.

Each evening, he stole a few minutes to scan the Associated Press's Massachusetts wire, checking for murders in Brockton, Massachusetts. He found plenty of them: A high school football star stabbed to death in a bar fight. A clerk shot three times in the chest in a botched convenience store holdup. A teenager kicked and beaten to death in a street gang initiation. A ten-year-old with a toy pistol gunned down by a nervous cop. But no blonde stabbed to death by a sex maniac.

After finishing his Friday shift, he downed

a couple of Killian's at Hopes, drove home, went to bed, and drifted off into a . . .

Rushing to catch a flight to somewhere, he sprinted to the gate and dashed into the airplane seconds before the door closed. He started down the aisle and froze. Every seat was occupied by a naked blonde. Their bodies, faces, makeup, and hairdos were identical. Stab wounds blossomed like roses on their torsos. Each one, Mulligan somehow knew, had been stabbed fifty-two times.

Kwame Diggs's voice burst from the intercom: "This is your captain speaking."

At three A.M. Mulligan startled awake, exhausted and drenched in sweat. His cell was playing "Dirty Laundry," his ring tone for Lomax.

"Mulligan."

"You awake?"

"I am now."

"Marvin from Barrington just won a hundred bucks for calling the WTOP tip line to report he saw two white males throwing Molotov cocktails through criminal-coddling Judge Needham's windows."

"You listen to WTOP in the middle of the night?"

"Couldn't sleep."

"Okay, I'm on it."

"Thanks. I'll call Gloria and have her meet

you there."

Less than twenty minutes later, Mulligan pulled onto Nyatt Road, just a short stroll from the Rhode Island Country Club in the upscale bedroom community of Barrington. The judge's two-story Tudor-style brick home was fully involved. Flames curled from the eaves and jitterbugged in the blown-out windows.

The judge and his family, Mulligan knew, were not at home. After his ruling on Diggs, they'd hightailed it to their vacation place on Sanibel Island in Florida. Good thing, because the Barrington Fire Department was not on scene yet. That was odd, because two of the town's fire stations were less than three miles away.

Five minutes later, TV vans from Channel 10 in Cranston and Channel 12 in East Providence came tearing down the street. Two minutes after that, Gloria pulled up, jumped out of her car, and started snapping pictures.

Another ten minutes passed before two pumper trucks and a rescue vehicle unhurriedly rolled up and turned into the long, tree-lined gravel driveway. The firemen climbed out of the pumpers and took their time unspooling hoses, connecting them to a fire hydrant, and dragging them across the wide, chemical-green lawn.

They waited until the roof collapsed in a shower of sparks before they sprang into action, spraying streams of water into the wreckage.

75

On Saturday afternoon, Chief Hernandez of the Warwick PD sported a blue baseball cap and a T-shirt emblazoned with the logo "Mercer Hardware Lions," the name of the preteen girls' soccer team he coached. He had his feet up on his desk and was sipping from a "World's Best Dad" coffee cup.

"What I'm about to tell you has to remain absolutely secret for now. Can I count on you to keep your mouths shut?"

"Yes," Jennings said.

"Sure thing," Mulligan said.

"The state crime lab completed the DNA testing on Thursday, and we've got a match."

"All right!" Jennings said.

"The results were sent to the New York State Police that afternoon. Yesterday, New York's Criminal Prosecutions Division drafted a warrant for Diggs's arrest for the murder of Allison Foley. At first, the judge they approached declined to sign it. He insisted that the DNA test be replicated by the New York crime lab. But when the urgency of the situation was explained to him, he relented."

"What happens now?" Mulligan asked.

"At five A.M. tomorrow, the Massachusetts State Police STOP team, which is what they call their SWAT unit, will hit the Diggs house in Brockton. Two New York State Police detectives will be present as observers, as will I."

"I want to be there," Mulligan said.

"You and Andy have both earned it," Hernandez said. "You'll ride with me, but you've got to promise to remain in the car until they drag Diggs out."

"Will do," Mulligan said. "Can I bring a photographer?"

"No, but you can bring a camera. Once they clear the house, take all the pictures you want."

At four thirty Sunday morning, the assault team assembled in the Cardinal Spellman High School parking lot two blocks from the Diggs house. Mulligan counted twelve state cops in body armor. One carried a breaching shotgun designed to blow dead bolts and hinges from exterior doors. The rest were armed with assault rifles. At four fifty-five, they jumped into their vehicles and raced toward the Diggs house, their bar lights dark and sirens silent. A New York State Police cruiser followed. Hernandez's car, with Jennings riding shotgun and Mulligan in the backseat, took up the rear.

The vehicles screeched to a stop in front of the one-story cottage on Ruth Road. Four STOP team members sprinted toward the backyard to cover the rear door. Four more raced to cover the side windows. The last four rushed the front entrance, tromping through Esther Diggs's petunia bed.

The breaching shotgun boomed, blowing the lock through the front door. The cops charged in, shouting, "State Police! Down on the floor! Down on the floor!"

And then . . . silence.

Hernandez, Jennings, and Mulligan waited in the car. They did not speak. Twenty minutes later, the cops walked through the front door and trudged down the front walk.

Alone.

Hernandez, Jennings, and Mulligan got out of the car and joined them on the sidewalk.

"He's not here," said the lieutenant in charge. "His mother says she hasn't seen him since Friday night."

"Aw, fuck," Hernandez said.

"Yeah," the lieutenant said. "And now he probably knows we're after him."

Early that afternoon, the Massachusetts State Police released Diggs's mug shot to the media, hoping the public could help with the manhunt. Hernandez, Jennings, and Mulligan met Gloria and Mason for a late lunch at Charlie's diner in Providence to talk things over.

"He could be anywhere now," Hernandez said.

"Anywhere includes here," Mason said.

"Think Susan Ashcroft is safe?" Gloria asked.

"Her husband has a gun, and he knows how to use it," Hernandez said. "And the Coventry police promised me they'd have a patrol car go by her place every hour from dusk till dawn until the bastard's in custody."

"What about Mary?" Mulligan asked.

"She's got me," Jennings said. "I almost hope the bastard comes for her so I can empty my revolver into him."

"What about Felicia?" Mason asked. He shouldn't be asking about her, he thought. He should be *with* her.

"I asked the Providence cops to watch out

for her," Hernandez said. "They say all they can do is have a patrol car drive by her place a couple of times during the night."

"Then I better sleep there until he's caught," Mason said.

"Diggs is twice your size," Mulligan said. "What good will you be if he breaks in?"

"He won't," Mason said. "He's a coward. He's never attacked a woman when there's a man around."

"There's always a first time," Jennings said.

"Do you have a gun, Thanks-Dad?" Mulligan asked

"No."

"Do you know how to use one?"

"No."

"I do," Mulligan said. "I'm still stuck working nights on the copy desk, but I usually get off around midnight. Get me a key to her place and I'll let myself in, spend the night dozing on the couch."

Mason pulled out his cell and called Felicia.

"Is this really necessary?" she asked.

"Yes," Mason said.

"I'm his lawyer. Why would he want to hurt me?"

"He probably doesn't," Mason said, "but let's not take any chances, okay? I mean, the guy *is* a homicidal maniac. Who knows what he'll do?" He took a deep breath and half whispered, "I need to know that you're safe."

They agreed that Mason would stay at her place until the danger passed. Reluctantly, Felicia agreed to give Mulligan a spare key.

As Mulligan strolled out of the diner, he was in desperate need of sleep. He'd worked the night shift on Saturday, then risen well before dawn for the abortive raid. But it would be hours before he could get any.

First he had to write a news story about the raid. Then he had to put the finishing touches on an account of the newspaper's investigation into the old New York killing and how it led to the new murder charge against Diggs. Lomax planned to start that one on page one, with a full page inside.

When he was done with that, it would be time for his evening copy desk shift again.

At midnight, nineteen hours after the raid on the Diggs house, Mulligan finished work and drove to Freyer's place in Newberry Village, a condo development in the Providence suburb of Cranston. The street was well lighted, and some of the front yards, including Freyer's, were bright with floods.

Fighting to keep his eyes open, he drove

down the street past her place and kept going, studying both sides of the street. Then he turned around and made another pass. When he was satisfied that no one was lurking, he parked on the street, pulled his .45 from its hiding place under the front passenger seat, tucked it in his waistband, and trudged up the front walk. He climbed the steps to the front stoop and inserted his key in the lock.

He found Mason dozing in the living room on a tan leather sofa, a pen in his hand and a yellow legal pad open in his lap. Beside him on the cushions, an aluminum baseball bat.

"Whatcha doin'?" Mulligan asked as Mason stirred awake.

"Working on the lyrics for a song I'm writing," Mason said.

"Want to sing it for me?"

"Not yet."

"Tell me the layout."

"Living room, kitchen, dining room, and half-bath on this floor. Two bedrooms and a bathroom upstairs."

"Checked the locks on all the doors and windows?"

"Of course."

"Where's Felicia?"

"Asleep upstairs."

Mulligan stifled a yawn.

"Why don't you head up, too? I've got this now."

"You can have the other bedroom," Mason said.

Oh? Mason was sleeping with Felicia now? That was news. No bragging. No bravado. The publisher's son was a class act.

"No thanks," Mulligan said. "Better if I stay down here."

Mason wished him good night, picked up the baseball bat, and trudged upstairs. Mulligan watched him go, then rechecked the locks on the front door and the downstairs windows. Off the kitchen, he unlocked a sliding glass door and stepped onto a small deck that looked over a treeless backyard. It was not fenced.

Thirty yards away, the back sides of a string of matching condos were dark, save for the blue light from a television flickering in one upstairs window. He dropped his hand to his waistband, felt the grip of his pistol, and stared into the darkness, looking for the glow of a cigarette or any sign of movement.

He stood there for a good ten minutes, then went back through the sliding doors and locked them. He turned off the lights, placed his .45 on the coffee table by the couch, pulled off his Reeboks, and stretched out on the leather.

He closed his eyes and listened to the sounds of the house. He heard nothing but the hum of the air conditioner, not liking the way it muffled the sound of a car gliding by on the street. He got up, found the temperature controls on the living room wall, and shut off the A/C. Then he returned to the couch, dozed off, and found himself on the death plane again.

A week crawled by. Updates on the manhunt appeared daily in the Rhode Island and Massachusetts newspapers and every morning, noon, and night on New England TV news broadcasts.

Late every afternoon, Mason met Felicia at her law office and drove her home. Every day after midnight, Mulligan drove to the condo, studied the street, let himself in with his key, checked the backyard and the locks, and settled down to sleep on the couch.

The daily manhunt updates never had anything new to report. Diggs had either fled the area or was lying low.

76

Tuesday afternoon, Mulligan ambled down the sidewalk past the governor's limo and shoved open the door to Hopes. Fiona was waiting for him at a table in back. He grabbed a shot of Bushmills and a Killian's chaser at the bar, took the seat across from her, and said, "What's up?"

"Thought you might want a scoop on the obstruction of justice investigation."

"I would."

"The A.G.'s office negotiated a plea bargain with Galloway and Quinn. They'll both admit to one count of perjury and one count of conspiracy to obstruct justice. They'll be sentenced to ten years in prison and be ordered to pay five-thousand-dollar fines. After the sentences are handed down, I'm going to pardon both of them."

"What about Warden Matos?"

"He won't be charged, but he's agreed to take early retirement."

"With full pension?"
"Yes."
"My tax money at work," Mulligan said. "How about the prosecutors who handled the assault case? They were in on it, too."
"The attorney general has found no evidence to proceed against them."
"Did he look for any?"
"Off the record?"
"Sure."
"Then, no."
"That all of it?"
"One more thing. Another guard, Paul Delvecchio, will plead guilty to one count of vandalism for destroying Mason's car. He'll be fined a thousand dollars and get a year, suspended. And he'll have to pay Mason twenty-eight thousand in restitution. I'm told the guards' union plans to take care of that for him."
"Swell," Mulligan said.

77

Tuesday night was a bitch. Statehouse reporters flooded the copy desk with political news, some of it so clumsily done that Mulligan felt compelled to rewrite it. Five people, one of them a local bank president, died in the rain in a three-car collision on Providence's treacherous Thurbers Avenue curve. And Sammy "Snake Eyes" Tardio, a Mob enforcer rumored to have turned rat, was shotgunned in a Federal Hill bar. Mulligan juggled copy with no time for a dinner break, surviving the evening on Cheetos and lots of weak coffee from the newsroom vending machines.

At midnight, just as the paper was about to be put to bed, a four-alarm fire broke out in an abandoned jewelry factory in the city's dilapidated Olneyville section. Fifteen minutes later, the police radio on the city desk screamed the news that the roof had collapsed, trapping half a dozen firemen inside.

Kit Murphy, the night city editor, held page one to get the story in the paper, then cursed a blue streak when the reporter at the scene called in to say he couldn't get back to file because his car wouldn't start.

"Have Gloria give you a lift," she said.

"No can do. She's already on the way back with her fire photos."

Murphy ordered him to call the copy desk and dictate the details over the phone. Mulligan spent twenty minutes pumping the reporter for facts and writing a hurried but passable story for the final edition. The last press run started an hour late, which meant overtime pay for the pressmen, the mailroom crew, and the delivery truck drivers.

"You're gonna catch hell for this," Mulligan said.

"I know," Murphy said, "but I don't really give a shit."

It was past two A.M. when Mulligan stepped out into the storm and fetched Secretariat from the parking lot across the street. The rain was coming down hard as he turned into Felicia's condo development in Cranston. A single downstairs light was on in her place when he drove past.

He continued to the end of the street and drove back, unable to see much through the rain-spattered windshield. He parked at the curb, grabbed his .45, and tucked it into his pants. Then he climbed the front stoop, quietly let himself in, and found Mason sleeping on the couch, the Louisville Slugger like a lover in his arms.

Eight miles south, Gloria rolled up to her house in Warwick, parked in the garage, went through the connecting door to the kitchen, and dropped her camera bag on the kitchen table. She was proud of herself tonight, proud that she'd stood in the rain without panicking to shoot some first-rate fire photos. She walked through the house, checking the locks on all the doors and windows. Then she skipped up the stairs, pulled off her clothes, and tossed them on the floor. She dropped into bed and immediately fell asleep.

Mulligan headed for the half-bath to drain the evening's coffee from his bladder. When he was done, he roused Mason and told him to go upstairs. Then he went out through the sliding glass doors, checked the backyard, came back inside, rechecked all the locks, and turned off the air-conditioning.

■ ■ ■ ■

In Warwick, ten miles to the south, Andy Jennings's two big dogs snored on his living room carpet. He sat on the floor beside them, cleaning their namesake, a Model 460 V Smith & Wesson. His other pistol, a nine-millimeter Walther, was already cleaned and loaded. When he was done, he loaded the Smith & Wesson with hollow-points, bade the pooches good night, picked up both pistols, and tiptoed up the stairs to the bedroom where Mary was sleeping. He put the guns on the bedside table and slipped under the covers.

Fifteen minutes later, he bolted awake. The dogs were barking.

Mulligan put his .45 down on the coffee table. Exhausted, he stretched out on the couch and listened to the house. All he could hear was rain battering the windows.

Suddenly, he was on the death plane again, but this time something was different. At first, he didn't know what it was. Then one of the blond women's eyelids fluttered. She opened her mouth to scream.

In Coventry, twelve miles to the west, Tim

Zucchi poured himself another cup of black coffee and settled down in front of the TV. His pistol, a nine-millimeter Sturm, Ruger semiauto, lay beside him on an end table. For two weeks now, he'd been going to bed at six P.M., getting up at eleven P.M., and standing guard until dawn. Each night, he TiVo'd all the late night talk shows and then watched them until it was time to go to work.

"Say something funny, asshole," he told Conan O'Brien. "I need help keeping my eyes open."

Mulligan startled awake. It wasn't just the dream that was different. Something was different *here,* too. The rain sounded louder now. The air stirred as if a window had been opened. He peered into the darkness.

He saw nothing.

After a moment, he sensed something huge padding toward him across the living room carpet. He swung his legs off the couch, picked up his .45, and snicked off the safety.

The gun had a will of its own. It boomed three times before Mulligan made a conscious decision to fire it. The something huge vanished in a red mist.

78

"If you were a better shot, you could have saved the criminal justice system a ton of money," Chief Hernandez said.

"He's gonna live?"

"The doctors working on him at Rhode Island Hospital seem to think so. I told them not to work too hard."

"Where'd I hit him?"

"You put one round in his left shoulder and another in his left lung. The third shot struck a picture of Freyer's mother on the living room wall. Got the old gal right in the liver."

It was early Wednesday morning, the sun just coming up. Hernandez and Mulligan were sitting in straight metal chairs on opposite sides of a scarred steel table in a Warwick PD interrogation room. Three detectives, two local and one from the Rhode Island State Police, leaned against once white walls stained yellow with cigarette smoke.

"Diggs was carrying a military-style combat knife with a seven-inch blade," Hernandez said. "Did you catch a glimpse of it before you fired?"

Mulligan hesitated.

"The smart answer would be yes," Hernandez said.

"Then yes. Yes, I did."

"Did he say anything to you?"

"No."

"But you were afraid for your life?" Hernandez asked, nodding his head to signal the correct answer.

"Yes, Chief. I was afraid for my life."

"And for the lives of the two people sleeping upstairs?"

"That's right."

"Okay, then," Hernandez said.

"How long are you going to keep me here?"

"In a hurry, are you?"

"I am. I've got to get back to the paper. I don't want to get scooped on my own story."

"You're going to be here all day."

"Aw, shit. What about Mason?"

"He'll be here all day, too."

"Sonovabitch!"

"Tell you what," the chief said. "We'll keep

a twelve-hour lid on this, give the two of you enough time to break the news."

"Thanks."

"Under the circumstances, it's the least we can do."

"How about a medal?"

"No."

"A commendation I can hang on my wall?"

"Don't press your luck."

79

A week later, Mulligan stepped into the elevator at the *Dispatch* with five men wearing identical black suits, white dress shirts, and purple ties. Three of them were carrying laptops. One of them got off with Mulligan on the third floor and headed for Lomax's office. The other four continued on to the upper floors, which housed the treasurer's and publisher's offices.

Mulligan walked to his cubicle, checked his messages, and found one from Lomax assigning him to write six obituaries for the next day's paper. Ninety minutes later, he was banging out the last one:

> Herbert "Party Boy" Walker, 57, of 22 Colfax Street, Providence, a patrolman in the Providence Police Department, died yesterday at Miriam Hospital after a long illness.
>
> Walker's dying wish, according to friends

and family, was to make it known that his enthusiastic consumption of cheap whiskey and oxycodone, along with his stubborn refusal to take the advice of his physician, had contributed to his early . . .

The man in the black suit was leaving the managing editor's office now. Mason watched him head for the elevator and then wandered over to ask Lomax what was up.

"Strangers are rummaging through the *Dispatch* looking for loose change," Lomax said.

"Who are they?"

"A pack of greedy corporate raiders negotiating to buy the paper."

"From General Communications Holdings International?"

"How the hell did you know?"

"I'm an investigative reporter. I know all kinds of stuff."

80

On Saturday night, Roomful of Blues, the legendary eight-man Rhode Island band, was on stage at Lupo's Heartbreak Hotel on Washington Street. Chris Vachon, the lead guitar player, was tearing it up behind a new frontman named Phil Pemberton. A veteran of the Boston blues scene, Phil injected soul into the band's familiar sound, his textured voice alternately aching with tenderness and threatening to wreck the walls.

Mulligan, Gloria, Mason, and Felicia were sharing a table, but not the check. Mason was springing for their night on the town. Felicia, who'd shed her lawyerly garb for party duds, wiggled to the band's insistent groove.

"Don't you hear that?" she squealed, clutching at Mason's hand. "How can you sit still?"

Under the table, Mulligan's right Reebok

was keeping time. Gloria stared at him, surprised by his rhythm, and tried to remember the last time she'd danced. Mason, looking somewhat distracted, held on to Felicia's hand and smiled in her direction as Phil launched into "Ain't Nothin' Happenin'." How wrong he was, Mason thought.

After Doug Woolverton's trumpet finished the tune with a sizzling flourish, Phil acknowledged the screams for more, then hushed the crowd.

"Got a triple threat for ya here tonight," he said. "Newport's own Edward Mason is in the house. He writes the news. He writes music. And if he hasn't lost his nerve, tonight he's gonna sing. This ragtime number he just wrote is something different for the band, but we ran through it a couple of times this afternoon, and we dig it. I think you will too."

Mason grinned at his shocked colleagues, winked at Felicia, and made his way to the stage. Travis Colby, the keyboard player, got up so the kid could take his place. Mason bent toward the mike and said rather jauntily, "Ladies and gentlemen, 'Providence Rag.' "

His fingers hit the keys, setting down a rollicking beat that made the audience hoot with surprise. When he began to sing, his voice wavered, hunting for a key. Once the rhythm kicked in, he found it and started to have fun.

Come on and hear the presses rising roar
Inking tales of sins and war
Oh ma honey, what we do
Provide you with a point of view
Oh ma baby, there's just no match
For the roar we roar at the ol' *Dispatch*

That mighty rumble that you hear
Rhode Island's favorite ragtime rag
The truth we tell will persevere
Rhode Island's favorite ragtime rag
Work up a cheer, and hoist your beer
For Rhode Island's favorite ragtime rag!

After Mason's debut, and a raucous ovation from the crowd, the band took a break. The newly minted performer walked back to the table through backslaps, toasts, and high fives. When he reached his seat, Felicia jumped up and planted a long kiss on his lips. Mulligan leaned in as if he were going to do the same, then laughed and gave his friend a brotherly clap on the shoulder.

"Two questions," Mulligan said. "Is this what you're gonna do when the paper is sold? And do you need a roadie?"

Mulligan drove home alone beneath a big yellow moon, Phil Pemberton's tender rendition of Sam Cooke's masterpiece "A Change Is Gonna Come" still singing in his ears. He left Secretariat at the curb, trudged up the stairs, and shouldered through his apartment door. He was grateful that Larry Bird was history, but he still longed for a big dog, one that would greet him with moist kisses and a thumping tail.

He was bone tired and a little drunk, but when he threw himself on his mattress, sleep wouldn't come. He'd never shot anyone before, but he was fine with that. He wished he'd shot straighter, that he'd blasted a hole straight through the place where Kwame Diggs's heart should have been.

Mulligan's mind raced, a slide show of death. He'd never been inside the murder houses, but he imagined the five long-ago victims lying in glistening pools of blood. He struggled to remember his best friend, Rosie, as she once was and not as a bundle of bones entombed beneath a marble slab. The pumping heart of the newspaper he loved was failing, too, sluggish rivers of printer's ink barely trickling through its veins.

Mulligan had always said that being a newspaperman was the only thing he was any good at — that if he couldn't be a reporter, he'd probably end up selling pencils from a tin cup. He figured begging would pay as well as the *Dispatch,* but it didn't sound like much of a plan.

September 2012

The pain in his chest is returning. He presses the red call button for the nurse. Ten minutes later, she still has not come.

He looks at the wall clock and realizes it has been only an hour since his last shot of Demerol. It will be another sixty minutes before the bitch will give him another one.

He picks up the remote and flips through the channels. *Celebrity Apprentice. The Golden Girls. Battlestar Galactica. Hillbilly Handfishin'.* Jesus, what a bunch of crap.

The cop stationed outside his door steps in, glares at him for a moment, then ducks back into the hallway. The cop, or others like him, will remain there, the man knows, until he's well enough to appear in court for his extradition hearing.

More channel flipping. Finally, he hits on something worth watching. *Jason X,* a slasher movie about Jason Voorhees, one of his favorite characters. He's never seen this one; it was made while he was in prison.

He slides his right hand, the one that doesn't have an IV stuck in it, under the coarse hospital sheet and gives himself a tug. His erection rises, then deflates. What the hell?

The drugs, maybe. Yeah. That must be it.

By the time the movie ends, his chest is on fire. He presses the call button maybe fifty times. Finally, the bitch comes in with his silver needle. The pain recedes.

He drifts off. . . .

He is behind the condo again, peering through the windows. The kitchen is empty. He sits in the wet grass and removes his sneakers. Then he pulls a glass cutter from his little black valise and carves a hole in the window. He reaches through it, unlocks the latch, raises the sash, and crawls inside.

He tiptoes out of the kitchen and pads across the living room rug. Someone is sleeping on the sofa. He slips the combat knife from the sheath on his belt and swings it in an arc, tearing out the sleeper's throat. There is a gun on the coffee table. A big, heavy pistol. He picks it up, sticks it in his waistband, and wipes his knife blade clean on the leather couch.

Then he turns and stealthily climbs the stairs. Somewhere up there, the girl of his dreams is waiting. He feels himself getting hard.

At long last, he will hear Felicia scream.

ACKNOWLEDGMENTS

In September 2011, Thomas H. Cook, one of the finest writers of my generation, accepted my invitation to lunch at a pub in St. Louis. He welcomed the chance to catch up with an old pal. I had something more in mind. For two hours, the Jedi prose master listened patiently as I droned on about my muddled idea for a third crime novel, prodding me with questions and offering priceless suggestions. A year later, when I completed the first draft, I was pleased with each chapter but not with the way they fit together. Something wasn't right, but darned if I could figure out what it was. I sheepishly sent the manuscript to Susanna Einstein, who is not only a great agent but the best story doctor I've ever known. She promptly identified the problem and offered a solution. As always, my wife, Patricia Smith, one of our finest living poets, edited every line of every page, adding music to my occasionally toneless prose. If not for their brilliance and generosity, this novel might never have been written. Every writer should have such friends.

The employees of Thorndike Press hope you have enjoyed this Large Print book. All our Thorndike, Wheeler, and Kennebec Large Print titles are designed for easy reading, and all our books are made to last. Other Thorndike Press Large Print books are available at your library, through selected bookstores, or directly from us.

For information about titles, please call:
(800) 223-1244

or visit our Web site at:
http://gale.cengage.com/thorndike

To share your comments, please write:

Publisher
Thorndike Press
10 Water St., Suite 310
Waterville, ME 04901